Distant Thunder

A Novel of the American Revolution

Timothy J. Krueger

The Langdon Maritime Chronicles, No. 1

First paperback edition 2023
By Quayside Press
457 S. Quay St., Lakewood, Colorado 80226

Copyright © 2023 Timothy J. Krueger

All rights reserved. No part of this book may be reproduced or used in any form or by electronic, mechanical, or other means, now known or hereafter invented, including photocopying and recording, or in any information storage or retrieval system, without permission in writing from the copyright owner, except for the use of brief quotations in a book review.

Cover art: *Shipping in the English Channel* (c. 1755), Charles Brooking (c. 1723-1759)

ISBN: 979-8-395-37199-7

Dedicated to my fellow adventurer in life, M.B.K.

Acknowledgments

Thanks are due to several persons who read this novel in manuscript and offered invaluable advice, whether historical, technical, grammatical, or stylistic. These include MB Krueger, Stu MacAskie, the Rev'd Elizabeth P. Randall, the Rev'd Sally K. Brown, Ross Jallo, Dr. Michael J. Kornelsen, and Rear Admiral Richard G. Heaslip, CB, Royal Navy.
Additionally, Dennis Johnson offered helpful assistance in navigating the world of publishing and actually getting this book to print.

Author's Foreword

THE EXPERIENCES of the Rev'd Thomas Langdon as presented in the ensuing narrative closely mirror those of an actual revolutionary-era clergyman, the Rev'd Jonathan Wiswall. The events surrounding his expulsion from his hometown of Falmouth (now Portland), Maine, are modeled directly on his life; but, although Wiswall went on to be chaplain in several British warships during the duration of the Revolutionary War – just as my own character does – his experiences from that point diverge, thus serving more as an inspiration than a direct model. Hence the alteration of the character's name.

Every book of historical fiction is a varying mix of those two components, history and fiction. Of the greatest authenticity in this novel is the progression of events, which follows closely the actual occurrences in New England during that fateful year, 1775. Most of the correspondence, resolutions, decrees, proclamations, minutes, ships' logs, and sermons are actual reproductions of existing primary documents. Even certain conversations (especially those of Vice Admiral Samuel Graves) were drawn directly from correspondence and translated into dialogue. Some documents, however – referred to in other historical writings but no longer extant – have been reconstructed. A handful of still others have been entirely fabricated where the movement of the plot calls for such liberties on my part. The Rev'd Langdon's journal is such an invention, aiding principally in allowing the reader a first-hand look into his thoughts as the plot develops.

Where the greatest latitude has been taken – and where the prevailing historicity of the document takes on its most fictitious nature – is in my portrayal of characters. My attempt was to make the main characters as historically accurate as possible; but, where the scarcity of actual documentation forced me to take interpretive license, consistency and plausibility in the context of other information was my guiding principle.

Uppermost in my mind at all times was an effort to present the coming of the American Revolution from the eyes of a man who initially, like most colonists, held a mixture of sentiments towards the increasing unrest; but later, through force of events and personal conviction, felt compelled to a defense of the government and crown. The Loyalist point of view has not been well represented in our civic and cultural lore. This is a great loss, not only to the cause of full, accurate, and objective history, but also to our true appreciation of the conflict and the varied passions it inspired. It is hoped that this depiction of an actual Loyalist, imbued with raw human emotions and palpable realism by way of a narrative treatment (such that it might draw a larger measure of the reader's sympathy than a more academic, scholarly approach) will go some small way towards rectifying that deficiency.

Timothy J. Krueger
Denver, Colorado
26 May, 2023

Chapter One.

It was on a frosty evening in mid-February, 1775 that the tranquility of Falmouth, in the Maine Province of the Crown Colony of Massachusetts Bay, was shattered abruptly by the sound of gunfire from the harbor. The din – that of small arms – came from His Majesty's Brig *Gaspee*, which had been riding at anchor for nearly a week in the small New England coastal town, revictualing to continue its patrol of the Maine coastline.

Among the many inhabitants of the town who stood up from their dinners and went to their front windows were the Reverend Thomas Langdon, minister of St. Paul's Church, and the Honorable Enoch Freeman, Esq., chairman of the town's Committee of Inspection.

The clergyman was a dark-haired bachelor of thirty-one years, born in Falmouth and educated at King's College, New York, where he had taken a Bachelor of Divinity degree in 1766. The following year he was selected by St. Paul's – the Anglican parish of his hometown – to be their next vicar, and was thus sent to England to be ordained a priest in the Church of England. He returned six months later to learn that his remaining parent had succumbed to illness during his absence, and thus that the small house on the western outskirts of town, in which he had grown up, was now his parsonage.

He was an affable man of medium height and slender build, and much beloved of his small congregation. For a man of the cloth, he was not especially dogmatic, and there were rumors that his education – which had included philosophy, history, music (he was a tolerably good flautist) and the classics as well as theology – had made him something of a latitudinarian when it came to religious matters. It was even whispered that he harbored "high church" sympathies under his elegantly powdered wig, even though the services over which he presided at St. Paul's were simple and eminently "low church." He was an impeccable dresser, cutting a fine figure around town, and was admitted by all as the closest thing in Falmouth to "a man of fashion."

The Hon. Enoch Freeman was an attorney by vocation, who had studied law at Harvard in the latter 1750s (although he never took a degree in it). He was nearly a decade older than the Rev'd Langdon, and a widower. He was substantially taller, easily topping six feet, and his tastes were simpler and his dress plainer than that of the Anglican clergyman; but he pictured himself an eloquent and charismatic leader of the Committee of Inspection, over which he was chairman. His election to the political position partially attested to this charisma. His demeanor was serious, some would even say dour, and it was generally acknowledged that he had never had a spontaneously humorous thought in his life.

Both men, after fruitlessly peering from their respective windows, threw on their great coats and ventured into the snowy street. Their paths crossed very near the quay.

"Ah, good evening, Mr. Langdon."

"Good evening, Mr. Freeman."

A small crowd of onlookers had already gathered near Pearson's wharf.

"What's all this, I wonder?" Freeman asked gruffly, his eyes focused on the shadowy form of the *Gaspee* a quarter of a mile out in the moon-lit bay. His face was illuminated briefly as a fusillade of musketry erupted from the brig's quarterdeck. "Surely it's too late for an exercise or drill!"

"Perhaps Lieutenant Hunter thinks it important to exercise his men in the art of nocturnal gunnery," said Langdon.

Not sensing that Langdon was jesting, Freeman replied, "Well, you'd have thought he would have sent word ashore to inform us, if that were — "

The next flash of small arms from the brig revealed a boat with four occupants pulling strongly towards an uninhabited, tree-lined portion of the shoreline.

"Is that boat their target?" Freeman asked with horror.

"It would appear so," Langdon said, seriousness replacing his earlier good humor.

"Do you think they are actually aiming to do execution?"

"I wonder who the people in the boat could be. Thieves? Pirates? Natives?"

"Deserters, more like," Mr. Freeman said.

The firing stopped when the boat reached shore. Langdon and Freeman could just make out the sound of excited voices aboard the *Gaspee* out in the harbor.

After some minutes had passed, and Langdon found himself becoming restive, he said, "My house is on the way back to yours. Why don't you stop, and I'll give you some tea."

"Lord, never tea! But coffee . . . if you've coffee . . .?"

"Of course I've coffee," Langdon replied.

"Then I should be delighted," he said.

"Good."

They were just approaching the Rev'd Langdon's home when a group of loudly shouting men appeared, carrying the bloodied body of a man through the town. Freeman stopped a boy who was a part of the entourage.

"We found the boat some ways up the beach," the excited youth reported breathlessly, "and it were empty but for a body, shot several times through. Riggs, who found him first, says he were dead, but others insisted he be brung to Dr. Coffin."

"Very proper," Freeman commended him. "Did Mr. Riggs, or anyone else, recognize the dead man?"

"No, sir."

"And there was nobody else near the boat? I clearly saw four in it before it reached shore."

"None, sir. They must have ran." The boy sprinted away to catch up with the group bearing the body, and a wintery silence re-exerted itself. Freeman and Langdon continued on their way, wrapped in their own dismal thoughts until their coats were hanging on hall pegs, a water kettle was simmering over the newly stoked fire, and they were seated comfortably before it.

"Having had the time to reflect, Mr. Freeman," began Langdon, "I am inclined to agree with you, that the men in the boat were deserters from the ship. Reports of desertions all along the coast are prevalent of late. There's not a single paper I read that does not include such an account. His Majesty is having a devilish time keeping his ships manned on the North American station."

"Well, with life aboard a man-o'-war being such a brutish thing, I'm not surprised," Freeman shook his head. "Many a man is there by force, having been impressed against his will; and there are many a convict and prisoner among 'em, too, you may depend upon it."

"Doubtless you are correct," Langdon said, placing two cups and saucers on an end table between their chairs. "Do you take milk or sugar in your coffee, Mr. Freeman?

"Neither."

"I hope you don't mind if I myself have tea?"

"Why should I?" Freeman asked.

"The vociferousness of your protest to my offer of tea," Langdon began with the hint of a smile, "seemed to betoken an objection on political grounds; that is, that tea is taxed."

"Where you choose to spend your money is your business, Mr. Langdon. If you wish to fill the pockets of corrupt crown ministers with your hard-earned wages . . ." he shrugged. Then another, albeit unlikely, thought occurred to him. "Unless I seriously misjudge you, Mr. Langdon, I am assuming that it is not smuggled tea you are serving."

"Never in life, my good Mr. Freeman!" said Langdon, taking mock offence. "How could you even think such a thing of a man of the cloth?!" He then became more serious. "Actually, it is appalling to me how blatantly this illegality is carried on, right under the nose of Mr. Lyde, our worthy customs collector."

Freeman grunted.

"The merchants' resistance to this insignificant tea duty astounds me, I must confess, Mr. Freeman," continued Langdon, watching Freeman out of the corner of his eye as he poured him his coffee. "Now, you and I are in full agreement on the issue that Britain has no right to tax us internally, and I share your abhorrence of the most recent acts of parliament, being vindictive and calculatedly condescending; but I consider this duty on tea as acceptable, being an external regulation of trade for the good of the empire as a whole. After the last war, in which we fought side by side with our British cousins, and were relieved to find that they considered us worthy of their protection from the French, we then turned a blind eye to the financial obligations of our protectors, and protested virulently to any minor duty or fee meant to lighten the already astounding burdens placed upon our English counterparts. We did not lift a finger to pay for those services rendered generously on our behalf, which were paid for by our English brothers and sisters."

"I do not see it that way, Mr. Langdon," Freeman shook his head and sipped his coffee. "We are worth more to Britain by our natural resources, and the goods and trade we provide to her merchants – making Britain the mercantile giant of the world – than any amount she spends on our defense. It's my firm opinion that parliament was not so much concerned with getting us to foot our share of the bill, as to assert their dominion over us," Freeman contended.

"I think you confuse cause and effect, Mr. Freeman," Langdon continued in a measured tone, stirring milk into his tea. "I do think parliament's initial intent was to get us to pay our fair share of the war's staggering expenses." He tapped his spoon gingerly against the side of his cup before laying it with a tinkle in the saucer. "It is well known that the average Englishman pays three-and-a-half times more taxes than any British American. It was only when resistance to parliament's initial proposal, the Stamp Act, grew to alarming levels that parliament, like a parent upbraided by an insolent child, felt compelled to re-affirm its right of legislative jurisdiction. This led, unfortunately, to a handful of overly stern measures, which have only inflamed the demagogues on this side of the Atlantic into ever more frantic – but still groundless – cries of oppression and tyranny."

"Well, whatever the chronological order of things, Mr. Langdon, the Boston Port Act, the Quartering Act, the Quebec Proclamation, and their like are established facts, and it's not only our right but our responsibility to oppose such acts of injustice. And, although we apparently differ on this, I consider the tea duty as among these injustices."

"Our difference is probably only one of degree, Mr. Freeman," continued the parson. "Pitched, unlawful protest on our part will turn a small injury into an inflamed wound, eventually infecting the whole body and preventing healing. Nothing is to be gained by it. On the other hand, there are legal avenues of protest at our disposal, such as lawful petition and reasoned complaint to the proper authorities. By such methods were the Stamp Act and the Townshend duties repealed, you will recall."

"Except for the duty on tea, of course," Freeman countered.

"Yes, but it is such a mere pittance of what used to be taxed. In fact, it is insignificant enough as not to affect our daily lives in the least."

"But allow parliament an insignificant breach of our liberties, and they'll soon accustom themselves to it and begin oppressing us with bigger and bolder strokes," Freeman argued.

Langdon laughed. "With all due respect, my good Mr. Freeman, I think you exaggerate. Your imagination has been inflamed by the likes of Samuel Adams, and you fancy that you see threats where there has previously been nothing but indulgence and mindfulness. Do you seriously think that Great Britain, with the greatest tradition and veneration of liberty of any state in Europe, and the most perfect form of government ever devised by mankind, would actually have any inclination towards real tyranny . . . much less believe that she would benefit from it?"

"The late acts of parliament to which you earlier alluded, Mr. Langdon, give me great pause, leading me to suspect that perhaps Mr. Adams isn't far wrong."

"Well," Langdon shrugged, sipping his tea, "we shall see, I suppose. How is your coffee?"

"Commendable."

"Not too strong?"

"No."

"And tax-free, as well," Langdon winked.

"Aye, that it is," said Freeman, draining his cup with satisfaction.

*

The Rev'd. Mr. Thomas Langdon's Journal

Monday, 13 February, 1775. (. . .) H.M. Brig *Gaspee*, riding at anchor here, fired at deserters in a boat after dark. The Hon[ble] M[r] Freeman came to coffee. Discussed taxation and politics amicably (he's among those who won't drink tea because it's taxed). Clear and cold, with a frost p.m.

TUESDAY, 14 FEBRUARY, 1775. Confirmed today that the four men in the boat were sailors deserting the *Gaspee*, one killed. The ship's captain, Liue^t Wm Hunter, had been unable to pursue them owing to their having taken the ship's only boat, and had thus resorted to the musket in an attempt to prevent their desertion. The boat was returned to the brig by M^{ssrs} Waite & Pearson, which garnered Lt Hunter's thanks and commendation. He also expressed his gratitude to those townspeople who had attempted to save the life of J^{no} Lutey, the deserter who had been killed; and asked that any information concerning the whereabouts of the other three deserters be passed along to him or any other King's officer the moment it was known. No one is deceived into thinking this would mean anything but hanging from the yardarm to any deserter who was found, and townspeople, indisposed to the violence necessary to the maintenance of discipline aboard a warship, are unlikely to satisfy the L^t's request, I suspect. J^{no} Lutey's body taken into the bay in a boat and buried at sea without prayers, though I offered to provide same. Lt Hunter replied that a deserter did not deserve the honours of a Christian burial. Did not wish to argue, though I disagreed. Said prayers on Lutey's behalf at Eve^{ng} Prayer in the church. Dined at Mrs Ingersoll's. Fair and extremely cold.

CHAPTER TWO.

TWO AND A HALF WEEKS after the *Gaspee* affair, on the evening of the 2nd of March, the Rev'd Langdon locked up St. Paul's Church after saying Evening Prayer, the cadences of the Magnificat going through his head, and made his way to the home of his childhood friend, Mr. Edward Oxnard, now a prominent merchant in town.

Langdon and Oxnard as adolescents were still remembered in certain circles for having gotten into every sort of boyish mischief imaginable, stealing apples from the Brackett orchard, skipping grammar lessons to fish or skinny-dip in Back Cove, and frightening the old widow Mrs. Brewster half out of her wits by climbing into a tree outside her bedroom window in the middle of the night and ghoulishly moaning the name of her dear departed husband. The latter business – in which they had been apprehended – had resulted in a censuring, not only from their respective families, but from the Town Council, as well.

Dinner was served soon after his arrival, and Langdon took his usual place at the table next to the Oxnards' little boy, a four-year-old, across from Edward and his wife Polly, who was about five months pregnant.

"You've heard of the disturbance in town earlier today, haven't you?" Oxnard asked once they had all been seated in his spacious, candlelit dining room. The quality of the furnishings spoke to Oxnard's success as a merchant.

"A disturbance? No," Langdon replied.

"A merchant ship from England arrived in port this morning, the sloop *John & Mary* of Bristol, with goods on board for Captain Coulson," said Oxnard. Langdon's eyebrows rose at the mention of the name, for Thomas Coulson was a parishioner of St. Paul's, and was in the last stages of building a ship for an English merchant.

"Goods from England?" Langdon inquired.

Oxnard nodded. "For the completion of Coulson's sloop."

"Let me predict what happened next:" Langdon leaned back in his chair as Polly set a plate before him of cod, boiled potatoes, and string beans. "The Committee of Inspection made inquiries."

"They did not just make inquiries. They met in the library chamber and voted with little debate that none of the goods be landed until an investigation be made, as to whether the goods were in violation of the Continental Association," Oxnard said.

Langdon shook his head sadly, tucking his napkin into his collar. Some six months previous, in September of 1774, delegates from eleven of the thirteen American colonies had met in Philadelphia, calling themselves the "Continental Congress," in order to debate the colonies' grievances with the crown. The resolves which resulted from this congress included a non-importation agreement called the Continental Association, whereby any colonist who imported goods from Britain would be open to public censure. To monitor the compliance of merchants from Massachusetts to Georgia, Committees of Inspection were created in each town of any size, the members of which were to apprise themselves of all mercantile activity in their respective localities, and to publish the names of any violators of the Continental Association.

Langdon had no objection to the basic idea – a mutual and voluntary resolve on the part of colonists to send a signal to Britain that they felt themselves the object of unfair treatment. But he disliked the creation of these Committees of Inspection, which spied on the actions of their neighbors, sticking their noses into others' affairs and stirring up the emotions of the masses. This sort of public censure smacked of mob justice, as far as Langdon could see.

"The committee adjourned until tomorrow morning at eight, at which time they have desired Captain Coulson and the master of the *John & Mary* – I think his name is Hughes – to attend," Oxnard concluded.

"I shall attend that meeting, I think. It is to be in the library chamber, as usual?" Langdon asked.

"Yes," Oxnard nodded. "Would you lead us in a blessing, Thomas?"

"By all means," the clergyman said. They bowed their heads and he recited a brief prayer.

No sooner had he finished than Oxnard asked, "Don't you find it presumptuous of the committee to mix themselves up in Coulson's business?"

"I'm not quite sure what to think, except that you did not attend very closely to my prayer, Edward!" they all laughed. After they had begun to eat, Langdon said, "I certainly feel for our friend Coulson, as he must continue working to feed his family; yet, if his work violates the Association, where is the line to be drawn between personal sacrifice and the public good? As a shipwright whose primary purchasers are British merchants, is he to allow his family to go destitute simply to retain a unified colonial posture toward Britain?"

"I don't know about 'the public good,' Thomas. I wonder just how effective – not to mention legal – this Continental Association is. I have my grave doubts as to its efficacy. Will it not, as evidenced by this affair, bring greater harm to us than to those whom it is intended to affect? I mean, this does much more immediate – and potentially irreparable – damage to Coulson, and Falmouth in general, than to the British merchant who placed the order, much less to Parliament or the Crown."

"A worthy point, Edward," Langdon said wiping his mouth with his napkin. "I am much concerned by the creation of these Committees of Inspection, which appear all too ready to pry into the affairs of free Englishmen, creating a more sinister form of oppression here in our midst than ever a distant Parliament posed."

"Precisely."

"At the very least, I am slightly comforted that the chairman of our Committee of Inspection, Enoch Freeman, is a rather level-headed man of some learning," Langdon observed. "I had him to tea some weeks ago. The night of the *Gaspee* affair, in fact."

"Yes, but it is to be remembered that he, and most of the rest of the current committee, were members of its insidious forerunner, the Committee of Correspondence, created by Samuel Adams to spy secretly on us and report who was fallow ground for protest, insurrection, and rebellion, and who was inclined to loyalty and defense of the government. Keeping track of people's private political sympathies borders on sedition, in my opinion; and for Mr. Freeman to have participated in such subversion of the constitution is enough to worry me," Oxnard said. He toyed with his food with his fork for a moment, then continued in a yet more agitated tone of voice: "It is all of a pattern, I fear. First we are informed that a Continental Congress has formed to tell us what our collective opinions are; then we are oppressed with Committees of Inspection which, to make up for their lack of official authority, are forced to rely upon the threat of angry mobs in order to accomplish their ruinous deeds; and now we've townsfolk – who were, I remind you, perfectly happy, reasonable, law abiding subjects not more than three months ago – boarding ships without warrants, preventing the landing of cargos and the carrying out of our lawful business, and presuming to force others to conform to their vile association! What will it be next, I wonder? Pledges of allegiance to their seditious goals, administered at the point of a pistol? All from a little threepence per pound duty on tea!"

Langdon remained silent, agreeing with much of what Oxnard said, but his mind was not entirely made up on the subject.

"Your food is getting cold, Edward," observed Polly. "The rest of us are nearly finished. May I offer you a second helping, Thomas?"

Langdon shook his head and thanked her, complimented the meal, then turned back to Edward, saying, "It's not just the tea tax. It's more the principle of the thing, I suspect: the fact that we are taxed by a Parliament in which we have no representation and therefore no way in which either to consent or to protest." He found it disconcerting somehow that, two weeks ago, he was defending the views of government to Mr. Freeman, a disgruntled colonist; and tonight he was defending the views of the disgruntled colonists to Mr. Oxnard, a decided friend of government. Perhaps it was the latitudinarian in Langdon that inclined him towards defense of an attacked party – or, as his critics might phrase it, his fence-sitting.

"But I remind you, Thomas, of the Stamp Act and the Townshend duties – both very unpopular with colonists after their imposition by Parliament. Yet, by way of lawful petition, orderly protest, and reasonable complaint, all these were repealed . . . except for the tea, of course. So much for this unfounded notion that Americans are not represented in Parliament! I would say that American interests have been readily served in Parliament up till now. It should be a lesson on how lawful subjects can effectively remonstrate against perceived grievances, rather than these 'Continental Associations' and 'Committees of Inspection' and 'Boston Tea Parties' . . . like the temper tantrums of some ill-bred child!"

"To the eyes of Parliament perhaps we are just a pack of ill-bred children," Polly offered.

"Well, our confirming their prejudices by such lawless behavior does us no credit. The selfish ingratitude of this people astounds me at times! They have not yet learned, that with rights also come certain responsibilities."

"If we're not careful, the rod of chastisement will soon descend . . . and I fear it will descend without discernment on the rebellious and the loyal alike," Langdon mused forebodingly.

"The rain falls on both the just and the unjust," Polly added.

"Well spoke, my good Polly; well spoke," Langdon commended her, the scriptural allusion sitting just at the edge of his recognition.

"And what will be the gentlemen's pleasure? Coffee or tea?" she asked, standing from the table.

"Tea," they both said with conviction.

*

THERE WAS QUITE A CROWD of townspeople gathered outside the library chamber when the Rev'd Langdon arrived the next morning shortly before eight o'clock, their breath rising in the brisk morning air like steam from a herd of cattle. "Good morning, parson," greeted several of his parishioners, to whom he returned the greeting.

At length the committee members arrived and, although it seemed that everyone would not fit into the spartan library chamber, they filed through the door, the members seating themselves around the long table in the center, the rest standing closely packed against the walls. The roll was called and all nineteen members responded.

"Gentlemen," began the chairman the Hon. Enoch Freeman, "Pursuant to the motion passed yesterday, were Captain Coulson and Master Hughes informed of our proceedings and desired to attend this meeting?"

"Yes, Mr. Chairman," said one Jedediah Cobb, a member of the committee. "I done informed 'em myself," he said.

"Good, and is either Captain Coulson or Master Hughes in attendance?" This was addressed to the occupants of the chamber at large.

"I am here," said Captain Coulson from among the onlookers, all eyes turning to the corner of the room from whence his voice came, "but Master Hughes has remained aboard his ship, it being much shattered during its crossing, and he having much to attend to in terms of repairs." Coulson was a tall, lanky man, his balding head bowed by habit given the usual lack of space between the decks of a ship, and rather shabbily dressed.

"Very well. Thank you for being so good as to attend, Captain Coulson," Freeman said. Addressing the committee, he continued, "The initial question before us for consideration is whether Captain Thomas Coulson's taking of the rigging and sails out of the *John & Mary*, and his using them to fit out the ship now under construction here, would be a violation of the Continental Association. Is there any discussion of the matter before a vote is taken?"

An immediate babble broke out from committee members and onlookers alike. "Order! Order!" Freeman boomed. "The chair recognizes Mr. Benjamin Mussey!"

"Thank you, Mr. Chairman," began the said Mussey when the group had been quieted. "I put it to the committee that the case is quite clear: The first article of the association reads, 'That we will not import, into British America, from Great Britain or Ireland, any goods, wares, or merchandise whatsoever . . .' And now from the tenth article, 'if any goods or merchandises shall be imported after the said first day of February, the same ought forthwith to be sent back again, without breaking any of the packages thereof.' And now from the fourteenth article — "

"We are all familiar with the provisions contained in the association, Mr. Mussey," interrupted Freeman.

"Yes, well, I just wanted to point out how clearly the matter before us conforms to its unequivocal language."

"That it does not," interrupted another member of the committee, one Daniel Ilsley. "If I might speak, sir?"

"Yes, the chair recognizes Mr. Daniel Ilsley."

"Mr. Chairman, the ship being built here by Captain Coulson was ordered several years ago by one Mr. Garnet, a merchant of Bristol, England. Since last Autumn it has been finished with respect to all things save the rigging and stores necessary for its transportation to England. Neither the merchant, Mr. Garnet, nor the Master of the sloop *John & Mary* was aware of the Association when shipping the said articles in December of last year – "

"So they say," shouted one of the members of the crowd.

"I therefore put it to the committee," continued Ilsley, ignoring the outburst, "that this case does not conform to the association in three respects: First, that it cannot be considered an importation, as it is meant to complete the property of a Bristol merchant, not an American; Second, that the said stores will, in effect, ship themselves back to England when fitted aboard the ship for which they are intended, without which she would be unable to cross the Atlantic as planned; and Third, that the articles were shipped and sent prior to the owner's knowledge of the association, thus exempting them from the prohibition."

"That's a lot of bullocks," barked Jedediah Cobb. "Aboard that sloop is goods from Great Britain; they arrived well after the deadline set by the Continental Congress – hell, they was shipped after the deadline, whatever the master might say – and if they's landed on American soil, no matter the purpose, they're an importation fair and square. Our duty's clear, and that's to send 'em back to England, unopened."

"Hear, hear," echoed several of the committee members and onlookers.

"But they are not an importation!" insisted Mr. Ilsley over the rumble. "Whatever Mr. Cobb might say, Mr. Chairman, the definition of an imported good is something used for consumption in the land to which it is transported. The rigging and stores are to be fixed to an Englishman's property – hence, as near to actual English soil as you can get in America. It does not matter that Americans are employed in the fitting out of such goods. In fact, it is to our benefit. That Mr. Garnet chose to have an American shipwright build his ship can only be to our advantage, for we get the emolument thereof."

"I'm afraid you err, my good Mr. Ilsley," intervened a softer-spoken member of the committee, an appropriately named John Butter. "In order better to differentiate between what is, and what is not an importation, I believe it is necessary to look at the intentions of the Continental Association itself. The intentions are, quite clearly, to show the British government our resolve against their lining their pockets with our lucrative trade, while simultaneously taxing us when they have no right to do so. In order to show our determination, we must turn any and all British ships, with whatsoever goods, away from trading in our ports."

"On the contrary, Mr. Butter," retorted Mr. Ilsley, "the intent of the Association is to legally injure British trade in order to send a message to Parliament that we are good and loyal subjects who feel ourselves unrightfully taxed. The Association must not be coercive, thus bringing deserved retribution upon our heads, but a simple refusal to accept imported goods. The sending of these goods back to Britain, however, is to break a contract that was made years ago, and is just about to be fulfilled; it is, therefore, no less than a criminal act. It would no doubt incur a loss to Mr. Garnet, but it will not bring any gain to us; whereas the fitting out of Captain Coulson's ship will provide the town with employment and revenue. If I am not mistaken, Mr. Garnet has been a good customer for many years, exporting English manufactured goods to us in return for lumber. After his ship is fitted out, he may continue purchasing our lumber – which he will certainly refuse to do should we insult him in this matter – but we shall no longer accept any of his manufactures until such time as Parliament reacts constructively to our grievances and the Association lifted. For that he will have Parliament to blame, not us. And to create a chorus of angry merchants in Britain, appealing to Parliament on our behalf, is as close to effective representation as we are likely to get in the short term. Clearly, if we are to debate the intentions of the Association, the solution as I have offered it will be more to our local benefit, as well as cause more harm to Britain in the long run, than any narrow interpretation on our part in the present." A few isolated heads nodded in agreement with Ilsley's words.

Mr. Freeman, the chairman, spoke at this point. "I put it to you, gentlemen, that it is not for us to interpret the intentions of the Association, but merely to follow its resolves. It would take us quite far afield to begin debating whether we or Mr. Garnet would stand to gain or lose more or less by the fitting out of Captain Coulson's ship. I recommend that we confine our comments to the *John & Mary*, her goods, and what our actions should be."

"Hear, hear," came a voice from immediately behind the Rev'd Langdon. "The chairman is quite correct in saying that our duty is not to interpret the Association, but merely to obey its resolutions."

Turning around, Langdon recognized Mr. Nelson, minister of one of the Puritan congregations in town. To himself, Langdon thought, "Just like a Puritan to advocate blind obedience," but out loud he said, "You speak as if the Continental Association were law, Mr. Nelson; as if it were a piece of approved legislation."

"Duly passed by the Continental Congress, yes," he stated.

"It is not. It is merely the resolve of one group of colonists who met together under the auspices of England's liberal tradition of allowing its citizens to gather peaceably. It is only by way of the freedoms granted to us under the British Constitution, Mr. Nelson, that they were allowed to meet at all, and talk about whatever they pleased. If a group of colonists meets together and agrees among themselves not to import anything from a certain country, that is their right as free Britons; but they cannot enforce their whims upon other free Britons, except by act of Parliament."

"Parliament is a brood of vipers and devils," spat Mr. Nelson. "I admit no authority but that of God Almighty and what is manifest in his Holy Writ; so when an earthly king violates my God given rights as laid out in the Bible, I will oppose him by authority of my heavenly King."

To himself Langdon thought, "You have just uttered treason;" but he actually said, "Pray show me where in the Bible it says that you have a God given right not to be taxed, or not to submit to temporal authority? I remind you rather of our Lord's words 'Render unto Caesar what is Caesar's, and unto God what is God's'."

"Would the clergymen kindly postpone their theological discussion until the business of the committee has been carried out?" called out chairman Freeman in a good-natured voice, drawing the laughter of the assembly. "Is there a motion to vote?" he asked. There was. "Very good. Mr. Parsons, would you read the resolution drafted by Mr. Mussey and his sub-committee?"

Mr. Parsons stood. "'That the taking out the rigging, sails, and stores from the sloop newly arrived from Bristol, and the appropriation of said rigging, sails, and stores to rig a ship under construction here by Captain Coulson, would be in violation of the Continental Association; and therefore that the said rigging, sails and stores for the said Captain Coulson's new ship, ought forthwith to be sent back again, without breaking any of the packages thereof.'"

The roll was called, and the members voiced their vote in response to the reading of their names. The resolution was passed, thirteen to five.

Freeman, who as chairman had not voted, spoke following the vote, addressing Captain Coulson. "You are aware of the result of this committee's deliberations, Captain Coulson. Do you agree to comply with the resolution just passed?"

"I beg leave to inform the committee," began Captain Coulson, stepping forward to make himself distinct from the crowd, "that the *John & Mary* is in such a state of disrepair that she will be unable to return to England before her faults are remedied. And, I regret to inform the committee further, her master has told me that in order to repair her adequately, the freight must be removed in order to heel her over, for she is in want of proper caulking and a few new boards under the water."

"She cannot be repaired with the cargo still aboard?" Freeman asked.

"Not according to Master Hughes, no," Coulson replied.

"The cargo can't be shifted?"

"No."

"Why not?"

"I have only Master Hughes' word as to that, Mr. Chairman. In such cases it is usual to lighten a ship as much as practicable, making it possible to heel her over in order to properly caulk and repair her bottom from the outside. It can't be done from inside."

A silence followed this pronouncement. The room seemed prickly with expectation.

At length the chairman said, "A number of knowledgeable persons to whom I have spoken have said nothing about the *John & Mary*'s need for such extensive repairs."

"Well, with all due respect, Mr. Chairman," Coulson rejoined, "you obviously haven't spoken with anyone what's been aboard the *John & Mary*; or maybe they were landlubbers, who think if a ship's got all her masts in a generally upright position, she's fit to go to sea!"

"That's quite enough, Captain Coulson." Freeman said coldly. "In the interests of a number of inhabitants of this town," he continued, "I propose that a committee of carpenters, riggers and caulkers be created to go aboard the *John & Mary* to establish her state of repair and seaworthiness."

"Just which inhabitants would that be?" Coulson demanded, his pique apparent to all.

"Beg pardon, Captain Coulson?" Mr. Freeman inquired.

"Who are these inhabitants in whose interest you are proposing to invade the property of a British merchant?" Coulson persisted.

"The constituency of this committee," Freeman stated.

"I recall no election of this committee, and therefore you have no constituency. Nor is this committee authorized to issue search warrants."

"This committee represents the interests of our colony in general, as established at the Continental Congress of last September, Captain Coulson," Freeman said. "And furthermore, it is not an invasion of property, but a justified investigation of a claim made by you in the name of Master Hughes which bears directly on the satisfactory conclusion of this matter."

"Yet, if I am not mistaken, it takes a valid warrant from an authorized Crown Court to enter and search private property." Coulson persevered. "And you propose to do this without such a warrant."

"I am not entirely sure that an examination of the state of repair of a vessel requires a warrant of the type you refer to. And I remind you that persistence along these lines – that is, resistance to a peaceful examination of the vessel by disinterested parties – will imply deceit on your part, Captain Coulson."

Coulson's anger bristled at this comment, but he opted not to reply.

The roll was called on Freeman's proposition, and it passed by the same margin.

Freeman announced in a conclusive tone of voice, "You have been informed of the committee's desires, Captain Coulson, founded on the Continental Association. I now move that this committee adjourn."

*

FRIDAY, 3 MARCH, 1775. (. . .) The Committee of Inspection seems bent on interfering with Falmouth's trade, and Falmouth's friends of gov^t seem bent on interfering with the business of the committee. Such division is unfortunate, as the latter group will injure our peace, the former our prosperity, neither of which is to be desired. I can see the right of both arguments, and if I were persuaded that either was wholly in the right, I suppose I would find myself in that camp; but, as I see that both have elements of rectitude, and both have elements of demagoguery (and no little self-righteousness), I cannot with comfort place myself in either camp. As a result, my overall demeanour, normally good natured and inclined towards optimism, is clouded over considerably.

Chapter Three.

SEVERAL MORNINGS after the Committee of Inspection's meeting, the Rev'd Langdon's breakfast was interrupted by a frantic banging on his kitchen door.

Opening the door while brushing away the crumbs clinging to his dressing gown, he found his neighbor, Mr. Page.

"What is it, Mr. Page?"

"There's been a tarrin'-and-featherin', Reverend," he exclaimed, short of breath.

"Good God, no!" Langdon exclaimed. "Where?"

"Just out o' town, at the Harris farmhouse."

"Was it Mr. Harris who was tarred-and-feathered?"

"No. Jeremiah Coffin it was."

"Jeremiah Coffin!" Langdon exclaimed. He was one of Falmouth's most prosperous citizens, a housewright by trade, brother to the highly respected Dr. Nathaniel Coffin. "How did it happen?"

"He was in Mr. Brackett Marston's public house last night, apparently, and said one thing too many to a group o' drunken men," Page replied. "Before anyone could stop 'em, they'd drug 'im off. 'Twasn't known 'til early this morning where they'd taken 'im and what they'd done to 'im."

"Where is he now?" Langdon asked.

"He's at his brother's, who's lookin' after 'im."

"I shall go there as soon as I am dressed, Mr. Page. I thank you for bringing me this news," Langdon said hurriedly, closing the door behind him and racing to his bed chamber.

Twenty minutes later he stood before the door of Dr. Coffin's home, where a number of people had gathered, shivering in the cold, early March morning air. An elderly lady who was a parishioner of St. Paul's Church recognized him and hurried to his side. "Thank God you're here, Reverend. None of us is safe anymore," she said resolutely, clutching his arm. "The madness has now reached our town as well, and we must each tremble with fear in our own homes for the lawlessness which is running loose over the streets!"

"There, there, Mrs. Ingersoll," Langdon reassured her, patting her hand. "I'm hoping it's not as bad as all that. Are people being allowed inside to visit Mr. Coffin?"

"Dr. Coffin has requested that people remain outside. A few are being let in, however. You'll no doubt be admitted, as the vicar, Mr. Langdon," she said.

Langdon went to the door and made himself known to one of the servants who, upon recognizing him, led him upstairs to a back bedroom. Lying upon the bed was one of the most horrific sights

Langdon had ever seen: a creature vaguely resembling Jeremiah Coffin, covered unevenly with hardened globs of black tar and mangled, tattered remains of goose feathers. Dr. Coffin and his two daughters bent over him, rubbing lard-covered cloths on his cheeks and forehead. Mrs. Coffin worked with a pair of scissors at what had been her husband's thick crop of hair, now matted and congealed into a solid mass. Jeremiah Coffin could barely move his arms or legs due to the dried pitch caked over his skin, and his face grimaced in what appeared to be excruciating pain at every movement.

Another of Dr. Coffin's daughters entered the room with a steaming bucket of hot water, taking it to the bedside. Upon recognizing the Rev'd Langdon, she curtsied politely, muttering a subdued greeting, then went to her uncle's side and began to work on a large glob of tar under his left armpit, looking like a heinous, black tumor. Langdon could not draw his eyes away from the spectacle for perhaps twenty minutes, by which time Mr. Coffin's head was shorn of hair and his face relatively freed of its tarry encasement.

Finally able to move his head and look around, Mr. Coffin said, "Good morning, parson."

"I fear it is anything *but* a good morning, Mr. Coffin. I am most dreadfully sorry . . ." Langdon said helplessly. "Who did this horrible thing?"

"So-called 'patriots,'" croaked Coffin in reply. "Sons of lawlessness, who call themselves 'Sons of Liberty' to disguise their real intent, which is to take liberty away from anyone who disagrees with them."

"But . . . why? Why did they do this to you?"

"Because I stand for keeping authority in the hands of the government, rather than in the hands of an angry mob," Coffin said.

"What brought it about?"

"I was in Marston's public house last night around ten o'clock, and just as I was about to leave, I overheard a conversation going on between two men at a nearby table, who were discussing the *John & Mary*. They were arguing about whether the stores for Captain Coulson's ship were an importation or not. Well, I'm fed up with such talk, so I went to their table, laid my hand peaceably on one of their shoulders, and said 'The real issue, gentlemen, which should be on the mind of every man concerned about his liberties, is not whether the goods aboard Mr. Hughes' sloop are an importation, but whether we're going to let a band of self-appointed meddlers tell us, free Englishmen, what to do! Perhaps, rather than discussing the contents of Mr. Hughes' sloop, you should be discussing whether the Committee of Inspection had any right to stick their infernal noses into the affair at all! The existence of that committee is a threat to all of our liberties . . . not least our privacy and the right to conduct our business free from interference. Members of the committee talk about Parliament interfering with our trade by imposing duties and tariffs, but that is negligible when compared to this committee's attempts at blocking our trade altogether!'"

"Lie still, Jeremiah! Do not agitate yourself," Dr. Coffin urged his brother.

Relaxing his muscles, he continued, "Well, these so-called 'Sons of Liberty' couldn't tolerate talk of that kind. What right do I have, after all, to state my opinion when it contradicts theirs? What's more, they are willing to use force to ensure that I keep my opinions to myself, whereas I am willing to allow them free expression of theirs. So, they took advantage of their rights and deprived me of mine."

"Who were these people?"

"A group of harbormen led by Calvin Lombard."

"And how did they . . .?"

"They forcibly took me out of town, to the Harris farmhouse. One of the lads had fetched a bucket of pitch from a harbor shed, and they heated it up in the barn, killed one of Farmer Harris' geese, plucked it, and you can see the result," explained Coffin, wincing as his brother removed a patch of tar from his abdomen to reveal an expanse of red and blistered skin beneath.

Langdon shook his head, unable to find words. He eventually went to the bedside and squeezed Mr. Coffin's hand. "You have no idea how this grieves me, Mr. Coffin. You shall be in my prayers."

"I thank you for your sympathy, Mr. Langdon. It is most generous of you to look in on me."

"You are in the best care in town. Your esteemed brother, ably attended by his three fair assistants, will no doubt see that you are on your feet again in no time."

"Of that I am most hopeful, Mr. Langdon. Thank you."

Langdon went immediately to St. Paul's and said Morning Prayer, including words for Jeremiah Coffin, as well as a supplication on behalf of all of Falmouth's inhabitants, that they be spared from any further violence and unrest.

*

THE REV'D LANGDON was among a group of persons who sat around Captain Coulson's dining table that evening, including George Lyde, the Falmouth Customs Collector, all very much disturbed by the day's events. Coulson's table was in his kitchen, and the appointments much more spartan than Edward Oxnard's.

"You know who is to blame for this," Edward Oxnard said. "The Committee of Inspection, that's who. Them and their fatuous behavior concerning the *John & Mary* that inspired the harbormen to their deed. When a community's leaders talk treasonous talk, the actual treasonous deeds are carried out by the unwittingly aroused lower classes."

"What beats me," Captain Coulson said, passing his hand over the top of his head, "is that the infernal committee of carpenters and caulkers was established 'in the interest of a number of inhabitants of this town,' as if the whole community were clamoring to board the *John & Mary*! I swear, what this committee won't do to justify their actions!"

"They have no legal authority," pointed out Oxnard, "so they must create any authority they can out of thin air."

"Their power is that of fear an' intimidation," Coulson added. "They can compel a certain level of compliance by threatenin' that any opposition could result in communal disapprobation, or even violence, such as that which happened this morning. It is evil an' ungodly, something which six months ago I would not have countenanced possible in this normally pious an' goodly populace!"

"You'd think the French had won the last war by the amount of tyranny and oppression about!" observed Oxnard. "That we are still Englishmen is not apparent by our liberties anymore!"

"Things have not gone that far, I think," Langdon countered quietly. "There is much lawlessness about, regrettably, but the English Constitution is still the law of the land, and I have every confidence that, because of its time-tested strength and perfection, our solutions will eventually be found by appealing to it rather than otherwise. There will be those who advocate its abrogation, but I cannot believe that the majority of thinking citizenry would consent to overthrowing the very thing that ensures our liberty, prosperity, and peaceable livelihoods, even if they agree with the so-called 'Sons of Liberty' concerning taxation and grievances with the crown. I believe a basic sanity will eventually prevail over the people of this colony when they realize the anarchy and lawlessness that would result from pitched protest against the crown, much less war or – God forbid – independence!"

Silence greeted the clergyman's reassuring words, and he realized that his colleagues did not share his optimism.

"So the committee of carpenters and such went aboard the sloop?" asked Oxnard of Captain Coulson.

"Yes, the very day after the Committee of Inspection met, so intent are they of convincing the world of their unrelentin' compliance with that unholy Continental Association. A group of seven of them – only two of whom I knew by sight. I wonder where they dug up such unquestioned authorities on nautical matters?!"

"And their findings?" Oxnard asked.

"The committee met the followin' day, and the carpenters reported that, in their considered opinion, the *John & Mary* might be made ready for sea in two days, without havin' to take any of the stores out of her."

After a doubtful silence Oxnard asked, "Do you think they are right?"

"Well, there's no question the sloop could be made ready for sea in two days – all they need is water an' stores for the return voyage. But whether she'll be in good enough repair to *complete* the voyage is another matter entirely," Coulson said. "It's akin to sayin' that that canoe out back of my house could be made ready for sea in two days. Or my house, for that matter! It's technically true, but ludicrous."

"And what did the committee do then?" Oxnard persisted.

"They drafted a resolution, voted on it, and sent a copy to me," Coulson replied standing from his place and going to his writing table in a corner of the kitchen. "After reviewing the situation in detail," he said, returning to the dinner table, "includin' a listing of every last hogshead of stores aboard the *John & Mary*, they write, 'Resolved: That seven days be allowed said Coulson, from this time, to repair said vessel, and to make the necessary preparations for sending her back; and if he does not at the end of that term (wind and weather permitting) send said vessel out of this harbor to proceed to Bristol, this committee will forthwith cause the truth of the case to be published, agreeable to the Continental Association.'"

George Lyde, the town's imposing Customs Collector, who had remained a silent observer till this point, asked in his deep voice, "Captain Coulson, on your word of honor, is the *John & Mary* in a state of such disrepair that it cannot safely proceed to sea?"

"On my word of honor as an Englishman an' a Christian, founded on my lifetime of occupation with ships an' the sea, the *John & Mary* is unfit for a voyage to England. To Boston, maybe, but never across the Atlantic," he replied with conviction.

"Could you find shipwrights, masters, carpenters and the like to agree with you, based upon an inspection of the sloop itself?" Lyde asked.

"Without a doubt, there would be a number of my fellow merchants alone who, upon even a cursory inspection, would support me."

"Then let us assemble as many of such men as we can find," said Lyde with decision, "send them to inspect the *John & Mary*, and submit a sworn deposition to the Committee of Inspection at their next meeting. We cannot allow their manipulation of facts to go unchallenged when we are able to determine the truth of the affair ourselves. This is our right as free Englishmen!"

*

IT HAD SNOWED SEVERAL INCHES the previous night and earlier in the day, so as the Rev'd Langdon made his way home from Captain Coulson's house, there was a chilling crunch under his feet. His attentions barely took note of it, however, for his mind was racing with thoughts and plans of a different nature.

He pondered the troubling things he had witnessed that evening. While he was inclined to agree with those who disliked the actions and demeanor of the Committee of Inspection, his overriding fear was of the increasing inability of either side to talk peaceably and respectfully with one another in an attempt to find a reasonable resolution to differences. And this portended hardening opposition, and perhaps even violence, among the citizenry, which was to be lamented above all.

He had seen this fracturing in his congregation, too. There was a small minority of people who were becoming increasingly vocal about disobedience to the crown, insisting that Langdon, and therefore the church, sanction their attitudes and behaviors as conforming to their God-given right to liberty and freedom from oppression. Whereas Langdon agreed with their right to these things, he argued that smuggling and rebellion against the government were neither effective nor morally appropriate modes of battling injustice. He was taking more and more criticism for this unpopular position.

Langdon was yanked from his thoughts as a shadow darted across his path several yards in front of him, disappearing between two houses. He neither slackened nor quickened his pace, having no cause for alarm, until he heard the crunch of many feet in the snow-packed road behind him. He cast a glance over his shoulder and saw several town youths, two of whom he recognized, following him.

One of them called out, "Look, boys; if it ain't the king's arse-kisser!" They burst out in derisive, adolescent cackling. Langdon attempted to ignore them, and made an effort to keep a steady, unvarying pace.

Their taunts, however, continued, and they closed in on him slowly. "Why don't you kiss my arse, Reverend Son of Despotism?" called one.

"Tory Dog, go home to your dear old poxed Lord North," cried another, referring to the prime minister.

"You can be a better loyalist toady in London than here, you tea-sucking Papist bishop's-spawn."

Langdon, his heart pounding in alarm but his clergyman's sensibility much offended by the last epithet, stopped and turned, saying, "Go home to your mothers, boys. You have little understanding of the grave issues to which you refer, and merely parrot the thoughtless, idle chatter of malcontents. Do not think I do not recognize you, young Master Pearson and your – "

A snowball flew from out of the darkness, astonishingly close to Langdon's right ear. He involuntarily ducked to the left, losing his balance in the slippery snow and falling to one knee. A ball of ice hammered into his shoulder, causing him to gasp, more from surprise than pain, and another pelted his cheek.

"Take that, you friend of tyranny!"

"Loyalist sycophant!" They ran off down the street and out of sight.

Langdon raised himself carefully, his cheek stinging. Turning to continue his way home, he mumbled under his breath, "Lord, forgive them, for they know not what they do."

*

The Rev'd Mr. Thomas Langdon's Journal

Tuesday, 7 March, 1775. I am much angered by the tarring and feathering of J^{er} Coffin, a known friend of gov^{t}. His brutal usage at the hands of harbourmen is an unfortunate sign of the times, when violence is seen as a fit expression of political opinion. I would be equally angry and disappointed had the harbourmen been friends of gov^{t} tarring and feathering someone who had spoken in opposition to the gov^t, but I have not seen examples of violence in that direction. Oxnard and the "Tory" camp (as the friends of gov^t are being called by their opponents – inaccurate appellation though it may be, as I know many of them to be Whigs) are however of the opinion – and I do not much disagree with them, I must admit – that it is the seditious example set by the town's leaders, most notably those on the Comm. of Insp^n, that incited the harbourmen to their heinous deeds. Perhaps it is because those angry with the govt feel unable to make themselves heard in any other way, but I do not think this justifies it. I myself was accosted this evening in the street by a group of young ruffians, most of whom I recognized as the sons of rebelliously inclined families, and, although I came away bruised, I was much *more* injured by their epithets of "Tory dog," "Loyalist sycophant," and the like. That I have come to be identified with the "Tory" camp is something of astonishment to me, for I see myself as standing up only for peace and mutual respect as a man of God; but if the latter is seen as intolerable to the opponents of govt, then perhaps it is inevitable that I be identified as such. *Lord Jesus Christ, assist me in being fair-minded, even-handed, and neutral in my dealings with my fellow men. Amen.* Mild a.m., Snow flurries and cold p.m.

Chapter Four.

AT THE EXPIRATION of the seven days set for Captain Coulson to dispatch the *John & Mary* from Falmouth harbor, the Committee of Inspection met again in the library chamber. The Rev'd Langdon, as someone conceivably perceived as disinterested in the affair, had been asked by George Lyde to deliver the deposition which had been sworn by fourteen persons experienced in things nautical, to the effect that the *John & Mary* was wholly unfit for an extended oceanic voyage. This he took folded in his breast pocket to the meeting.

The chairman, Enoch Freeman, called the meeting to order, summoned Captain Coulson, and asked that Mr. Parsons, the secretary, read aloud the resolve which had been agreed at the previous meeting.

"Agreeable to the opinion of this committee, Captain Coulson, have you sent the *John & Mary* out of this harbor?" It was a rhetorical question, for anyone who cared to look out the window could see the *John & Mary* moored exactly where she had been these last two weeks.

"I have not," answered Coulson.

"And what is your reason, Captain Coulson?" inquired Freeman.

"The *John & Mary* is in no shape to put to sea. She is in want of repairs. 'Twould be the height of folly to send such a dangerously unseaworthy vessel out to brave the vicious elements of the North Atlantic in winter."

"Are you aware, Mr. Coulson," interjected the chairman, "that the findings of the select committee of riggers, carpenters and caulkers contradicts that assertion?"

Coulson looked at Langdon, who, being duly signaled, broke into the proceedings. "If it please the committee . . ." he said, standing from his position among the onlookers and taking the deposition from his coat pocket.

"What is it, Mr. Langdon?"

"I wish to submit the following deposition for the committee's consideration in this matter." He approached the large table around which the committee was seated. "It may go some little way towards explaining Captain Coulson's inability to comply with the committee's late resolve."

The deposition was unfolded by Freeman, who read the first few lines, inspected the signatures at the bottom, and looked with irritation at the clergyman. He folded it again, and said "It will be taken into consideration, Mr. Langdon, but our business today – "

"May I trouble the chairman to have the deposition read aloud to the committee at large, as it may have considerable bearing on the ensuing discussion," Langdon insisted.

Freeman took a deep breath, trying to dispel his mounting anger. He clenched his jaw, then said, "Very well. Mr. Parsons, will you read the deposition submitted by the Rev'd Mr. Langdon?" he handed the sheet of paper down the table to the secretary, who stood and read it aloud:

"'Stephen Miliken, ship's captain; Richard Harris, ship's captain; Joshua Eldridge, shipmaster; Wesley Simmons, merchant; William Campbell, shipmaster; Abijah Church, ship's carpenter; Edward Oxnard, merchant; Thomas Pagan, merchant; James Tileston, shipwright; Benjamin Waite, merchant; Jeremiah Pote, merchant; Thomas Cumming, merchant; Abraham Osgood, merchant; and Josiah Dornett, Comptroller of Customs; all the aforesaid being citizens of Falmouth, in the County of Cumberland, in the Province of Maine, in the Colony of Massachusetts Bay, having personally appeared before me, William Tyng, Esq., Sheriff of the County of Cumberland; and being duly sworn on the Holy Gospels of Almighty God, did depose and say: That having gone aboard and inspected the sloop *John & Mary* of Bristol, John Hughes master, they have found her in an unfit state to be sent to sea; that a number of loose boards under the water, and a desperate want of caulking throughout most of the hold, resulting in the collection of nearly as much water as the pumps are able effectually to unship, leave her in a state which would prove dangerous to her crew and cargo should she find herself in rough seas. It is therefore recommended by the deponents that the goods in the hold be removed, and she thoroughly repaired, before sending her to sea. Sworn this twelfth day of March, 1775, before me, William Tyng, Esq., Sheriff of the County of Cumberland.'"

A silence followed upon the conclusion of the reading, and the deposition was passed back to the chairman. "Well, Captain Coulson," Freeman began, "if the *John & Mary* is in such a pitiable state of repair, have you attempted to remedy this situation?"

"As you have just heard, Mr. Chairman, the sloop cannot be repaired until the goods have been removed from the hold, and – "

"But the finding of this committee's select group of carpenters, riggers and caulkers, who were aboard the *John & Mary* two weeks ago, found that the sloop's need of repairs did *not* require the removal of the cargo."

"That is, with all respect, Mr. Chairman, not an accurate assessment of the sloop's seaworthiness. I was informed by Captain Hughes, master of the *John & Mary*, that those carpenters an' caulkers were not aboard his ship above ten minutes, an' gave only a cursory glance into the hold, whereas the deponents in the statement submitted by Mr. Langdon were aboard for upwards of forty-five minutes, inspecting very thoroughly every inch of her bottom."

"It remains, however, Captain Coulson, that you have made no attempt whatsoever to repair the sloop." the chairman insisted.

"As the deposition states, Mr. Chairman, it would be purely futile, as the cargo *must* be – "

"Well, Captain Coulson, if the goods must be removed from the *John & Mary*, have you made efforts towards procuring another vessel for the reshipment of the goods back to Bristol, agreeable to the desire of this committee?"

Captain Coulson bristled at this question, and said, "With all due respect, Mr. Chairman, that is an utterly preposterous, and impossible, proposition."

"Pray tell why it is impossible?"

"You seriously want me to hire another vessel than the two already in question? In short, you expect me, because of this confounded Association, not only to forego revenue which is rightly mine by virtue of the contract I made with Mr. Garnet of Bristol early last year, but also to go to the *additional* expense of procurin' *another* vessel, to send back stores which I am in need of right here in Falmouth?! This would be taking bread out of the mouths of my children! No, sirs," Coulson shook his head emphatically, nervously wringing his hat in his large hands, "I remain unconvinced that the reshippin' of these goods is for the benefit of the town, the colony, or even the cause of liberty in British North America. The only vessel other than the *John & Mary* in which I will consent sendin' the stores back to England is the sloop for which the stores are intended in the first place."

"I must agree with Captain Coulson," interjected committee member Daniel Ilsley. "Mr. Chairman, the logical thing would be to allow Captain Coulson, with the help of Falmouth's men, to transfer the stores to his sloop, rig it properly, allow time to repair the *John & Mary*, then send them *both* back to Bristol. We will have fulfilled our duty to the Association, as well as having looked after the welfare of many of our own townsmen in the process."

Jedediah Cobb rocketed from his seat in protest. "That's clearly ag'inst the Continental Association! To rig the sloop would be to make an importation of them stores, and thus be in direct contravention of the resolves of the Continental Congress. The captain's only option remains to send them stores back in the *John & Mary*, and quit delayin' about it."

"Well, then we're right back where we started," Captain Coulson retorted . "Any mariner worth his salt will tell you that you'd be responsible for the murder of the *John & Mary*'s crew, Mr. Cobb! I, however, would not send my worst enemy out in that leaky barrel of a sloop!"

"Let us hope you will not have that opportunity, Captain Coulson," said Daniel Ilsley. Only one laugh – and that quickly stifled by an onlooker – was to be heard.

"I am to assume therefore," Freeman said, "that you have no intention of reshipping these goods to England in any manner whatsoever?"

"Other than in a thoroughly repaired *John & Mary* – or better yet, if I were allowed to use the cargo to complete the fitting out of the sloop for which the goods were intended, an' *thereby* send 'em back to England – no, I have no intention of sendin' 'em back."

"Mr. Parsons," Freeman said, "let the record show that Captain Coulson has neither attempted to repair the *John & Mary* nor endeavored to procure another vessel in which to reship the goods to Bristol, and can provide the committee with no assurances that he will send them back in any other manner than he at first proposed. Now – "

"Mr. Chairman," came the voice of Langdon from his place among the onlookers standing around the committee table, "I cannot restrain myself from observing that the actions of this committee are becoming more imperious with each sitting. As a man of God, I am much saddened at this apparent loss of compassion from persons whom I have heretofore found to be – "

"This is not your church, I beg to remind you, Mr. Langdon," snapped Freeman. "The committee's behavior is not under examination here, but that of Captain Coulson."

Langdon shrank back as if he had been slapped.

After a moment of uncomfortable silence, Freeman turned to Coulson and asked in a low voice, "Do you realize, Captain Coulson, what you are forcing us to do by this resistance of yours?"

"I am not forcing you to do anything."

"I think this committee has been more than patient in our

handling of this matter, and very generous in offering you several avenues of compliance to the Continental Association; yet at every turn you have defied us, insisting on a course of action which will not only hurt the cause of liberty in these colonies, but ultimately your own interests as well. Have you no – "

"With all due respect, Mr. Chairman – "

"*Do not interrupt me, Captain Coulson!*" the chairman bristled. "Have you no regard for the plight of the oppressed peoples of these colonies, and the urgency of stiff measures such as the Continental Association? And even if you don't, and it is left to more perceptive and perspicacious individuals to guide this people's affairs, have you no regard for your fellow citizens and family, who will ultimately suffer from your obstinance? Indeed, by your recalcitrance, Captain Coulson, you are prolonging this period of strife, and delaying that time when our quarrels will find their resolution. Your stubbornness grieves me, Captain Coulson. And, if you do not reverse the inflexibility of your position immediately, I have no choice but to recommend that this committee find you in violation of the Continental Association, and to entreat the citizens of this town and colony to disavow any further dealings with you until such time as you retract your views. How do you respond?"

"I beg leave to point out, Mr. Chairman, that there is considerable dissension on these matters. First of all, to speak to as many of your points as I can recall, it's not my intention to defy this committee or any of the citizens of this town. By standin' firm, as I do, on the issue of the stores an' rigging aboard the *John & Mary*, I'm merely defyin' what I'm steadfastly persuaded is an ignorant an' ruinous course of action. Secondly, I must disagree with you most pointedly on the question of what is the most 'perceptive and perspicacious' course of action for the inhabitants of these colonies in relation to the mother country. I put it to you that it is those who share your treasonous opinions who're prolongin' a resolution to our present difficulties with the crown, an' not the good an' loyal subjects of His Majesty who feel as I do."

"How dare you accuse me of treason!" hissed Freeman.

A number of voices saying "Hear, hear!" rumbled through the chamber.

"You have one more chance to retract, Captain Coulson, otherwise – "

Still stinging from what he felt was the chairman's unwarranted savagery towards him, the Rev'd Langdon exploded, "I cannot believe my ears!" All eyes turned at once to him as he approached the committee table. "This is the very Inquisition!"

"Would the Reverend gentleman – "

"No, the Reverend gentlemen will *not* sit down," Langdon retorted. "Did you not take note of the tarring and feathering a week ago of Mr. Jeremiah Coffin, one of the principal inhabitants of this town? And do you think the mob that did that horrible deed would have done so without the example which this committee has given to our once peaceful and harmonious society?"

"Lamentable as that was, it is irrelevant to the business of this committee, Mr. Langdon. Now, will – "

"It is *directly* relevant to your proceedings, gentlemen! Regardless of your views on current political affairs, do you not see that you are inflaming the under classes with simplistic ideas of violence and unrest? You, the educated and well-placed members of our once congenial community – beneficiaries of the English constitution and mercantile system, not to mention the tradition of liberality and freedom which have ever been hallmarks of our history – you are ideally situated to influence the general moral tone of our society. Yet you have incited the masses to violence, as that is their only method of collective expression."

"Mr. Langdon –!"

"Did you not see the printing in the town's newspaper several days ago of an advertisement instructing the making of gunpowder? And the publishing of a resolve of the Provincial Congress in Cambridge last February encouraging the manufacture of firearms and bayonets? Do you not see that this is akin to putting a burning match into the hand of a child in a hay loft? If this committee were interested in promoting the welfare of the inhabitants of this town and colony, it would work to prevent the publication of such incendiary items – or at least would repudiate such as injurious to the interests of prosperity and harmony – rather than promoting them."

"Mr. Langdon, I demand – "

"When you self-righteously accuse Captain Coulson of hindering the cause of liberty in this colony, yet continue insisting on your own prerogatives to pry into the private affairs of your neighbors, where you have no business, I find serious hypocrisy in this behavior, gentlemen, and I implore you to alter the tenor of your activities *before it is too late!*"

"Order, Mr. Langdon! *I demand order!*" the chairman shouted above the din of objection which had steadily risen during the clergyman's monologue. Between clenched teeth, Freeman said, "One more word, Mr. Langdon, and I shall forbid you from ever attending any meeting of this body again!"

"Hear, hear!" murmured several of the committee members. Langdon wiped his brow with a handkerchief and slowly moved back into the crowd of onlookers. Two by two, all eyes returned to the chairman, who said quietly but with firmness, "Now, unless you make an indication to the contrary, Captain Coulson, be hereby informed that, within the next week I shall bring to a vote before this committee a resolution declaring you a violator of the Continental Association as expressed in its eleventh article. If there be no further business, I move that this meeting be adjourned."

General chaos followed the adjournment as members and

onlookers grouped together in search of allies for the battle lines which had been clearly drawn. Freeman extricated himself from several enthusiastic members, who saw him as the obvious leader of their cause, and intercepted the Rev'd Langdon as the latter made his way out of the chamber.

"Do you have a moment, Mr. Langdon?" Freeman inquired sternly.

"Yes," Langdon said somewhat hesitantly, unsure of what to expect.

"Let us step over here . . ." Freeman said, moving away from the door through which many of the occupants of the chamber were exiting. "Mr. Langdon," he began, picking his words carefully and avoiding looking directly into the clergyman's face, "I am very concerned by what appears to be your alliance with Captain Coulson and his party."

"Why, Mr. Freeman! I am allying myself only with peaceable behavior," Langdon protested. "In fact, I deplore the taking-of-sides which has arisen over this whole affair."

"Then why did you submit that deposition?" Freeman demanded.

"Because I am a servant of the truth. Justice is only served when *all* the facts are known, not just those that conform to one party's view."

"But you are playing directly into the hands of the friends of government. I had thought we agreed on the injustices committed by government against the colonies," Freeman argued.

"We do. But that does not make me an *enemy* of government," Langdon stated. "On the contrary, it persuades me that we must redouble our efforts to rectify those wrongs, not pout like recalcitrant children. If we kick and struggle against every gesture from the mother country, how are we to differentiate a slap from a caress?"

"Please have done with your clerical moralizing, Mr. Langdon!" Freeman insisted. "The situation calls for a much more rational, clear-headed assessment than such metaphors allow for."

"On the contrary, I have always been of the opinion that metaphor tells one much more about the essence of an issue than ever scientific dissection does."

"I would enjoin you," continued Freeman with growing impatience, "not to get yourself involved with Coulson or the other Tories in Falmouth, like the Customs Collector, Mr. Lyde, or Sheriff Tyng. It is destructive to civic morale and unity, and their influence is inciting people to take sides one against another, and giving rise to partisanship, even amongst families and friends."

"On that score I most profoundly disagree, Mr. Freeman," Langdon shook his head. "Take the tarring and feathering of Mr. Coffin – was it Mr. Lyde, Sheriff Tyng, or Captain Coulson who incited that tragic offence? No, it was those who would rebel against their king and country . . . the very people over whom *your* committee is having such a profound and disturbing influence. It is *you* whom I would encourage to cast your attention towards civic morale and unity, and the dangerous effect you are having on it; and to have done with *your* clerical moralizing about injustice and tyranny."

Before Freeman could reply – even before it was clear whether he intended to – Langdon turned on his heel and left the library chamber, filled with indignation.

*

THE REV'D MR. THOMAS LANGDON'S JOURNAL

TUESDAY, 14 MARCH, 1775. (. . .) I will not compare myself with Our Saviour in saying that my indignation was righteous – that is for God alone to judge. But I was certainly more enraged than I have ever been during the comm^t meeting and for several hours afterwards. I pray to God that it was not solely due to stung pride. No, I must hope it was in reaction to what I witnessed in the comm^t that caused me to feel as I did. Mr. Freeman no doubt has fixed me firmly in the so-called "High Tory" camp after today's proceedings. Yet I hope I may yet demonstrate to him and those under his influence that I am not committed to one faction or another, but to what is right and best for our town and society; and where one side tramples on God-given and gov^t-sanctioned rights in an overzealous attempt to manipulate the process of affairs in their favour, I will oppose them. *Lord Jesus Christ, guide me with Thy strengthening hand; show me the right path amidst confusion; lead me into that place where I might be of service to Thy Holy Will through reconciliation and not division; through moderation and not controversy; through calmness and not fear. Amen.* Overcast but warm. Showers p.m

Chapter Five.

"There is only one thing for it, I'm afraid," said William Tyng, Sheriff of the County of Cumberland, as he sat with several other guests at the Rev'd Langdon's dining room table, sharing a pot of tea that evening. His well-worn three-cornered hat lay on the table at his elbow, thus revealing a head of sparse hair, unkempt strands snaking in disarray over his balding crown. "I am writing to Governor Gage in Boston, informing him of the disturbances here, and requesting that a warship be sent to this port. That'll put the fear of God into 'em!"

"I wholeheartedly agree, Sheriff," Edward Oxnard said

enthusiastically. "I'll affix my name to your letter, should you wish it." Everyone at the table, excepting Langdon, made the same offer, which Tyng accepted.

"How do you propose sending this letter?" Oxnard asked.

"I've a trusted friend going to Boston day-after-tomorrow. I'll give it to him, with instructions to destroy it should he feel it were in jeopardy of falling into malicious hands."

"So that means," Oxnard calculated on his fingers, "that the letter will be in General Gage's hands, Lord willing, by early next week. The 20th at the latest."

"Correct," Tyng replied. "And judging by the promptness with which he responded to the Marshfield affair last month, and the couple of days it would take a vessel to sail from Boston to Casco Bay, wind and weather permitting, we might expect some sort of action or reply by the first of April."

"What makes you think," asked Lyde in his deep voice, "that Gage will pay any attention to us at all? Aren't we rather ancillary to the main theatre of affairs in Boston?"

"Well, there's no harm in trying," offered Oxnard, "and according to newspaper reports from all over New England, and a few places more distant, Boston is no longer the only seat of unrest."

"All the more reason for us not to get our hopes up," said Lyde. "I gravely doubt that Governor Gage will actually do anything for us. The few thousand British regulars and handful of warships assembled at Boston are far too few to meet the growing tide of unrest and violence in a territory stretching thousands of miles from Halifax in the north to the Carolinas in the south. Indeed, we are on the very fringe, and therefore even less important from a strategic viewpoint."

"I will emphasize in the letter the one aspect of our situation which I think will be of some interest to the commanders in

Boston," Sheriff Tyng began. "It is rumored – nay, even reported – that Admiral Graves has ordered the requisitioning of any vessels which are in danger of falling into rebel hands and used as potential privateers against His Majesty's forces. I think their Lordships will be quite interested to hear of Captain Coulson's unfinished sloop, which would be quite a prize in the hands of the rebels, and they will send a warship directly to assist in its completion, probably ordering it back to Boston where the admiral can keep an eye on it, and possibly even pressing it into His Majesty's service."

"Better that than a rebel privateer, although I wish it could simply be completed in peace and sent back to Bristol, as I'm sure Captain Coulson himself would wish," Mr. Lyde said.

"A rebel privateer?" Langdon interjected with incredulity. "That assumes armed conflict to a degree unimaginable to me!" he said. "I mean, I cannot imagine a rag-tag band of untrained and undisciplined colonists forming an army – much less a naval force – which would come anywhere near to threatening the armed might of Great Britain. It would be madness on the part of any man who dared it!"

"Oh, with all due respect, Mr. Langdon," Sheriff Tyng said somberly, "I think, given adequate munitions – and Americans have demonstrated their talent for smuggling all too well lately – they could pose a significant threat to any group of regulars; and, although it seems less likely at sea, I'd warrant a flotilla of a half-dozen privateers between here and Boston could wreak havoc with the merchant trade, requiring a British squadron ten-times as large to counteract."

The clergyman shook his head. "I cannot believe it would ever come to that!"

"Then you are being willfully blind," said Tyng. Silence greeted his pronouncement.

Langdon shook his head in resignation. "It is sad how easily men are caught up in the spirit of violence. Even those who tout reason and compromise above everything find themselves, when the issues become too emotionally laden, wishing for a forced resolution to the conflict. They say to themselves, How much simpler and more satisfying to coerce our adversaries into compliance, rather than having to persuade them; to have, in other words, our disturbances decided by a contest of arms. How easy it is even for a man of peace to resort to the sword when it appears to suit his end. Yet how wrong we are. How terribly, lamentably wrong!"

"Be that as it may, Mr. Langdon, a British warship in the harbor would not have to use its force to return a number of this town's inhabitants to a right use of their reason, not to mention restore the King's honor in these parts!" Sheriff Tyng insisted, to which Mr. Oxnard heartily agreed.

"Well, I must be off," Tyng said after a pause. "Important business tomorrow in Brunswick, and I've two hours on horseback ahead of me. Thank you very much for the tea, Mr. Langdon." He nodded to the other gentlemen, who expressed likewise that they would be taking their leave, and soon the house was empty.

As Langdon picked up the cups and saucers, his mind coursing along the uncomfortable channels of the evening's conversation, he only reluctantly assented to the thought that the present unrest could escalate to the level of armed conflict depicted by Sheriff Tyng, which disturbed him greatly.

What his own actions in that event would be, he could not tell. It went without saying, of course, that he would remain a law-abiding person, advocating moderation, compromise, and reason in the great debates of the day. But, as such persons were being increasingly cowed into silence and intimidated into submission by those who were inclined toward rebellion, he was not sure that persistence in this vein would be ultimately profitable. But would it be any more profitable for him publicly and vocally to oppose the rabble-rousers? He was unconvinced.

His washing up completed, Langdon went to his study. Wednesday nights were normally reserved for the composition of his sermon for the following Sunday, and it had become so much of a habit that, despite the lateness of the hour, he felt he ought at least to read and ponder the lessons for the day to get a start on it.

He lit several candles on his desk and opened his prayer book to the table of lessons. He perused the Old Testament lesson, then continued on to the New Testament lesson, which was from the 13th chapter of the Apostle Paul's Epistle to the Romans. It read:

> Let every soul be subject unto the higher powers, for there is no power but of God: the powers that be are ordained of God. Whosoever therefore resisteth the power, resisteth the ordinance of God: and they that resist shall receive to themselves damnation. For rulers are not a terror to good works, but to the evil. Wilt thou then not be afraid of the power? Do that which is good, and thou shalt have praise of the same: For he is the minister of God to thee for good. But if thou do that which is evil, be afraid; for he beareth not the sword in vain: for he is the minister of God, a revenger to execute wrath upon him that doeth evil. Wherefore ye must needs be subject, not only for wrath, but also for conscience sake. For this cause pay ye tribute also: for they are God's ministers, attending continually upon this very thing. Render therefore to all their dues: tribute to whom tribute is due; custom to whom custom; fear to whom fear; honor to whom honor.

Langdon sat thoughtfully, the Bible open on the desk before him. One phrase kept echoing in his mind: 'Ye must needs be subject, not only for wrath' (by which Langdon surmised was meant 'not for fear of the consequences'), 'but also for conscience sake.' This was an appeal to the individual's sense of what was right and wrong. Far too often, Langdon thought, Christians were told that their religion was a code of behavior, of commandments, admonitions, and prohibitions that were not open to discussion. Yet scripture's frequent appeals to individual reason were usually overlooked. He felt that it was not what people did that was so important as what they valued. And Christ's own words, pointing out that lust of the eye was to commit adultery in the heart, demonstrated that the sin was committed in the intent and not the deed – in the mind and not with the hand. Indeed, the purely physical – the atoms and vapors that make up the visible world – was morally neutral and benign. For instance, are the atoms of the hand which commits a theft or a murder guilty of the crime? No, it is the spirit or soul – the *animas* – of the criminal which is guilty.

This appeal to the conscience, exhorting the reader to be subject to the 'powers ordained of God,' was in effect an appeal directly to the individual. It was an invoking of a code of ethics – a matrix of competing motivations and interests – and not just a commandment of unarguable finality. And it therefore appealed all the more to Langdon, forcing him to wrestle intellectually with it far more than if it were a simple directive.

Langdon was startled by the extent to which the passage applied to their present situation, and the ambivalence he felt in knowing which course of action he should take. He felt almost as if a door were closing behind him, preventing him from turning away from this new realization. Unlike many men of the cloth who claimed direct communication with God, he found the thought laughable – at least he had never heard anything like a divine voice in his head. Yet Langdon felt a growing conviction as strong as any he'd ever had, and acknowledged that this could perhaps be interpreted as divine guidance.

Langdon took several sheets of paper from his drawer, opened his ink bottle and began writing. The sermon flowed with unusual ease, and he worked steadily, stopping only to replace the candles when they began to sputter. When he had affixed the period after the final 'Amen,' he laid down his pen and rubbed his eyes. He looked at the clock across the room. It was difficult to bring it into focus, but eventually he made out that it was nearly 3 o'clock in the morning, which startled him.

A warm sense of satisfaction suffused his breast, coupled with the conviction of rectitude. The sermon was written; the die was cast. "Here I stand," he thought, quoting an earlier Christian at a critical crossroads, "I can do no other."

*

ON THE FOLLOWING SUNDAY, to ensure that the New Testament reading would have the greatest chance of being clearly heard in the church, Langdon asked George Lyde, the stentorian Customs Collector for Falmouth, if he would be the reader. His booming voice and commanding manner of speech were perfectly suited, Langdon knew from experience, to the peculiar acoustics of the church building. In addition, there was a certain significance in having the town's Customs Collector read this passage.

Concerned as he was about the reception of what was to be a possibly controversial sermon, Langdon passed the first part of the service in a state of great agitation, which reached a climax as Mr. Lyde approached the front of the church to read the lesson from Romans.

Standing in the pulpit some minutes later, with a deep breath, he began.

"I am sometimes approached by people, parishioners and non-parishioners alike, who suggest to me that, perhaps the scriptures are not always timely, or relevant to modern life. Why should we, they say, find anything significant in genealogical lists, or exhortations to wash our feet before sitting down to a meal? As an Englishman, what is there with which I can identify in the experiences of a Moabite servant-girl, or a Jewish king? Indeed, certain portions of the scriptures seem less important to our moral and religious edification than others. But at times there comes a passage which is so timely as to jar the reader with astonishment, impressing upon him the indefatigable working of the Holy Ghost in the pages of scripture. Romans chapter 13 is one of these, being as relevant to us in Massachusetts today as to the first-century Christians for whom Paul wrote his epistle over seventeen-hundred years ago. And its message is unequivocal. 'Let every soul be subject unto the higher powers,' it reads, and from the context we know that the Apostle is referring to one's rulers.

"The early Christians in Rome were subject to pagan rulers, compelling them not only to worship a pantheon of pagan gods and goddesses, but often the emperor himself. These new Christians very rightly questioned whether they ought to pay homage to a government so grossly anti-Christian, and to support it with their tribute and taxes. What was Paul's reply to their questions, however? 'The powers that be are ordained of God,' he assured them. 'Whosoever resisteth the powers, resisteth the ordinance of God. They are God's ministers; Render therefore to all their dues; tribute to whom tribute is due; custom' – take note, ye who avoid the customs collectors for your smuggled goods – 'custom to whom custom is due; fear to whom fear; honor to whom honor.'

"If Paul should advocate this to a people groaning under the pagan subjugation of Imperial Rome, how much more would he advocate it to us, the fortunate subjects of a beneficent, magnanimous and – above all – Christian monarch? If Paul could suggest to a people persecuted by their rulers, that these very rulers

– the Emperors of Rome – were 'ordained of God' and 'ministers for good,' and that those who resisted them 'shall receive to themselves damnation,' how much more should that apply to us, whose rulers are the sworn upholders of these very principles? One could easily be inclined to forgive a man for not respecting rulers who have threatened him with persecution and even death; but for an Englishman to withhold tribute from his good and gracious sovereign, this is even more assuredly to 'receive to himself damnation.'

"Some may ask, But what of our grievances? Does not a person have the right – nay, the *responsibility* – to protest unjust measures, and to resist the imposition of such by his rulers, no matter how good and benevolent they might be? Yes, we've every right to protest, to make our views and feelings known, to advocate alternatives. Thanks to the liberality of our constitution, we are granted numerous legal and civilized channels by which to do this, and many of these have proven their efficacy in recent years. But to resist one's rulers – and I'm persuaded that Paul is speaking specifically of illegal, subversive, and blatantly seditious acts, such as we've seen all too frequently of late – this is what Paul threatened would bring about damnation. When a man ceases to respect his ruler; when he refuses to pay tribute; when he recommends his ruler's overthrow; when he commits violent acts against those who continue to respect their ruler; *that* is when his protest has gone too far and become twisted and sinful."

As he spoke the last three words, he noticed a family halfway down the right side of the church whose father had directed them to collect their things to leave.

"The Apostle Paul speaks also to those of us who grumble at the sending and assembling of His Majesty's troops and warships in Boston at this tumultuous time. 'If thou do that which is evil,' says the Apostle, 'be afraid; for he *beareth not the sword in vain:* He is the minister of God, a revenger to execute wrath upon him that doeth evil.'"

The family was on its way down the aisle towards the west doors, and several other individuals had begun to edge their way out of the pews. "The troops and warships assembled at Boston are the very instruments described by St. Paul, ready to execute wrath on them that do evil. And who can deny that there exist at this time forces which are doing evil? Who can deny that there are those who, by their lawless resistance to the 'powers that be,' are bringing damnation not only upon themselves, but upon *all* of us? Who can deny that this country – and this colony in particular – has seditious factions within it, refusing to pay tribute, suggesting that resistance is the only course of action open to us, forming societies to spy upon those who disagree with them, tarring-and-feathering those who oppose them; and who, in their blatant, ill-considered defiance, are bringing us all to the very brink of pestilence, retribution, and even war!"

The west doors banged shut after another group of congregants had taken their leave. What remained of the congregation looked up towards the pulpit with a mixture of fear and astonishment. Langdon set aside the rest of his prepared sermon and moderated his tone, convinced that those who were left would not benefit from any more of the same.

"But take heart, you who have remained loyal," he smiled down on them. He could almost hear the sighs of relief as the parishioners of St. Paul's recognized their old rector once more. "For Paul tells us that our ruler is the minister of God to us for good. 'Do that which is good, and thou shalt have praise of the same.' Remain steadfast in your convictions – not merely out of fear of the wrath which will surely come, 'but also for conscience sake,' as the Apostle tells us. Remain unflagging in your loyalty, my brothers and sisters, paying tribute and custom and honor to whom these things are due, and you shall surely be rewarded." He paused, gauging whether his conciliatory words had reassured them to any degree. "In the name of the Father, and of the Son, and of the Holy Ghost, Amen," he concluded, and descended from the pulpit.

*

THE REV'D MR. THOMAS LANGDON'S JOURNAL

SUNDAY, 19 MARCH, 1775. (. . .) I grew a little more impassioned than I had intended, or even believed possible, in today's sermon. In fact, I must confess to this private record of my thoughts and deeds, that I invoked the passage from Romans in a little more slavish fashion than is my wont. It is ironical (but perhaps my just desserts) that I will be branded a 'high Tory' because of a sermon which does not conform absolutely to my rather latitudinarian approach to Holy Writ. I would prefer it if my public reputation rested on a sermon of which I could be more theologically and hermeneutically proud than this one! But, such is the fickle nature of public life. (. . .)

CHAPTER SIX.

SOON AFTER DAWN on 11 April many of the citizens of Falmouth were awakened by the sound of pounding hammers through the town. The Hon. Enoch Freeman, upon hearing them, smiled with satisfaction and turned over in his bed, falling back asleep.

The Rev'd Thomas Langdon, on the other hand, arose in great consternation. Looking out of his bedroom window he saw a man wearing a cloth cap nailing a poster to a fence post.

Hurriedly dressing, he soon stood outside reading the bill. That there was a pleasant feel to the air, promising a warm spring day, did not occur to him. It read:

Committee of Inspection
Falmouth, Mass., 10 April, 1775

> To hold a man up as an object of general detestation, to deprive him of the benefits that result from society, is disagreeable, is painful; but, on the other hand, to neglect the interest of our Country, to disappoint the just expectations for our constituents is dishonorable and base. The Committee of Inspection of the Town of Falmouth, therefore come forward, to discharge the duty they owe the public, and the trust reposed in them by their fellow-citizens.

There followed an account of the Coulson affair from the arrival of the *John & Mary* on 2 March, through each of the committee's various meetings up to 15 March. The final paragraphs then read:

> It appeared that Captain Coulson had not taken due care to get the said Sloop repaired, nor had endeavored to procure another, in which to reship the goods to Bristol, and would give the Committee no assurance that he would send them back.
>
> We, the said Committee of Inspection, do therefore, agreeable to the directions of the said Continental Congress, as expressed in the Eleventh Article of their Association, hereby publish the name of the said Thomas Coulson, as a violator of the Continental Association.
>
> By order of the Committee:
>
> The Hon[ble] Enoch Freeman, Chairman

Downhearted after reading it, Langdon almost failed to notice that there were a number of people hurrying in the direction of the harbor. He stopped someone and asked where it was they were all going with such haste.

"A warship has entered port," was the excited reply. Langdon immediately joined their ranks and made his way to the waterfront, burning with even more curiosity than the hanging of the bill had inspired. His emotions were fluctuating violently as he approached the quay, going from almost uncontainable dejection to soaring elation upon observing the most majestic sight he thought he had ever seen. The British Union Jack, flapping lazily at the stern of the slowly approaching man-of-war, its sails, yards, and fittings in exceedingly good trim, filled him with a surge of patriotic pride, despite his conviction that the presence of a warship would spell more trouble for the town in the long run than it would resolve in the short.

His Majesty's Armed Ship *Canceaux* approached Falmouth in the faint early morning airs under a light press of sail, and even though she was yet thousands of feet away, the voice of a man in her bows testing the shallowness of the bay and calling out depths every half-minute was clearly audible to the silent gathering of watching townsmen. She was substantially larger than the *Gaspee* had been, and, more importantly to the landsman's unpracticed eye, she was not fore-and-aft rigged, like the latter schooner, but ship-rigged, with three masts of square sails mounted on horizontal yards. Her lines were graceful and dignified, her paintwork and upkeep impeccable, her handling skillful and easy. She made a dramatic contrast to the *John & Mary*, for instance, which was a larger ship, but, like a typical merchantman, ungainly and wide, very functional and basic in her lines, and with very little attention paid to her physical appearance, which was patched, stained, and unkempt. A handful of that merchantman's men lined her rails, chatting animatedly and obviously quite pleased as they watched the *Canceaux* come closer. The merchantman's master, Mr. Hughes, could be seen near the stern, telescope to his eye, examining the approaching warship.

It took the *Canceaux* twenty minutes to reach a point some cables from the shore. With an apparent ease which belied the true difficulty of the tasks involved and which spoke very well of the discipline and competence of her commander, the sails disappeared, the anchor was dropped, and the stern of the ship swung round 45 degrees, thus presenting its broadside to the town.

Langdon remained a spectator of these goings-on for about an hour all told, until the day was well enough advanced to reveal an overcast but relatively warm spring day.

Enoch Freeman, quite in contrast to his satisfaction at daybreak with the sound of hammering in his ears, turned a pale shade of white upon hearing the news of the *Canceaux*'s appearance. He made coffee with some difficulty, his hands shaking, and, as he sat silently at the table with his cup, he cursed: No sooner had he brought the Coulson affair to a conclusion, in the hopes of declaring victory and thereby furthering the cause of American liberty (and perhaps his own local political career), than his hopes were dealt a serious challenge by the appearance of a warship, the commander of which doubtless had political ideas quite contrary to his own.

*

LIEUTENANT HENRY MOWAT, commander of the *Canceaux*, sent a communication ashore early in the day to request the coming aboard of Sheriff Tyng, Captain Coulson, and Mr. Lyde, the Customs Collector, thus confirming to the Rev'd Langdon that the ship's appearance was a result of the sheriff's letter, sent over a fortnight ago. These three attended Mowat aboard his ship around noon, and were invited to lunch with the commander in his cabin.

Lieutenant Mowat was a short, stocky Scotsman of about forty years with an intense gaze and a determined air. He wore no wig, although most of his guests did, and had very closely cropped sandy-colored hair.

The *Canceaux* was too small a ship for the great cabin to have stern windows, and its inhabitants had to stoop in order not to bang their heads against the deckhead beams; but there was a table in the middle, set quite commodiously with four places, and Mowat directed them to their places. Mowat's cabin steward, a negro named Penfold, passed quietly behind them, serving food and removing used dishes.

Having confirmed to them upon their first coming aboard that he had been sent in direct response to their letter requesting aid, Mowat proceeded to update them on the general state of affairs in Boston.

"I have been engaged for several years in surveying the New England coast in order to update the Admiralty's charts of the region," he began in his thick Scottish burr. "This December, however, in consequence of disturbances in Portsmouth, New Hampshire, Vice Admiral Graves sent Captain Barkley of the *Scarborough* and myself with the *Canceaux* to the Piscataqua River, where our sudden and unexpected appearance before the town prevented a great number of cannon being carried off by rebels.

"In January Governor Wentworth of that place was very desirous of having a ship close in to the town, to prevent continued rioting by the populace, so Captain Barkley ordered me to fulfill the governor's wishes. A pilot, supposedly knowledgeable of the harbor and its environs, was brought on board to maneuver us into a location that would satisfy the governor. The pilot turned out to be a rebel sympathizer, however, for he anchored us in a place at high water which was not deep enough at low tide to keep us afloat.

We were therefore benipped in the spot for an entire day, Captain Barkley providing whatever assistance he could."

"What happened to the rebel pilot who ran you aground?" Lyde asked.

"He had left the ship before the ebbing tide revealed our predicament; and although Governor Wentworth put out an immediate search for the man, he could not be located," Mowat explained.

"Thereby proving his guilt," remarked Lyde.

"Aye," Mowat agreed. "At the next high tide but one (the intervening one was too weak), we were finally able to get off the bottom and were warped into deeper water, where we determined that the only damage to us was to the false keel, and the metalwork at the bottom of the rudder. Admiral Graves, when he heard of the incident, ordered me at Captain Barkley's discretion to Halifax to have the damage repaired. Captain Barkley considered the damage too insignificant and the *Canceaux*'s presence too greatly needed to dispatch me at once, however, and waited instead until things might calm down. As you can guess, things have never calmed down. In late March, however, orders arrived from Graves requiring me to come at once to Falmouth, before continuing to Halifax, due to the disturbances described in your letter, Sheriff Tyng. Hence, my presence."

"And what do you intend to do now you're here?" Lyde inquired.

"See to it that Captain Coulson's sloop is finished and sent round to Portsmouth or Boston; and meanwhile, keep the peace," he responded.

"You will go on to Halifax afterwards?" the Customs Collector persisted.

"Yes, after my business here is finished," Mowat said.

"And when will that be?"

"It depends on how quickly Coulson's sloop can be finished. A fortnight, given adequate muscle," he replied. "Three weeks at most."

"I see," said Lyde. "Although, ever since Coulson has become the target of the Committee of Inspection, he's had difficulty getting harbormen to assist him, even when offering double the usual wage."

"I should be able to provide a few of my crew to assist, at any rate," Mowat stated.

After a short silence, Mowat asked, "Tell me, what is the general attitude among the townspeople toward government, this whole affair with Captain Coulson's sloop aside?"

"It is frighteningly anti-government, stirred up considerably by the Committee of Inspection," Lyde replied.

"Ah, that's the body which has found Captain Coulson in violation of their Association? Chaired by – the name was mentioned in your letter, Sheriff Tyng."

"Enoch Freeman."

"Yes, that's right. Enoch Freeman. Is he a very dangerous man – a demagogue?"

"Not . . . exactly," Lyde said slowly. "He is not a rabble-rouser, like the infernal Samuel Adams; but he is certainly to blame for giving this Coulson affair the amount of publicity it has received, and for making sure the popular attention did not wane due to disinterest in the affair."

"I see. Are there other leaders of sedition in Falmouth?" Mowat inquired.

"Freeman has many supporters, and, I'd reckon, no shortage of men who would readily shoot him in the back and fill his shoes should he waver in his resolve," Tyng replied, "but they have all rallied around Freeman for the moment, anyway."

"And where do the town's other leaders stand?" Mowat

continued his interrogation.

"Jedediah Preble, the chairman of the Town Council, probably leans towards the rebels, but has not yet shown his colors," Tyng replied, "and the most prominent merchant families are split – the Pearsons and Cobbs are mostly rebels, but the Oxnards, Waites and Ilsleys are friends of government."

"And the clergy?"

"Ignominiously seditious!" exclaimed Lyde. "With the exception of the Rev'd Mr. Langdon, of course, rector of St. Paul's, the English church. He is, in fact, a most eloquent man, well worth your acquaintance, Captain Mowat. He wavered at first, but he has recently come out strongly in favor of loyalty and reason in public affairs. A most persuasive conversion, I might add, bringing a few of the fence-sitters and faint-hearted with him, I'm informed."

"Did he indeed?" Mowat nodded with approval. "Well then, I shall do as you recommend and make his acquaintance ere I leave port."

*

IN FACT, HE INVITED the Rev'd Mr. Langdon, along with the Hon. Enoch Freeman, Jedediah Preble and George Lyde, to the *Canceaux* for dinner the following evening. Mr. Preble declined the invitation with regrets, but the remaining three attended.

The ship's gig was sent to collect the townsmen at Pearson's wharf. The midshipman in command of the boat, Mr. Larkin, could immediately tell which of the three he liked most. His eyes passed quickly over Mr. Lyde, pinched and elderly; and, although they paused briefly on the serious and almost sinister Mr. Freeman, owing to a decided nervousness on his part, they finally came to rest on the Rev'd Langdon, whose bright face communicated a boyish excitement. Mr. Larkin's approval was strengthened when, having reached the *Canceaux*, the youthful clergyman declined the use of the bosun's chair, which both Lyde and Freeman availed themselves of, and climbed up the ship's side under his own power, then watched with interest the operation of hoisting the other two on board from there.

Langdon looked around with curiosity, it being his first time aboard a warship. He was surrounded by a spectacle of extreme order and cleanliness, which conflicted slightly with his only other nautical experience, when he had taken passage to England and back on one of the Oxnard's merchant ships in 1767 for his ordination. The eight cannon, lashed into their places along the deck, were another sign that this was a very different kind of ship. But there were many sights and smells which brought back strong reminders of that passage: the sloped wooden deck beneath his feet, the great masts and their miles of ropes and cordage stretching above his head, the capstan and other deck fixtures, the odors of tar and sea salt.

Contrary to his expectations, he did not sense a sullen and brooding crew, resentful of or inured to their cruel treatment at the hands of a malicious tyrant; but a jovial, happy lot who smiled at each other, doffed their hat to him as a man of the cloth, and stepped to their duties with alacrity and a willing nature.

They were shown into the great cabin once Lyde and Freeman were safely aboard, where they found Mowat and a tall, lanky stranger, who turned out to be the ship's surgeon, Dr. David Bailey, his jet-black hair tied neatly in a queue at the nape of his neck.

"I have taken the liberty of inviting my ship's surgeon, Dr. Bailey, to fill the place of Mr. Preble," Mowat explained as he introduced them. They were offered sherry, which they drank sitting down due to the low ceiling above their heads. The steward

Penfold padded quietly around them as they ate.

The conversation was at first somewhat stilted, with careful avoidance of controversial topics and a studied restraint on all parts; but it soon became freer, especially as the sherry, and the wine which was served with dinner, loosened tongues and lowered inhibitions.

"Tell me, Captain Mowat," asked Freeman at one point, "how does one survey a coastline?"

"Ah," a smile crossed the mariner's face, indicating his obvious fondness for the topic. "Maritime cartography is a very slippery science, incredibly susceptible to error," he began, launching into such a detailed explanation of mathematical theorems, angles, distance calculations, the difficulty of contending with unknown or variable ocean currents, the use of telescopes and other instruments, the inexactness of "casting the lead," etc., that he soon left his guests far behind in their comprehension of the topic.

Having lost interest, Langdon turned to Dr. Bailey, who sat on his left, and asked quietly, "What sort of medical cases do you have among the hands at this moment, Dr. Bailey?"

"The men of the *Canceaux* are a healthy lot, in general," he replied, "with only the usual collection of lacerations, bruises, hypothermia – that before the recent warm weather, anyway – acute stomach complaints, blisters, boils, the re-occurrence of venereal sores . . ."

Freeman, who sat across the table from them, cleared his throat loudly, making it apparent he did not appreciate this line of conversation whilst he ate. Dr. Bailey's face reddened with embarrassment.

Langdon, regretful of having caused the obviously sensitive young doctor any discomfort, quickly changed the subject by asking, "What is your background, if I may be so bold?"

"I was raised in Lincolnshire but studied medicine as an

apprentice to my uncle in Blackheath, then did a special course at Cambridge . . . nothing extensive. Just enough to get a surgeon's warrant from the Navy Board," he explained, not very loudly and without much pride.

Langdon, sensing that talking of himself would be less uncomfortable for the apparently shy doctor, said, "I went up to King's College in New York, and, although I learned a great many valuable things there, and do not regret my having done so, I have always had the feeling that an industrious man with a great deal of self-motivation could make his way just as well – in fact, better in some cases – than someone who, by dint of memorizing a few things and demonstrating this in written examinations, obtained a sheet of parchment saying he was a bachelor or doctor of this or that subject."

Dr. Bailey smiled vaguely.

"You are probably just such an industrious, self-taught person, I'd warrant," Langdon observed.

"Very kind of you to say so," Dr. Bailey replied politely.

Admitting defeat in his attempts to strike up a separate conversation, Langdon turned his attention back to Mowat, who was now talking about the natural suitability of Casco Bay as a ship's harbor.

"I assume that you have not come here simply to enjoy the sheltered benefits of this natural harbor, Captain Mowat, so what brings you to Falmouth?" asked Freeman in a manner which struck the Rev'd Langdon as mildly abrupt.

"I will not dissemble, Mr. Freeman," Mowat said matter-of-factly. "My orders are to assist Captain Coulson in the completion of his sloop, and to escort the vessel back to Boston once it is finished. In the meantime, I am to give whatever assistance I can to the friends of government in these environs, and to keep the peace."

"How did you hear about Captain Coulson's sloop?"

"From my orders, of course."

"Yes, but where did that information come from?"

"I am unable to provide such information."

"To protect your informers, no doubt," said Freeman, avoiding eye contact with the Rev'd Langdon and Mr. Lyde by spinning his wine glass between his fingers.

"You would perhaps be surprised, Mr. Freeman," stated Mowat evenly, "at the number of people in this town who do not consider the providing of freely accessible information to proper governmental authorities as a thing to be ashamed of."

Freeman did not respond, a hint sullenly.

"As for you, Mr. Freeman," Mowat continued, causing Freeman visibly to stiffen, "you could be of the greatest benefit to the peace of Falmouth by using your influence to persuade townsmen, particularly harbormen and merchant crews, to assist in the completion of Captain Coulson's sloop. Ever since you have embroiled Coulson in the efforts of your committee, I hear that no harborman will lift a finger to assist, even when offered twice the usual wage. Your influence would sway them, Mr. Freeman. Not to mention that it's the quickest way of getting me out of your hair."

"Never," Freeman stated, shaking his head. "I must remain staunch in my support of the Continental Association."

Mowat paused, then said, "Very well. Do as you please. A spirit of fairness, however, compels me to inform you that your name is known to General Gage and Admiral Graves as the major leader of sedition in Falmouth, Mr. Freeman. I am merely giving you fair warning that this is so, and that you still have opportunity to reconsider your path."

"Is that what this little dinner is all about? To intimidate me with threats?"

"Oh, come, Mr. Freeman!" Mowat said, his voice tinged with anger for the first time that evening. "I am a King's officer; this is a town in His Majesty's Kingdom; you are a local official, just like Mr. Lyde here, and the Rev'd Langdon; we are all Britons. The custom of naval officers inviting local port officials to dine with them is immemorial. Do not imagine that you see threats in a matter of social etiquette."

"You do not see your words as a threat, then?"

"More of a favor, actually."

"A favor," he sniffed. "It is tactics like this which feed American notions of British tyranny, condescension and intimidation," Freeman said.

Mr. Lyde snorted, drawing all eyes to himself. "What you, through your committee, Mr. Freeman, have done to Captain Coulson – the public censure, incitements to communal disapprobation, the ruination of his livelihood, opening him and his family to mob-sanctioned hatred and violence – this is not tyranny? Whereas Mr. Mowat's little dinner here is? You have a very interesting definition of tyranny, Mr. Freeman."

"Gentlemen . . ." Lieutenant Mowat held up a hand. "Let us not allow what has been a pleasant evening to be sullied with acrimony." He then called for port wine, and conversation returned to more studied and stilted topics.

Just prior to taking leave of the ship, the Rev'd Langdon invited Lieutenant Mowat and any of his officers to attend services at St. Paul's on the coming Sunday, which happened to be Palm Sunday. Mowat bowed graciously and said that he would convey the information to all of his officers.

He, Mr. Larkin, and Penfold were indeed present on the following Sunday, the officers sitting in the front pew and Penfold immediately behind them. To Langdon and most of the congregation it was a great pleasure – and a mark of considerable pride – to have King's officers in their midst. The deep blue of their uniforms, the white facing of Mowat's lapels, and the extremely shiny gold buttons glistened in the spring sunshine which streamed through the windows of the church. Penfold had a rather sweet tone to his tenor voice, Langdon noted while singing the hymns, and, after the service, as the parishioners were standing about the churchyard chatting and enjoying the clement weather, the rector quipped to the steward, "You would make a valuable addition to our rather pitiable choir, Mr. Penfold, should you care to leave the navy and join us." He winked at the smallish black man.

In a foreign accent that Langdon could not identify, Penfold said, "I would be nothing but a detriment to it, having never studied the art, reverend sir."

Mowat said, "You have a choir much to be envied, as far as my very untrained ear could ascertain, Mr. Langdon."

"Well, let us be thankful that the ear of God is more attuned to the hearts of the singers than to their voices," Langdon commented obliquely. "As for myself, I would give anything to obtain a pipe organ for St. Paul's. On my occasional excursions to Boston, and when I was studying at King's College, New York – not to mention when I was in England for my ordination – I can scarce describe the tears that have welled up in my eyes at that most glorious of sounds: A well-trained choir and a fine organ raising their harmonies to heaven! The cost of an organ, however – not to mention its transport from England . . ." Langdon shook his head.

"There are no organ builders in America?" Mowat asked.

"No. Not yet."

Mowat assumed a distant look, and Langdon realized that Mowat had tired of the topic of music. Mowat glanced about himself somewhat distractedly. Langdon quickly concluded with, "I do hope you will be able to join us next week, Captain Mowat. Easter Day."

"I shall make every attempt, Mr. Langdon. A very good day to you." And with that, they returned to their ship.

*

The Rev'd Mr. Thomas Langdon's Journal

PALM SUNDAY, 16 APRIL, 1775. (. . .) Lieu^t Mowat impresses me extremely as an officer. I have learned that he is from the Orkney Islands of Scotland – hence an "Orcadian" (I had not heard this word before). The *Canceaux* is a model of efficiency and (as far as a warship can be, I suppose) communal felicity. She is a ship of 8 cannon (and various smaller armaments), with a crew of 45 men, although Lieu^t Mowat told me he was "a half-dozen or so" under complement. It is difficult to imagine the force which a mere handful of men can wield given the right tools. There is something both comforting and unnerving in this: Comforting if they are there to protect you in the enjoyment of your rights and freedoms; disturbing if they wield their influence in a way that is against one's interests. And, while the presence of the *Canceaux* is salutary to my comfort and reassurance, I am very well aware of (and yet try not to gloat over) the discombobulation it is causing the rebelliously inclined, anti-gov^t forces in Falmouth. I refrain from gloating not wholly out of pure motives, but also self-serving ones, for the tables may be turned one day soon, if the *Canceaux* departs before our disputes with the Crown are settled. I would venture to hope (perhaps vainly) that others will have the same decency not to gloat over my misfortunes. In any case, however, I am bound to "do unto others as I would have them do unto me," regardless of whether I am accorded the same in return. *Teach me mercy, O Lord, when I am strong, that I might be afforded mercy when I am weak. Amen.* Weather sunny and glorious, with many pleasure boats in the bay.

Chapter Seven.

Four days later the Rev'd Langdon hosted a dinner at his home which included Lieutenant Mowat, Mr. and Mrs. Lyde, Edward and Polly Oxnard, and Dr. Bailey, surgeon of the H.M.S. *Canceaux*. Langdon had engaged the assistance of several women of his church for the preparation and serving of the meal.

After much small talk of a convivial nature, Mr. Lyde abruptly cast an icy pall over the group when he asked, "Mr. Mowat, sir, will it come to war?"

Mowat shifted uneasily in his chair. "In my honest opinion, Mr. Lyde, yes. Protest is grown to such a pitch in most places as to drown out the calmer voices of reason."

"And if, sir, it does come to war, what will be the outcome?" Lyde persisted.

"A resounding victory for British arms, I must of course believe; but it is impossible to tell."

"If it comes to war," Langdon observed, "any outcome will be a defeat, as needless blood must be shed on both sides. And war always brings hardship and suffering to the innocent, no matter who the victor is."

"Hear, hear, Mr. Langdon," Mrs. Lyde said. "There is nothing to be gained in warfare. Even if the government wins, it will leave a divided and embittered populace in the colonies, impossible to govern in the long run."

"While I do not necessarily disagree, Mr. Langdon," interjected Mr. Lyde, "perhaps it is the only way forward, disagreeable though it may be. Not that I'm advocating war; but, should it come to that,

I think the rebels will field an army in name only. It will be soundly drubbed by clearly superior British regulars in its first engagement, which will thus remind the greater part of colonists of the peerless and invaluable protection we enjoy from our mother country, and which we would be idiots to do without, not to mention oppose."

"I wonder whether the government has any options but war?" put in Edward Oxnard.

"Of course it has, Edward!" Langdon exclaimed.

"Well, I ask you, would a complete acquiescence in the matter of taxation on the part of Parliament avert with any permanence the inexorable march toward war? Or would it merely delay the process slightly, emboldening the insurrectionists to acts of even greater resistance and defiance?"

"Do away with all taxes and these selfish countrymen of ours would be dancing in the streets," Langdon insisted. "Their resistance to taxation has become something of an obsession; a madness!"

"On the contrary," Oxnard continued, "Get rid of the issue of taxation and the malcontents would look for something else, in my opinion. They have set their sights on separation and independence. Take the thorny and impractical issue of American representation in Parliament – a thing that will never happen."

"You astonish me, Edward," Langdon said. "Is not representation exactly what so many have been clamoring for, for years?"

"Have you ever actually considered what would be involved in the representation of Americans in Parliament?" Oxnard asked. "Firstly, it would require a *closer* association with the mother country than the opposite . . . and it is almost incomprehensible to me that the rabble-rousers would see such a thing as positive. Our status would have to be upgraded from colonies to provinces, or actual counties of Great Britain, each providing a certain number of representatives to Parliament according to population. This would necessitate either a massively increased number of members in Parliament (by one-third, as there are three million American colonists to eight-and-a-half million inhabitants of the British Isles), or a radical re-drawing of English districts. Either one would mean the reduction of the overall numerical importance of each British member. I cannot imagine the average Englishman – or Scotsman – " he nodded at Mowat, "assenting to such a dilution. And this would still not provide for any American representation in the House of Lords, unless the peerage be opened to Americans, thus creating a thing abhorrent to most colonists: an American aristocracy. In addition, the paying of higher taxes, as the English pay, would, out of fairness, have to be extended to us upon full inclusion into the ranks of Parliamentary participants, thus incurring exactly that to which the Americans are most violently opposed, only far worse. In addition, the Church of England would become the established church of *all* the colonies, meaning that bishops and dioceses would have to be created, and that a church tax to support the state church would be obligatory even to non-Anglicans, just as it is in England. To summarize, American colonists are some of the most fortunate and enviable men on the face of the globe, having nearly every privilege extended by the English constitution through the might of her arms, the prosperity of her economy, and her tradition of individual freedoms; yet having virtually *none* of the onerous burdens and responsibilities which most other Englishmen must pay to possess these very same privileges. This refrain the rabble-rousers raise about 'no taxation without representation' is a sham. It actually means, 'no taxation, full stop.' It is as unreasonable and self-serving an assertion as I have ever encountered."

All sat in silence following Oxnard's monologue. "You have clearly given this issue much thought, Mr. Oxnard," said Mowat eventually. "I am impressed. I had not envisioned how complex it really is. And possibly intractable."

"Perhaps a firmer resolve to militarily defend the government's prerogatives at an earlier stage would've done the trick," began Mr. Lyde randomly. "To have, for instance, sent a force of twice the present strength about six months ago . . . perhaps this would have silenced the dissenters, and disallowed them a chance to organize."

"More likely," Oxnard shook his head, "it would have given the demagogues increased pretext to preach the gospel of liberty from so-called oppression, thereby swaying public opinion against government all the more swiftly."

The sound of someone pounding insistently on the front door startled the gathered company.

"Who in God's name could that be?" Lyde asked, attempting unsuccessfully to let irritation mask his deeper uneasiness. Langdon arose apprehensively.

"Don't answer it alone, Mr. Langdon," Mowat said, standing. "I'll come with you."

Langdon was at first relieved to find that it was Thomas Pagan, a parishioner of St. Paul's, at the door. "Mr. Langdon, sir, there's dire news . . . oh, hello Captain Mowat, how do you do?"

"Come in, Mr. Pagan," Langdon stepped back, opening the door wide. "What is your news? Come into the dining room and tell everyone at once: I have some guests."

"A horseman from Portsmouth has just come into town," Pagan began once he had greeted everyone. He stood wringing his hat nervously in his hands as he spoke. "There's been an armed engagement – " a collective gasp went round the room. "between British troops and what everyone's calling 'minutemen,' or colonials. A number of British troops, some are saying a dozen companies or so, last night ventured under cover of darkness from Boston to Lexington, where they were met by a group of these 'minutemen.' The British fired into them, apparently without provocation – "

"I highly doubt that," Mowat stated calmly.

" – and killed two-score of 'em, or so." Another gasp. "The British then retreated to Boston, but their heels were dogged by swelling ranks of rebels, firing from behind trees and fences, killing or wounding fifty or sixty or more before they got back to safety."

"Good Lord!" Lyde exclaimed.

"God have mercy on us all," breathed Langdon softly.

"The number of casualties cannot be accurate, surely?" Lyde scoffed.

"Gentlemen," said Mowat with calm authority, "the first reports of an event are always inaccurate, and modified slightly with each retelling – "

"I've told you everything just as I heard it from John Waite," protested Mr. Pagan.

"Doubtless you have, sir; but we must keep our heads about us and remember that it is advisable to await more level-headed accounts in the days to come, especially the official British report, before forming a judgment of what took place."

"Let us hope and pray you are correct, Captain Mowat," Lyde said gravely.

"I must return to my ship and put it under arms just in case anyone in town is carried away by the news and gets it into their heads to do something foolish. Mr. Langdon, it was a great pleasure to sup with you in your home, and I regret that it must be ended thus."

So saying, he and Dr. Bailey took leave of the parsonage. The other guests soon followed suit, and Langdon sent home the ladies who had prepared and served the meal, escorted by the Lydes and Oxnards. He overruled their protests and assured them he would clear everything up himself.

Before he began, however, he went to his study and fell to his knees in front of his desk chair, praying fervently and pleadingly for the minds and souls of his fellow countrymen.

*

THE REV'D MR. THOMAS LANGDON'S JOURNAL

EASTER SUNDAY, 23 APRIL, 1775. It was the bleakest Good Friday in memory; and the joy of Easter was so dim as almost to be imperceptible. The sermon I gave today was, I think, a model of restraint and moderation, holding out the olive branch of peace and the scales of reason to anyone who yet had the wherewithal to take them. But those most needful of hearing my words were certainly not the ones to darken the door of an Anglican church, perceived as being the very embodiment of the English hierarchy and loyalty to the crown. Indeed, the congregation I gazed down upon from the pulpit was much reduced in number from that which I was accustomed to addressing, even from just a week before; and they huddled nervously in their pews, looking like cowering mice ready to flee at the first sign of an approaching cat.

As reliable accounts of the recent engagement at Lexington and Concord have reached Falmouth these past few days, we have learned that General Gage was informed of a cache of illegally horded munitions in Concord, and that troops of the 10th Regiment of Foot had been dispatched to destroy or confiscate same. On the way there, in Lexington, they were blocked in their progress by a group of armed and hostile "minutemen," having awakened and assembled themselves by an industrious system of mutual notification which had been secretly developed over the last few months for just such an eventuality (note to ponder: is this treasonous? Seditious, certainly). The British ordered the group to disperse, which they refused to do. Then shots were fired – accounts differ as to who fired them – which resulted in an exchange of volleys, leaving a handful of dead or wounded among the colonials. The armed rabble then dispersed, allowing the regulars to continue on to Concord, where they destroyed the said magazine of military stores, and thence set upon their return to Boston. By this time bells were ringing and word was spreading throughout the countryside, and many opportunists had taken up their muskets and pistols to join in the sniping from behind trees and fences at the withdrawing regiment. In all, by the end of the day, the casualties on both sides, including both dead and wounded, exceeded fifty.

What is more disturbing than the lamentable loss of life, however, is the effect the incident has had upon the populace of our town. The words of that great man William Pitt, the Earl of Chatham (would that he were again Prime Minister in these troubled times!), uttered in the House of Lords some three months ago, are more true than he could possibly have imagined: "The very first drop of blood that is spilled will not be a wound easily skinned over; it will be *irritabile vulnus*, a wound of that rancorous and festering kind, that, in all probability, will mortify the whole body."

The armed rabble around Boston, inflamed by bloodlust, has reportedly grown to an alarming size, attracting every malcontent and lowlife of the region; and they have laid unofficial but effective siege to the army in Boston, disallowing any communication or trade by land. Rumors abound of plans and stratagems to capture the British warships in Boston harbor; to throw up great entrenchments and siege works in Charlestown, Roxbury, Dorchester Heights and Boston Neck; to bombard and drive the British troops from the city into the ocean.

If the *Canceaux* did not rest reassuringly within sight of nearly every house in Falmouth, I and the other loyalists of the town would be quaking with fear at this sudden unleashing of madness and anarchy in our midst. Even so, the rebellious contingent of Falmouth takes enormous encouragement from the news, and anti-gov^t enthusiasm has become more pronounced. Those who have kept silent about current affairs, unwilling to profess even just a leaning one way or the other, are now compelled by ruffians in the streets, and by unspoken but ominous threats from the town's ascendant rebels, to declare their allegiance and suffer the consequences.

Lexington and Concord has worked as a catalyst, in effect giving permission to the "Sons of Lawlessness," as Mr. Lyde calls them, to initiate violent acts against the representatives and friends of gov^t. I maintain that these "Sons of Lawlessness" make up a minority of the population, perhaps one-third; but they are able, by their fomentation of threats of violence and harm, to intimidate the moderate second-third of the population into either silence or unwilling acquiescence, merely to avoid harm being done to them. The remaining third are those of us who are zealous and outspoken in the defence of our liberties, unwilling to let a mob of troublemakers dictate to us our political sentiments or behaviours. *Lord God of compassion, have mercy on your wayward people, who like lost sheep have gone astray, every one to his own way; and so guide the minds of those who take counsel for our affairs, both on these shores and in England, that they might remain calm in the face of this first, awful bloodshed. Amen.*

Chapter Eight.

LATE ON THE FOLLOWING EVENING there was a knock on the Rev'd Langdon's door. He went with no little apprehension to the front window and, parting the curtain gingerly with an outstretched finger, observed one of the town's boys standing at the door, a piece of paper in hand. Langdon scanned the street for other boys, to see if any mischief were perhaps afoot, but seeing none, and recognizing the boy as one of the sons of Jeremiah Pote – a respectable merchant whom Langdon knew to hold sentiments which leaned towards loyalty to the crown – he determined he was safe.

"Yes, Master Pote?" he asked, opening the door only a little, and keeping the ball of his foot propped against it at the floor.

"Message, sir," he proffered the note.

"From whom?" Langdon inquired, taking it.

"From Mr. Lyde, the Customs Collector."

"Thank you. You are very kind," he said, closing the door, curiosity replacing suspicion. After he had bolted the locks securely, he went into his study and unfolded the letter. Placing it under a candle to throw some light upon it, he read,

> Mon., 24 April, 1775
> Nine o'clock, p.m.
>
> Rev'd Mr. Langdon,
> Strong evidence suggesting a concerted plan by certain Sons of Lawlessness to take myself and Mr. Dornett prisoner has persuaded us to go aboard the *Canceaux* for protection.

Please come immediately to the wharf. If you see two lanterns in the shrouds of the mizzen mast, you will know we are safely aboard. If not, go to my residence, and if I am not there, I have been apprehended in my attempt to get to the ship. Inform Captain Mowat of our disappearance immediately. In the latter case, please take whatever measures might be necessary to ensure the safety of our families, who remain secured in their respective dwellings, but whose well-being in that event would be in grave doubt.

I am, reverend sir, your most grateful servant,

G. Lyde.

Langdon stuffed the note into his coat pocket and hurried outside, going to the waterfront quarter of the town. With relief he spied two lanterns hanging in the shrouds of the *Canceaux*'s mizzen mast. Walking back to his house, he went by both Mr. Lyde's and Mr. Dornett's dwellings. There being no signs of unrest, he refrained from taking any action.

The next day, at the behest of Lieutenant Mowat, the Committee of Inspection issued a guarantee of security for Lyde and Dornett in the carrying out of their occupations. They therefore returned to shore and resumed their duties entering and clearing ships and their cargos – a very necessary occupation in a town the principal activity of which was commerce.

The incident nonetheless disturbed the Rev'd Langdon and other loyalists greatly. Together with the revelation that Mowat intended to depart Falmouth with the *Canceaux* within another fortnight, as Captain Coulson's sloop was nearing completion, Edward Oxnard felt compelled to pen the following memorial, on which he had collected the signatures of 17 other persons, representing nearly 60 of Falmouth's inhabitants:

Falmouth 2d May, 1775

To Henry Mowat Esqr. Captain of His Majesty's Ship *Canceaux*. The Memorial of us the Subscribers, for themselves and many other faithful Subjects in the County of Cumberland,

Sheweth: That since the arrival of His Majesty's Ship under your command, we have been relieved by your spirited conduct from those anxieties natural to persons who oppose the enemies of our happy Constitution; and by your courteous and kind behavior to all the friends of Government, flattered ourselves with the pleasing prospect of a continuance of your protection. But those agreeable sensations are entirely vanished, and we are reduced to the last degree of despair, by your information that when Captain Coulson's ship will be ready for sea you are immediately to leave this place – and consequently us – a prey to the sons of rapine and lawless violence. We therefore entreat that in your goodness you will remain with us till we can make known our deplorable situation to General Gage, which we shall do without delay.

We further entreat you will be so obliging to represent our dangerous situation to Admiral Graves – and as we are now deprived of sending a petition to his Excellency by land and having no effectual method of conveyance by water, we beg you will suffer an officer and a few men from your ship to proceed for that purpose in a boat we have procured for such a service.

[Signed:] Thos. Oxnard, Merchant; Nath'l Coffin, Physician; Joshua Eldridge, Shipmaster; W. Simmons, Merchant; Wm. Campbell, Ship Master; Jos. Dornett, Comptroller of Customs; Thos. Coulson, Merchant; Robt. Pagan, Merchant; Edwd. Oxnard, Merchant; Wm. Tyng, Sheriff of the County of Cumberland; Thos. Pagan, Merchant;

Thos. Langdon, Minister of the Church of England; George Lyde, Collector of Customs; Benjn. Waite, Merchant; Jer. Pote, Merchant; Thos. Cumming, Merchant; Abrm. Osgood, Merchant; Jereh. Coffin, Housewright.

*

OXNARD AND LANGDON delivered this letter to Mowat on Tuesday evening, the 2nd of May, and were invited to stay aboard the *Canceaux* for dinner. In the great cabin this night were, apart from Mowat and his shore guests, Dr. Bailey, a certain Midshipman Barker, and Mr. Hogg, the master of the *Canceaux*.

"What manner of vessel have your friends procured for the purpose of proceeding to Boston?" Mowat asked, referring to the memorial they had just delivered.

"A single-masted, 20-foot dory, or cutter," Oxnard replied.

Mowat nodded. "Well, I have decided to agree to your request of providing three men and an officer for the purpose of sending your boat to Boston. I have some papers and reports to send to Admiral Graves myself, and this would appear to be the most effectual way of accomplishing that."

"I speak for all the friends of government in Falmouth when I say that we are very much obliged to you, Captain Mowat," Oxnard said, his voice quivering with emotion.

"I shall put the three men under Master Hogg here. I suspect it will take them about a week to complete the trip to Boston and back," Mowat explained.

Hogg said to Langdon, "As one of me official duties, I see to the young gen'lemen's education," he nodded at Mr. Barker who, at 16, was one of the ship's three midshipmen. "As I shall be gone for a week, the cap'n 'n I were wondering whether you could see your way to coming aboard once or twice to give a lesson to the midshipmen. History, or grammar, or . . ." he cast about for a subject he thought a parson might be in command of, "doctrine, perhaps . . ." he seemed not as enthusiastic about the last-named subject.

"With the utmost pleasure, Mr. Hogg," said Langdon, genuinely touched. "I beg you to forgive my ignorance of nautical matters, gentlemen, but what is the function of a master aboard a warship?"

"Why, to navigate the ship," Hogg replied.

"The master is responsible for knowing the ship's position at all times, and for setting the best course for our destination, once the latter is communicated to him by me," Mowat added. "And in a ship of this size, with no lieutenants or other commissioned officers, he also serves as second in command."

"I keep the ship's log, as well," Hogg pronounced with a touch of pride.

"I perceive that you are a considerable figure on board, sir," Langdon said.

"I trust you are referring to his status and not his girth," Dr. Bailey commented, chuckles erupting around the table.

"I have gathered by way of certain sources, Mr. Langdon," Mowat observed after Penfold had cleared the dinner plates, the wine bottle had been sent round again, and conversation was becoming looser, "that you are a musician of some accomplishment,"

"Well, I'm not so sure I would describe . . ." began Langdon, shrugging.

"One of the reasons I asked Dr. Bailey to dine with us tonight is because he is a musician, as well," Mowat continued, ignoring the clergyman's protestations of humility. "A flautist,"

"Really! How extraordinary," Langdon exclaimed, "for I, too, am a flautist! We shall have to play a few duets, if opportunity warrants it in future," Langdon said. "I have a small volume of violin duets which I purchased when I was in London for my ordination in '67 – little arrangements of works by Dr. Arndt, C. F. Abel, Christian Bach, William Boyce, *et cetera*. Aside from the occasional violin double-stops, the parts are perfectly suited to a flute."

"By all means, yes," Dr. Bailey assented.

A voice on the deck above cried out "Boat ahoy!" The response was too distant to make out, but Mowat instantly cocked his head in the direction of the sound.

Little more than a minute had passed when there was a knock on the cabin door. Before Lieutenant Mowat had had opportunity to grant leave for the person to enter, the *Canceaux*'s senior midshipman, Mr. Larkin, burst through the door and reported breathlessly, "Boatswain's compliments sir an' there's a boat approaching with Sheriff Tyng aboard. Says it's urgent he speak to you."

"My compliments to the boatswain, and bring Sheriff Tyng here as soon as he is aboard, Mr. Larkin," Mowat said.

"Aye aye, sir," he turned to leave as precipitously as he had arrived.

"And, Mr. Larkin . . ." Mowat said authoritatively, halting the thirteen year-old in the already half-closed doorway.

"Yes, sir?"

"No matter how important the news you bear, wait to enter the captain's cabin until given leave to do so. A King's officer keeps his composure even in an emergency."

"Aye aye, sir. Sorry sir," the midshipman said, touching his forehead in salute.

When the door had closed, Mowat explained to Langdon, "The son of a friend of mine, whom I agreed to take aboard last year. A good, eager lad, but he does rather lose his head when he gets excited."

Sheriff Tyng soon arrived. He held his well-known, battered, three-cornered hat in his hands, revealing his bald pate, moist with perspiration.

"Good evening, Sheriff Tyng. Will you join my guests and me in a glass of port?" Mowat asked. Penfold was pouring the dark red liquid into cordial glasses standing on a tray.

"Oh, no, thank you, Mr. Mowat," Tyng replied, nodding to Mr. Hogg, Dr. Bailey, and the parson.

"What is your news, sheriff?" Mowat asked, adding hastily, "I assume my guests may remain in the room?"

"Why yes, of course: The whole town knows of it by now," he said, nearly as breathless as Mr. Larkin had been. "An armed party of two-hundred men led by a Colonel Samuel Thompson has taken a King's contracting agent prisoner up the bay in Brunswick – "

"Edward Parry?" Mowat asked.

"The very man," Tyng replied with some surprise that Mowat should know the name already.

"Damn," was Mowat's simple reply.

"And that's not all," Tyng continued. "Thompson has confiscated the five-hundred masts procured by Mr. Parry in that and neighboring ports; he has taken five other men, prominent friends of government in Brunswick, into custody, one of whom has reportedly been buried alive; and here's the worst of it: He's taken possession of two merchant sloops in Brunswick, and reportedly plans to use them to capture or destroy the *Canceaux* and Captain Coulson's sloop."

"Who are these two-hundred men he has with him, and how well are they armed?" Mowat inquired.

"They are local men, it seems, with their own hunting pieces, and identify themselves each with a bough of spruce in their hats," Tyng replied.

"A body of militia, or a hot-headed rabble?" Mowat pressed.

"More like the latter, I think," Tyng said.

"The easier to disperse with a cannon-shot, then." His confidence reassured his guests to some degree. "Are they still in Brunswick, to your knowledge?"

"They are; although word of their deeds is encouraging a number of people in Falmouth to arm themselves and assist them should they come here," Tyng said gravely. "Word is that the Town Council is to meet first thing tomorrow to discuss the news."

"What do you think the likely outcome of that meeting will be?" Mowat asked.

"Lord only knows!"

"I am indebted to you, sheriff, for this valuable information. I will take whatever measures are necessary to protect not only my ship and those vessels under my protection, but all friends of government in this town," Mowat said with finality.

"And we are all inestimably appreciative of that, sir, as the memorial prepared by Mr. Oxnard attests," Sheriff Tyng said, bowing his balding head.

Mowat turned to his steward and said, "My compliments to Mr. Larkin, and would he please inform me of the state of the wind and tide." The steward bowed and left the cabin. Turning back to Sheriff Tyng, Mowat asked, "Are you familiar with Brunswick, Sheriff?"

"Quite familiar," Tyng replied confidently. "That is," he said, a cloud of doubt passing over his face, "perhaps I should say that I am familiar with the landward approaches, not the seaward approaches, if you get my meaning . . ."

"That could be quite useful to me. Would you consent to remain aboard, Sheriff Tyng, and potentially make an excursion with the *Canceaux* to Brunswick tonight?"

"I would be honored to be of whatever service you should choose, Mr. Mowat, sir," he said.

The steward reappeared. "Mr. Larkin's respects, sir, and the wind is westerly and gentle but unwavering; and the tide is an hour past low-water mark."

"Excellent. Is your boat still alongside?" Mowat asked.

"Yes. A group of harbormen who I asked to await me."

"Harbormen, eh? Are they known to you?"

"Not by name, no."

"Would you say they are friends of government?" Mowat inquired.

"I should highly doubt it, as most men of their class have been seduced into becoming so-called 'Sons of Liberty' by the example of our Committee of Inspection."

"Then I am going to make the following suggestion, unusual as it may sound:" Mowat turned to the clergyman, quite unnerving him with the unexpectedness of the address, "Mr. Langdon, you are of a build similar to our esteemed sheriff here. If you were to exchange your outer clothing and were to pull the sheriff's hat down over your face, Mr. Langdon, you could easily pass as Mr. Tyng in the darkness, and take his boat back to shore. I want them to think that the sheriff has returned ashore, and thus to raise no eyebrows. I intend to slip our cable and leave silently, when the moon has set and there is no light, and slip up the bay towards Brunswick to investigate. I don't want word to get across land to Colonel Thompson and his men. If there's continuing mischief about, I intend to surprise them. Would you be willing to do this, Mr. Langdon?"

Langdon blinked in shock. "I . . . I am. I shall do my utmost to impersonate the good sheriff." He was surprised to feel a hint of excitement coursing through his veins in addition to the expected fear.

"Excellent. And Mr. Langdon, you could do me an additional service if you were to attend the Town Council meeting in the morning and observe the goings on. If you are able, influence them into condemning Colonel Thompson's actions as treasonous and inflammatory. Then I would like you to return aboard as soon as I've returned, which should be sometime tomorrow morning, with a report. Understood?"

Langdon nodded.

"Very well. If you would be so kind as to exchange your outer garments, gentlemen, and we shall be about our business."

He and the sheriff went into the *Canceaux*'s tiny chart room adjacent to the great cabin, where they exchanged their outer garments, including their breeches and waistcoats. The sheriff was several inches taller than the clergyman, so his things looked slightly baggy on Mr. Langdon, but that was better for their deceptive purposes than the other way around.

Emerging back into the cabin, Langdon said, "This will have to do," looking down at himself doubtfully. Penfold, as cabin steward, stepped forward to straighten a stray part of his clothing.

"It will do quite well in the dark, Mr. Langdon, as long as you keep the hat pulled low over your eyes," Mowat assured him. "In the main, people see what they expect to see, and are not very observant. Are we ready?"

"I think so, yes," Langdon replied.

"Very well. I'm going to slip anchor as soon as your boat has reached the dock, Mr. Langdon. Mr. Hogg, call all hands to sail, if you please, but quietly, quietly, mind: Not a peep out of the men as they move to their stations."

"Aye aye, sir."

Mr. Langdon accompanied the master on deck.

"Fare ye well, Mr. Tyng," said Hogg loudly at the side with a great wink of his twinkling eye.

"Thank y- . . . Thank'ee, Mr. Hogg," he said, altering his voice and manner of speech to fit the more rustic sheriff.

Hogg cupped his hands and said over the side, "Boat thar! Sheriff Tyng coming aboard."

"Aye, aye," came a voice from below.

Langdon turned, a jolt of terror shooting through his body as he looked down into the boat. He hoped he would not recognize any of the men. Grasping the rail, he spun his weight around to begin his descent. Looking at his feet as he sought out the steps, he realized how shiny his shoes looked in comparison to the sheriff's dingy boots and muttered a curse to himself.

Once he was seated in the boat, he kept his face low and facing outboard, as if looking at the water. His heart was beating so loudly in his breast that he felt sure the two oarsmen sitting opposite him must hear it. He dared not look at them, however, for fear of revealing his identity.

After the boat had pushed off from the side of the *Canceaux*, Langdon was startled by the address of the coxswain, asking him, "Pearson's wharf again, Sheriff Tyng?"

"Yes, thank you," he said, his voice sounding to himself like it was steeped in terror. The coxswain made no reply.

The boat ride seemed interminable to Langdon, and the approach of the dock was painfully slow. He began to wonder whether the sheriff had already paid the men a fare, or whether it was expected at the conclusion of the trip. He cursed himself for not having thought of asking Tyng about the financial arrangement. He supposed he would just have to assess the situation once they arrived. If the coxswain looked expectant for his fee, Langdon would pay him; If he did not, Langdon would mutter a brief thanks and be out of the boat and hoofing it as quickly as possible out of sight.

His anxiety reached a fever pitch as they approached the dock. Langdon almost jumped when the coxswain barked, "Up oars!" The oars came up and were held almost vertically as the coxswain steered the boat up against the dock. One of the oarsmen reached out and caught one of the piers of the dock, and the other reached a hand toward Langdon. Langdon wondered at first whether he was holding out his hand for the payment; but finally interpreted it as a proffering of assistance. He took the offer and stood up, gauging his step out of the boat. To his vast relief, the coxswain said, "'At'll be two shillings, sir."

Langdon reached into his pocket, thankful that he had the required fare, and placed the coins without a word into the coxswain's upheld palm.

"Thank'ee, Sheriff Tyng,"

"Not at all," he muttered, turning and walking toward the land. The sound of his shoes on the hollow planking of the dock echoed unusually loudly in his ears, and he tried not to betray his anxiousness to get out of sight by walking too rapidly. Nevertheless, he breathed a great sigh of relief as he disappeared around the corner of first one building, then another. In another five minutes he was home, safe and sound.

*

THE FOLLOWING MORNING, a mere glance into the bay sufficed to tell Langdon that the *Canceaux* was already returned from her mission to Brunswick – if, indeed, she had left at all.

A little later in the morning he squeezed himself into the meeting house with half of Falmouth, it seemed, and, although he could see very little of the proceedings, he could identify most of the voices which spoke.

Jedediah Preble, the long-bearded chairman of the Town Council and, as the closest thing to a mayor, one of the most influential men in Falmouth, called the meeting to order, asking a Mr. Bryant to tell what he had learned yesterday while in Brunswick. The said Bryant related a story much like Sheriff Tyng's (omitting the far-fetched detail of someone being buried alive).

When Mr. Preble opened the matter for discussion, Langdon was favorably impressed to hear the amount of doubt – indeed, disapprobation – among the council members for the plan of Colonel Thompson to take or burn the *Canceaux*. It seemed to indicate that, aside from the Committee of Inspection, at least some of the town's responsible denizens were not as far gone as Langdon had begun to fear; or at least that, in the face of a real threat to a King's ship, they were unwilling to support such outright treason.

The council seemed in one accord that any attempt against the *Canceaux* was rash and injudicious; that it would likely provoke Vice Admiral Graves to blockade the town, thus stopping its trade – which would be ruinous to the town's welfare – or even possibly to take more drastic measures. Furthermore, Lieutenant Mowat was praised by members of the council as "a gentleman whose conduct since he has been here has given no grounds of suspicion that he had any design to distress or injure us. On the contrary, he has afforded assistance to sundry persons and vessels in distress."

It was therefore moved and carried that the following actions be taken: The council would write to the Committees of Inspection at Brunswick and Georgetown, desiring that they prevent as far as possible Colonel Thompson's leaving their district; secondly, write by express to Thompson himself, requesting that he desist from any attempt on the *Canceaux* or its tenders, "as it would throw the town into the greatest confusion imaginable;" and thirdly, that the council would urge the inhabitants of Falmouth to provide no assistance whatsoever to Thompson or his cohorts should they come to Falmouth.

Langdon left the meeting house at the conclusion of the debate and, passing by his house to collect his flute and the book of violin duets he had mentioned to Dr. Bailey, made his way to Pearson's wharf, as instructed. At his appearance a boat put off immediately from the *Canceaux*'s side, and within a quarter of an hour he was aboard the warship.

He quickly learned that the *Canceaux*'s mission to Brunswick had not accomplished everything Mowat had wished, the ship running aground at one point in the dark, shallow waters of Casco Bay. "Luckily, the tide was on the make, so we soon floated free," explained Master Hogg. Upon arriving in Brunswick, they found no evidence of unrest, and the band of persons under Col. Thompson had moved to the southward – towards Falmouth, in fact – soon after sundown. A shore party led by Mr. Hogg and Sheriff Tyng located the five-hundred masts that had been confiscated by Thompson and his men, overpowered the single guard, and, unable to take them away, set fire to the lot of them. The *Canceaux* then slipped back down the bay to Falmouth, arriving just before dawn.

"Word of your foray has apparently not reached Falmouth yet," Langdon observed, "else I suspect I'd have heard of it in the Town Council this morning." Langdon went on to report the favorable result of the meeting, the news of which satisfied Mowat very much.

Langdon then helped Mowat write a number of letters before noon, the most important (and most interesting) of which was to Vice Admiral Graves; and, after having lunch with Mowat and Dr. Bailey on deck to take advantage of the beautiful weather, they spent the afternoon transcribing a lengthy, technical document describing in great detail the "State and Condition" of the *Canceaux*, which Mowat was going to include with the letters to the admiral. It did not present a positive picture, describing the ship to be low on provisions, in want of munitions, and dangerously undermanned with but 38 hands aboard, and even a handful of these on loan to Captain Coulson for the completion of his sloop.

Anticipating that there might be the necessity of more shore parties in the coming weeks, Mowat had decided to send

Midshipman Samuels in charge of the boat to Boston, rather than Mr. Hogg.

After Mowat had done with Langdon's services, he and Dr. Bailey tried their hands at a flute duet, to the amusement of a number of the crew who stood listening on the lower deck outside Dr. Bailey's small cabin. The pair struggled through a piece by William Boyce, and did tolerably well for two persons who had never played together before, nor had really practiced their respective instruments in several months.

"Would you be interested in performing the Boyce on Sunday in St. Paul's Church as a voluntary before the service?" Langdon asked the doctor.

"Very much so, yes."

"Good, then why don't you have dinner with me in my home this Friday evening, and we will rehearse it again."

"I should be delighted."

*

The Rev'd Mr. Thomas Langdon's Journal

TUESDAY, 2 MAY, 1775. (. . .) I am continually astonished that our present tranquility rests on the shoulders of some 43 souls – the officers and crewmen of the *Canceaux*. Perhaps I should have known better; but when one thinks of a king's ship, an armed vessel, one envisions ranks upon ranks of sailors, marines, officers, and domestics, even though one knows perfectly well that such a number could not possibly physically fit into so confined a space. One's feeling comes into conflict with one's knowledge: in other words, expectation is shaken by fact. How much of life, I wonder, would not be upbraided and transformed by this equation, were we to allow it? How many of our notions and opinions of things seemingly firm and transfixed – even of things we deem eternal – would be shaken if we were to allow them to be honestly examined? I suspect that, when we have been translated into glory in God's heavenly presence, by far the greater number of our beliefs and opinions will fall under the onslaught of divine truth than otherwise. We can but rely on the grace of God's mercy to accept our feeble and petty efforts at understanding, in the hopes that they will, at the last, be deemed sufficient. But then, that is what the Redemption is about: God will judge us through the mediation of his most blessed Son, who took our insufficiencies to the Cross and buried them forever. *We thank thee, heavenly Father, for the redemption of our manifold deficiencies in the death and resurrection of your Son: Help us to be ever mindful of the grace shown so undeservingly to us, even as we are, through our selfishness, blinded to its continual presence all around us. Amen.* Overcast and threatening rain.

CHAPTER NINE.

ON THE FOLLOWING DAY Sheriff Tyng, Midshipman Samuels, and three hands from the *Canceaux* set off before dawn for Boston, bearing with them voluminous documents, including a letter from George Lyde to the Commissioners of Customs, the memorial to Mowat prepared by Oxnard, a letter from Mowat to Graves introducing the memorial, a handful of other letters from Mowat to various officials and acquaintances in Boston, an official letter from Mowat with the "state and condition" of the *Canceaux* for Admiral Graves, and a letter from Sheriff Tyng to General Gage.

On Friday, as planned, Dr. Bailey went ashore with his flute in the late afternoon, and he and Langdon rehearsed the Boyce for nearly an hour, until it was virtually without technical flaw. One could have argued that their expression or articulation was lacking, but their accuracy was of a high degree, their tuning reputable, and the tempo steady and unwavering.

When dinner was ready – Langdon had engaged the help of Mrs. Ingersoll in preparing the meal – they sat down.

"Captain Mowat kept the people under arms all last night, in preparedness for a potential attack," Bailey said.

"Was there occasion for him to expect an attack?" Langdon inquired.

Bailey shrugged.

"I suppose one can never be too careful," Langdon remarked.

"Indeed," Bailey nodded. His dark, almost black hair was drawn back into a tight queue for the evening, tied at the nape of his neck.

In an abrupt change of topic, Bailey asked, "Why are you not married, Mr. Langdon, if I might be so bold? I mean, you are a man of position and substance, possessing all things requisite to marriage."

"You flatter me," Langdon replied smilingly. He reflected a moment, then said, "I am a man of curious habits, lending themselves to privacy, like reading and study, music, and writing. Indeed, my position as minister of St. Paul's provides me with perhaps more social contact than I actually require. Thus, my way of life occasions little need for constant companionship." Langdon paused, pressing the tips of his fingers together. "And what about you, Dr. Bailey? Are you married?"

"No."

"And possessed of those same qualities you listed as being requisite."

Bailey nodded. "I am a naval surgeon. I have been aboard the *Canceaux* now for nearly two years, and do not look to return to England for yet another. Men of naval careers are too long distant from their homes, in my opinion, to be proper spouses."

"Yet the vast majority of mariners are married, I'd warrant," Langdon pointed out.

"Aye, I'm sure that's true," he agreed.

"Assuming, therefore, that Cupid should strike you with one of his darts, would you drop your noble pretense of bachelorhood for conjugal bliss?" the parson inquired.

Bailey chuckled, his face turning slightly red, then said "I'm surprised to hear a man of the cloth invoke pagan gods."

Now it was Langdon's turn to laugh. "Your avoidance of my question is masterful, Dr. Bailey! Distracting a religious man with a comment calculated to raise his ire! I beg leave, however, to point out that I did not *invoke* Cupid, but merely *alluded* to him."

Bailey laughed but did not reply.

Before their conversation could resume, their attention was drawn to the sound of a number of men's voices, raised in anger, passing by the house. They looked at each other in alarm, rising to peer out the nearest window. Mrs. Ingersoll came from the kitchen, a look of great agitation troubling her features.

The tail end of a large group of armed men passed by the house in the direction of the wharves. "I do not recognize any as townspeople," Langdon observed.

"If my sight were not so much deteriorated in the last few years," Mrs. Ingersoll said, shaking her head, "I'd swear that one of those was a farmer with whom my late husband used to deal."

"I suspect your eyesight still does you credit, Mrs. Ingersoll. They are country people, if I am any judge," Langdon observed. Bailey remained silent but watched the disappearing group with no little consternation.

"I suggest we escort Mrs. Ingersoll to her house, Dr. Bailey," Langdon stirred himself to action, "She lives only a few houses from here. Then, if we deem it safe, I'll walk you to the waterfront, where you can make your way back to the ship. I apologize for abruptly ending our evening in this fashion."

"No apologies, Mr. Langdon; this is the third dinner at which we have been present that has been interrupted by outside events. It is but a regrettable necessity in these times, it appears."

He took his flute, and Langdon, insisting that they leave the dishes and things as they were, held the door for them.

They saw Mrs. Ingersoll without incident to her home, but upon approaching the waterfront, they heard quite a low tumult of voices, and, occasionally, when gaps between buildings allowed it, they could see quite a crowd milling about, casting glances at and pointing in the direction of the *Canceaux*. The occasional pistol or musket was brandished to lend teeth to the shouted threats.

"Death to Captain Mowat!" was one call they heard, among many others of an even more violent, insulting nature. King George, Lord North, and General Gage came in for particular vilification; but, as these latter were not physically vulnerable to their attacks, the general epithets regarding loyalists and "Tories" were far more upsetting to Langdon and other loyalists within their hearing.

It was a very disturbing spectacle to both men, the one because it prevented his return to safe quarters aboard ship; the other because it represented a populace at large rising up to disturb the peace and tranquility of this once sleepy and contented town. More than anything he had seen so far, this troubled the parson, and signaled that irresistible change was afoot, which would touch all their lives in a profound, and perhaps even a violent manner.

Langdon caught Bailey's arm and pulled him into the shadow of a wood-sided shed. "Look, let's go back to my house," he whispered. "If they disperse in a few hours, you can go back to the ship then. Otherwise, I have a guest bed where you can sleep. We'll bolt all the doors and leave the lights out."

The doctor readily acquiesced.

Once back in the house they cleared the dishes from the table and washed them. They sat in the study and conversed for an hour or two on various topics by the light of a single candle; then, as there were still voices to be heard around town at midnight, Bailey agreed that it would be most prudent to spend the night on shore.

By morning the rabble had dispersed, and they could see the *Canceaux* with her broadside to the town as they walked to the wharf.

"Ah, Mowat's clapped springs on the cables and hove her to," Bailey observed with satisfaction.

"Good for him," Langdon said. It was more the tone of the doctor's voice than an understanding of the nautical jargon that engendered the parson's hearty agreement, for, in truth, he had little idea what the meaning of the doctor's words were.

Dr. Bailey waved very broadly at the ship, his arm extended far above his head. A responding wave from the quarterdeck of the *Canceaux* indicated that he had been sighted. He looked along the waterfront quarter of Falmouth. "Well, things appear to have calmed down," he said.

"Yes, indeed," Langdon agreed, "probably because the rogues got tired after a while and yearned for the comfort of their beds."

"Yes. More revolutions have ended because of that than anything else, probably," he smiled.

"Indeed," Langdon nodded. "I hope Mowat did not worry about your not returning last night."

"I'm sure he appreciated that it was more prudent of me to remain ashore," Bailey said.

After a moment of silence, and a boat had put off from the ship's side, Bailey said, "In spite of the unexpected inconveniences and things, I very much enjoyed our time together, Mr. Langdon – "

" – Thomas. Call me Thomas," Langdon insisted.

The hint of a smile graced the doctor's face. "And you must call me David," he said.

When Bailey had clambered aboard the boat and waved goodbye from the sternsheets – and several sailors had tipped their hats to Langdon ("G-day, Reverend"), pleasing him that they recognized him – the parson turned and made his way back home.

He pondered the custom of two people moving to the use of Christian names. It not only demonstrated the comfortability and familiarity between the two parties, but, more importantly, symbolized the removal of ranks and distinctions like 'Dr.,' 'Rev'd,' and 'Mr.' from between them, indicating that they appreciated each other as equals.

*

AS THINGS REMAINED RELATIVELY CALM for the next 24 hours, Dr. Bailey came ashore Sunday morning, and he and Langdon played the Boyce duet as the opening voluntary at service, which excited much comment after the conclusion of the morning's activities. Much more comment, in fact, than the sermon, which did not surprise – nor displease – the parson.

Indeed, Langdon was somewhat hesitant about the sermon to begin with, a portion of it falling more into the category of pastoral counsel than religious instruction. Because he considered it to be godly advice, encouraging his parishioners to make up their minds firmly in the conflict which was to come, and to resign themselves to the consequences, he considered it "meet and right" to append a personal, political and non-religious address to the end of his sermon, as follows:

"It is now become too plain to be any longer doubted," he had said, "that a union is formed by a vocal and growing minority, almost throughout this whole continent, to oppose the supremacy, and even the lowest degree of legislative jurisdiction, of the British parliament over its colonies; and that preparations for war are making with a vigor which the most imminent dangers from a foreign enemy never could inspire.

"It should seem astonishing that a country of husbandmen, possessed every one, almost, of a sufficient share of landed property, in one of the finest climates in the world, living under the mildest government, enjoying the highest portion of civil and religious liberty that the nature of human society admits, and protected in the enjoyment of these, upon the easiest of terms, by the only power on earth capable of affording that protection; that a people so situated for happiness should throw off their rural simplicity, quit the peaceful sweets and labors of husbandry, bid open defiance to the gentle entreaties of that parent state which nursed their tender years, and rush to arms with the ferocity of savages, and with the fiery zeal of crusaders! And all this for the redress of purely chimerical grievances.

"For, alas! if arms must decide the unnatural contest, success cannot be purchased without many a tear, on the part of the victor as well as the vanquished. Many a fond wife will be plunged into all the bitterness of woe upon reading the name of her affectionate spouse among the number of the slain; many an anxious parent will be afflicted with the melancholy tidings of the death of a son; many a beloved child will listen with an heart-felt anguish to the sad story of his father's fall. And all this load of misery may be dreadfully accumulated by the languors of disease and the frowns of poverty, touching not just the soldier on the field of combat, but the entirety of our once happy society.

"The immediate causes lie obvious to every observing eye. By the help of that single word, *Liberty*, demagogues have conjured up the most horrid phantasms in the minds of the common people, ever an easy prey to such specious betrayers. These demagogues –

often under the name of politicians, who make it their profession to be agitators of the masses – have so misconstrued the march of events that the unmeaning merchants, laborers, and farmers – who had really no interest in matters of controversy – now fancy they see civil and religious tyranny advancing with hasty strides across their continent.

"I am far from considering American colonists, either by nature or habit, warlike people. But there is in us an enthusiasm for politics, like that which religious notions inspire, that drive men with an unnatural impetuosity. 'Liberty' among Englishmen is a word the very sound of which carries a fascinating charm. The colonists fancy this precious jewel is in danger of being ravished from them. However ill-founded this apprehension may be – for what principle on earth can provide so much liberty as that upon which the English constitution is founded? – the effect on their minds is the same as moral certainty would produce, thus making it futile to speak reason to them. Seized by the dementia of the times, they make a voluntary sacrifice of themselves, their wives, children and fortunes, at the shrine of liberty, and fondly imagine they recommend themselves to heaven and posterity by thus heroically preferring poverty and distress to the most inconsiderable abridgement of liberty. They will not and cannot examine the truth of the situation until they are frightened enough to do so. Then and only then will they pause and reflect, questioning the propriety of their conduct, and attentively viewing the certain evils into which they find themselves to be rushing. I am so well convinced that our countrymen, at least a majority of them, act under the power of mere delusion, rather than from positive vicious intent, that I most ardently wish to see them brought back to a sense of their duty, with as little havoc and bloodshed as may be.

"We, my friends, are faced at this time with a simple choice:

either to be borne along with the apparently irresistible torrent, intimidated by the threats of our countrymen into an involuntary compliance with their treason; or to risk life and limb, home and property, in standing firm for the authority of a benevolent government which has heretofore been our sustenance and protection. The choice has been forced upon us. We must make our election soon."

Bailey stood at the parson's side after the service, accepting the parishioner's compliments, for which Langdon was very relieved and thankful, as this allowed parishioners to greet him and give their respects without feeling the necessity of commenting on the sermon.

When they had all gone and Langdon was removing and hanging up his cassock in the sacristy, he thanked Bailey for his contribution to the service and suggested they stroll around to Back Cove, a scenic portion of the neck of land on which Falmouth was situated. Bailey said that Tuesday would be more convenient for him, and, thus agreed, they took their leave of one another.

*

The Rev'd Mr. Thomas Langdon's Journal

Sunday, 7 May, 1775. I am finding that David Bailey and I are becoming something like friends. It is a rather new and pleasant sensation – one that I have not really experienced since childhood with Edward Oxnard; and, although the latter and I are still acquainted, our lives have taken such different paths – and our minds, too – that the intimacy which we shared as boys is no longer much in evidence. It has taken my befriending another, and reawakening those dormant feelings, to make me realize how distant Edward and I have grown, which makes me wonder whether I have not become, as a clergyman, distant and aloof from those whom I formerly called friends. Perhaps, despite all my arguments to the contrary, I am a lonely man.

Add to this the discomfort I feel at the thought of becoming so close to someone who, with his imminent departure, will also disappear from my life, and I have a growing sense that I *am* a lonely person, without someone I can really call *friend*. David, who is engaging, witty, and intelligent, with an element of social grace and reservedness that I find comfortable and attractive, has made me begin to realize that the simple rusticity of most of my acquaintance is not something I can warm to. I do not look down upon, despise, or judge in any negative way this rusticity; but David has compelled me to recognize that, for true intimacy, I require a little more social refinement and intellectual animation than what is typically to be found in Falmouth. If any of my acquaintance were to read this, they would immediately accuse me of elitism or arrogance; but I do not, in my heart of hearts, think it is so. Perhaps only God can be impartial in this judgment, however. Partly cloudy and mild.

Chapter Ten.

It was a fine early summer's day, with a fresh breeze and clear skies, when the Rev'd Langdon looked out his window to assess the weather in reference to his planned stroll with Dr. Bailey along Sandy Point.

They had agreed to meet at Pearson's wharf at noon, and the boat that would be carrying the doctor from the *Canceaux* would then take them both around the cove to the back of the neck. They would send the boat back to the ship, returning by foot to the parson's house for dinner.

These plans in mind, Langdon was surprised to find Lieutenant Mowat in the boat with Dr. Bailey when he arrived at Pearson's wharf.

"Hello, gentlemen," Langdon greeted them.

"When hearing of our outing," Bailey said in explanation, "Lieutenant Mowat became very jealous, and I could not restrain him from accompanying us."

"Oh, by all means, we are honored," Langdon said, stepping into the boat, expertly steadied by the four oarsmen, and seated himself on the bank opposite Mowat and Bailey.

"Truth to tell," Mowat said as the oarsmen shoved off from the pier and began pulling strongly out into the bay, "In my capacity as marine cartographer, I thought it an excellent opportunity for innocently surveying the rear approach to the town, should there ever come a necessity of knowing its geography."

"Ah. Such as . . . ?"

Mowat shrugged. "Oh, a number of scenarios come to mind which might occasion a landing of sailors or marines in secrecy: the interruption of a seditious meeting, the dispersement of a rabble, the protection of persons threatened with mob violence, the rescuing of prisoners or hostages, the burning of a building which is being used to store munitions . . ."

"I see, yes," Langdon said. Mowat had more than adequately satisfied his curiosity. "You must join Dr. Bailey and me for dinner at my house after the walk," he insisted.

"That is most kind in you, Mr. Langdon, but I would not wish to impose."

"Not at all. I'll simply have Mrs. Ingersoll add another cutlet or two to the skillet."

The boat pulled along the front of the town, giving its occupants a fair view of it, and then around the point, where it dropped them at a place that Langdon pointed out.

Aptly named, Sandy Point was the broadest beach near Falmouth, and as they walked up it, Langdon observed, "I used to swim all along this beach as a boy during summers."

Mowat stopped and looked out into Back Cove. "How deep is it? – say, thirty feet out from here?"

"About six feet at low tide."

Mowat looked to shore now, particularly at a large grove of trees. Langdon could see the mental machinery at work and could imagine the thoughts going through his head. Indeed, for an instant Langdon fancied he could almost see a nocturnal landing of marines from boats. As he followed in his mind their pretended path as they splashed through the water onto the beach and towards the thick grove of elm trees, he caught sight of something which made his imaginings seem suddenly uncannily palpable – a great disturbance of the sand, and numberless footprints in the dirt beyond the reach of the tide.

He walked across the beach to examine them. Mowat and Dr. Bailey came up to him and looked down at the footprints and followed them with their eyes into the underbrush where they disappeared.

"These look rather freshly made," Langdon observed.

"Who do you suppose made them?" Bailey asked.

Mowat raised his eyes and looked in the direction which the footprints led: directly into the grove of trees.

"I assume it was them," Mowat said. Langdon and Bailey followed his gaze and were startled to see a group of men advancing quickly towards them. Langdon actually gasped at the sight. They were heavily armed, and each had a bough of spruce stuck in his hat, thus indicating who they were. Langdon looked desperately behind him and out into the cove, as if to seek an escape route, or to see if the *Canceaux*'s boat was still in sight.

"Don't you move," shouted one, apparently their leader, a pistol in his hand. The armed party reached the three stunned men and surrounded them.

"Mr. Thompson, I presume," Mowat said to the leader.

"Colonel Thompson."

Mowat was silent in reply.

"An' you, I presume, is Cap'n Mowat of His Majesty's Sloop *Canceaux*," Thompson said with mock respect in a thick backwoodsman's brogue.

"Correct," Mowat said, his outward calm reassuring Langdon and Dr. Bailey slightly. "But it is a ship, not a sloop."

"Oh, now isn't we impressed!" Thompson said, causing his men to laugh menacingly. He was a tall, gangling man with extremely unkempt and knotted hair protruding from under his hat, and his face, hands, and clothing were filthy, having obviously not been shaved, washed, or changed in days. "An' who, pray, might yer companions be, Cap'n Mowat?"

"This is Dr. Bailey, surgeon of the ship under my command; and this is the Rev'd Mr. Thomas Langdon, vicar of St. Paul's Church, Falmouth," Mowat said, indicating each in turn.

"Oh, what a perdy catch I've made!" Thompson exclaimed.

"If you are intending to detain us or take us prisoner, Mr. Thompson, as your use of the word 'catch' would seem to indicate, I would remind you that, as I am a King's officer, it would be considered treason. An offense punishable by hanging," Mowat said calmly.

"It's Colonel Thompson, as I already done 'minded you . . ."

"Pray, by whose appointment and authority are you a colonel?" Mowat inquired.

"By the Provincial Congress o' Massachusetts, that's who," Thompson snapped. "But see if I cares whether you call me 'Colonel' or 'Mr.' You can call me anythin' you bloody damn well please, what you bein' my pris'ner an' all," Thompson said, spitting on the ground at the feet of Mowat.

"Aside from the treason which I have already mentioned, Mr. Thompson, taking me prisoner would be a very injudicious act. If I do not return to my ship, with my companions, the master of the *Canceaux* has orders to fire on the town," Mowat said.

"Well, that was mighty fore-sighted o' ya', Cap'n Mowat, to give such orders, was'n 'it? Fact is, I thinks yer bluffin', with yer fine English an' flowery threatenin's," Thompson said.

"I happen to be Scottish; and, as a matter of fact, Mr. Hogg, the master of the *Canceaux*, has had standing orders for a week or two past, that if ever I were taken hostage, he is to lay the town in ashes," Mowat stated, looking Thompson directly in the eyes. Langdon himself wondered whether he was bluffing.

"Well, we'll just have to see 'bout that, won' we." He gestured to a couple of his men, who, after checking the prisoners for weapons, prodded them with the muzzles of their muskets to follow Thompson towards the grove of trees.

Langdon's heart pounded in his ears as they made their way silently into the grove. Glances at both Mowat and Bailey communicated nothing to him. He tried to force images of being shot in the woods from his mind but was not wholly successful.

They were taken into the copse and made to sit on a fallen log, a number of the rebels surrounding them to ensure they did not attempt an escape.

When at one point Langdon began to whisper a question to Mowat, one of their captors hissed venomously, "Pipe down, there, you English dogs!" Mowat visibly bristled at being called a dog (not to mention English), the muscles in his jaw tensing, but he controlled his emotions and remained silent.

A number of men were posted as sentries at the edge of the grove, and a handful of others were sent into town with orders that the prisoners couldn't overhear.

Mowat, Bailey and Langdon were disallowed from conversing with one another, and remained motionless for nearly an hour into the early afternoon.

It was nearing two o'clock when sentries approached Thompson to announce that "a number of gentlemen from the town" were desiring to speak to him. Thompson at once ordered that they be brought into the grove.

Enoch Freeman and Jedediah Preble soon appeared, very somber expressions on their faces. They stood talking with Thompson at the far edge of the grove, which was too distant for the captives to overhear everything, but near enough to make out that Freeman and Preble were pleading with Thompson to release the prisoners, as continued detainment would bring harm to the town. Thompson, however, was adamant, repeating over and over again that "divine providence" had thrown them into his hands, and that to deliver them up would be to waste a great opportunity. He was quite inflexible, and grew rather angry with Preble and Freeman, saying he had thought better of them than to be such "high Tories," which label they protested vehemently. Their voices had risen enough that the captives now had no difficulty in hearing every word.

Freeman reminded Thompson of his reply to the Town Council's express of the previous week, wherein he agreed to desist in designs to destroy the *Canceaux*; and that to be consistent with that intention, he would have to release his hostages. This reminder, however, incensed him even more, and, with more epithets and curses than decent language, he vilified their presumption of having written to him in such a tone, and did they not realize it had been the effrontery of their express which had been the very thing to convince him that Falmouth needed to be chastised for its arrogance and neutrality, and forced to see that there was now pitched warfare between Britain and her colonies, and only a clear declaration of allegiance either for or against independence would win the day?

"Do you mean to say that your return message, agreeing to lay aside any designs of destroying the *Canceaux*, was dissimulation – in other words, a lie?" Mr. Preble demanded angrily.

"There is policy in war," Thompson replied vaguely.

Preble was nearly seething with rage at this pronouncement, and an outburst looked inevitable until the timely arrival of one of Thompson's sentries interrupted their disputation. The sentry brought with him Jedediah Cobb, and apologized to Thompson that he had not asked permission, but that Cobb's information seemed important enough to warrant an immediate hearing.

"Well?!" Thompson shouted impatiently at Cobb.

"Mr. Hogg, master of the *Canceaux*," he said, "has heard that Captain Mowat is in the custody of Colonel Thompson, and has therefore sent word ashore that he will fire upon the town if the captain is not returned aboard by six o'clock."

Langdon looked at Mowat, but the latter's features remained implacably expressionless.

Preble and Freeman looked imploringly at Thompson, hoping this news would sway him. He hardened his lips, however, and said, "They has to do more than fire a few cannonballs into the town to think I's gonna give 'em up."

Preble and Freeman growled with exasperation. "What do you propose to do with them? Why keep them hostage?" Preble inquired angrily.

"Jes' think what a ransom they'd fetch, especially the Cap'n there," Thompson said, his eyes gleaming with greed. "That'll set an example o' what'll happen to other Tories an' royalist dogs."

"Good Lord!" Preble exclaimed. "This is the end of us!"

Freeman laid his hand on Preble's shoulder to calm him, then said, "We will return to the town now, Colonel Thompson, and try to go aboard the *Canceaux* to confer with Mr. Hogg. In the meanwhile, do nothing rash, which we would all later regret. We'll return by five o'clock to see if you've thought better of your intentions."

"Don't bother," Thompson said, cursing under his breath as they left the grove in the direction of the town. He kicked the dirt in anger once they were out of sight and made remarks about how they would have to pay for their "high-handed Toryism."

*

ANOTHER THREE HOURS of virtual silence were spent in the grove. The prisoners were party to occasional conversations supposedly out of their hearing, in which some of Thompson's men debated the advantages of killing or ransoming them.

At a little past five o'clock, as promised, Messrs. Preble and Freeman reappeared, this time with four other men, all members of either the Town Council or the Committee of Inspection, namely Jedediah Cobb, John Waite, John Butter and Moses Pearson. These six reported that they had spoken with Mr. Hogg, and that he seemed in earnest concerning his threat to fire on the town; and they implored Colonel Thompson to release his prisoners in the interests of, if not the town – as he seemed to care little for it – then of patriotic unity.

Thompson refused, saying that if Hogg actually fired so much as a single musket-ball into the city, he could not be held responsible for his actions. "For each ball fired, I'll execute a prisoner."

"You infernal fool!" Mr. Preble shook his head in disbelief.

Freeman, his teeth clenched in anger but exerting an extreme effort to control himself, said menacingly, "Don't you see that that would provoke a war? The execution of a King's officer is not just murder; it is treason! It would deal a mortal blow to the righteous cause of liberty, and none would stand by you. It would make us the laughingstock of London, bickering amongst ourselves like this."

"A war is just what we needs, I been reckonin' for a long time now," Thompson replied with chilling calm. "Words an' more words ain't gonna solve our problems no more, but steel an' shot."

The air was suddenly filled with the distant thunder of a cannon. Freeman pulled a watch from his pocket. "Six o'clock," he pronounced.

Everyone else was silent, waiting for further reports. There were none.

"A warning shot, perhaps?" asked one.

"Aye, a warning shot," broke in Lieutenant Mowat, all eyes turning towards the prisoners. "You've another hour, then my orders to Mr. Hogg are to destroy the town."

"At the cost o' yer lives," said Thompson threateningly.

Mowat did not reply.

Colonel Thompson turned to Freeman. "You can report to your precious Mr. Hogg that for every cannonball fired into the town, I cut off one o' the fingers of a prisoner, starting with the medicine man. Thirtieth shot and I begin executing 'em."

Preble ejaculated, "Savage!"

Freeman's jaw tensed, but he said nothing.

Colonel Thompson said simply, "It's gettin' dark. I'm movin' the prisoners to Marston's Pub." He began calling orders to his men. The six representatives of the town went their own way in frustration.

*

BRACKETT MARSTON'S PUBLIC HOUSE was located on the outskirts of town. It was a large house, surrounded by apple orchards from which its locally famous cider ale was produced; and Langdon knew that Mr. Marston was a champion of rebellion, and might therefore be a secret ally of Colonel Thompson.

It was twilight by the time they arrived at the house. Colonel Thompson's men filled the main, public room of the house, and immediately clamored for food and drink. The prisoners were taken to the cellar – the easier to guard – and arrangements were made to feed Thompson's men in rotation, so that several could always be left on guard. The prisoners were informed that if they wished to eat, they would have to pay for it out of their own pockets: Mr. Marston's hospitality did not extend to them.

As seven o'clock approached, the Rev'd Langdon grew extremely agitated. "Do you think Hogg will fire, given the ultimatum issued by Thompson?" he asked. His hands were like ice.

"Hard to say," Mowat said. "The stakes are risen pretty high on both sides, although I think Mr. Thompson is too stupid to realize it. It does not enter his brain that the brutal murder of two King's officers and a minister of the Church of England, coming so soon on the heels of the incident at Lexington and Concord, would leave government little option but to assume a posture of warfare against her colonies. On the other hand, Hogg is bound by orders to brook no insult to the King's honor, our lives notwithstanding."

Bailey leaned against a wooden beam, Langdon paced agitatedly back and forth, and Lieutenant Mowat sat on an empty keg, outwardly calm as the hour of seven approached and passed. It was nearly a quarter past, and no cannon-fire had been heard, when the door to the cellar was opened, and Enoch Freeman was admitted. He descended a few steps, then turned and said to Thompson, who stood at the top of the steps, "You said you would remove your guard so that I could confer in privacy."

There was a moment of silence. "How can I trust you, bein' a high Tory an' all?"

"I am a patriot and no Tory."

Colonel Thompson looked spitefully at Freeman, as if examining his intentions, then jerked his chin to one side for the guard to come up. The guard ascended the stairs and Freeman descended into the candle-lit darkness of the cellar. The door closed behind him.

"I've been aboard the *Canceaux* to talk with Master Hogg," Freeman began, addressing Mowat, "and he is willing to delay a bombardment until I have had a chance to speak with you, and perhaps work out an agreement."

Mowat nodded. "Very well. Proceed."

"As you have seen, Colonel Thompson is unwilling to listen to reason, and adamant in his insistence upon detaining you as his prisoners; yet he has no clear conception what to do with you in the long run to further his ends."

"Well, what sort of agreement do you have in mind, that might be acceptable to Mr. Thompson?" Mowat asked.

"I doubt if there is one, truthfully. But I have two possible avenues in my mind. The town is in an uproar, with people evacuating their homes and fleeing into the woods in anticipation of a bombardment. Ten miles away, in Gorham, there is a company of over a hundred militiamen commanded by Colonel Edmund Phinney. Rumor has it that they're on their way here, having heard of the commotion. I don't know Colonel Phinney personally, but chances are he is more reasonable than Thompson; and, commanding about three times as many men, it is to be hoped that he will be able to enforce a rational resolution to this situation."

"However, that is only a hopeful assumption, I take it, Mr. Freeman?" Mowat asked. "He could turn out to be just as ignorant and strong headed as our Mr. Thompson."

"Unfortunately, yes."

"And the second avenue that occurred to you?" Mowat prodded.

"Well," began Freeman furtively, casting an apprehensive glance at the door at the top of the stairs, "I don't think Colonel Thompson was aware when he put you in this cellar that there is another exit."

Mowat's eyes brightened.

"Behind those barrels is a crawl space that leads to a storm door in the ground at the side of the house. Thompson has guards stationed only at the front and rear doors of the house. Neither is within sight of the storm door, and, it being a dark night with townspeople fleeing their houses into the orchards and woods in anticipation of bombardment, it could very well be that, if you can get out of the door, three men scurrying into the trees would not excite comment."

"Excellent," said Mowat turning to the barrels in question. "And you must come with us, or you will be murdered by Thompson for aiding our escape."

"No," said Freeman. "Once you are safely away, I will return upstairs and attempt to distract them further."

Mowat considered him for a moment. "I think that highly unwise; but you must do as you think best."

Bailey and Langdon by this time had begun to try and drag the indicated barrels away. Neither of them being particularly brawny men, they were slow in their work.

While watching them, Mowat asked Freeman quietly, "How did you find things aboard the *Canceaux*?"

"Calm and disciplined. I overheard idle words among some petty officers about mounting a rescue attempt, but I think Master Hogg is not listening to such talk."

"Good," Mowat said simply. "Let us talk in normal tones, in order to disguise any sound they may make moving barrels." Freeman nodded. "I must admit, Mr. Freeman," Mowat continued, slightly louder, "that you have impressed me today. Your sentiments are not what one might call loyal; but you are not a rabble-rouser like some of your countrymen."

"I consider myself loyal, Mr. Mowat," Freeman rejoined. "Loyal to the tradition of freedom which the English constitution has heretofore granted us with such liberality. I do not hide the fact, however, that I believe this liberty has lately been curtailed, not least in parliament's insistence on punishing us for our unwillingness to satisfy the greed and vanity of corrupt ministers."

"All governments have faults, Mr. Freeman," Mowat observed, "as do all its ministers, for they are but men. Isn't it a far greater thing to identify and seek to rectify the faults in a government you already have – especially one so liberal in its attitude towards individual liberty and self-correction as the English – than to throw it off and try to form something new, with all the uncertainty and potential for failure that that implies? What if someone like our Mr. Thompson here were to develop a great following, and then, when independence was won, find himself in a position of influence? It frightens me to think what the American colonies have in store for them if they throw off the centuries-old, finely tuned system of checks and balances written into the English constitution, and wager their livelihoods on some untested and potentially anarchistic group of usurpers down in Boston, or New York, or Philadelphia. Won't this be the throwing off of a mild, distant tyranny (as you perceive it) for a palpable, immediate, and much more alarming one close at hand?"

"You speak eloquently, Captain Mowat," Mr. Freeman admitted. "If I had more confidence in the benevolence of the king, and the lack of corruption in parliament, I could almost acquiesce to your logic. But I have seen too much desire on the part of the crown's ministers, both in Westminster and Boston, to prove their rectitude and supremacy rather than to think of the colonists' welfare."

Having listened while he worked, Langdon said while wiping the sweat from his brow, "Proving their rectitude seems to be the fault of more than the government. These self-appointed colonial leaders speak of liberty, praising it and putting it on the tongues of the common man, but what they actually do, with their spying, the acts of violence they perpetrate, the tarrings and featherings, the confiscation of property, and now the taking of prisoners . . . their actions are anything but indicative of a veneration for true liberty!"

Mowat gestured subtly to Langdon not to become agitated, and said, "You rest a moment, Mr. Langdon. I'll assist the doctor."

Three barrels had been rocked carefully and quietly to the side, revealing the wood of a rough and unfinished door behind them, almost invisible in the shadow of the shelf above it. Bailey, stooping beneath the shelf, pulled on what appeared to be a makeshift handle. Slowly it began to give way, scraping inward across the floor. The removal of another barrel proved necessary before it could be opened wide enough to admit entrance.

Mowat turned to Freeman when Bailey announced that the door was clear. "You are certain you do not wish to accompany us, Mr. Freeman?"

He nodded. "It would label me a Tory."

"Very well. Let me say that this deed will be remembered, and rewarded, if opportunity presents itself. I admonish you, in the coming days of unrest, to consider the consequences of war. Being a Scotsman myself, I am not unsympathetic to anything that appears to be high-handed treatment from Westminster; but never would I advocate violent overthrow of what is, when all's said, a decent and well-meaning government."

"Thank you, Captain Mowat," Freeman said.

The prisoners had to stoop more than double in order to fit through the crawl space. They heard Mr. Freeman continuing to talk softly behind them, to give the illusion that conversation was still taking place in the cellar.

Langdon had taken one of the candles from the cellar with them. After practically crawling twenty or thirty feet along a moldy and damp space, choked heavily with cobwebs, they arrived at the end. There was a wooden door in the ceiling of the passage, through the cracks of which the twinkling stars could be seen. Langdon extinguished the candle as Bailey applied his eye to one of the larger cracks and gained as great an angle of view as possible. "Can't see too much, but I've got one corner of the house in view, and it appears deserted."

"Let's have a go at it then," Mowat said.

The doctor tested the door. "It appears locked," he said with dismay.

"Any locks would be on the inside, surely," Langdon said. "It must just be jammed."

"Let's force it," Mowat said urgently. "Come, time is of the essence. Chop, chop!"

It proved easier than expected for the three of them to force the door, and the wooden planks swung upward and outward with what seemed like a deafening groan of long-neglected hinges. With nary a pause, not even to look around, the doctor hoisted himself out of the crawl space and turned to assist Langdon, who clambered a little less gracefully out of the hole. The two men reached in and grasped the shorter, stockier lieutenant, one under each arm, hoisting him out in the blink of an eye.

Then all three turned and ran headlong into the darkness of the orchard, their hearts pounding so loudly in their ears and their feet in the grass that, even if someone had challenged them with a shout, they would not have been able to hear it.

Chapter Eleven.

Their breasts heaving as they gasped for air, Mowat, Langdon, and Bailey came to a stop after running for what must have been a full five minutes. Reasonably assured that they had not been pursued, and their panic having mellowed into a dull fear, they stopped to assess what was next to be done.

"We must get back to the ship somehow," Mowat said between gasps.

"Yes," Langdon and Bailey said simultaneously.

"But how?"

None spoke for a few moments as their brains raced and their breathing slowed.

"If we go back through town, we are sure to be seen," Bailey said.

"But there are no boats to be had elsewhere," Langdon observed.

"You don't know of any loyalist families living on the outskirts of town who might have a boat in their possession?" Mowat asked the clergyman.

"The customs collector, George Lyde, has the customs boat; but it is moored at Pearson's wharf."

"Right in the middle of town." Mowat said, shaking his head. "What about Josiah Dornett, the Comptroller? He lives, I am informed, on the extreme north side of town. Does he have a boat?"

Langdon considered this idea. "I have a plan," he said at last. "We will go to the Dornett residence – although, once it is discovered that we have escaped, the Dornett's is one of the dwellings we would most be expected to resort to. If we reach it in time, however, we could perhaps persuade Mr. Dornett to go into town, row himself to the *Canceaux* in the customs boat and inform Master Hogg that we should be picked up by a ship's boat in Back Cove."

"Excellent idea, parson. Which way to Mr. Dornett's?"

They stood in a grove near the Dornett residence little more than quarter-of-an-hour later, taking care to remain silent and obscured until they had assured themselves that the house was not being watched by Thompson's men. Earlier, on their way, they had heard the alarm being raised in town, and assumed that their escape had been discovered. Freeman must have distracted them rather effectively for it to have taken them a full 20 minutes.

"The house appears to be unmolested," Mowat whispered after several minutes of observation. "Perhaps Mr. Langdon should go to the door alone, being the best acquainted with the comptroller."

"All right," Langdon nodded.

"We'll whistle something like a bird call should we see any suspicious persons around the house while you're inside," Dr. Bailey said just before Langdon slipped away from them.

"*You'll* whistle something like a bird call," whispered Mowat to the doctor. "I haven't the faintest idea!"

Langdon, crouched to almost half his height, made his way as silently as possible towards the house. Every snap of a twig or crunch of leaf under his foot made his heart leap into his throat; but he found himself without event standing on the rear doorstep of the house. A single light seemed to come from an inner room. He tapped gingerly on the door.

No one seemed to stir from within. Cringing, he tapped a little louder. The flickering light, probably that of a candle, was immediately extinguished. He tapped yet again, trying to think of an inconspicuous way to communicate that it was he, the parson, and that Mr. Dornett had nothing to fear. Tapping for a fourth time, he thought he saw a figure move within the house. He leaned closer so that his face could be more easily seen through the window. At last he heard the latch moving in the door, and then it opened a crack.

"Mr. Langdon, is that you?" a hoarse whisper came from inside.

"Josiah! Yes, it's me!"

The door opened, the parson passed silently through it, and Dornett quickly bolted the lock after him. "Word around town is that you were taken prisoner with Captain Mowat by an unruly mob from Brunswick," he said, looking perplexed.

"I was, and Dr. Bailey, too, the ship's surgeon. But we've escaped. The others are in the woods out back."

"Lord! And you've taken refuge on *my* doorstep!"

"We must get back to the ship, Josiah. Since your house is slightly remote from the town, and we knew you to be trustworthy, you were naturally our best – "

"And that's probably just what Colonel Thompson is thinking, too!" Dornett snapped, casting an apprehensive glance out the window.

"We're sorry to have to throw ourselves at your feet, Josiah; but we *must* get aboard ship. Our idea was that you, not being involved in this affair, could perhaps slip into town, take the customs boat out to the *Canceaux* and inform Master Hogg where to collect us. We would meanwhile repair thither and remain concealed until they arrived. Do you think that's possible?"

Dornett bit his lip in thought. He was obviously not enthusiastic about the idea. "I'm not exactly uninvolved, as you say, being a King's official and therefore suspect in their eyes; but . . ." He hesitated. "Perhaps I could go along to the Waite residence – they're just a couple streets over. John Waite has two strapping sons who might not excite suspicion if observed putting off in a boat in the middle of the night."

"That would be excellent. Tell them to instruct Hogg that we should be found in Back Cove, at Sandy Point. They should hang out a lantern and, let's see, blink the shutter twice every minute or two. Once we've been assured it's them, we'll leave our cover and come to the water's edge where they will be able to see us. Got that?"

"Sandy Point, Back Cove," recited Dornett, "blink the shutter twice every minute or two . . . is that it?"

"Exactly right. We are eternally grateful to you, Josiah."

The Comptroller merely nodded.

"I will go back to Captain Mowat and Dr. Bailey. We will make our way to Sandy Point. Our lives depend upon you, Josiah."

"And mine on pure luck," he said. He reached for the door. The sound of a whippoorwill came to them through the night air. Langdon grabbed Dornett's arm before he could turn the handle.

"Oh God!" ejaculated Langdon. "That's Dr. Bailey, signalling that someone suspicious has appeared!"

Dornett uttered a curse. There came a loud rap at the front door, startling them both nearly out of their skins.

"Hide yourself here," Dornett whispered as he looked around himself for his candle. "I'll see who it is, and try to send them away."

"Good luck," Langdon said.

The knock came again, louder. "I'm coming, already," he said aloud, disappearing into the hall.

Langdon secreted himself behind a curtain, straining his ears to follow Dornett's actions. He heard the front door open, an annoyed comptroller demanding to know who it was who called at such an hour, then the voice of another, more muffled, inquiring after information regarding the whereabouts of Captain Mowat and the Rev'd Langdon.

"Haven't you heard?" Langdon heard Dornett reply with irritation. "They've apparently been detained for questioning by a group of patriots newly arrived from Brunswick. That's what I've heard, at any rate. The town's abuzz with the news. I'm surprised you haven't heard it by now! You have? Well, why the devil come asking me, then?"

There was a snippet of conversation Langdon couldn't make out, then Dornett said, "Ah, escaped, have they?"

More muffled voices.

"Yes, all right," Dornett bid them goodnight, and the door closed. Peeking out from behind the curtain, Langdon saw the flickering light of the candle fade away as Dornett made his way up the stairs, presumably to his bedroom. Admiring his cunning, Langdon was reminded of the verse from Matthew where Jesus admonished his disciples to be "wise as serpents and harmless as doves." Soon, this time without light, he heard the stairs creak as Dornett returned. "I think they've gone," he said.

"Well done, Josiah."

"In the customs business, where one is constantly on the lookout to recognize subterfuge and lying, one gets pretty good at it oneself," he said.

"Godspeed," Langdon said, feeling this was more in keeping with a clergyman than "Good luck" had been. He opened the back door slowly, in order to give Mowat and Bailey plenty of opportunity of seeing him and therefore warning him if suspicious persons were still about. Hearing nothing, he crept furtively out and made his way back through the underbrush.

He explained the plan to them, then indicated what he felt would be the way to Sandy Point which would afford them the most cover, although it was not the shortest.

"That's for the better," whispered Mowat, "for I should be very much surprised if we shall not have to wait at Sandy Point for a wee time before being collected, even if we crawled all the way there on our bellies!"

*

The lieutenant's prediction proved quite correct, and the three refugees had been shivering with cold for two and a half hours by the time a boat appeared around the point, a lantern blinking the agreed code.

With relief they made their way from the thick underbrush to the beach, waving. "Ahoy there, Canceauxs!" Mowat called hoarsley. A clamor broke out in the boat as its coxswain, Midshipman Barker, issued an order and altered course for the beach where they stood. The lantern was shuttered.

As the boat approached, Mowat suggested they wade out to meet it. The three therefore waded into the icy cold water until they stood in it up to their waists, shivering uncontrollably in the damp night.

Just as strong hands were reaching over to haul them into the boat, a cry was heard from on shore, striking terror into their hearts. The three refugees were unceremoniously dumped into the bottom of the boat, and Midshipman Barker issued orders for their hasty propulsion away from the shore. Not half a minute had passed when the report of a pistol was to be heard, then another. One of the two shots splashed directly abaft the boat, dousing Barker with a small plume of salt water.

Raising himself to one of the benches, Mowat saw two men on the beach, presumably some of Thompson's men, reloading their pistols. In the couple minutes it took them to ram the powder, wad, and shot into the barrel of their pistols, the boat had achieved a distance of some hundred yards from the beach. When the first of the men leveled his arm and pointed the pistol at the boat, Mowat said, "Down, all!"

A splash several yards from the boat followed closely on the heels of the muffled report of the pistol. "Stay down!" he hissed when several oarsmen sat up to resume their task. "There are *two* of 'em."

The second proved even more ineffective, as none could trace the fall of its shot.

"Give way all! Together!" came the voice of Midshipman Barker once more. The boat was virtually out of range of the men on the shore when their third shots came.

Mowat said, "I think we're out of harm's way now, Mr. Barker. Make a course for the ship."

"Aye aye, sir."

Thus free of threats from the shore, and allowing himself to relax for the first time in more than twelve hours, the Rev'd Langdon felt himself overcome with uncontrollable shivers. He leaned over the side of the boat and retched ineffectually, his stomach already empty.

"We'll be on board in twenty minutes, sir," Midshipman Barker said comfortingly.

"And then we'll get you into some warm, dry clothing, Thomas," Bailey said through his own chattering teeth.

Once aboard, Mowat shook Master Hogg's hand heartily, commending him for his steady conduct that day. Hogg muttered a few words of modesty but could not hide a sort of beaming smile at this praise.

"Come to my cabin in a quarter-hour, Mr. Hogg, and we'll discuss the situation in detail. I must first get into some dry clothing."

Langdon went with Bailey to his tiny cabin. Thrusting a folded garment at him, Bailey said "Wear these slops until you can get some clothing of your own."

Suddenly overcome, Langdon asked tremulously, "I wonder how that shall be done?" After collecting himself, he asked quietly,

"Do you suppose I shall ever set foot in Falmouth again?"

"Of course you will!" said Bailey. "Once this so-called Colonel Thompson and his men are got rid of, you'll be snug as a bug in your house again."

Langdon nodded, though without conviction.

"As for getting your clothing right away, we'll send word ashore in the morning to some of your friends, and ask them to go along to your home and bring out some of your effects. And until you're ashore again, this cabin will be yours, and I – "

"No, David!"

"– and I will sleep in the medicine dispensary – there's quite enough room to sling a hammock there – and feel quite at home," Bailey assured him, silencing further protest with a wagging of his finger.

Chapter Twelve.

DESPITE HIS EXHAUSTION, the Rev'd Langdon found sleep difficult aboard the *Canceaux* that first night, partly because he was not at all used to sleeping in a hammock, and the ship seemed never to sleep itself; but mostly because his mind was a hive of unrest. But eventually he slept, the sound of footfalls on decks and ladders, and the creak of the ship's beams as she rocked at anchor, appearing in his troubled dreams.

Langdon was startled awake not long after dawn by the sound of pistol fire, first distant, as from on shore; then startlingly close at hand, as if from the very deck above.

When he had extricated himself with little grace from the hammock, a terrific neck ache making him wince with pain, he dressed in the slops he had been given, and emerged on deck.

It was soon learned that, in the night's tumult and confusion, a group of townsmen, in search of Mowat, Bailey, and Langdon, had broken into Captain Coulson's abandoned house (his family had days ago taken up residence aboard his nearly finished sloop), had found a keg of New England rum in the cellar, and one of the many who had become drunk – Calvin Lombard, who had been ringleader of the group responsible for the tarring-and-feathering of Jeremiah Coffin last March – had gone to the waterside with a brace of pistols and fired at the ship. Mr. Hogg, who had had the watch, ordered the fire returned, but with no real aim to do execution.

Langdon soon smelled the heady odor of fresh coffee coming from the ship's galley beneath the forecastle, and before he had had opportunity to inquire whether he might be able to have a cup, Midshipman Barker announced, "Captain's compliments, sir, and would you join him for coffee in his cabin."

"By all means, Mr. Barker," he said warmly.

Mowat sat at the table, a metal pot at his elbow. He offered the parson a cup. Langdon accepted gratefully, and apologized for his clothing and appearance.

Mowat waved it away as unimportant. "I trust you slept well?" he asked, indicating to the ubiquitous Penfold that he pour him a cup from the pot.

"As well as might be expected, I suppose."

"You'll get used to it ere long, I assure you. Pretty soon you'll be able to sleep through a fleet battle!" he chuckled.

"Have you yourself had opportunity to sleep through any battles?" Langdon returned playfully.

After draining his cup and holding it out to Penfold to pour another, Mowat added more seriously, "I was only a part of one such battle, Quiberon Bay, in '59."

"Indeed!" Langdon said with astonishment.

"I passed my lieutenant's examination in '58, and was commissioned fifth lieutenant of the *Dunkirk*, a fourth rate of 60 guns. She joined Sir Edward Hawke's fleet the next year, and was at Quiberon that November."

Langdon remained silent, partly in awe, partly because the hot coffee had provided something of a pleasantly numbing effect.

"There was such a gale and such heavy seas," Mowat continued, "we weren't able to open the gun-ports on the lower deck, and were thus effectively just a 28-gun ship. The *Thésée*, a French 74, did venture to open hers, and she sank almost immediately with all hands."

"Dear me!"

"But talk of this sort, interesting as it is, is not why I asked you to come aft, Mr. Langdon. Aside from welcoming you aboard, I was hoping to employ your services again as a secretary," Mowat said.

"By all means," Langdon assured him. "While I am aboard, you may call upon me for anything of that nature, and I shall be more than happy to comply. It is the least I can do in exchange for your protection."

"Very well, I want you to write a letter to Freeman for me, demanding that the town turn over the man who fired at the ship this morning," Mowat said. "I'll look it over when you're done and sign it."

"Do we have any word as to Mr. Freeman's fate at the hands of Colonel Thompson?" Langdon inquired.

"Aye," Mowat replied. "Mr. Lyde, the customs collector, has already been aboard this morning, bringing news of the night's goings-on. Mr. Freeman is alive and well, it turns out, mostly because Colonel Phinney of Gorham arrived soon after our escape and was finally able to talk some sense into Colonel Thompson. Mr.

Freeman, whom Thompson had imprisoned upon learning of our escape, was released in exchange for pledging to pay £158, which Thompson said was to provide for the provisioning of his men.

"I'm sorry to say," he continued in a quieter voice, "that your house, along with that of the Coulsons, was broken into by the mobs, and most of your valuables taken."

Langdon was silent for a moment, then said, "Well, I'm to be most thankful for my life, which I do still possess this morning. As for worldly possessions, I suppose there's something to be said for being more careful about storing up treasures in heaven than on earth."

"Aye, quite," Mowat replied.

"Although I rue the loss of my books. And my flute."

"Those are all probably still there, along with your clothing, which we will send for immediately. Mr. Lyde has already said he would look in and see what could be brought away in the custom's boat."

"Then . . . you don't think I'll be going ashore again myself?"

Mowat hesitated, feeling sadness for the clergyman. "You are certainly to be the judge of that, Mr. Langdon," he began. "You have your roots there, your parish to care for, your house and history . . . You must weigh these things against the apparent fact that many of your kinsmen have risen up against their government and will plainly not abide anyone who disagrees with them to continue peaceably in their lives and trades. If I am any judge, a general war looms mere months, perhaps even weeks, away. A man of your convictions is now forced into making a choice between leaving his home to enjoy the benefit of the king's protection, or remaining in his home and foregoing that protection until peace can be restored to the whole of the country. That is what I unfortunately believe."

Both were silent for a time. Langdon reflected that the theme of his last sermon at St. Paul's was now being preached to him through Mowat's words.

"George Lyde and his wife have asked for my protection, as well, and will be coming aboard later today or tomorrow, with many of their possessions. They will remain with me until I get to Halifax, where they will establish themselves for the duration. The Coulsons, as you have heard, have taken refuge aboard their sloop, which is now finished . . . as far as it's going to be, anyway. The *John & Mary* will be setting sail today, having finished her business and repaired her bottom. We'll all be setting sail in the next couple days, and I'll escort Coulson's sloop to Portsmouth, where Captain Barkley of the *Scarborough* can look after it. Then I'll be off to Halifax. As for your future, in view of these things . . ." he stopped, not sure as to whether the melancholy clergyman could bear to hear any more.

"Yes?" Langdon asked.

"Well, firstly, I continue to be in need of a captain's clerk, but I fear you are so overqualified for such a position that I hesitate to mention it. The salary is paltry – less than £2 per month in a sixth-rate such as the *Canceaux* – but it is something you could occupy yourself with during the remainder of this conflict.

"My second suggestion is this: With your particular combination of talents and interests, you might prove a very attractive man to Vice Admiral Graves. Not only does the flagship not have a chaplain, to my latest knowledge, but, I happen to know that the flagship's purser died last month, and the admiral's clerk was appointed in his place. There may still exist, therefore, a vacancy in the area of admiral's clerk. In addition, a flagship usually has an entire raft of midshipmen and other youngsters aboard, so with your education and learning, you would make an excellent schoolmaster. I do not know whether Graves has a schoolmaster already. I will, if you wish, write to the admiral on your behalf, recommending you for any or all of those positions in the flagship, H.M.S. *Preston*."

Langdon continued to be silent, the enormity of these considerations weighing on him.

"Think about it a wee while," said Mowat quickly in his comforting Scottish accent, "and inform me at your leisure of your determination. As I've said, I would be more than happy to write a letter of high commendation for you, should you wish it.

"As for matters nearer to hand," Mowat continued, "I want you to write, as I've said, a letter to Freeman about turning over the man who fired at the ship this morning."

Langdon, rousing himself, nodded, "I will. And may I write a letter or two of my own, to be delivered by whomever you have appointed to deliver your letter?" Langdon inquired.

"Yes, of course," Mowat replied.

"Thank you. I've a parishioner or two – one an elderly widow, another a woman with child – after whose welfare I wish to inquire," he explained. "And a friend to whom I would like to wish farewell."

*

MOWAT WAS VERY PLEASED with Langdon's product half an hour later, and, after signing it, sent it and the parson's hastily penned notes ashore with Midshipman Barker.

Midshipman Barker, upon returning aboard, told Mowat that the town was in a complete, uncontrollable uproar. Homes and shops were being plundered in the name of liberty, abandoned houses were being used for barracks – and there were now a number of them, including the Coulson's, Tyng's, Lyde's, Dornett's, Pagan's, Oxnard's (Edward and Polly had taken refuge at the home of parents in Biddeford, Langdon learned), as well as

Langdon's parsonage — and that destruction of the *Canceaux* was on everybody's lips. In fact, a stranger, potentially sacrificing his own safety, had approached Mr. Barker courageously and told him that he had overheard plans for bringing "fort guns" to the town to destroy or drive off the *Canceaux*.

Around noon the Lydes came aboard, three boats laden to the gunwales with their belongings. They also brought a number of Mr. Langdon's clothes, a single trunk full of books, and his flute in its wooden case. Langdon felt tears pricking the corners of his eyes at the sight of the flute case.

Dr. Bailey and the exiled clergyman sat on the quarterdeck in the afternoon, enjoying the sun and keeping an eye on the movement of the rebels in the town. They had been advised that to sit on deck might not be the safest of things to do, should more of the rebels take it into their demented heads to fire at the ship. Assuring themselves, however, that, at such a distance they could be hit only by extreme chance rather than deliberate aim, they took the risk.

Shortly before three o'clock, they watched as the *John & Mary* got under way. "Just in time, it would seem," Bailey observed, "what with the rebels being so bold as to fire at us, now." It took an hour in this moderate breeze for the ungainly ship — now made marginally more beautiful by the unfurling of its pyramids of dingy white canvas, glowing in the afternoon sun — to clear the harbor and move out into Casco Bay.

Before she had quite disappeared, however, a single pistol shot was heard in the direction of Captain Coulson's sloop. Both Dr. Bailey and Langdon leapt to their feet, and, Midshipman Larkin, the officer of the watch, directed several armed men into the shrouds, should the situation necessitate a return of fire. Lieutenant Mowat appeared on deck almost immediately. "What is it, Mr. Larkin? Whereaway?" he asked, holding out his hand for a telescope.

"From Captain Coulson's sloop, sir. Impossible to determine the cause yet," he said, giving Mowat a telescope handed him swiftly by the Master, who had also appeared from nowhere. "I've taken the liberty of sending some muskets into the shrouds, sir."

"Very attentive of you, Mr. Larkin," Mowat said as he examined Captain Coulson's sloop through the telescope.

"Deck thar'," came the lookout's cry from far overhead. "Boat rowing towards shore. Looks like one o' ours."

"It is one of ours," Mowat observed, still peering through the telescope. "It's the jollyboat I lent Captain Coulson the day before yesterday to complete his fitting out. And those don't look like his men manning it!"

Langdon squinted in the direction of Captain Coulson's sloop, trying to pick out the boat in the late afternoon glare. The sun being in the west, it was necessary to shade his eyes when looking towards shore. He soon spied it, however, a froth of water around its bow as it pulled hastily towards the docks.

"Mr. Randle!" Mowat called to the *Canceaux*'s gunner. "Prepare to fire one of the six-pounders to bring them to. I suspect our boat is being stolen. Mr. Hogg," Mowat turned and looked for the master, who stepped forward immediately. "Assemble a boat's crew and take the gig to pursue the jollyboat. Make sure the men are well-armed, for you may have to cut it out by force."

"Aye aye, sir," Hogg said, jumping to the task with loud orders this way and that.

Mr. Randle, the gunner, had assembled a crew of his mates, and within minutes, the jollyboat having almost reached shore, one of the *Canceaux*'s larger cannons fired, a tongue of fire lashing out of its barrel at the almost deafening crash, followed by a prodigious amount of smoke, which only lazily drifted away due to the lightness of the breeze. The power and violence of the gun, leaping backwards like a chained animal as it fired, sent a thrill up the clergyman's spine.

He was not able to determine the fall of the shot, or how close it came to its mark. It was not much intended to hit the boat, Langdon suspected, but merely to be a show of force.

Mr. Hogg's crew of eight in the gig were soon rowing with haste in the direction of the wharf where the jollyboat was just docking. Mowat watched the proceedings silently but intently for the next twenty minutes through his telescope, having climbed a few yards up into the mizzen shrouds.

The gig returned alone to the *Canceaux* half an hour later. When she had come alongside and Hogg had climbed aboard, he reported that the jollyboat had been taken from the water and hauled overland into the town. Hogg had opted not to pursue, thinking the risks too great of putting a mere handful of his men into the midst of what was sure to be a growing and bloodthirsty mob, attracted by the sound of gunfire.

"Very prudent of you, Mr. Hogg. Mr. Langdon," Mowat called out, much surprising the parson.

"Yes, captain?"

"Come to the chart room if you would be so kind. We are to write another letter to Mr. Freeman," he said, turning towards the main hatch. "Mr. Larkin," he called as he was disappearing below, "Keep an eye on the town, and leave the gig manned." He stopped on the ladder, another idea having occurred to him. "In fact, have a swivel gun mounted in the bow of the gig. Inform me immediately of any boat that moves, and don't hesitate bringing anything to, either with a warning shot or sending the gig in pursuit."

"Aye aye, sir."

"Now, Mr. Langdon," Mowat began once they were in the chart room and a pen and paper had been taken from the map cabinet, "Take something of this sort down, please:

"*'Mr. Freeman, A jollyboat belonging to H.M.S.* Canceaux *was taken* this last hour from Captain Coulson's sloop, by a group of men who refused to heave to when pursued, and who carried the boat to some unknown location ashore. This theft has reduced my patience to its last degree. If the boat is not returned to this ship immediately,' --underline that word, 'immediately'-- 'drastic actions will result – '"

Langdon interrupted: "How about *'I shall have no alternative but to take drastic action . . .'?*"

"Yes, excellent. Make it so. Now a new paragraph: *'Furthermore, I have heard rumors that some persons think to bring cannon or other fort guns into Falmouth to drive the* Canceaux *from port. I have no doubt that you are aware that this would mean the instant reduction of the entire town to ashes.'* Another paragraph: *'As the presence of such illegally assembled mobs from neighboring localities – that of Mr. Thompson foremost among them – has brought nothing but trouble to Falmouth, I suggest your committee meet and pass a resolution for the raising of a local militia to dispel the said mobs, being unwelcome and deleterious to the town's welfare.'* Then end the letter with the usual, *'I am, etc., etc.'* Write it up formally, plus a copy for the Admiral, and I'll sign it. We might make an honest man of Mr. Freeman yet!" With these words, he sprang back on deck to leave the parson to his task.

The letter was sent ashore by Mr. Barker under a flag of truce. Its reply, which came with Mr. Barker almost half an hour later, merely read "A town meeting is to take place tomorrow morning at eight o'clock, where your letter will be read."

*

"QUITE AN EVENTFUL FIRST DAY aboard the *Canceaux*, what?" Mowat asked Mr. and Mrs. Lyde towards the end of dinner that evening. Mowat had given up his cabin to them (much to the fastidious Penfold's annoyance, as it happened – especially when Mowat told them to make use of Penfold as if he were their personal servant), taking the adjacent chartroom for himself, but they had graciously assented to Mowat's reclaiming it for dinner, as long as he didn't mind the various personal effects which lined the walls, in the process of being sorted and re-packed by Mrs. Lyde. Thus, he had invited the ship's passengers – the Lydes and the Rev'd Langdon, as well as Dr. Bailey – to join him.

"Very eventful indeed," Mr. Lyde nodded. "I shall always remember the 11th of May, 1775."

"My husband tells me that we will be sailing very soon," Mrs. Lyde said by way of inquiry.

"That is correct, Mrs. Lyde," Mowat inclined his head. "Providing I get no orders to the contrary."

"And what will become of Falmouth when we leave, I wonder?"

"That is impossible to tell, of course," Mowat shrugged. "Either the rebelliously inclined will gain the upper hand due to our absence, thus forcing the loyalists to conform or flee; or our absence will cause the mobs to lose their interest in the town, and they will head south to Portsmouth or Boston where there are more opportunities for annoying His Majesty's forces, leaving Falmouth to go about its business."

". . . without a customs collector, I might add," observed Mr. Lyde wryly. "I am gone, and Mr. Dornett and his family are staying with friends up the coast in Woolwich, waiting and seeing."

"Well, let us hope it becomes possible for them to return in time," Mowat said. "In fact, I pray it will be possible for all of you to return to Falmouth eventually – but it will not be for many months, I fear."

"Let us hope your prayer comes true," Mrs. Lyde said.

"We are British, having all been born and raised in Massachusetts," Mr. Lyde said emphatically. "If the colonies throw off their British association, then we must remove to a portion of our country which has not. Perhaps, then, to Canada."

"Your sentiments do you great credit, Mr. Lyde. Gentlemen and Mrs. Lyde:" Mowat stood, taking his glass of wine and holding it out in front of him, "The King!"

"The King!" all returned the toast, and drained their glasses heartily.

*

The Rev'd Mr. Thomas Langdon's Journal

Thursday, 11 May, 1775. On board H.M.S. Canceaux anchored in Falmouth Harbor (. . .) The Lydes brought me a case of clothing, my flute, a case of books – including this journal, which, thanks be to God, had not been taken – and also a report of the state of my house, with many windows broken, all the silver and other valuables gone, several pieces of furniture missing, other pieces broken up and being used as kindling by Colonel Thompson's men. Mrs. Lyde told me it was altogether a tragic shambles. What evil times we are heir to. I am pleased to hear that Mr. Freeman has not fared as ill as I'd feared; although £158 must be several years' earnings for him, and no small hardship. His actions were very brave, and he must now find himself a man without a faction, as he has no doubt alienated the more rabid contingent of rebels, while not yet rehabilitating himself in the eyes of royal officials or loyalists. I rather fear his time as a figure of much influence around town has ended. He was an influence for ill when he had that power (and perhaps that is why he will be made to suffer henceforth); but now, when he could be a force for good – for moderation, that is – his authority is discounted by having been fair-minded to those whose blood is clamored for by the angry mobs.

As for my own standing and future, I hardly dare think about it. Mowat is persuaded that I should abandon hope of returning to

Falmouth anytime soon, and therefore that I should look for a temporary place serving His Majesty's armed forces as chaplain, or clerk, or schoolmaster. Although I can see that he is right, and should be grateful for his offer of assistance, my emotions recoil, and I have not yet accepted that all is lost for me in Falmouth. How can one's life and livelihood, one's vocation and career, be so stable and edifying one day, and a month later be utterly stripped away? All I have striven to build at St. Paul's – all the work I have done amongst the people of the parish – all the attachments and relationships I have nurtured over an entire lifetime – I find it difficult to accept that they are now utterly gone. The shock is almost too much to bear. The grief would be intolerable, if I could only feel it as I should; but I can feel nothing but a vague sense of having to survive from day to day, from meal to meal, even from hour to hour. Perhaps this is a blessing, this deadness of emotion that is creeping over me. *Lord, assist me in this most awful hour; sustain me with your bountiful spirit; strengthen me when I am powerless; lighten my darkness when I am unable to see my way forward. Amen.*

Chapter Thirteen.

THE TOWN COUNCIL forwarded a copy of their minutes to Lieutenant Mowat after the meeting the next morning, Friday the 12th, which outlined the discussion that had taken place. On the count of the jollyboat, it was resolved that the council would do their utmost to find and return it; and concerning driving the armed mobs out of town, whether by raising a local militia or by passing a resolve to offer no aid or support, the minutes read, "that the town disapproved of the proceedings of the armed body, but that we were unable to resist them."

Several days before this, Mowat had doubled the lookout, giving them specific instructions to watch the motion of the rebels, and report anything suspicious. Now he ordered that the gig with the swivel mounted in the bow and its crew be held in readiness on the seaward side of the ship, ready to push off in the blink of an eye, should it need to be sent in pursuit of something. The four cannon of the larboard broadside, which faced the town, were also kept ready at all times, and could be loaded and fired at literally a moment's notice.

On Friday evening it was heard that the rebels had begun to disperse after a day of light rain, but when Saturday dawned, intelligence reached Mowat that Thompson and his men were still about.

"Can it really be only six days ago that Dr. Bailey and I played our flute duet in church?" Langdon asked Mowat over coffee on Saturday. "It seems like an age, so much has transpired since then!"

"Mmm," Mowat grunted, obviously pre-occupied with some other thought.

"Are you sending any communications ashore, today, Mr. Mowat?" Langdon queried.

"I do not anticipate any, why?"

"I would like to send a note to the wardens of St. Paul's – if they're still in town – that I will not be coming ashore tomorrow for service, and include a note to be read to the congregation, should anyone show up," he explained.

"Would you like to read prayers aboard the *Canceaux* tomorrow?" Mowat asked. "The men would appreciate it, I'm sure. I haven't rigged church for quite a long time."

Langdon indicated that he would be more than happy to do so, then descended into silence to ponder the strange nautical phrase Mowat had used, "to rig church."

*

Mowat had a conference later that day with Master Hogg, at which he asked Langdon to be present.

"Mr. Langdon, pray tell me if this sketch of Back Cove as I remember it is correct," Mowat said, pushing a sheet of paper across the table to him, upon which was sketched in ink a fairly accurate depiction of the place in question. Langdon told him as much, pointing out one or two minor modifications.

"And you said that at high tide, it is six feet deep about thirty feet out from the shore?"

"At least."

Mowat turned to Hogg. "When we walked along the beach it was nearly low tide, and the bottom was sandy and gradual right up to the edge of the beach. It would be a smooth approach anywhere along there, and an easy landing."

Hogg nodded, studying the drawing.

"There will be a high tide just after one o'clock a.m., and I consider that an ideal time for the landing, as we've discussed," Mowat said.

Langdon inquired hesitantly what was afoot.

"It seems Mr. Thompson and his men are still in the area, although most of the rest of the mob have dispelled. I've heard they are hiding in the very same grove of trees in which they held us prisoner last Tuesday. I'm sending Hogg at midnight with twelve men and the gig, the swivel still mounted in the bow, to see if they can't surprise them and take Thompson prisoner," Mowat explained. "His actions have warranted it, I think, and I'll take him before Admiral Graves and Governor Gage personally, to try him for treason."

"Twelve men against thirty-some?" Langdon asked.

"In the middle of the night, twelve armed sailors can seem like an army. Plus, a couple men are to be left in the boat, manning the swivel. One blast from a swivel into a group of men can pretty much decimate the lot."

"Ah?" He had thought to utter a knowing murmur, but it had come out as a question.

"A swivel fires something called 'canister,' and in this canister are placed many small musket balls, or even nails, bits of useless metal, etc. When fired, it sprays projectiles in a general direction, mowing down everything in its path. It is useless, obviously, against the hull of a ship, or other solid targets; but it wreaks havoc on human flesh."

"Aha," Langdon said.

"So if things go badly for Hogg, and his men must retreat to the boat, a single deftly handled swivel can fend off the assault of dozens of men until the boat can shove off and head back to the ship."

"I see. Well, I wish your men luck. Thompson and his toadies deserve what's coming to them," Langdon said, astounding himself in saying such a vengeful thing, and repenting of it immediately in his mind.

He remained awake that night, and on deck, pacing along the larboard rail with Dr. Bailey. They watched at half-past midnight as Hogg and his men put off quietly from the starboard side of the ship (and hence concealed from the shore). The oars of the gig had been muffled with cloth tied around them, thus reducing the splash and sound of their use, and the men had been heavily armed, each with either a musket or pistol, and a cutlass or dirk of some kind. The ship felt strangely empty once they were out of sight. The *Canceaux* was already seven or eight under her complement of 45, minus the three who had gone in Captain Coulson's boat with Sheriff Tyng and Midshipman Samuels to Boston. Having fifteen more out of the ship left little more than two dozen people aboard, including her passengers. Langdon commented on this to Dr. Bailey, who agreed that the ship seemed disconcertingly empty.

Every dozen turns or so up and down the deck, the clergyman stopped by the light of the binnacle to consult his pocket watch. One o'clock came and went, and no gunfire was heard.

Langdon discussed quietly with Bailey about Lieutenant Mowat's generous offers regarding employment in the navy, either in the *Canceaux* or the *Preston* under Vice Admiral Graves.

"That's a very fine offer, Thomas," Bailey said, "yet I sense a certain reticence to take him up on it."

"Yes. I'm not quite sure why, really. Perhaps an unwillingness to accept the fact that I must leave the only living I've ever known."

"Well, I encourage you to take up the offer, especially regarding the admiral. At the very least, it will bring your name to his attention, and such a rare opportunity should never be turned down. Preferment is everything in the service. Promotions are as often made on the basis of personal acquaintance with one's superiors as merit. That is why Mowat, as capable and thorough-going a seaman as you're ever likely to find in the service, is still a lieutenant, in command of an eight-gun armed ship, at 42, when others, fifteen years his junior and with half his ability, but blessed with uncles and fathers in the admiralty or parliament, have been made post-captains."

"What if I have no interest in promotion, however, or making a career of it, but merely wish to serve His Majesty during the space of the conflict, until such time as I may be able to return to serve a church ashore?"

"I should still not pass up a chance to become admiral's chaplain or clerk," Bailey said without hesitation. "Of course, I would very much welcome your remaining aboard the *Canceaux*; but, for your own comfort and advancement, I would look quite favorably on a berth in the flagship. I don't know much about ecclesiastical practices, but I suspect having been chaplain to an admiral could do some good later in trying to find a living ashore."

"I suspect you're right," Langdon conceded.

"And you're likely to get a larger berth on a larger ship, too," he winked.

At two o'clock the lookout announced quietly that a boat was approaching the ship. The officer of the watch, Midshipman Barker, ordered his men to ready their weapons, then hailed the boat. It was the gig, returning from its mission. Lieutenant Mowat came on deck, and Master Hogg reported that the grove was empty, although there were signs of a recent encampment, which looked abandoned.

"Good. Well, let us hope the Thompsonites have quit Falmouth, then. We shall no doubt find out tomorrow."

*

Sunday dawned fair, and at ten o'clock church was rigged. Langdon read morning prayers for the men and gave a brief sermon on one of the appointed readings. Langdon found it a particular pleasure to read that prayer found in the back of the prayer book in the section labelled "Occasional Prayers," which was to be used specifically at sea. He had never before had opportunity to read it aloud, and it seemed particularly fitting to what appeared the beginning of a career at sea, however brief it might be. The prayer had that Elizabethan cadence which he so much loved; for, what Shakespeare was to literature, the Book of Common Prayer was to Christianity.

> O eternal Lord God, who alone spreadest out the heavens, and rulest the raging of the sea; who hast compassed the waters with bounds until day and night come to an end; Be

pleased to receive into thy Almighty and gracious protection the persons of us thy servants, and the fleet in which we serve. Preserve us from the dangers of the sea, and from the violence of the enemy; that we may be a safeguard unto our most gracious Sovereign Lord, King George, and his dominions, and a security for such as pass on the seas upon their lawful occasions; that the inhabitants of our land may in peace and quietness serve thee our God; and that we may return in safety to enjoy the blessings of the land, with the fruits of our labors, and with thankful remembrance of thy mercies to praise and glorify thy holy Name; through Jesus Christ our Lord. Amen.

Langdon found himself involuntarily affected as he recited the words 'that we may return in safety to the blessings of the land.' Not a few of the men noted his quavering voice at that point, and Mowat, knowing that sailors often considered the presence of a chaplain aboard ship unlucky, approved of their attentiveness and sensitivity to their guest and passenger.

It was determined later that day that Thompson and his men had indeed quit the area of Falmouth, and their whereabouts were unknown.

"The time has come," Mowat pronounced upon hearing this news. "Mr. Hogg, prepare the ship for sea. We will sail at first light tomorrow. Inform Captain Coulson to do likewise. If he indicates he has insufficient men to set sail, send a half-dozen of our people to him, reminding him that we are to have them back once we reach Portsmouth, and he shall be responsible for finding additional hands thereafter."

Before sundown that Sunday evening, May 14th, 1775, the Rev'd Langdon spent a long, silent hour looking at that town which had been his home for all but three of his 32 years. He offered up intermittent prayers for the town and himself, spaced widely by his rambling and very emotion-laden thoughts. When Dr. Bailey approached him at one point, as the edges of the western clouds over the town were brilliantly illuminated with the golden light of an already disappeared sun, he found the parson with tears glistening on his lower eye-lids with the reflection of the sunset. The doctor remained respectfully silent for a moment before announcing quietly that Mr. Mowat had invited them for dinner with the Lydes.

Langdon wiped his eyes, apologizing. Bailey smiled with understanding. "As a medical man, I am persuaded that the shedding of tears is a healthy thing. It lubricates and cleanses the eye-balls, and shows that your inner emotional workings are in order, my good Thomas."

"You comfort me, David," he smiled, turning to accompany him below.

"Have you ever noticed," Bailey observed a few minutes into the meal, "how, in America, Church of England families are peopled for the most part by persons with New Testament names – Thomas, John, James, Peter, Paul, Stephen – but that the dissenting Protestant and Puritan sects give their children Old Testament names – Enoch, Isaac, Benjamin, Daniel, Jacob, Isaiah?"

"Not to mention Jedidiah, Ezra, Jabez, Peletiah, Josiah, Abijah, Mordecai . . ." added Langdon.

"Why is that, I wonder?" Dr. Bailey asked.

"An interesting question," Langdon observed. "Perhaps..." and he launched into a series of denominational speculations, even while recognizing that Bailey had asked this on purpose to distract him from his melancholy thoughts. And he liked him all the better for it.

*

THE FOLLOWING MORNING Langdon was awakened at dawn by the boatswain's call for "All hands to make sail!" Not wanting to miss the occasion, he arose and emerged on deck in a relatively unkempt, unshaven state. It was grey and overcast, but a warm breeze from land promised brighter weather later, perhaps. He saw Mowat standing on the quarterdeck, and, approaching him, asked where he might be able to observe the proceedings without getting in the way. Mowat indicated the lee taffrail, where the parson duly positioned himself.

The various details of sailors were at their places: a half-dozen at the capstan to raise and make fast the anchor, a dozen strung out along various yard arms, ready to unfurl sails, and the remaining dozen scattered about the deck and shrouds at various locations, ready to perform duties of which Langdon had no concept at that point.

Mowat and Hogg stood by the tiller – the *Canceaux* was too small a ship to have a wheel, and the rudder was thus controlled by a tiller, much like in any small boat. They discussed various things in low tones.

"Did Coulson respond to our word last night, that we would be setting sail this morning?" Mowat asked at one point.

"No, sir," Hogg said.

"But the message was sent?"

"Yes, sir. By Mr. Larkin, sir."

"Well, the buggers still look asleep. At least they have not indicated that they need any men." He took a telescope from Midshipman Larkin, who stood nearby, and trained it on Coulson's sloop.

"Mr. Randle!" he called, clapping the telescope shut and handing it back to Larkin.

"Yes, sir?" the gunner replied, being one of the men at the capstan.

"Be so good as to fire a signal gun. I don't think Coulson's men are awake!"

"Aye aye, sir," he saluted, and called to assemble his mates.

"Mr. Larkin, I doubt Coulson can read naval signals, but ready the signal to weigh anchor, just in case. Perhaps he has an old king's sailor aboard."

"Yes, sir."

"Mr. Aiken!" Mowat called to the boatswain. "You may commence weighing anchor once Mr. Randle has fired his gun." Lowering his voice he addressed the master, who stood nearby. "Mr. Hogg, you may carry on."

"Aye aye, sir," he said stepping forward, puffing out his chest as he oversaw the crew's activities.

Mowat joined Langdon at the taffrail, resting an arm on the rail itself. "The winds are light and variable, and no one has any idea what sailing qualities Captain Coulson's sloop will have, this being its first time to sea. I doubt we'll make it much past Cape Elizabeth by sundown."

"That little progress?" Langdon asked with astonishment, Cape Elizabeth being but six or eight miles by sea from Falmouth.

Mowat simply nodded. As it turned out, they did not even make it that far. Coulson's sloop was ready to set sail half an hour after Mowat's first gun. The light and variable winds which prevailed all day, and the inexperience of much of Coulson's crew (he had had to resort to the employment of willing landsmen once the procurement of further seamen proved impossible) kept progress to a minimum, and Mowat ordered that both ships anchor under the lee of Hogs Island at dusk, and ordered Hogg to send two seamen and a midshipman to Coulson's sloop to assist her progress on the morrow. A moment of mirth occurred when Mowat asked the name of the island, and hearing that it was called Hogs Island, inquired of the master how he had gotten an island named after him.

"If the cap'n had not been so busy these last weeks ashore," Mr. Hogg replied, "he would have noticed me pawning the ship's valuables in order to purchase the island," which produced a hearty laugh from the crew within earshot, and which was repeated to the rest at dinner by their messmates.

The following morning, Tuesday the 16th, both ships got under way at dawn, and, as the breeze had freshened considerably overnight, and was north-westerly – and also, presumably, due to the presence of a midshipman and two able seamen on the sloop – they made great progress that day, the coast seeming to float by to starboard as they sailed south towards Portsmouth.

It felt good, Langdon reflected, to get the wind under their coat tails, so to speak, and to be in motion at last, free of Falmouth and all its painful memories. Before Mowat invited him for coffee to the chartroom, they had passed Cape Elizabeth, and before it was time for Dr. Bailey and the parson to take their lunch on deck, in the shadow of the mizzen topsail, they had left Biddeford in their wake. Captain Coulson's sloop proved to be a fine sailer, and the *Canceaux* was hard pressed at times to stay ahead of her.

Langdon was very pleased to find that he did not become seasick now that they were truly under way. He had once been seasick while on passage back to Falmouth from London after his ordination, at which time he was convinced he was going to die, so grave seemed his complaints and so lugubrious his spirits; but, despite his worries as the *Canceaux* ploughed through the waves towards Portsmouth, he felt unaffected, and was able to put down a hearty lunch.

Around three o'clock in the afternoon, with Kennebunkport in view to windward, the lookout shouted, "Deck thar', sail to leeward, two points off the larboard bow!"

Mowat asked the lookout for a report, and, after a few minutes of observation, he announced it was a brig sailing almost directly towards them.

"Mr. Hogg," Mowat said to the master, who stood by the tiller, "let her fall off a point, that we might be brought on a course to intercept. Mr. Randle, load and run out the port guns, if you please. Mr. Barker, signal Captain Coulson's sloop to keep company, then prepare to raise the colors at my signal."

Within half an hour, the brig was several leagues ahead of them, a point off the larboard bow. "Mr. Hogg, bring her up a point, and take in all but the main topsail. Mr. Barker, raise the colors, if you please."

The Union ensign burst open in the wind as the midshipman hoisted it up the mizzen halyard, fastening it when it flew just above the spanker boom.

"Mr. Randle, you may fire a gun across the brig's bow when you bear," Mowat called through cupped hands to the gunner on the forecastle. Mr. Randle, in response, sighted along the barrel of the gun, and then, once he and his mates were clear of the gun's anticipated recoil, put his piece of slow match to the touch hole. A second later the gun leapt backwards, belching smoke and flame as it hurled its six-pound ball in the general direction of the brig.

Soon the *Canceaux* was virtually dead in the water, broadside on to the brig, which dipped its own colors and took in its sails to indicate it would submit to being spoken to.

Taking a speaking trumpet from a rack near the binnacle and placing it to his lips, Mowat called over the thirty yards of rolling water, "Ship ahoy!"

Her master, also speaking through a trumpet, replied she was the *Charming Nancy* of Biddeford, returning thence from Savannah with a cargo of raw cotton. Mowat, having no visible reason to doubt the claim of the brig's master, let her pass with a wave, and resumed his course for Portsmouth.

This being his first direct experience of Mowat as a commander of a King's ship at sea, Langdon was thoroughly engrossed in what proved to be an unremarkable incident. His admiration of the captain grew, for even this rather insignificant incident called Mowat to a thorough-going vigilance, unalloyed by either lethargy or expedience.

Langdon retired to his hammock at about ten o'clock that evening, having word from Mowat that they would probably be anchoring some time after midnight off Kittery Point, beyond which was the entrance to the Piscataqua River and Portsmouth harbor. The area was too fraught with sandbars, reefs, and rocks to attempt a nocturnal entrance into the harbor. Mowat forewarned him that, by pre-arrangement with Captain Coulson, the signal to anchor was three guns. "You will no doubt be awakened by it in the wee hours of the night, Mr. Langdon, so bear it in mind."

To say that he would be awakened was quite an understatement. It turned out that the cannon used for the first signal gun at three o'clock, a.m. was the one on the deck immediately above his head. Its roar, and the rumble of its recoiling carriage across the reverberating planking, was such a deafening, startling thunder that he shot bolt upright in his hammock, knocking his forehead against a deckhead beam. His physical reaction to this impact and the resulting pain was to lurch to the side, which caused the weight of his body to unbalance the hammock, and he ended up spilling in a heap of bedding and night-clothes onto the deck. He felt himself lucky to have emerged from the incident with little more than a vicious red bruise on his forehead.

He was awakened about an hour later by more clattering about on deck. He could not imagine what occasioned the activity, and listened to it for what must have been a quarter hour until he fell back asleep.

The next morning, after he had arisen (and discovered that the bruise on his forehead had swollen to the size of a musket ball), he went on deck and followed the eyes of everyone, who looked to shoreward. At first, all he saw was the green and pleasant prospect of the New England coastline, brilliantly illuminated by the early morning sun from behind his back. Then he saw Captain Coulson's sloop, heeled over to an alarming degree, and what seemed dangerously close to the shore.

Midshipman Larkin approached him. "Captain Coulson's sloop dragged her anchor during the night and trailed on shore. Mr. Hogg and several of the ship's boats are employed in attempting to warp her off."

"What do you mean by 'warp her off,' Mr. Larkin?" Langdon asked.

"They pass a line to a boat, which – " he gasped upon catching sight of the parson's disfigured forehead. "Mr. Langdon, sir, your forehead . . ."

"I had a nasty bump in the night," Langdon said cryptically, too embarrassed to say anything more.

"You should see Dr. Bailey at once, sir," he insisted. "Let me show you the way," he took the clergyman's arm as if he were an invalid.

"I know very well where Dr. Bailey is to be found, thank you," Langdon snapped, jerking his arm from Larkin's grasp. He immediately repented of his temper, however. "I'm sorry, Mr. Larkin. I have slept very poorly these three nights aboard, and I am apt to be irritable, as you might imagine. I will take you up on your thoughtful suggestion," he said, then turned quickly to go below.

He found Dr. Bailey shaving in his dispensary by the light of a lantern, leaning over a tiny mirror wedged against an interior wall by a book. Dr. Bailey, hearing him approach, threw a towel over his naked shoulders, and bid his friend good morrow. Langdon apologized for interrupting his morning toilet and bade him carry on.

As he finished, he suggested Langdon send to the galley for a pot of coffee, which he did. He then pointed out the welt on his forehead and was in no wise encouraged by the doctor's quick intake of breath. Langdon described how it had occurred, and Dr. Bailey procured some ointment from a small jar in a locked cabinet, which he applied gingerly to the tender lump. "This should take down the swelling a bit and lessen the pain."

"Have you heard about Captain Coulson's sloop running on shore?" Langdon asked.

"No."

"Well, apparently her anchor dragged. They're trying to . . . what's the word? . . . warp?"

"Trying to 'warp her off,' no doubt. That usually means the ship's anchor is taken by a boat away from the ship, dropped, and then, by use of the capstan, the people drag the ship free of the ground," Dr. Bailey explained.

"Not only are you my physical balm this morning, David; you are a veritable encyclopædia of nautical information."

"Well," he shrugged as he relocked the cabinet, "after one's been aboard ship for a few years, one rather absorbs the terminology by constant exposure. I've made no study of the subject, I assure you."

Their coffee arrived and they talked of trivial topics for a while.

Then, gathering his courage, Langdon said, "I suppose my moment of decision is nearly at hand."

"You mean as to whether you will go on to Boston or remain aboard the *Canceaux*?"

"Yes," he replied. "Let us assume I take Mowat up on his offer of a letter and go to Boston. I have no assurance that Admiral Graves will so much as notice me. Then where would I be?"

"Well, Mowat has offered to make you his clerk," reasoned Dr. Bailey. "We may be in Halifax for a month or so, undergoing repairs, but I suspect we'll be back in New England waters by

August. If the admiral has failed to appoint you by then, either to his flagship or to one of the other ships in the squadron, I'm sure Mowat will be more than happy to take you back. Why don't you ask Mowat if you may arrange it so?"

"Yes, I suppose I will," Langdon said.

The boats – including two that came out from Portsmouth harbor to assist, sent by Captain Barkley of the *Scarborough* – finally got Captain Coulson's sloop off the ground just before noon; and, in company with the *Canceaux*, they all sailed into the harbor and moored.

*

The Rev'd Mr. Thomas Langdon's Journal

Wednesday, 17 May, 1775. On board *Canceaux* Anchored in Portsmouth Harbour. (. . .) And so, quite literally with a puff of wind, I am removed from out of Falmouth, a development unlooked for and unwanted, but having become necessary through force of events. I cannot help but wonder what will become of my parishioners. Will the Oxnards be driven from place to place because of Edward's outspoken opinions? Will Polly be forced to give birth while they are exiled from their home? Will poor Mrs. Ingersoll, nearly 70, survive what will surely be the hardships to come, no longer having me and the other congregants of St. Paul's to rely on? I feel as if I am abandoning them. The weight of this collective misery weighs heavily upon me. The sum of human suffering affecting this continent is intolerable.

And more than that, I am angered – at times I am flown into an inexpressible RAGE – when I consider the cause of all this turmoil, and the unnecessity of it all. I am filled with fury when I observe the sheer selfishness of a certain segment of the population, who would prefer to inflict everyone around them with misery, rather than suffer the tiniest of perceived grievances, the most frivolous and self-righteous sense of having been wronged by a distant government. Rather than attempting to rectify this error in peaceful, legal (and in the end, I am persuaded, much more effectual) channels, they rise up in protest, kicking and screaming like children when told they may not have another sweet, thrashing about indiscriminately in all directions, irrespective of whom they strike in their mad, unreasonable passion; and then, when the parent exerts a little strength to restrain and discipline the unruliness, they cry "Oppression!" Do these rebels not care about the peaceful, fruitful society they once enjoyed? Are they so blind as not to see with what misery they are blighting this once prosperous and happy shore? Are they incapable of perceiving that they are promulgating, in infinitely greater degree, that for which they fault the government, namely the abridgment of liberty? If 'Liberty' were food, they would be snatching it from the mouths of their brethren because they perceived that the government had withheld a single pea. Yea, for want of a pea, they throw over the entire meal!

When I am subject to such rages, I am clearly not myself. I very wrongly flew at one of the midshipmen this morning for nothing more than trying to mother me. Faced with an utterly uncertain future, having suffered the deprivation of my livelihood, grieving the loss of attachment and sense of belonging I once enjoyed, I am forcing those around me to share in my misfortune. *Have mercy on me, O Lord, a sinner; help me to distinguish in myself the righteous indignation you felt against the money-changers in the temple, from the prideful, malicious, spiteful anger of those who shouted "Crucify!" in the streets of Jerusalem. Give me a greater sense of your presence as I am cut off from associations and friendships in which I formerly took comfort. Teach me thereby to have a greater reliance on the assurance of your divine providence of all that I could ever need or want. Through the merits of your Son, our Saviour, Amen.*

Chapter Fourteen.

"Man the gig, Mr. Hogg, to take me to the *Scarborough*," Lieutenant Mowat ordered soon after anchoring. Captain Barkley had lost no time in signalling that "commander should repair on board forthwith."

"Mr. Langdon, join me in the chartroom, if you would," Mowat said as he descended the ladder. The clergyman followed him quickly. "Now, what is your decision, Mr. Langdon? I can make arrangements with Captain Barkley, should you wish to go to Boston. If so, I must know now."

"May I pose one further question, Captain Mowat?"

"Of course."

"If I should decide to go to Boston, and the admiral takes no notice of me, despite your letter, would you consent still to take me on as your clerk, howsoever I might reach you again?"

"Why of course. I should be only too glad of it," he said. "I shall include a request in my letter that the admiral, should he not find a place for you, provide transport for you to Halifax. There is a frequent intercourse of His Majesty's ships between those two ports."

"I am decided, then," Langdon said, "and would be grateful to you for your proffered letter of recommendation to Vice Admiral Graves."

Mowat was aboard the *Scarborough* for upwards of an hour. When he returned, he informed Langdon that it had been decided he should transfer to the *Sphynx*, sloop, which Barkley intended to send to Boston in convoy with several merchant vessels loaded with provisions that had been apprehended in the last week. That would not be for some days, however, so Langdon was welcome to remain aboard the *Canceaux* until such time as the convoy was ready.

The dory in which Sheriff Tyng, Midshipman Samuels, and four of the *Canceaux*'s men had sailed to Boston two weeks previously put into the Piscataqua on May 23 on its return trip to Falmouth, and, finding the *Canceaux* there, came alongside. Coming aboard, Sheriff Tyng wondered whether he would be continuing to Falmouth in the dory.

"No, I think I will be throwing you onto the mercy of Captain Barkley at this point, Sheriff Tyng, in getting you back to Falmouth. As for me, I glad of having my midshipman and seaman back aboard. The fate of this dory is now in Captain Barkley's hands."

As it happened, Captain Barkley directed that Mowat proceed to Halifax when he had watered and revictualed the *Canceaux* agreeable to his wishes, as wind and weather permitted. He directed that the dory be taken in tow, and that, as the *Canceaux* came near Casco Bay on its way to Halifax, that Tyng be put aboard the dory to sail himself (as he agreed he was capable of doing on his own) into the bay itself.

It was while they lay at anchor in Portsmouth that the squadron heard the devastating news of the taking of Fort Ticonderoga and Crown Point in the early morning hours of May 10. These fortifications controlled the waterway of Lake Champlain in upper New York, and its approaches to Canada. In the middle of the night, apparently, a certain Colonel Ethan Allen and a group of brigands referred to as the "Green Mountain Boys" had stormed the small sleeping garrison, which surrendered immediately, misled into thinking that the marauders numbered much more than they actually did. It was a victory of little tactical significance, moderate strategic significance (as it opened the way to Canada), but profound moral significance, heartening the rebels mightily in their resolve to resist, and disheartening loyalists and friends of government in like proportion.

*

THE REV'D LANGDON spent much of his remaining time aboard the *Canceaux* in the company of Dr. Bailey, conversing on a multiplicity of diverse topics, and playing flute duets. They found that their views on certain issues were very similar, save that of religion, for which the doctor regretfully confessed an apathy.

"I was raised in the home of dissenters, you see," he explained. "A rather puritanical strain of Methodists, directly descended from George Whitefield's followers, in fact. I was thus beset at an early age by my elders' enthusiasm for tendentious religious debate and stubborn schismatic opinions, damning all who disagreed with them to everlasting perdition. As it happens," he pointed out, "I concur strongly with what you said a few nights ago about the nature of most dissenters."

"When we were speaking about the prevalence of Old Testament names among them?"

"Yes. Dissenters, more inclined to believe in divine vindictiveness, take this trait upon themselves. Not to mention an overly acute judgmentalism, and animosity towards those who do not agree with them. Thus, since achieving adulthood, I have voluntarily exempted myself from such contentious debates, and have gradually grown more and more disillusioned with the entire subject of religion." He did not raise his eyes to look at the parson during this last statement, and Langdon sensed how brave it was of him to express such things to a clergyman.

"That is perfectly understandable, David."

"I must say that, excepting you, most Anglican clerics that I have met, while less universal in their damnation of their foes, nevertheless employ the same strains of inflexible arguments that my dissenting forebears invoked."

"I hope my influence on you in this respect has not been a negative one, David, reflecting badly on the Church of England."

"No, I assure you. Although we've studiously avoided talking of religion on most occasions, you have not struck me as at all judgmental or strict in your temperament."

"You should have heard a sermon I gave in early March!" Langdon quipped. "Lost a quarter of my congregation in one fell swoop!" They both laughed.

Another topic which they studiously avoided during those ten days, almost as if by prior agreement, was their impending separation. There was a sensitivity on both parts which caused them to remain silent on the issue. It was not until the day before Langdon's departure from the *Canceaux* that the topic was finally broached.

Dr. Bailey asked Langdon whether he would like to do some fishing, to which he enthusiastically agreed, it being a very pleasant day. Lieutenant Mowat consented to their using the gig for the better part of the fore- and afternoon watches, the larger pinnace and the Falmouth dory being used in the final victualling operations of the ship. They took turns at oars and tiller respectively, maneuvering across the bay and up into the mouth of the Piscataqua river. They managed to go a short ways upstream because the tide happened to be coming in, thus considerably mitigating the strength of the river's current.

Once they were above the town of Portsmouth, they put their lines into the water, and managed, with what scraps of bait the ship's cook had provided, to boat a handful of scrawny, unappealing fish which they returned immediately to the water as inedible.

"I hope I am not being too personal," Bailey said at one point, after a long period without so much as a nibble on the fishing lines, "when I say that I shall sorely miss you when you are gone, Thomas."

Langdon smiled, unable to think of an appropriate reply.

"I have grown rather attached to our times together," the doctor continued.

"I, too, have grown quite fond of them."

"I hadn't been aware until now how devoid the *Canceaux* is of anyone of my intellectual equal." He paused. "I mean to say that, until our conversations, I hadn't realized how much I've missed the company of a kindred mind." After an extended, somewhat uncomfortable silence, Bailey continued, "I'm beginning to regret having counseled you, as I did, to go to Boston, although I know it was right to have done so." Another silence. Then, with a smile which was not a little forced, he quipped, "So, when you are vicar of that fine church," he pointed to a tall steeple in the highest part of Portsmouth, "sitting in your stall listening to an anthem or voluntary – or when you are the first American bishop! – I hope you think back to my wise counsel, and thank me for it, having offered it not out of my own self-interest, but for your good."

"No doubt I shall," Langdon smiled. "Although, as for being a bishop . . ." he shrugged, saying the word 'bishop' with mock distaste. Made aware of his own sorrow at their parting, which he had managed to disguise up to now, he said weaky, "I imagine that wars do these sorts of things, throwing people together and pulling them apart again, whenever the exigencies of the service call for it." He felt pathetically unequal to the task of responding adequately to the doctor's touching words, though he wanted to communicate that he reciprocated such feelings. "I suppose it is too much to hope that we will ever serve in the same ship again…"

"Unlikely, I'd have thought."

After an uncomfortable silence, Bailey said with mock bluffness, "Well, I appear to be getting rather red in the sun. I suggest we return to the ship." Soon they found themselves alternating duties at the oars again, talking of this and that as if the foregoing conversation had never taken place.

*

THE FOLLOWING EVENING, the wind beginning to veer away from the east, Langdon's things were transferred from the *Canceaux* to the *Sphynx*, as both were to sail at first light the next morning, the former for Halifax, and the latter, in conjunction with the *Minerva* and another storeship with provisions for the army, to Boston. Lieutenant Mowat invited the parson for dinner one last time Saturday evening. Mr. and Mrs. Lyde, Dr. Bailey, Midshipman Mowat and Sheriff Tyng thronged the great cabin's familiar table.

Mowat raised his glass to Langdon during the meal. "To the admiral's next chaplain," he said to agreement all around the table.

Langdon was rowed to the *Sphynx* at dawn and remained on deck to observe the group of ships as they set sail. The *Sphynx*, a tiny armed sloop of no substantial cannon but a number of swivels and small arms, was commanded by a rather temperamental, unkempt young man named Lieutenant Fraser. The *Canceaux* set sail at the same time, and was a beauty to behold from a distance, her sails appearing uniformly as if controlled by a single hand. As the ship's prow swung out towards sea the yards came round at a precise and measured rate, conforming perfectly to the motion of the vessel itself. Langdon saw the figure of Bailey, he thought, standing at the taffrail watching the *Sphynx*. He waved, and the figure returned the gesture.

Langdon was, despite his ignorance of such things, quite

astonished at the differences he sensed aboard the *Sphynx*. He had begun to assume that all King's ships were peopled with crews like Mowat's highly regimented, happy lot, and he had decided that his previous overwhelmingly negative prejudices concerning the dismal life aboard a man-of-war had been quite wrong. Aboard the *Sphynx*, however, he realized he had not been so mistaken after all.

He allowed for the fact that the *Sphynx*'s crew of 15 had not been together for long and had been drawn from various other ships around the fleet that could spare a hand or two. One would thus not expect the kind of warmth of camaraderie that characterized the *Canceaux*'s men, the same forty people having been together for the better part of a decade. But the atmosphere aboard the *Sphynx*, and the intercourse between officers and men, was much less spirited, and therefore much less efficient. The boatswain was harsh in his use of the end of a rope across bare backs to "encourage" the men to their work, accompanied by insults and threats of punishment. The men, as a result, were surly and silent, carrying out their duties perfunctorily.

Due to the adverse and light airs of that morning, progress was slow, and they did not pass Kittery Point, which protected the entrance to the harbor, until several hours later. The *Canceaux* (due to better handling, Langdon assumed) was a mile ahead as the *Sphynx* passed the point but was still in sight. It was not until the sloop had turned south about half-an-hour later – the wind freshening once they were out of the lee of the land – that the *Canceaux*, hull down and just a small, bright pyramid of canvas on the eastern horizon, finally disappeared in the offshore summer haze.

Langdon had not moved from his place at the larboard rail the entire morning, foregoing breakfast in order to watch the *Canceaux*'s disappearance. He wondered vaguely – but quickly dismissed it from his mind as he turned to go below to his berth –

how long Dr. Bailey had watched the *Sphynx*.

*

THE REV'D MR. THOMAS LANGDON'S JOURNAL

SATURDAY, 27 MAY, 1775. H.M.S. *SPHYNX* AT SEA BETWEEN PORTSMOUTH AND BOSTON. (. . .) My thoughts are uneasy as I approach Boston. Though I have Mowat's letter to the admiral, I have no guarantee that he will pay me any heed, and then where will I be, with little money and no arrangements for lodging? Perhaps I should not have left the *Canceaux* after all. The associations I had formed should perhaps have been far more important to my decision than any other considerations. *Out of the depths I call to you, O Lord. Lord, hear my voice.*

CHAPTER FIFTEEN.

DESPITE OCCASIONAL VISITS TO BOSTON, Langdon had never before entered it by sea. The approach was so confusing that he could well appreciate why it could only be done during the daylight, and then only with the proper wind; for islands – and therefore lee shores – were on every hand. As they sailed southwest through Broad Sound the day after setting sail from Portsmouth, Langdon witnessed one of the most stirring sights he had ever seen: a very large warship with two decks of guns, her ports open in the warm afternoon sun, riding placidly at anchor. She was so much larger than any ship he had ever seen as to take his breath away. Compared to the *Canceaux*, with her four small cannon per side, she was gargantuan, with thirty-some blackened snouts protruding from the opened ports.

"The flagship, H.M.S. *Preston*, I assume," Langdon commented confidently to Lieutenant Fraser, trying to appear knowledgeable.

"No, the *Boyne* of 70 guns," he returned. "Largest ship on this station." The manner of his correction felt unnecessarily abrupt.

Soon thereafter, steeples, roofs, and gables came into view beyond another island, and this, Langdon realized, was Boston. The bay before it contained a veritable forest of masts, for at least a score of vessels were anchored there, and of these, three appeared to be warships, two very nearly as large as the *Boyne*.

"Williams, ready the salute," Fraser called.

As they rounded Governor's Island several minutes later, what passed for the *Sphynx*'s gunner and a couple of his mates began firing a stately salute of small arms – 11 guns spaced out with five seconds between each, as befitted a Vice Admiral of the Blue.

When they had done, and Williams was taking the muskets below deck, there suddenly boomed a cannon from across the harbor. All eyes turned to the puff of smoke, which was just dissipating in the wind near what Langdon now identified as the flagship. A large white flag at its mainmast dipped down and back up again.

To Langdon's utter astonishment, Fraser – a look of almost uncontrollable anger on his face – took several large steps across the deck, his shoes thudding ominously on the planking, and cuffed Williams across the face.

"You idiot!" he shouted. "God damn your eyes, you blind, pox-marked whoreson!" He took hold of the quailing man's collar, and jerked it violently while he gesticulated towards the flagship. "Can't you see the flag's white?! Two more guns, you villainous swine. I'll have you swinging from the yard-arm if you ever miss such a thing again!"

The gunner, with remarkably calm hands after such a berating, but his eyes hardened with hatred, re-loaded two guns, and the additional shots soon rang out.

Fraser, who had rejoined the parson near the rail, muttered under his breath, "Since when has Graves been promoted a Vice Admiral of the White? He'll probably have me in irons for such an insult. God damn that gunner for his insolence. He probably noticed it all along, but said nothing in order to embarrass me in front of the whole blessed fleet. They've got it in for me, this lot, they do." He left off his mumbling and brooded silently, chewing vigorously on his lower lip.

The *Sphynx* came to anchor none too gracefully, Langdon noted, with sails flapping ineffectually about, and the anchor itself getting tangled in its own rope at the cathead, thus causing the sloop to drift alarmingly to leeward for a moment until it could be disentangled and dropped. Langdon was frankly appalled, and – although he had nothing to do with it – embarrassed to be associated with such a show of incompetence before the admiral. He wondered if it were an ill-omen regarding his coming to Boston.

Langdon at length asked, "Pray, what is the name of that ship over there?" He thought it a neutral question and was hoping to divert Fraser's attention from the late scene of indignation.

"That's the *Somerset*, of 64 guns," he responded, his mood changing abruptly.

The flagship, the *Preston* of 50 guns, was marginally smaller than either the *Somerset* or the *Boyne*, yet of great visual similarity, its many guns arranged on two decks. The only other warship in view was substantially smaller, the *Glasgow* of 20 guns, which was remarkably similar to the *Scarborough*, Captain Barkley's ship in Portsmouth.

"It perhaps demonstrates my ignorance, Mr. Fraser," Langdon continued carefully, "but, I suppose I always assumed the flagship was the largest ship in the fleet."

"Only a bloody landlubber would think such a thing," he stated sullenly, apparently either unaware or unconcerned that he spoke so offensively. "On foreign stations such as this, where such large ships as the *Boyne* are virtually useless except as floating harbor batteries, a fourth-rate like the *Preston* is more suited as a flagship."

"What is a 'fourth-rate'?" Langdon ventured to ask.

"50-gun ships," Fraser answered. "Too small anymore to lie in the line of battle, they are often fitted out as flagships, meaning they have cabins for both admiral and captain and their numerous retinues. They were very popular ships at one point, especially on distant stations like this, Jamaica, the West Indies, or the East Indies. The *Somerset* there, for instance, although she's a third-rate and somewhat larger than the *Preston*, is probably not fitted out to be a flagship."

Langdon asked again: "So the rates indicate the size of a vessel, as determined by the number of guns?"

"Every ship of 20 guns or more is classified into one of six rates. These were established by Anson in the '40's. First rates are the largest, with 100 guns or more on three gundecks; then on down to the third-rates, which are the most numerous among line-o'-battle ships, like the *Somerset* and *Boyne*; fourth-rates are less common, often employed on distant stations like this one. Fifth- and sixth-rates are one-decked vessels, like the *Glasgow* there. Anything smaller is usually classed informally as a sixth rate to determine pay-rates, complements and the like, although technically they're not. Like the *Sphynx*, here."

"Or the *Canceaux*?" Langdon asked.

Fraser nodded.

The *Sphynx*'s only midshipman – relatively elderly for the rank at 24 years old – had been standing for a number of moments at Fraser's elbow. At the conclusion of their conversation, Fraser finally turned to the midshipman and barked ill-humoredly, "Yes, Barton, why are you hovering there like an insect at a picnic?"

"Flagship has signalled 'Captain repair on board forthwith,' sir," he reported, saluting.

"Well, don't just stand there gawking, man; acknowledge the signal and have my gig swayed out," he demanded.

When Barton had gone to do as he had been gruffly bidden, Langdon said, "May I ask your advice on something, Lieutenant Fraser?"

"Yes?" he asked suspiciously. Langdon suspected he was unused to having people ask his advice.

"As you may have been informed, my reason for coming to Boston is to introduce myself to the admiral. I have a letter of introduction from Lieutenant Mowat to that effect. Would you advise that I send it directly to the admiral – by you, for instance, right now – hoping that he would summon me in response; or do you think there a higher chance of my achieving my goal if I go unbidden to the flagship and offer it to him in person?"

"You want to see the admiral?" he asked. "What for?"

"It is a personal matter," Langdon said, not wishing to give this dislikable man any more information about himself than was absolutely necessary.

"Well, I wish you luck," he said derisively. "That is to say, I doubt you'll get any closer to him than several separating bulkheads will allow, so you can do as you please. I'll be happy to deliver the letter, if you wish, although I doubt he'll read it. Or you can take your chances and come with me now. As you wish."

"I'll come with you, then, if you don't mind," Langdon said, hiding his dejection.

Once they were in the boat and had commenced the trip across the harbor, Langdon asked, "Have you ever met the admiral before?"

"On one or two occasions, yes," Fraser replied, checking his coat for stains or flecks of dirt. "My crew's probably smirking, thinking of the reprimanding I'm going to be getting for not firing the proper salute. By God, they'll be sorry for their impudence."

"Have you ever heard of him being offended by such niceties as improper salutes?"

"Rank is everything in the service, Mr. Langdon, hardly a 'nicety.' It is what gives us authority to do what we do. Without rank and the authority it gives us, our efforts would be but 'sounding brass and tinkling cymbals, signifying nothing,'" he observed.

"Ah. You are familiar with the Scriptures, I see," Langdon commented, recognizing the quotation.

"Every morning and evening I read the scriptures, Mr. Langdon; upon rising and going again to bed. And it is my duty as a Christian and my honor as a commander in the King's service to be able to read it aloud to the men on Sundays. You may depend upon my frequent quotation of it," he stated sanctimoniously. Then, with nary a breath, he lashed out visciously at one of the sailors who had missed a stroke with his oar, "Look smart about your duty, you slovenly dog! The admiral's probably watching us through his stern windows."

Langdon knew he was expected, as a man of the cloth, to commend the officer's godly sentiments; instead, Langdon said, "Your quotation – from the thirteenth chapter of Paul's First Epistle to the Corinthians – was used originally in relation to charity, not authority."

Fraser looked at the clergyman with surprise, astonished that Langdon should argue with him rather than praise him. "Well, they're much the same thing in the end, aren't they?"

"Are they?" Langdon inquired, noticing Fraser's finger tapping irritatedly on the boat's gunwale.

"Well, charity is meaningless without it having authority to transcend, is it not?"

"I fail to see your meaning."

"If a man of no importance shows you charity, it means nothing. If, however, a man of much authority and power shows charity to someone who, by the divine order of things, is wont to expect nothing but reward or punishment for either doing or failing to do his duty, then charity has real potency, coming unexpectedly and without warrant, does it not?"

"Would you describe our Lord during his life on earth as a man of authority and much power?" Langdon asked.

"Moral authority, and divine power, yes."

"Hmm. And here I thought he was just a carpenter who associated mostly with the lowly."

Fraser snorted dismissively. "You are a typical colonist, with your provincial ideas and simplistic notions."

Langdon, although angered, did not reply. He had made his point.

The boat reached the flagship's side in another moment, and Fraser preceded the parson with a sneer up the ship's side. When he was out of sight, one of the boat's crew touched Langdon's sleeve. When he turned to look, the sailor grinned widely, winked, and said "Good on ye, parson." Langdon nodded to him, then observed all the men of the boat looking at him with mixed expressions of mirth and approval. He imagined that this story would be told and retold by the sailors of the *Sphynx* in the coming days, and he found that he was pleased about it.

He turned his attention to the flagship. The *Preston*, being much the largest ship he had ever boarded, loomed intimidatingly above him like a massive cliff to be scaled. Luckily, he needn't ascend its full height, as part way up was an entry port. But it was the first step that was always the most treacherous, as the small boat bobbed alongside, moving at a different rate and in a different direction than the ponderous hull of the flagship.

"Do ye wish fer a bosun's chair, parson?" asked one of the boat's crew.

"No, that will not be necessary, thank you," he replied, not wanting the indignity of being hoisted aboard like a barrel.

"Well then, when the boat reaches the top of 'er rise, and pauses there like, that's when ye make yer move," he was instructed. "We'll be 'ere should ye miss."

And miss he did, dousing one leg up to the calf in salt water and nearly losing a shoe to the deep, only to feel strong arms catch and support him until he could gain his footing. He ascended the ship's side with great care, one slow step at a time, until he reached the entry port and trod thankfully on deck. He waved his thanks to the men looking up from the boat, which now looked perilously far below, and then turned to assess his new surroundings.

He was relieved to find that Lieutenant Fraser was no longer in sight. A midshipman, however, stepped up and said, "Mr. Cuthbert Collingwood, sir, at your service." He was a round-faced youth of about 18 years of age.

"Thank you, Mr. Collingwood," Langdon said. "I am the Rev'd Thomas Langdon, late of Falmouth, in the Maine province of Massachusetts. I have a letter of introduction from Lieutenant Mowat, commander of H.M.S. *Canceaux*, for Vice Admiral Samuel Graves. What is the likelihood of my seeing the admiral?" he inquired.

"We shall see, Mr. Langdon. May I have the honor of delivering the letter?"

"Indeed, I should be most grateful to you, sir." He extracted it from the breast pocket of his coat and placed it in Mr. Collingwood's outstretched hand. "Although, if he is with Lieutenant Fraser just now, I would be loath to interrupt them."

Langdon noticed a hint of amusement pass over the midshipman's features. "But far be it from me to instruct you in your business, Mr. Collingwood."

Leaning towards him with the hint of a smile, in the manner of sharing a confidence, Collingwood said quietly, "Lieutenant Fraser is a man of little consequence, sir. I shall deliver it immediately."

Langdon inclined his head.

"If you would care to go up to the quarterdeck and wait, Mr. Langdon. The view of the harbor is much better from there." And with that, he disappeared below.

As Langdon stood on the quarterdeck – a real one, in this case, the forward part looking down on the upper deck – he was quite impressed by the relative grandeur of this ship, the atmosphere being much more formal and stately than any King's ship he had yet been aboard. He noted how quietly the *Preston*'s crew went about their business. They appeared to be aware that, in the cabin so close to where they carried on their various tasks or held their hushed conversations, the affairs of the fleet were being dealt with, which required their collaboration in the form of respectful silence.

Not three minutes had passed when Collingwood appeared on the quarterdeck. "You are in luck, Mr. Langdon," he said. "The admiral will see you now."

They passed Fraser coming out of the admiral's cabin as they entered, but no words were exchanged. Upon entering the admiral's cabin, Langdon's earlier impressions were augmented by the luxury of its appointments, there being a plush oriental rug over a goodly portion of the deck, a beautiful cherry-wood Queen Anne table in the middle of the room with ten chairs around it, a large wooden desk against one wall, and, most glorious of all, the grand stern windows wrapping around the rear of the vessel. Most of these were open to allow a circulation of air through the room on this pleasant early summer afternoon. The table in the middle was covered with papers, and a servant sat scribbling hastily at it.

The admiral himself was utterly unlike Langdon had imagined him. He was a tall, heavy man, showing all of his sixty-two years, with fleshy jowels that shook when he spoke. He had small, piercing eyes and very large hands. He stood beside his desk in a fancy, gold-embroidered waistcoat, without an overcoat due to the heat, and was saying animatedly in quick, clipped syllables to a lieutenant, "You are to remove the stores from Noddles Island as soon as possible. Their safety there is far from certain, even for another night."

Collingwood and Langdon remained stationary and waited patiently for the admiral to notice them. When he had done with the lieutenant, who saluted and departed, he turned and looked with a sort of jovial irritation. "Ah, Mr. Collingwood, you've brought the parson." He picked up the letter of introduction from Mowat and moved in front of the desk as the midshipman led the parson closer.

"The Rev'd Mr. Thomas Langdon, sir," Collingwood announced.

"It says here, Mr. Langdon," he tapped the letter with the backs of his fingertips, "that you have a clear hand and a fine turn of phrase at your command." He focused his small eyes intently on Langdon. "You do not use colloquialisms or provincial, backwoods colonialisms in your speech, do you?"

"No, sir," Langdon shook his head. "I have my Bachelor of Divinity degree from King's College, New York, and employ only the purest King's English."

"You've a colonial accent, however," he observed.

"That is not evident in the written word, sir. Much less in my handwriting," he replied smiling. "The Memorial from some of the Principal Inhabitants of Falmouth to Henry Mowat, brought to you by Sheriff Tyng a week or two back, was copied out by me."

"Oh, Tyng. Spirited man, but a most ghastly smell. Still, I could do with a score more of his like for every one of these infatuated New England towns." He turned and went behind his desk again. "Now, as Mowat no doubt told you, my purser died in April, and I appointed my secretary, Mr. Gefferina, to the position. I am therefore in need of a secretary with an indefatigable hand. Does your hand tire when you write, sir?"

"The length of my sermons should demonstrate the contrary," the parson quipped.

"Do they now," the admiral replied unsmilingly, deflating Langdon's expectation of a chuckle – except for something like a choked cough from Midshipman Collingwood. Graves continued. "Later in the week there are to be two courts-martial, and they produce a damned lot of paper, so I could use an extra copyist. Let that be your test. If you perform to my satisfaction during these trials, I shall appoint you my secretary."

He sank his substantial bulk into the chair, yet still seemed to tower over the desk. "Now, as for a chaplain," he looked Langdon square in the eyes, "I have little patience with religious enthusiasm, Mr. Langdon, and I find it a bad influence on the people to have an agitator in their midst. A damned nuisance, in fact. When I took command of the *Duke* back in '56, my predecessor had a hellfire-and-brimstone chaplain who put dangerous notions into the heads of the people. I sent him packing as soon as I could, and the air aboard ship improved instantly. I have avoided having a chaplain ever since, but, as you're not the first parson who has come to my attention by being driven from his home for his loyalty, I'm willing to fill the vacancy. You are not an agitator, are you, Mr. Langdon?"

"Far be it, sir," Langdon assured him. "I think you will find – "

"If you keep your sermons short and devotional rather than inspirational, Mr. Langdon, I'll allow you to perform Divine Service on Sundays and collect a chaplain's salary."

"I would be honored, sir." Langdon bowed his head in gratitude, and in so doing his weight shifted slightly. He was mortified to hear his wet shoe gurgle with moisture. Looking at the source of this sound, the admiral saw a small puddle of water on the deck around Langdon's shoe. After pursing his lips disapprovingly, he looked back down at Mowat's letter.

"Now, Mowat mentions school-mastering. I recently received permission from the admiralty to purchase several small vessels for His Majesty's service. I have already bought two, and plan on a few more. This is, however, depleting my ship of officers, forcing me to promote men from the lower deck. These are in desperate need of some refinement. Sailors, on the whole, like their officers to be gentlemen, and often resent anyone promoted from out of their midst, finding it difficult to follow orders from a man they consider their equal. If I could provide such newly made officers with enough education to make them seem like young gentlemen, I'll have done them some good. What subjects did you read when you were at, what was it called, King's College? Other than religion, that is."

"I did substantial reading in most of the humanities, sir, including history, philosophy, classics, literature, oratory and grammatics."

"No natural sciences?"

"No," he conceded.

"Pity," Graves said. "But, no matter; they'll get that sort of education — navigation and mathematics, at any rate — from the sailing master." He looked back down at the letter from Mowat lying on the desk in front of him. "Mowat is very complimentary of you, Mr. Langdon. I think highly of Lieutenant Mowat, and very much approve of his intrepid and officer-like conduct at Falmouth. Although I am disinclined to trust colonists, if what he says of you is accurate, and it proves itself of a standard requisite to the commander of an entire station rather than of a small armed ship, I can make use of you, sir. You'll be given a berth in the wardroom."

"I am honored, sir," Langdon repeated. "My things are yet aboard the *Sphynx*. Will it be possible to have them brought aboard the *Preston*, sir?" Langdon said.

"We'll have them sent for, and you will report to me at two bells in the forenoon watch tomorrow."

"Yes, sir. And thank you, sir," Langdon said.

"Mr. Collingwood, would you see to Mr. Langdon? Send for his things, and meanwhile introduce him to the men of the wardroom."

"At once, sir," he said, and, saluting, they left the cabin.

"Excuse me, Mr. Collingwood," Langdon said as they made their way to the entry port on the gundeck. "When is two bells in the forenoon watch?"

"Tomorrow morning at nine o'clock," he said.

They encountered Lieutenant Fraser waiting at the entry port. Collingwood approached him. Fraser avoided Langdon's eyes.

"Compliments of the admiral, Mr. Fraser, and would you be so good as to have your boat bring Mr. Langdon's trunks to the flagship?" Collingwood said. Although merely a midshipman, his deportment carried so much natural authority that he commanded Fraser's acquiescence as much by the force of his character as by an admiral's command.

Fraser did not look happy about it. The news of Langdon's transfer to the flagship embittered him. He feigned enthusiasm, however, and said, "By all means, Mr. Collingwood, at once." Then he disappeared over the side without another word.

*

THE REV'D MR. THOMAS LANGDON'S JOURNAL

SUNDAY, 28 MAY, 1775. ABOARD H.M.S. *PRESTON* IN BOSTON

HARBOUR. (. . .) There is very little that makes me angrier, in general, than religious enthusiasts who have a ready biblical verse to prop up whatever doctrine they choose to espouse. The hypocrisy of such men is too evident to be generously assigned to lesser motives. As I witnessed in the experience of David Bailey, such persons drive thinking men and women from the Church by giving it the face of self-righteousness, judgementalism and self-justification.

Who would have thought that my appointment to the various positions Mowat envisioned would be so easy? And I stood in front of the admiral with one leg sopping wet, yet!

I am very happy to find that the admiral has such a high opinion of Mowat, which raises both men in my estimation. I know very little of how such things work, but I hope that Graves has the good sense to promote Mowat soon. I have heard the phrase "making him post," which I assume means advancing him from the rank of lieutenant to post-captain. Mowat, as a lieutenant in command of a ship, is entitled to the address of "captain," but this privilege lasts only as long as his command, until he is "made post," at which time the rank of captain is made permanent, whether he is in command of a ship or not. I shall be very careful never to abuse my position with the admiral; but, if I find it in my power to praise Mowat in front of Graves, I shall do so whenever I can.

Chapter Sixteen.

"Captain Robinson," said George Gefferina, the *Preston*'s purser, who had just met Langdon himself moments earlier, "may I introduce the Rev'd Mr. Thomas Langdon. Mr. Langdon, this is

Captain Robinson, the flag captain."

Langdon was astonished at the flag captain's youth, looking little more than the parson's own thirty-two years of age, despite thinning hair. Langdon was suddenly reminded of the midshipman aboard the Sphynx, who could not have been too many years Robinson's junior, yet of a greatly inferior rank in the fleet.

"Very pleased to make your acquaintance, Mr. Langdon," he said with a wide smile. "What brings you aboard the *Preston* on this very fine last day of May?" he asked as they stood sipping sherry in the wardroom, awaiting the proper moment to take their places at the table for dinner.

"Admiral Graves has appointed me his chaplain, and I am hoping additionally to be of use as either the admiral's secretary or the schoolmaster," Langdon replied.

"Or both. All three, in fact," Mr. Gefferina said hopefully. "He was recommended by Mowat to be my replacement, and the admiral is considering him. He is apparently to be put to the test at Captain Bishop's court-martial next week."

"I see. Well, you've very large shoes to fill, Mr. Langdon, I'm sure you've been told," Captain Robinson remarked.

Gefferina – a man of rather diminutive stature – laughed, "Very large shoes, indeed! The very idea is comical." He spread his hands as if placing his small shoes on display. Mr. Gefferina was possessed of vaguely Italian features, with wavy hair as black as pitch, a complexion just slightly less pale than the average Briton's, and large, dark eyes. Langdon wondered about his parentage.

"Well, I wish you luck, Mr. Langdon," Captain Robinson said, looking over his shoulder as those present began following the first lieutenant's lead in taking a seat. "The *Preston* could no doubt use such a versatile parson."

Captain Robinson was the guest of the wardroom that evening, there being four lieutenants, the marine captain and his lieutenant, the surgeon, the purser, the master, and Langdon. All but the final two had a servant standing behind his chair, refilling glasses, placing and removing dishes as became necessary through the meal.

Langdon sat in a very tight space – there were eleven at a table designed to accommodate ten – and he was seated on the side where the extra chair had been added, between Mr. Gefferina the purser and the third lieutenant, John Graves. Having earlier learned that the *Preston*'s second lieutenant was one Samuel Graves, Langdon leaned over to Gefferina and asked quietly "Are either of these Lieutenant Graves any relation to the admiral?"

"Both, as a matter of fact," Gefferina whispered back. "And there's another one, as well – a Thomas Graves, who was, until just a few days ago, commander of the ill-fated *Diana*, of which you will certainly get an earful, serving at his court-martial," Gefferina informed him.

"I see," Langdon said, refraining from inquiring further, although his curiosity was piqued.

"Things are not yet quiet on Noddles Island, I hear, Mr. Graves," Mr. Gefferina said to the third lieutenant.

"I fear not," he said.

"I've heard mention of this Noddles," Langdon said. "What was the nature of the trouble?"

"Noddles, an uninhabited island in the bay," Graves began, "was being used by the admiral for the pasturing of several dozen cattle that had been providing milk and meat to the navy. Last Saturday night about five-hundred rebels landed on Noddles Island and set about burning our hay and attempting to drive the livestock into the bay. Marines were landed to drive them off, and a schooner – the *Diana* – was sent up the Mystic River to cut off their escape by water. The tide was turning, however, and the breeze was failing, so the admiral signalled her to return. Before she had extricated herself from the river, however, the breeze failed utterly, and she was becalmed between the mainland and the island. The admiral sent a number of ships' boats to tow the schooner out of the river. The rebels, meanwhile, who had by this time escaped from the island, had brought a couple of field pieces down to the mainland shore, and set about bombarding the *Diana*, thus preventing any boats from coming near her. She consequently drifted aground, and, although she returned a spirited fire, her commander – "

"Thomas Graves?" Langdon asked.

"Yes – he's my elder brother – he was obliged to abandon the *Diana* after dark, and escaped with his men into the *Somerset*'s boats, which had approached the schooner under cover of darkness for that purpose."

"Did he lose anyone?"

"Only two wounded, surprisingly," he replied. "A testament, I think, to the poorness of American gunnery. Or, divine providence," he added hastily, perhaps mindful that he was speaking to a clergyman. "There were, however, two killed in the *Somerset*'s boat, and a number of wounded. And the marines had many more casualties from the previous skirmish ashore, exceeding ten dead, I believe, and many more wounded."

"Dear me," Langdon said, shaking his head.

"Around three in the morning, the rebels perceived that the *Diana* had been abandoned and thus went aboard, plundered her, and burned her. The flames were visible throughout the harbor until daylight on Sunday morning."

Langdon shook his head again. "Was the *Diana* a significant loss?"

"She was one of the smallest vessels in the fleet, but, as the admiral is hard pressed to patrol and defend the station – which extends from Halifax to Georgia, mind – the loss of any vessel, no matter the size, makes it that much more difficult," John Graves responded.

"I'm very sorry to hear of it, Mr. Graves," Langdon said, not quite sure what else to say.

*

LANGDON'S SLEEP was quite fitful and light. Each vessel had its own peculiar maelstrom of sounds to get used to. The creaking of the *Preston*'s planks and boards, because she was a considerably larger and slightly older ship than the *Canceaux*, was of a much deeper pitch. One improvement, however, was that having a berth in the wardroom decreased the amount of noise quite remarkably compared to what he had experienced aboard the *Canceaux*.

He was up very early, unable to sleep once he had awakened around five o'clock. Excitement over his first day as admiral's secretary contributed to his insomnia, he was sure. He sat at the main table in the wardroom, where dinner had been served the previous evening, and read by the light of a lantern swinging from the deckhead. At about six-thirty, he watched as the steward brought washing bowls full of warmed water for the lieutenants, and took them away again. Langdon accepted one such bowl, and, returning to his berth, washed himself thoroughly for the first time since leaving the *Canceaux* four days ago. He recalled the admiral's comment about Tyng's 'ghastly smell,' and did not want to lead the admiral to believe that it was a trait peculiar to colonists.

He took his breakfast informally with an odd assortment of persons, including the purser, Mr. Gefferina.

"How did you sleep?" the latter asked.

"Not overly well," Langdon confessed.

Gefferina nodded. "Well, at least you're not seasick. My first week aboard a ship was spent retching over the rail until I was so miserable and exhausted, I literally collapsed, only thus getting my first good night's sleep."

"Yes, I thank God that I am not sick. I was seasick once many years ago, on passage from England back to Falmouth, my home. Well, my former home."

"You've been to England, then?"

"Yes, to be ordained." Langdon replied.

"You couldn't be ordained in America?"

"It requires a bishop to ordain a priest in the Church of England, I'm sure you are aware. There are no Anglican bishops in America, and thus, for an American to be ordained, he must go to England. This I did in '67, being ordained by the Bishop of London, under whose jurisdiction all the colonies fall."

"Why doesn't the church send a bishop to America?" he asked.

Langdon erupted with a laugh, amused that Mr. Gefferina should be so ignorant of such a publicly controversial issue. "Have you not heard what a royal stink the dissenting colonists have made on that score? The last thing the non-Anglican colonist wants is for parliament to create an American bishop and send him here, as it would smack of the establishment of religion, a thing they assiduously detest. They would almost rather pay their cursed tea tax than have a bishop!"

"I was not aware," said the purser.

A cannon roared out from overhead, nearly causing Langdon to dump his tea in his lap.

"Good God, what was that?!" Langdon asked, fearing some hostilities.

"A signal to the fleet of some kind," Mr. Gefferina said. "It's one of the more unpleasant aspects of being posted to a flagship: Interminable, damnable, deafening signals." Gefferina addressed a marine lieutenant at the other end of the table, who was just finishing his breakfast, "Mr. Harris, do you know what that signal portends?"

"A lot of bloody hassle, that's what," he commented, pulling on his red coat as he prepared to leave.

"A marine exercise?" Gefferina guessed.

"No. We're removing all the stores from Noddles Island," he said as he disappeared from the wardroom.

"Say, has anyone mentioned the name Troutbeck to you? He's chaplain of the *Somerset*," Mr. Gefferina said a moment later.

"Why, no," Langdon replied. The steward appeared in the wardroom, and Langdon, who desired more tea, tried to attract his attention.

"He is quite a notable cleric, I'm told," Mr. Gefferina continued. "He has written a volume of sea sermons, or some such thing."

"How do you mean, 'sea sermons?' Are they sermons *about* the sea, or to be read *at* sea?"

"I'm not certain, now that you make that distinction," he replied. "You'll have to make his acquaintance when you have a chance, and . . ."

The steward reappeared, and while Mr. Gefferina continued talking about the Rev'd Troutbeck, Langdon again made futile attempts to secure the steward's attention.

". . . I suspect he'd be more than happy to let you see his sermons, should he carry extra copies about," Mr. Gefferina assured him.

"So they are published and printed?" Langdon asked.

"Yes. I saw a copy when I accompanied the admiral to the *Somerset* once for a court-martial."

"Speaking of which," Langdon interjected, "are you to have anything to do with the courts-martial I'm supposed to attend later this week?"

"I suspect I will."

"What will I be called upon to do?" the parson asked. "The admiral mentioned copying, but . . ."

"Yes, it's mostly copying, although . . ."

The steward appeared again, and the clergyman's physical

gesticulations became very pronounced.

"Mr. Averall," Mr. Gefferina shouted. The steward turned to them.

"Sir?" he asked.

"You are very inobservant today. Mr. Langdon here will fall out of his chair soon if you do not bring him some more tea. And make sure it's hot."

"Aye aye, sir."

"What was I saying?" Gefferina asked.

"About what goes on at a court-martial."

"Ah, yes. Well, it depends on the crime being tried, and the rôle to which you are appointed. You will merely be a copyist at the upcoming trials, but in due course you may have increased duties. At a trial in late February, for instance, I was appointed Deputy Judge Advocate for the court-martial of Lieutenant Hunter of the brig *Gaspee*, for the murder of one of his seamen, who was shot while deserting – "

"Shot while deserting?!" Langdon exclaimed. "In Falmouth?!"

"That was the place, yes," Mr. Gefferina answered.

"I was there when it happened!" Langdon said. "Witnessed the whole thing! I saw the dead man himself, being carried through the streets."

"You don't say!" Mr. Gefferina said, looking genuinely astonished. "Well, when Lieutenant Hunter got to Boston a week and a half later, he requested the court-martial himself. He was, of course, acquitted. The trial was a mere formality and was relatively straightforward. It was therefore thought appropriate that I could serve as Deputy Judge Advocate, rather than a commissioned officer. But the upcoming courts-martial are not so trivial. One is for disobedience of the admiral's orders by a captain – Captain Bishop, of the *Lively* – and the other for the loss of a ship – the *Diana*. There's always a court-martial when a ship is lost. It's required by the admiralty."

"So the admiral will be trying his own nephew in the case of the *Diana*," Langdon observed.

"The admiral, as superior officer of the station, does not sit in judgement at a court-martial. Five or six other captains are selected to hear the evidence, determine the guilt or innocence of their peer, and pass sentence. The admiral must adhere to their judgment," he explained.

"I see. Well, it will be a new experience for me, at any rate."

"You should have the steward ready a pot of hot water for you to soak your hand in when you get back. You've never written in your whole life the amount you'll write that day, you may depend upon it!"

*

AMONGST THE REV'D LANGDON'S first duties for Vice Admiral Graves was to copy orders for Lieutenant Fraser of the *Sphynx*, directing him to return to Portsmouth, New Hampshire, and remain under Captain Barkley of the *Scarborough* until the *Canceaux* returned from Halifax. The orders for Captain Barkley which Lieutenant Fraser was to convey were also copied by the new secretary, as well as a number of other orders for different ships of the fleet.

On Sunday, June 4, which was Whitsunday – and also His Majesty King George's 38th birthday – Langdon performed divine service for the first time aboard the *Preston*. He was inwardly very pleased that the first service at which he officiated as a chaplain in the Royal Navy took place on such an auspicious day.

The New Testament reading being the eighth chapter of Romans, Langdon chose as the text of his sermon the 38th verse (coincidentally, he noted, His Majesty's age), which read:

For I am persuaded, that neither death, nor life, nor angels, nor principalities, nor powers, nor things present, nor things to come, nor height, nor depth, nor any other creature, shall be able to separate us from the love of God, which is in Christ Jesus our Lord.

Langdon identified the current conflict, and the passions it inspired, as one of those forces that threatened to separate mankind from the love of God; but men had the assurance that this could not happen, and they were to take heart from that.

Even though the admiral did not attend service, Langdon kept the sermon short and largely devotional in nature, in keeping with the admiral's stipulation. A number of the sailors and one or two of the officers approached him afterwards, either complimenting him on the sermon or saying that they were glad of having a chaplain aboard.

Mr. Gefferina's prediction for the courts-martial, which took place on June 5 and 6 aboard the *Somerset*, was correct concerning the soreness of the parson's hand afterwards. The sheer number of documents which required copying was staggering, including each item of written evidence, orders preceding or relating to the incident in question, depositions by observers or involved parties, the sworn statements of the witnesses, not to mention the proceedings of the court-martial itself, the verdict and sentence of the court, and the letters from the admiral to the admiralty reporting the result. Mr. Gefferina assisted briefly one day in the court-martial of Captain Bishop, but otherwise Langdon worked by himself. Captain LeCras of the *Somerset*, as the senior captain of those present in Boston at the time, was the president of both trials.

Lieutenant Thomas Graves was honorably acquitted of wrongdoing in the loss of the *Diana*, but Captain Bishop was reprimanded before being reinstated to his command, his failure to follow an order from the admiral ruled as an error of judgment rather than an intentional disobedience.

Langdon had the pleasure of meeting the Rev'd Mr. Troutbeck, chaplain of the *Somerset*, while he was aboard her, and, although their time for conversation was limited, the latter did indeed give him a copy of his sea sermons.

Reporting to the admiral's cabin the following morning, his hand sore and throbbing, Langdon was expecting to receive either commendation, correction, or admonition concerning his secretarial duties at the trials. Langdon's own opinion of the quality of his service being high, he had every confidence that Graves would be satisfied and officially name him admiral's secretary. Graves assigned him his tasks for the day without comment, however. As Langdon turned to leave the cabin with his stack of papers to be copied, Graves suddenly said gruffly, "Oh, by the way, Langdon, I heard your sermon through the skylight Sunday, as I was sitting here: It was just the thing that's wanted."

"Thank you, sir," Langdon said, suspecting it would be the closest thing to commendation he would ever receive from the admiral on his performance as chaplain.

*

THE REV'D MR. THOMAS LANGDON'S JOURNAL

WEDNESDAY, 7 JUNE, 1775. H.M.S. *PRESTON* IN BOSTON HARBOUR. (. . .) I suppose I am to assume that my appointment as admiral's clerk is official, as the admiral made no reference to my performance at the courts-martial, but simply handed me the days' work. I was very gratified with his comment on my sermon on Sunday, however, which was to say that it was "exactly what was wanted."

I was astonished to learn that a chaplain supplements his salary out of the pockets of the crewmen, which perhaps explains why most sailors consider it undesirable to have a chaplain on board. Each contributes (involuntarily, so I wonder that it can be called a "contribution") one groat (fourpence) annually from his already meagre wages, and the total is what is given to the chaplain. Hence, my basic pay as chaplain is 18 shillings a month (just over £10 *per annum*), plus a groat for every sailor, which, in the case of the *Preston* amounts to another £12 *p.a.* That's almost £2 per month, which is very nearly half my salary as vicar of St. Paul's. I do not yet know whether I will be entitled to draw the salary of a clerk, over and above the chaplain's salary (that would place me roughly on a par with my former income); or whether I should content myself with what I have.

Although I miss the *Canceaux*, where I grew to learn practically every crewman by name; and I miss my status as honored guest of Mowat at nearly every dinner; and although I sorely miss my conversations with David; I am finding that my life as clerk and chaplain aboard the *Preston* agrees with me very much, and that I shall be very happy in such employment for the remainder of this conflict, even if it should take several more months, or even a year. Clear and sunny, 80 degrees of temperature at midday.

Chapter Seventeen.

The first week of June was one of punishments, for, in addition to the reprimand of Captain Bishop issued by the court-martial, two marines from the *Falcon* were tried for desertion, and a marine officer of the *Somerset* was tried for drunkenness. All were found guilty; the marines were sentenced to 200 lashes each from every ship in the harbor ("flogging round the fleet"), and the marine officer was dismissed the service.

At dinner in the wardroom that evening Marine Captain Johnson – one of the more macabre of the officers – calculated that the marines had received some 1000 lashes each. It was a wonder that one of them survived the ordeal, the other having succumbed part way through the day. Langdon had been appalled by the spectacle as the long boat came alongside the *Preston*. The crew was mustered to witness punishment, and all watched grimly as the 200 lashes for each was meted out by the boatswain and his cat-o'-nine-tails. The backs of the men – who were both mercifully unconscious by the time they reached the flagship, one of them perhaps already dead – were masses of red, twisted flesh. The ghostly white of bone showed through at the shoulder blades, and blood ran in rivulets down their trousers and ankles. It was all Langdon could do to keep from retching at the sight.

The following day, as Langdon was copying orders for the sloop *Nautilus*, which was to sail for New York on the morrow, the sound of distant gunfire interrupted his work. He stood from the chart room and made his way onto the quarterdeck, where already a number of people had gathered. Captain Robinson climbed into the lower shrouds and, shading his eyes from the noon-day sun, squinted to the northwest, in the direction of the noise. His coattails flapped noisily in the relatively stiff breeze.

The chaplain stood near young Midshipman Collingwood, of whom he asked his opinion concerning the source of the gunfire.

"'Tis from on shore, I believe," Collingwood said. "Probably from Charlestown. Small arms, certainly. Judging from the intervals between shots, not more than three or four separate pieces," he surmised.

The captain, looking round and catching sight of Langdon's tall conversation partner, who stood out from most others, said, "Mr. Collingwood, take a glass aloft and see what you can make out."

"Aye aye, sir," he said, springing to his task. When he made his report a few moments later, saying he could see or determine nothing with either telescope or the naked eye, Langdon returned to his work.

Mere moments after sitting down, however, the rumble of a cannon could be heard, drowning out the crackle of the musketry which had kept up a constant popping ever since. The musketry halted for a number of minutes before starting up again, and continued for another quarter hour. At that time, another cannon shot punctuated the afternoon, and everything fell to silence.

Several hours later a report was delivered to the admiral from the sloop *Glasgow*, which had fired the cannon shots; and, because Langdon had copied the letter for the admiralty in London, he was able to repeat the account that evening at dinner to the wardroom members.

"Three officers from the army's 43rd regiment of foot were apparently rowing about the harbor for their pleasure, when they lost an oar overboard, and the wind caught the boat such that it prevented them from retrieving it."

"They handle oars about as well as they handle their drink," said Second Lieutenant Samuel Graves, after which followed a number of similar jokes and much laughter at the expense of the army.

When this had subsided, Langdon resumed. "Today's exceptionally strong wind drove their boat towards Charlestown, where a number of rebels gathered and began firing at them."

"The red uniforms making a nice target, I'm sure," said Mr. Gefferina.

"As they neared the shore, they had no choice but to abandon the boat and swim for the Boston side, which was by now perilously distant. The nearby *Glasgow* sent a boat, which the rebels took to firing at, as well. The men of the *Glasgow*, however, unheeding of the shot, fished the officers out of the bay. They then observed that the boat the hapless officers had been in had stuck on a sand bar before reaching shore, so they valiantly went in, swivels blazing, and brought it off. The *Glasgow* fired a cannon shot or two at the shore to disperse the rabble, as well, which seemed to have the desired effect. In the end, not a person on our side had been scratched, for all the expenditure of shot and powder on the part of the rebels."

"Good marksmanship, that," said Third Lieutenant John Graves sarcastically.

"I'm sure the distance was great," First Lieutenant Alexander Graeme said in his Sottish burr. "We must not underestimate the rebels, nor grow complacent by believing them to be harmless. I'd have thought Lexington and Concord would have taught us that," he said, fulfilling the sailor's rather apt nickname for him, which was 'Old Grim.'

*

"LET'S TAKE STOCK of what's before us, shall we, Mr. Langdon?" Vice Admiral Graves said the following morning when his clerk appeared in his cabin at the usual time. They seated themselves at the Queen Anne table in the center of the cabin. "We've a rather large project on our hands by the end of the month, and that is to prepare and compile a disposition of the entire fleet under my command – every ship from Florida to Nova Scotia, its location, its current orders, its commander, complement, and condition. This is required every six months, on the first of January and July. This will involve poring over old copies of my orders, of letters sent and received from all ships, etc. If we get started on that as we have time between now and the end of the month – this gives us almost three weeks – it will not be such a massive undertaking at the end.

"Secondly, the frigate *Cerberus*, in which Generals Howe, Clinton and Burgoyne recently arrived, is to be sailing back to Spithead on the 18th of June. I plan to send a number of letters and dispatches to the admiralty in it, acquainting them of the various actions surrounding the Noddles Island affair, the loss of the *Diana*, the results of the courts-martial, the unrest in Piscataqua, and various other recent events since the latter part of May. You can help me with the Falmouth incidents. We must also inform General Gage of the opportunity of sending whatever dispatches he may have for England. This will again require the preparation of many documents.

"Thirdly, in addition to today's general business, there is a special request I have of you. General Gage has prepared a proclamation which, in a meeting yesterday, I told him wanted turn of phrase and a bit of altering, and that I had just the man to do it. He gave me a copy of it," he handed the document to the parson, "and I'd like for you to smooth its coarseness, shorten it a bit, and sharpen its rhetoric so that it fairly stings the ear. It will be placed up as a broadside throughout Boston and Charlestown, and as many copies as can be printed will be sent into the provinces and given to ships as they sail for their various North American stations. I therefore want it to be as succinct as possible.

"Finally, General Gage has requisitioned and fitted a couple of sloops for His Majesty's Service, which I am to man. Added to the fact that I've already placed several of the *Preston*'s officers in other ships, and am about to give Mr. Collingwood his lieutenant's commission in the *Somerset*, this will leave me quite shorthanded in the way of commissioned officers. I'm therefore making midshipmen of four young, comparatively bright, able-bodied seamen, and would be most obliged if you would begin a course of study with them in ancient history, philosophy, geography, and literature. The master will give them their mathematics and navigation. Here are their names." He passed Langdon a slip of paper whereon were written the names Charles Tyler, Scory Barker, Gerald Gibbons and John Mason.

"I'm very glad to hear that Mr. Collingwood is to be promoted, sir," Langdon remarked, "but sad that he'll be leaving the *Preston*. He was the first to greet me aboard the flagship and seems a fine officer and gentleman."

"Indeed, he has the stuff of an admiral in him if he keeps his head. Now, I've given you quite a lot of secretarial minutiae, for which I'm very glad to have you aboard. Any questions?"

Langdon shook his head.

"Then why don't you start with General Gage's proclamation, and, by the time you've polished it up, I'll have some of today's orders ready for – " He stopped at the sound of cannon fire in the distance. "What the devil is it now!" he exclaimed, going to peer out the stern windows. "The *Somerset*'s fired off a few guns. God only knows why. I'll hear about it soon enough. Probably another group of American colonists annoying His Majesty's subjects going about their lawful business," he shook his head.

Still looking out the stern windows of the ship, his back to Langdon, Graves continued, "Let me enlighten you as to my position, Mr. Langdon." He was silent for a moment, as if composing his thoughts. "Although I am increasingly feeling that a swift interposition of military power is the only means left to restore these deluded, infatuated rebels to a right use of their reason; yet, I am hemmed on the one side by vague orders from the admiralty about enforcing the late parliamentary acts without initiating offensive operations; and on the other by insufficient ships and men to launch an attack that would show the rebels how their impudence will be rewarded. While the rebels are able to carry on war as vigorously as possible, I have orders which warn me against acting offensively for fear of widening the gap between colonists and crown. My requests for reinforcements, and clarification of the scope of my authority as regards military intervention, are met constantly with reluctance, miserable stinginess, and silence. Meanwhile, I am criticized for lack of spirit and zeal by those who would have me burn and lay waste to the whole country." He turned to face Langdon. "What, in God's name," he asked quietly, but with evident frustration, his hands open in front of him, "do they expect me to do?"

Langdon remained silent for a moment, honored by the admiral's confidence, but unsure of how to reply. Then, as the silence persisted, Langdon braved a question that he had been formulating. "In the current climate of rebellion, sir, under what circumstances would you think it appropriate for the commander of a king's ship to use military force against colonists?"

"There are a few very clear cases when it would be appropriate to use force; for instance, if a king's ship is attacked, its officers threatened, or its crew fired upon. A less defined but nevertheless appropriate use, in my view, would be if a commander, having received reasonable advices that an attack was planned by an identifiable body of rebels, struck first, for the protection of his ship and crew," Graves answered.

"Would you go any further, sanctioning, say, an attack upon a rebel installation which posed a theoretical threat to a king's ship?" Langdon persisted.

"Well, the rub comes in the area of public opinion, you see. I think the admiralty or Westminster would look favorably upon any British military action which could not be construed by the rebels as aggressive or provocational. Self-defense is the safest and clearest case, of course. However, the thing about these rebels which maddens me most – and, in confidence, impresses me –is their talent for demagoguery, and their ability to manipulate public opinion through clever turn of phrase and the invocation of civil and religious sentiments. They seem quite adept at wresting the mantle of martyrdom to their own side. We need to begin returning not only fire with fire, but persuasion with persuasion. It may already be too late to wage a war of words, but we should nevertheless enlist every weapon to our cause which could possibly be of value. That is one reason, quite frankly, why I took you on, and suggested that Governor Gage submit his proclamation to your verbal skills."

Langdon thanked him and continued his line of questioning. "Could the proclamation not be considered a fair warning of British intentions to intensify and widen the scope of their use of force? The first sentence seems fairly unequivocal on that score," he said, "this bit about 'to prove they do not bear the sword in vain.'"

"It's a step in that direction, certainly, Mr. Langdon; but not even a royal governor can issue edicts contrary to those of parliament or the crown," the admiral replied. "And, what's more, this proclamation is meant to be the last offering of the olive branch, and thus would not serve very effectively as a justification for future use of force."

"I see. I will do what I can, sir."

*

Governor Thomas Gage's Proclamation of 12 June, 1775, as amended by the Rev'd Mr. Langdon

By his Excellency the Honourable Thomas Gage, Esq., Governor in Chief, in and over His Majesty's Province of Massachusetts-Bay, and Major General of the same.

Whereas ~~the infatuated multitudes~~ [many colonists], who have ~~long suffered themselves to be conducted~~ [been influenced] by certain well known incendiaries ~~and traitors~~ in a fatal progression of crimes against the [constitutional] authority of the state, have at length proceeded to avowed rebellion; and the good effects which were expected to arise from the patience and lenity of the King's government are now rendered hopeless; it only remains for those who are entrusted with ~~supreme rule,~~ [maintaining domestic tranquility,] ~~and~~ [as well] the punishment of the guilty [as the protection of the well affected], to prove [reluctantly that] they do not bear the sword in vain.

The infringements which have been committed upon the most sacred rights of the crown and people of Great Britain are too many to enumerate on the one side, and are all too atrocious to be palliated on the other. All unprejudiced people who have been witnesses of the late transactions in this and neighbouring provinces will find, upon ~~a transient review~~ [an honest examination], marks of premeditation and conspiracy that would justify the fullness of chastisement. The authors of the present ~~unnatural~~ revolt, ~~never~~ [rather than] daring to trust the cause or their actions to the judgment of an impartial public, have uniformly placed their chief confidence in the suppression of truth. The press, that distinguished appendage of public liberty, and when fairly and impartially employed its best support, has been invariably ~~prostituted~~ [used] to the most contrary purposes, until, to complete the horrid profanation of terms and of ideas, [even] the name of God has been introduced in the pulpits to excite and justify devastation and massacre.

A number of armed persons, to the amount of many thousands, assembled on the 19th of April last, and, from behind walls and lurking holes, attacked a detachment of the King's troops who, not expecting so consummate an act of frenzy, made use of their arms only in their own defence.

Since that period the rebels, deriving confidence from impunity, ~~have added insult to outrage;~~ have repeatedly fired upon the King's ships and subjects, with cannon and small arms; have possessed the roads and other communications by which the town of Boston was supplied with provisions; and, with ~~a preposterous parade of military arrangement~~ [the illegal assembling of an armed body] affect to hold the army besieged, while part of their body make daily and indiscriminate invasions upon private property, and with a wantonness of cruelty carry depredation and distress wherever they turn their steps.

In this exigency of complicated ~~calamities~~ [circumstances], I avail myself of the last effort within the bounds of my duty[, to spare the effusion of blood]; to offer, and I do hereby in His Majesty's name offer and promise, his most gracious pardon to all persons who shall forthwith lay down their arms and return to the duties of peaceable subjects~~, excepting only from benefit of such pardon Samuel Adams and John Hancock, whose offences are of too flagitious a nature to admit of any other consideration than that of condign punishment~~.

Likewise, all such as shall take arms after the date hereof, or who shall in any wise protect or conceal such offenders, or assist them with money, provision, arms, or ammunition, shall be deemed rebels and traitors, and as such will be treated.

To these inevitable[, but I trust salutary] measures, it is [a far more pleasing part of] my duty to add the assurances of protection and support to all who, in so trying a crisis, shall manifest their allegiance to the King and affection to their state, so that such persons as may have been intimidated to quit their habitations in the course of this alarm, may return to their respective callings and possessions; and stand distinct and separate from the ~~parricides~~ [opponents] of our constitution, till God [in his mercy] shall restore to ~~his creatures in~~ [the people of] this distracted land, that system of happiness from which they have been ~~seduced~~ [misled], the religion of peace, and liberty founded upon law.

Given at Boston this twelfth day of June, in the fifteenth year of the reign of His Majesty George the Third, by the Grace of God King of Great Britain, d[D]efender of the f[F]aith, &c. *Annoque Domini* 1775. By his Excellency's command, Thos. Flucker, Secretary. GOD Save the KING.

*

"I FELT," Langdon said to the admiral later than afternoon, as the latter was looking at Langdon's emendations, "that it was not so much in need of verbal improvement, as softening. Many of the words and expressions could not but have the effect of further offending, and thereby achieving the opposite of what is intended."

"Yes, I quite agree," Graves said. "Very nicely done, Mr. Langdon. I shall send it back to the Governor, and we shall see which suggestions he will adopt."

As it happened, very few of the suggestions were adopted by Gage, and the proclamation that was published, posted, and distributed, was far closer to the original than Langdon felt was prudent. Graves did not seem to notice this, and thought the final proclamation was quite strong.

*

IN REPLY TO THIS PROCLAMATION, on the 15th of June, a broadside with the author identified simply as 'Sydney' was printed in Salem and spread all around Boston, addressed to "The Soldiers and Seamen serving in the British Fleet and Army in America." A copy falling into the hands of Gage was conveyed to Vice Admiral Graves.

"Mr. Langdon, the proclamation has engendered a reply!" he exclaimed jovially as his clerk entered the cabin Friday morning, June 16. It was the first time Langdon could remember seeing the admiral smile with genuine mirth, much less laugh aloud.

"Listen--:" he placed a pair of small, round spectacles on his nose and read, in a tone of mock urgency. "'Gentlemen: Your situation is very unhappy, being dishonoured by the most infamous service, and under the command of the most vile and miserable wretches that ever disgraced the name of Briton. General Gage, to his eternal infamy, has commenced a thief, robber, murderer, and common butcher of his fellow men; he has violated the most solemn compacts, and become an apostate to every thing that is honourable or virtuous. Admiral Graves has added to the crimes of a common pirate' . . . do I look like a pirate to you, Mr. Langdon?" he laughed. Langdon could not help but join in the mirth.

"Where were we . . . oh, yes, 'Admiral Graves has added to the crimes of a common pirate, that of forcing Americans, whom he hath pressed, to act against their own countrymen. Turks and Indians would scorn such rascally conduct.' Imagine, Mr. Langdon, even Turks would not act as I have! '. . . and surely every British soldier and seaman must detest such an odious scoundrel. Gentlemen, the Americans will entertain a respect for you, and consider you as their brethren, and wish to live in harmony with you . . .'"

". . . unless you disagree with them," Langdon added.

"Just so, yes. '. . . and to make you free citizens of America. May you soon be freed from the service of tyrants, become the glorious defenders of freedom, and join the victorious Americans.'

Lovely piece of work, that, isn't it? I like the 'odious scoundrel'-bit. You may refer to me in the future, with my blessings, Mr. Langdon, as 'that odious scoundrel.'" Again he fell to laughing. "I think perhaps we should have this reprinted at our expense and distributed to every man-jack in the squadron. Very little could inspire their loyalty and excite their competitive spirit more than to have a pack of rebellious Americans refer to their commanders as 'the most vile and miserable wretches that ever disgraced the name of Briton.' Some of our sailors may well agree, but they reserve the right of expressing it themselves, and don't look kindly on strangers doing it for them." He gave the handbill to Langdon. "Keep this for your personal archives, Mr. Langdon. You're partly to blame for it, you know."

"And proud of it, sir," Langdon said, although the fact that most of his attempts at softening the language had been ignored.

"As you should be!"

*

The Rev'd Mr. Thomas Langdon's Journal

Friday, 16 June, 1775. H. M. S. *Preston* in Boston Harbour. (. . .) Although the admiral is under the impression that the proclamation benefitted greatly from my suggestions, and is quite proud of my involvement, only three or four of the more minor amendments were actually adopted in the final rendering. I must say that I am disappointed, and cannot but wonder whether Gage felt that my changes, coming from a colonist, were an attempt to subvert his will, or to dilute his authority. The final proclamation as published came across, in my opinion, as unnecessarily arrogant and insulting, and I think it will be seen to have had a more negative affect on colonist's attitudes than otherwise, sadly. And I am perhaps now *persona non grata* in the governor's circle, for all I know. For myself, I little care what the governor thinks of me; but I would not wish to compromise the standing of the admiral.

Chapter Eighteen.

Langdon started into full consciousness at the sound of cannon-fire. He realized it must have been going on for some considerable time, as his dreams had been of distant thunder and an approaching storm. By the infinitesimal amount of light creeping under the door jamb of his berth, he suspected it was not yet dawn, and hence about four o'clock in the morning.

As the sound of gunfire neither let up nor slackened over the course of the next quarter hour, he decided to rise and determine the cause.

He emerged on deck around five o'clock. It was already quite warm, and he could tell it was going to be a hot day. The starboard rail was lined with people, officers on the quarterdeck, sailors on the main deck and forecastle. He saw Mr. Collingwood – it was his last day aboard – and approached him. Langdon had earlier congratulated him on his impending promotion.

"Again I find myself plumbing the depths of your nautical expertise in asking you what the source of the gunfire is, Mr. Collingwood," the chaplain quipped after he had gained a place at the rail next to the newly made lieutenant.

"Perhaps I should write a treatise on identifying distant gunfire," Collingwood returned, an enthusiastic youthful laugh in his throat. "This time it is not small arms but cannon – probably nine-pounders – and it comes from one of our ships, the *Lively*."

"Nine-pounders? You astonish me! You can tell all that just from the sound?"

"No," the lieutenant chuckled. "I simply happen to know that the *Lively* carries long nines."

"Aha! Just trying to impress me, then."

"Indeed," Collingwood smiled. He became serious again. "It appears the reason for the *Lively*'s cannonade is that the rebels have begun throwing up a redoubt on the hill behind Charlestown – see that black spot at the top of the closest hill? It looks like a volcano hiccupped overnight and left a black stain of lava at the very top. That's apparently five or six hours of ambitious work with spades and shovels, turning a pasture into a fortification."

"And a soon-to-be battlefield, no doubt," added the dour Lieutenant Graeme ('Old Grim' – Langdon has since learned that he, like Mowat, was an Orcadian), in his Scottish accent, who stood at Mr. Collingwood's other hand.

"I am impressed," Collingwood continued, "by their industry. No one will ever be able to fault Americans for lack of energy or ingenuity." Then, after a pause, he said, "A midshipman arrived from the *Lively* a few moments ago. He's with the admiral as we speak, and will no doubt shed some light on the situation," Mr. Collingwood concluded. Third Lieutenant John Graves came on deck and joined the little group of officers observing the distant goings on.

"Isn't that Breed's Hill?" Graves asked, squinting across several miles to the neck of land.

"I thought Breed's was the tallest one – the one behind it," Collingwood countered.

"No, I think Bunker Hill is the tallest. That one's Breed's," Old Grim said with finality.

"Well, at any rate, the rebels have been damned fools, erecting their works on the second-tallest hill," Lieutenant Graves remarked, spitting over the side into the bay. "And, as far as one can tell from here, they've failed to fortify the thinnest part of the neck – the landward end. Put a couple gunboats on either side of that and send a detachment of marines onto it, and you've virtually cut off their escape."

"Perhaps they *have* fortified the neck," Mr. Collingwood ventured.

"I doubt it. It looks to me like they've moved the better part of a thousand men onto the hill to fortify it . . . which, according to most accounts, is about half of what they've got around Boston altogether. If that's the case, I predict the American rebellion will be over by sunset."

Lieutenant Graeme gave a low whistle. "I'm no army tactician, nor do I wish to sound like a nay-sayer, gentlemen; but even assuming the rebels are routed today, and the siege of Boston is thereby lifted, I doubt very much the rebellion will subside. I think it will take an extended blockade of New England's ports to choke off the rebellious will."

"And not just New England anymore," Mr. Collingwood interjected. "Did you hear of the Governor of Virginia, Lord Dunmore? He was forced to retreat aboard the *Magdalen* last month. He fled Williamsburg with his family and went aboard the warship for protection from the mob. That's in Virginia, mind you – the supposedly loyal South!"

"That will soon be Governor Wentworth's position up in Portsmouth, as well," Lieutenant Graves stated.

"The rebellious spirit is an infectious one," Mr. Collingwood observed, "spreading like the plague once it has caught hold in a place."

"It's time for a tourniquet, then," commented Lieutenant Graves.

"It's too late for a tourniquet," said Old Grim. "The infection has spread through most of the body. And you saw how ineffective the tourniquet was with the Boston Port Act, which was parliament's attempt last year to isolate what they perceived as the seat of the rebellion."

They fell silent, looking at Charlestown neck and the cloud of smoke building to leeward of the *Lively* from her continual firing.

"What measures, then, do you submit would be more effective, Lieutenant Graeme?" Langdon asked, speaking for the first time in this conclave of lieutenants.

"I'm of the opinion that the ministry is undecided just how to proceed," Lieutenant Graeme began. "On the one side there are those who advise the king and Lord North to be conciliatory, investigating ways to accommodate the colonists in their grievances; on the other side there are those who counsel them to send a major force to quell the rebellion in an instant. So what do they do? Neither one completely. They make small gestures towards both, thus cancelling each other out. The attempts at reconciliation are nullified by minor reinforcements and legislation calculated to punish; yet these attempts at showing a strengthened resolve are entirely unequal to the task at hand. I am of the opinion that government should make up its mind on one of these strategies and attack it wholeheartedly. If it is to be reconciliation, then the ministry should make a serious attempt at addressing – and redressing – the American's perceived grievances: lift the Boston Port Act, the Fish Bill, the tea tax, the Quartering Act; and send a powerful delegation to negotiate a compromise, where the colonists do their part in supporting the empire, and Britain fulfills her duties as the mother country. If, however, it is to be a forceful putting down of the rebellion, then the king should authorize the sending of another 20,000 troops and three-dozen warships, and we will have done with these insurrections in a matter of months."

"I personally pray for the former," Langdon said after thanking him for his frank opinion.

"Well, you are a colonist," Lieutenant Graves observed.

"I prefer to think my opinions are a result of my personal convictions, Lieutenant Graves, not my place of birth," Langdon rejoined.

"But what of those who say, Mr. Graeme – and there are many – " continued Graves, choosing to ignore Langdon's comment, "that to send such a large force overseas would strip Britain of her home defenses, laying her open to a France ever watchful for the opportunity of recovering her losses in the last war?"

"The troops are not needed at home if the channel fleet is kept in readiness to prevent an invasion; and the line-of-battle ships necessary to protect against an invasion are of little use in America. Hence, equip and send every frigate, sloop, brig, and schooner that can be fitted out at a moment's notice, plus the troops, and Britain's bulwarks still remain adequately shored up by way of the channel fleet."

The clomp of shoes on the deck behind them made them turn. Midshipman Saunders – who was the admiral's frequent message bearer – stood saluting the first lieutenant. "Admiral's compliments, sir, and would you and the chaplain be so good as to attend him in his cabin forthwith."

The admiral was a virtual model of perpetual motion from the moment the marine sentry announced their presence. Graves scurried about the cabin as several servants brushed a uniform, polished his black shoes, and powdered his wire wig.

"Graeme," he said forcefully, "signal the fleet to sway out all ships' boats in preparation for sending them to the Boston wharves, as well as to ready their marines for a potential amphibious operation. Also, signal the *Falcon*, *Glasgow*, *Symmetry*, and . . . and . . . the *Boyne*'s tender..."

"The *Spitfire*, sir," Graeme offered.

"Yes, and the *Spitfire*; signal them to join the *Lively*, anchored in the Charles River Estuary so that their guns bear on Charlestown and the breastworks on Bunker Hill. Signal the battery on Copp's Hill to ready themselves to join the bombardment, but not to do so until specifically ordered. Also, sway out and man the gig and the launch, in readiness for my own use.

"Langdon," he turned on his clerk now. "Write something to General Gage which pledges the navy's unwavering assistance in whatever manner he may think fit in dislodging the rebels from the hill. Add something to the effect that it is my firm opinion that the rebels must not be allowed to remain, as they pose a threat to the security of the town as well as the ships in the harbor by holding such a position. I'll glance at it once you've finished it. Have Midshipman Saunders deliver the letter to Province House in the gig and inform him *to wait for a reply*. I'll not let Gage keep me in the dark on this day, as he would doubtless prefer if left to his own devices."

As Langdon sat scribbling in the chart room, he reflected on the admiral's words. He had heard rumors that Gage's and Graves' relations were somewhat strained, but the letters he had copied as secretary – at least one a day for the last two and a half weeks – had shown nothing but the most extreme cordiality and respect between the two commanders.

The letter was ready by half past five o'clock, approved and signed by the admiral, and Midshipman Saunders was duly dispatched in the gig.

"Have breakfast with me, Mr. Langdon," the admiral bade once Saunders had been sent. "As you are so lately come to Boston," he said once they were seated at the great table, napkins spread across their laps, "let me apprise you of why it frustrates and angers me so much in seeing the rebels entrenching on Breed's Hill.

"The very day after that senseless to-do at Lexington and

Concord – as my sailors and marines were covering the retreat and removal of the army across the Charles River into Boston – I went to General Gage with a proposal, complete with plans drawn by myself, for the seizing and fortifying of the heights surrounding Boston. Any idiot can see that Breed's and Bunker Hills to the north, and the Roxbury and Dorchester Heights to the south, are the most desirable locations from which to command not only the city but the harbor as well. I pointed out how imperative it was to seize and defend these, as cannon placed at the heights would be able to rake the entire town and inner harbor with a withering fire. Further, I recommended the evacuation of Charlestown and Roxbury of their inhabitants, as they pose threats to Boston by their nearness, and burning them to the ground. Nothing but ill can come of having such clusters of buildings, and the refuge they afford to skirmishers and snipe-shooters, so near at hand to the encampments and ships around Boston.

"Well, the general in Gage was overruled by the governor in him – which would have been all well and good *before* Lexington and Concord, but, once the rebellious scoundrels had had the audacity to fire on King's troops, the general should have risen to the fore. Gage, however, would have none of it. He told me my plan was 'too rash and sanguinary.' He said he was fearful that Boston's townspeople might rise up in protest if he attempted to take Roxbury, and that the popular will would turn against him if he were to burn the property of private, neutral colonists.

"I granted him the extremity of burning the towns, but still pressed him to occupy Dorchester Heights and Bunker Hill. When he continued to object, I said that he should at least fortify Bunker Hill, as it was already in our possession, and would involve no costly maneuvers to invest it, as Dorchester Heights might. He disliked the idea, however, of having a small pocket of troops separated from the main body and exposed, as he thought it, to raids and enemy mischief. I told him I thought it quite a safe position if adequately fortified, and even offered placing a vessel or two at his disposal for the defense of the position, but he would have none of it.

"Finally, facing his damnable intransigence in not taking advantage of clear and present opportunities, I told him I was in that case mightily concerned about the safety of the *Somerset*, which once lay where the *Lively* is now, in the Charlestown ferry roads. She could only be removed from the position on a floodtide, and then only by warping if the wind were not favorable, which made her terribly vulnerable. I was determined that she was potentially in danger, so I sent the *Lively* to the position, having a much shallower draft than the *Somerset*. I pressed upon Gage the necessity of constructing a fort on Copp's Hill inside Boston, which faces Charlestown and Bunker Hill from the south. I offered to construct it, supply it and man it from my own resources. This he finally consented to. The erection of this battery – by an admiral – afforded much amusement to the garrison, particularly among those who did not readily perceive the intent. It was christened soon by the name of 'the admiral's battery,' and is always spoken of with a wink and a smile. But witness, Mr. Langdon: – the only battery in Boston capable of returning any fire on Bunker Hill this morning happens to be the one which I built, and that only because I was pleased to make a fool of myself in their eyes. Well, let them smirk and chuckle now, now that I've done the work of *both* the navy *and* the army!"

He bit into a piece of toasted bread, but, finding it burned, tossed it with disdain onto his plate.

"This whole thing could have been avoided had I been taken seriously two months ago," he continued, wiping the crumbs from his mouth with his napkin. "But no, I was despised by Gage's father, whom I had the dubious pleasure of being acquainted with in

England many years ago, and now I am the butt of jokes among the governor's staff, as well."

Langdon suddenly realized that the presence of such long-standing acrimony might be another explanation for the rejection of his suggestions in the wording of the proclamation a little more than a week ago.

"Well, let them joke. I've half a mind to remove my ships to the outer harbor, pointing out that they are now vulnerable to guns the rebels might choose to place in their redoubt on Breed's Hill, and let Gage deal with the rebels by himself. It might serve him for his haughtiness."

He fell silent for a moment. The steady, measured booming of the *Lively*'s cannon in the distance crept back into their consciousness, bringing the admiral back to a sense of what was to be done.

"But my duty calls me to offer whatever assistance I can, for the good of king and country, overlooking the snubs – both personal and those of the service – that I and my squadron daily endure." He paused, assessing the chaplain's reactions to all this information. "So, there you have it right from the old horse's mouth: the background to the well-publicized animosity existing between the governor and his admiral."

"I am flattered by your confidence," Langdon responded politely. "Your foresight does you great credit, sir."

Graves grunted, meaning no disrespect to his secretary, but exhibiting his bitterness over the whole affair.

*

AT 9:20 A LIEUTENANT JORDEN, naval *attaché* to the governor, was rowed to the flagship to report to the admiral about the governor's council of war, at which he had been present as representative of the navy.

"So what will the Royal Navy be required to do, Mr. Jorden?" Graves asked somewhat sarcastically. Langdon and Captain Robinson were present.

"There's to be a landing at Morton's Point around noon under the command of Major General Howe, for which the navy is respectfully requested to provide as many boats and oarsmen as possible. The continuing bombardment of the rebels' breastworks from the various vessels and batteries involved, is also much appreciated," Jorden reported.

"Doubtless," muttered Graves.

"In addition, Major General Howe wonders about the possibility of bringing the *Somerset* into range of the hill. He is willing to meet you aboard her, should you think there a chance of success."

Graves rubbed his chin thoughtfully. "I'm virtually certain it's impossible, but I will be more than happy to meet the general aboard the *Somerset* at his convenience. Mr. Langdon, sketch a note to Mr. Howe to that effect, would you?"

"Yes, sir," said Langdon, sitting down at the great table to write as the conversation continued.

"What was the . . ." the admiral struggled to find the right word, ". . . *mood* of the council, Mr. Jorden?"

"There was a certain amount of friction, sir. Especially from Major General Clinton, who argued for immediate action. He proposed taking the rebels from both front and rear before their works could be completed or reinforcements could come up from Cambridge. The only possible avenue of retreat, he pointed out, lay across the Neck, and, although the mill dam prevents a landing on the Charles side of the peninsula, a floating battery or vessel could be brought up to rake the Neck and thus prevent anyone from getting across in either direction. Then, while Howe led an assault up the front of the hill, Clinton would take 500 troops up the

Mystic River and 'put the cork in the bottle,' as he put it, occupying the Neck. Or, failing that, to land the said contingent at the Charlestown wharves, march them around the south side of the peninsula to the enemy's rear, and thus accomplish the same thing."

Graves pursed his lips and nodded. "Sensible plan."

"Howe agreed on the necessity of acting quickly, but both he and General Burgoyne felt that Clinton's complicated plan accorded the rebels too much esteem as soldiers and afforded them too much time. Equipping, preparing, and positioning the pinning force would take several hours, if not an additional day, thus allowing the rebels to make greater progress in the digging of their earthworks at the top of the hill. Burgoyne was of the opinion that they should simply attack immediately, and that the rebels would not stand and fight. A frontal assault was all that was needed to send the routed rebels scurrying back to Cambridge."

Graves grunted.

"In the end, Gage decided to go with Howe's plan, and put him in charge of the noon assault. General Clinton stormed from the room, I'm afraid to say," Jorden said. "That's when Howe approached me about the *Somerset*, sir."

"It's to be noon, then?"

"I respectfully pointed out to them that high tide would not occur until three o'clock, sir, but they did not apprehend my point."

"No, of course not. What could God possibly do to thwart the resolve of four major generals of His Majesty's army, eh? Well, your efforts are to be commended, Mr. Jorden."

"Thank you, sir."

"Are you finished, Mr. Langdon?"

The secretary held up the document for the admiral's persual. He signed it and gave it to Mr. Jorden. "If you would be so good as to deliver this to Mr. Howe, sir, I would be most obliged."

*

Vice Admiral Graves, despite his heavy build, astonished the Rev'd Langdon by springing lithely down the ladder from the entry port and stepping with calculated ease into the bobbing launch, ignoring the proffered assistance of eager oarsmen – which assistance Langdon himself gratefully accepted, remembering his brush with disaster when first coming aboard the *Preston* two and a half weeks ago.

While he expected the hot temperature to moderate once the boat pulled away from the side of the flagship, it became even hotter, unprotected from the direct sun and with little breeze to move the air. By the time they found themselves aboard the 64-gun *Somerset*, where General Howe, who had arrived some moments before, stood in conversation with Captain LeCras on the quarterdeck, Langdon was sweating profusely.

"Ah, Vice Admiral Graves," said Howe upon the approach of the admiral. He was a surprisingly youthful looking, tall, slender man, his dark hair pulled into a tidy queue at the nape of his neck. His starched red uniform was impeccable and of the latest fashion. "How good to see you again," he said with a broad smile which struck Langdon as slightly supercilious.

"This is Mr. Thomas Langdon, my secretary," Graves said.

"Pleased, I'm sure," he said, inclining his head slightly.

"I wish to repeat my offer in person, if I may: that of the ungrudging assistance of the navy in dislodging the rebels, and to coordinate our efforts on this momentous day," Graves said.

"You think it a momentous day?" Howe asked without exhibiting very much interest, but looking Graves unflinchingly in the eyes.

"I believe the vast majority of the rebels on the neck can either be killed or captured, resulting in a great victory if it is done properly and our execution equals our planning," Graves replied.

"Ah," Howe said. It seemed to be his way of acknowledging that he had heard Graves' words but did not necessarily concur with them. "Well, there's no question that the rebels must be driven from their crude earthworks, as they could threaten Boston itself with bombardment from there; but whether driving them from their holes on that hill will be considered a great victory for the cause of government, I very much doubt it. It strikes me as a tiresome but necessary burden, with little more reward than keeping them from breathing down our necks."

"You are a much better judge than I, certainly," Admiral Graves said carefully. "Nevertheless, I think it simply good sense that, having determined an objective, one accomplish it in the most strategically advantageous manner. Hence, having determined it necessary to drive the rebels from Bunker Hill, we may as well take advantage of the situation and capture the whole lot of them, lock, stock and — "

"I thank you for your advice on military matters, sir, but I am here to get your advice on maritime ones." Howe said abruptly, smiling disingenuously.

"Quite so," said the admiral quietly, his facial expression hardening.

"What is your opinion concerning bringing the *Somerset* within range of the redoubt?"

"It is not necessary to have an opinion when it is a matter of mathematics, sir," Graves rejoined tartly. "As the coming tide at three this afternoon is not to be a very high one, as tides go, it will be improbable that the Somerset, with such a deep draft, can be brought into anything like effective range."

"And the *Preston?*"

"Although a smaller ship, she draws nearly as much water as this one, I'm afraid."

"Can it not be attempted?" Howe asked.

Graves and Captain LeCras exchanged a quick glance. "By all means, general." The admiral nodded to LeCras, who turned without expression to his first lieutenant.

"How many vessels do we have that can get within range, then?" Howe asked as Captain LeCras went about giving the orders which would set the ship in cautious motion towards Charlestown Neck and Breed's Hill.

"The *Lively* and *Glasgow*, both of 20 guns, the *Falcon* of 14, and the *Spitfire* and *Symmetry*, of six or eight guns each. I've already ordered them into place."

"Which puts what weight of metal against the hill?" he inquired.

The admiral rubbed his chin as he calculated. "Just over 250 pounds, I'd say."

"And the *Somerset*, with her lower deck 24-pounders, would add, what, 500 pounds of shot?"

"560," Graves stated.

"Damn!" General Howe exclaimed. "Imagine what damage we could do with a single broadside from this ship! The others are a great help, the *Lively* and *Spitfire* and whatnot – and I'm thankful for their presence – but we must get this ship within range. It would triple the amount of metal we could put against the rebels."

Graves said nothing, which effectively communicated that he knew very well it was impossible. "There is the Copp's Hill battery," the admiral observed after a moment, running a finger distractedly under his collar due the growing heat of the day. "Its 24-pounders deliver nearly 200 pounds of shot with every salvo."

Howe did not reply, further angering Graves with his arrogance.

Half an hour later, after the leadsman had called out a frighteningly shallow depth under the keel of the *Somerset*, Captain LeCras said to the admiral, "We ought go no closer, I think, sir."

"Quite so, Captain LeCras. Yet we are still several cables from a point at which I think the guns were within range of the rebel earthworks. You may take her back out to safe water."

Howe, aware that he had been defeated, simply smiled and said, "I thank you for the attempt, Admiral Graves, and would you direct the boats of the squadron to repair to the Boston wharves, that we might begin preparations for the landing?"

"At once," Graves replied. "And good luck with the assault," he added, calling over the side to the departing general.

*

The Rev'd Mr. Thomas Langdon's Journal

SATURDAY, JUNE 17, 1775. BOSTON HARBOUR. (. . .) I am quite surprised and distressed to find the level of animosity that exists between the army and navy in Boston. And, although I will be seen as favouring the admiral due to my association with him, yet I cannot but assign the greater blame to the arrogance and disdain of the army over and against the navy. Admiral Graves began the day with every appearance of cooperation and solicitude, offering assistance before any request was made; issuing orders of cooperation before the army had even settled on a plan of action. And the episode I witnessed on the quarterdeck of the *Somerset* between Graves and Major General Howe left me quite as angry as the admiral himself. Perhaps Graves should not have offered advice on what is perceived as a military rather than a naval operation; but I would have thought that his opinions, second only to those of the governor himself, should have been consulted in the matter, especially as the operation was to commence, and largely to be carried out, with naval support. The coolness and, indeed, diffidence with which Graves was treated by the haughty young general left me with a very bad taste in my mouth. The opinions of other naval officers seems to concur with mine, according to a conversation with Lieu^{ts} A. Graeme, J^{no} Graves, and C. Collingwood,* in which I took part early in the day, so I am supported in holding them. Perhaps Adm^l Graves' treatment by Howe should have been my first foreboding of how the events of the day would turn out.

ADDED IN DIFFERENT HANDWRITING, DATED SEPT. 1820:

*These three lieu^{ts}, as it happens, all became admirals and had distinguished careers in the Navy. J^{no} Graves commanded several sloops during the remainder of the American war, was made post in 1783 and given command of the *Sandwich* (90). He died a Rear Adm^l in 1811. Alexander Graeme, who later became the Sixth Laird of Graemeshall in the Orkneys upon the death of his elder brother, captained several sloops before being made post and given the *Pearl* (32) in 1779, and the *Tartar* (28). In 1781 he took command of this same *Preston* (50), in which he was present at the Battle of Dogger Bank, where he lost an arm and was paid off. He returned to active duty in 1795 and was promoted Rear Adm^l shortly thereafter. He served until 1802 before retiring, and died an Adm^l of the Blue in 1818. Cuthbert Collingwood is best known for his association with Lord Nelson: they met when they served together as lieu^{ts} in the *Lowestoffe* in 1777; Collingwood succeeded Nelson in command of the brig *Badger* in 1779; succeeded Nelson again in the frigate *Hinchinbroke* (28); then saw out the American war in command of several other ships. With the resumption of hostilities in 1793, he was flag captain of the *Barfleur* (98) under Rear Adml Bowyer at the Glorious First of June, 1794, and commanded the *Excellent* (74) at the Battle of Cape St. Vincent, 1797. Promoted to Rear Adm^l in 1799, he was second-in-command to Nelson at the Battle of Trafalgar, 1805, leading the windward column into battle in the *Royal Sovereign* (110), and taking command of the fleet upon Nelson's death. Raised to the peerage as Baron Collingwood, he continued to serve until his death in 1810, when he was laid to rest next to Nelson in St. Paul's Cathedral. That the Rev'd Langdon should be serving with three future admirals of such distinction must be counted as something of a curiosity, if not a marvel.

Chapter Nineteen.

Lieutenant Graeme supervised the arming of two scows – large, flat-bottomed boats – with a 12-pounder cannon in each, and these were manned by marines and sent off Charlestown neck to prevent any more rebels from coming across from the mainland, and to harry their expected retreat. The *Glasgow* and *Symmetry* were ordered to approach the neck as nearly as possible, taking great care not to run aground, and assist the scows in their objective. Meanwhile, the *Lively*, *Falcon*, and *Spitfire* kept up their bombardment of the redoubt, although at a slackened rate, for Admiral Graves worried that overuse of the guns would cause their overheating and cracking.

Graves also secretly ordered the vessels to prepare for the heating of shot, and sent orders to the Copp's Hill Battery to ready carcasses for firing.

The battleships *Boyne*, *Somerset*, and *Preston* were ordered to provide the smaller vessels with reinforcements for the relief of their gun crews, and to send replenishment of shot and powder from out of their stores.

At 11 o'clock the flagship signalled the squadron to send all boats to the Boston wharves. The admiral retained the *Preston*'s gig for his own use, but every other boat – and there must have been two dozen – set out across the bay at this point for Boston, to join the veritable fleet of small boats requisitioned by the army for the day's coming amphibious operation.

The sun had grown very warm, and the breeze which had earlier promised to offer some relief had died almost entirely away, leaving a sticky oppressiveness to the air which would make the army's work very warm.

Langdon stood on the quarterdeck much of that early afternoon when he was not required by the admiral. At a little past one o'clock the first boats put off from Boston, filled with red-coated soldiers. Within ten minutes the bay between Boston and Charlestown Neck seemed solid with red. It looked from the flagship as though one could walk straight from one neck of land across the bay to the other, all on the backs of the infantry. By two o'clock, the boats having each made two or three trips across the bay and back, over 2,000 regulars had landed on Charlestown Neck and were forming on the beach. The location of the landing was quite a disappointment to Lieutenant Graeme and Mr. Collingwood, who continued to be the clergyman's companions on deck.

"Just like a general to think of nothing more creative than a frontal assault," muttered Old Grim. "Rather than landing them behind the rebels, thus trapping them in their own bunkers, like self-dug graves, he is going to march right up the hill from the front, exactly as the Americans want him to do."

"Perhaps this is just the pinning force, or the diversion, and he'll land others behind the rebel entrenchments after this," Mr. Collingwood offered.

"According to what I heard Lieutenant Jorden report to the admiral, that's apparently what General Clinton suggested, but his plan was overruled as more complicated than the situation deserved," Langdon observed. Lieutenant Graeme grunted, as if to say he was not surprised.

"Tell me, gentlemen, what is a carcass?" Langdon inquired.

"'Tis a thin metal shell that looks like a cannon ball, but is filled with combustibles, designed to explode in flames on impact," Lieutenant Graeme explained. "Why?"

"Well, I overheard the admiral sending orders to the Copp's Hill battery to ready their carcasses for firing. When the admiral said 'carcasses,' I, of course, had visions of them bringing up the corpses of cows and sheep, for a sort of medieval catapulting exercise. I had no idea there was a special sort of ammunition with that name."

Collingwood and Graeme looked at each other significantly.

"That could mean only one thing," Graeme said.

"What is that?"

"That he intends to ignite something."

"Charlestown," Collingwood said quietly. Langdon suddenly plumbed their meaning. Hadn't the admiral at breakfast this very morning told Langdon about his plan to burn Charlestown and Roxbury to the ground? Now he was waiting for the opportunity to do so in the heat of battle. Langdon wondered whether Graves would have the cheek to do so in disregard of Gage's wishes, should the governor continue to disapprove.

His thoughts were interrupted by Vice Admiral Graves himself, who appeared suddenly with Midshipman Saunders and called, "Mr. Langdon, come along: We're going to Charlestown."

Fifteen minutes later they disembarked on the beach in the midst of the better part of Britain's armed forces in North America. With the help of a subaltern they found their way to General Howe, who stood before a makeshift table, surveying a handful of maps which were unrolled upon it.

Catching sight of Graves – a blue uniform in a sea of red – Howe stiffened and said, "Good day, admiral. What brings you out of your floating fortresses?"

"I've come to see if I can be of any further assistance as you carry out your work, sir," he replied.

"Very good of you, sir," Howe said. "As a matter of fact, your appearance is quite timely. As you can see," he pointed northwest across the grassy slopes of the northern part of the neck, "the rebels have extended their line from the redoubt clear to the beach. My plan of a flanking maneuver around the north end is thus somewhat frustrated. If, however, you would order the floating batteries stationed in the Charles River to move around to the north, into the Mystic River, and fire on their exposed lines from behind, they'd break and run like rabbits, leaving the path of advance open to my men."

"It would probably take the better part of an hour for the batteries to reach the new position," Graves observed, "and, what with the tide being about to turn . . ." he stopped, aware that it made him sound uncooperative.

"I am awaiting my reserves at this moment anyway," Howe looked over Graves' shoulder towards Boston.

"Very well, I shall see to it," Graves said, turning to Midshipman Saunders and repeating the order in nautical terms, such that the marines manning the batteries would know just what was required of them. Saunders ran off to the beach.

Howe turned back to his charts. At that moment a marine corporal approached from the southwest and saluted.

"Major Pitcairn's respects, sir, and he wishes to inform you of much fire coming from Charlestown directed at the army's left wing. He suspects that there are townsmen or rebels hidden behind fences and buildings who are taking advantage of the cover afforded them and will continue harrying His Majesty's troops as they advance up the hill towards the redoubt. Major Pitcairn asks if it might be of service to send a detachment into the town to drive the rebels from their cover?"

Howe shook his head. "I am doubtful of the efficacy of storming the town, as we would probably sustain more casualties than we would inflict. Tell Major Pitcairn to remain in place for now, and to protect his men as much as possible from the fire. And to keep me informed of any developments."

"But as we ascend the hill, sir, they will have the opportunity of firing at us from behind, which Major Pitcairn respectfully submits will play great mischief with his unit, sir, and – "

"General, if I may suggest . . ." Graves stepped forward.

"Yes, Admiral Graves?" Howe inquired.

"If you wish, I could have the town set afire by having heated, incendiary shot and carcasses fired into it."

Without hesitation, Howe said, "Yes, that should do the trick. Thank you, Admiral Graves. Please see to it."

Moving slightly away from the general's circle, Graves said to Langdon, a look of barely disguised satisfaction on his face, "Mr. Langdon, order Captain Bishop of the *Lively* to fire heated shot into the town; then go on to the Copp's Hill battery and tell them to begin firing carcasses into Charlestown. They have standing orders from me to that effect; merely tell them to put them into action. Understood?"

"Yes, sir," Langdon said, turning and making his way back to the beach, where he commandeered a boat and its crew in the name of the admiral.

After delivering the orders verbally to the *Lively*, which he shouted up to the deck from the boat, they continued to the wharves of Boston, where Langdon disembarked and made his way up Copp's Hill to the battery, which had fallen silent. Moist with the sweat of his exertion, he glanced quickly over his shoulder and saw that the troops were advancing up the hill and had come to within a couple hundred yards of the redoubt. The battery on Copp's Hill was no doubt cautious not to fire at the rebel works with friendly troops so close. The crimson ribbon of their perfectly formed line stood in brilliant contrast to the sunny green of the hillside's grass. There came an almost uncanny silence, putting Langdon in mind of how accustomed he had grown to the steady booming of cannon and tattoo of drums which had been sounding ceaselessly all day. Now the air seemed to stand still as every eye in Boston watched the slow, inexorable march of the British redcoats toward the brown earthworks and fenced barricades of the rebel defenders.

Langdon forced himself to turn and continue his way up to the battery. He was astonished to find the men of the garrison bantering playfully with each other, seemingly unconscious of the weighty events occurring on the opposite side of the bay. They apparently thought their work completed for the day: the redoubt would soon be stormed and carried by the redcoats, the rebels would break and flee, and the troops would pursue the routed force halfway to Cambridge. The acrid odor of burnt gunpowder and singed wads hung about the battery, making Langdon's eyes water and his nose sting. He caught sight of two high-ranking army officers standing at the parapet, observing the goings on and talking quietly with each other. An inner voice told Langdon these were Major Generals Clinton and Burgoyne.

Langdon delivered his orders to the commander of the garrison, a navy lieutenant, at the conclusion of which he noticed a cloud of black smoke – different from the whitish-grey smoke of gunpowder – eddying lazily around the *Lively*, telling him that she had begun firing heated shot into Charlestown. The air being as still as it was, the cloud hung about the vessel tenaciously. Langdon caught sight of tongues of flame licking out the windows of a waterfront building in Charlestown. The incendiary shot was having the desired effect.

"Looks like old Graves got his way after all," one of the generals commented with amusement. Langdon suspected it was Burgoyne, as he was the handsomer of the two, and Burgoyne was famous for his dashing good looks.

"Certainly can't fault him for tenacity," said the other, whom Langdon presumed was Clinton – actually slightly taller than Burgoyne, but of a heavier build and rounder features.

"Stubbornness, more like."

"Howe's in command of the right flank?" Clinton asked.

"Yes. I fancy I can just see him at the head of his line."

"And General Pigot, in command of the left, is merely to make a feint at the redoubt until Howe has carried the right flank and can turn in on the redoubt," Clinton observed.

"That's the plan," Burgoyne said.

"Lord, the right flank must be no more than thirty yards from that fence row now, and there's nary a shot from either side!"

"The rebels are showing extraordinary discipline," Burgoyne observed.

"Yes, surprising, isn't it?"

A smile of amusement crossed Burgoyne's face, and he quipped, "Perhaps they haven't any ammunition – " Before he could finish, however, the fence row erupted into a flame of fire and grey smoke. The look of amusement on Burgoyne's handsome features transformed itself immediately into one of grim horror as the British line was seen to shudder and stagger, stopping dead in its tracks. By the time the crackling and popping sound of the rebel musket volley reached their ears, the British line had begun to move slowly forward again, leaving at least a dozen killed or wounded behind, looking like splotches of red, crumpled in the grass. A second volley from the wall, however, completely shattered the British line, and it broke into tiny pieces as men fled individually and in terror from the field, back towards the beach where they had initially formed their lines.

"Lord . . . !" Clinton was heard to gasp. "Where's Howe?"

Langdon, who suddenly felt sick to his stomach at the horrifying spectacle – he had just witnessed, he told himself, scores of men being killed – could however not turn his eyes away and stood transfixed. Isolated puffs of smoke and the rolling sound of musketry along the left flank soon attested to the fact that Pigot's feint on the redoubt had commenced. This front, too, was forced to fall back after a heated exchange of fire with the redoubt. It retreated in much greater order than the right flank – thankfully, but by design. The sight tied Langdon's stomach in knots, and the normally unflappable General Burgoyne had taken a fancy linen handkerchief from his pocket to dab at his forehead. Clinton's hand was over his eyes – to shield them from the sun or as a sign of despair, Langdon could not tell.

In the intervals between the deafening sound of cannon, which hurled carcasses into Charlestown from Copp's Hill and red-hot shot from the *Lively*, there came the sound of human voices from the battlefield. Langdon was not sure which he found more excruciating: the piteous cries of countless British wounded as they crawled helplessly through the long grass back towards the beach, or the exultant whoops of delight from the rebels, who stood and threw their caps in the air out of joy at having made the finest army in the world retreat.

"Hit 'em again, Howe," Burgoyne was heard to say through clenched teeth, revealing that he feared Howe – if indeed he was still alive – would perhaps consider the battle already lost and return to his boats, nursing his wounds.

An agonizing quarter hour passed as the British regiments reformed themselves on the beach. A stream of boats filled with wounded began making its way over to Boston – a stream which was to continue without interruption throughout the remainder of the day.

Langdon was filled with equal portions of elation, dread, and pure hatred of the rebels when the British line – thinned by about one-tenth, but tidily redrawn – began its slow march again, across the grass toward the fencerow on the right, and up the hill to the redoubt on the left.

By now the town of Charlestown was generally ablaze, sending a cloud of brown smoke drifting upwards, caught by the all-but-non-existent breeze and bending eastwards out towards the harbor. The cloud partly obscured the lower part of the battlefield from Langdon's sight, but the upper portion, where the troops neared their objectives again, was clearly visible from Copp's Hill.

Langdon found his fists tightly balled, his brow furrowed, his teeth clenched, his entire being willing the British troops onward to the utter destruction of the rebels, hiding behind their obscene earthworks. A small part of his consciousness was appalled at the feelings of hatred welling up in him against his countrymen, and the utterly violent and evil desires he wished upon them. He reflected briefly on the ugly effect that witnessing this warfare was having on his normally peaceable nature, but he soon forced such thoughts from his mind, superstitiously fearing that they might somehow have a negative effect on the outcome of the battle.

Again there was the agonizing waiting, the anguish of hope, the fear of catastrophe, the expectation of a titanic clash, all clutching simultaneously at the heart of the observer. It seemed almost brutal how the rebels refrained from firing until the British line was within a mere thirty yards of their objective, allowing them so close before ripping into them with everything they had. For several minutes the brilliant flashes of gunfire along the rebel entrenchments were like a continual sheet of lightning, the firing an uninterrupted crackle of sound. The British line staggered, writhed, continued drunkenly forward; but the opposition was still too stiff. Units broke and ran, others persisted until abandoned on all sides and forced to fall back. Companies dispersed into individuals, breaking ranks and fleeing for safety, ignoring pleas from their officers to hold to their formation; and all the while, the number of fallen, both wounded and dead, multiplied among the red-coated soldiers in the green grass. It looked to Langdon like there could be as many as two hundred prone soldiers lying in the grass, some writhing or crawling, others completely still.

Burgoyne cursed, and said, almost as if grasping at straws, "See how the rebels ceased firing immediately when the British turned, rather than pursuing them with shot? And look how every moment the trickle of rebels fleeing the back of the bunkers increases? Their ammunition is virtually spent, I'm persuaded. Howe *must* try once more!"

"That's no way to win a battle: keep throwing your line at the enemy until they've spent their powder," Clinton observed under his breath. Then a moment later, he said louder, "Look at the leftmost portion of Pigot's regiments – which is that, the 47th?" He pointed to a group of men on the beach next to the furiously blazing town.

"Yes, that's the 47th," Burgoyne confirmed.

"They appear to be leaderless, milling about, some climbing into boats. I don't see an officer of any rank among them."

Burgoyne was silent.

"I'm going over," Clinton said without further hesitation.

"You're what?"

"Someone's got to rally that regiment. You can explain to Gage why I've left without orders," Clinton said with resolve, beginning to climb down from the parapet.

Langdon moved towards him. "Excuse me, sir. There's a boat from the *Boyne* just down the hill at the quay, which is at my disposal," he explained quickly. "Take it. Tell them Mr. Langdon, secretary to Admiral Graves, told you to do so."

"My thanks Mr. Langdon," shouted Clinton over his shoulder as he disappeared from sight through the bulwark of the battery.

Langdon's eyes met General Burgoyne's. "So you're the Rev'd Mr. Langdon," the general said when Clinton had gone.

Langdon nodded, not knowing what to expect.

"I suppose this confirms what my mother always told me about never speaking ill of others, for you never know who might be listening. An humble-looking private citizen standing nearby turns out to be the admiral's secretary." He affected a rather convincing hangdog look of penitence. Langdon smiled but remained silent. "I noted with approval your additions to the governor's proclamation of a week ago," Burgoyne continued.

"Thank you."

"Damn lot of good it appears to have done us, however, what?" he gestured with genuine pity in his eyes to the catastrophe transpiring across the harbor. Langdon turned his eye back to Charlestown. He watched as the boat bearing General Clinton put off a minute or two later from the quay and began pulling strongly towards the conflagration which indicated the location of Charlestown.

After another quarter hour, with reinforcements arriving in one direction as wounded were ferried in the other, the British formed again, this time in columns rather than lines – thus presenting less of a target to the waiting rebels. General Clinton had arrived in the midst of the wildly disorganized rabble which had been the 47th regiment, and, heartened by his sudden and unexpected appearance among them, they rallied to form columns for the third attempt on the redoubt.

"They'll do it this time," Burgoyne said – Langdon wondered if the comment was directed at him – as the British columns marched up the hill once more. The troops on the right flank – which had taken the greater beating previously – were purposefully thinned by Howe in order to bolster the left flank. It didn't take a general to explain to Langdon that his strategy seemed to have changed.

"What incredible bravery," Langdon heard himself say, shaking his head in disbelief at the tenacity and courage it must take for a soldier, clad like a target in a woolen uniform on this sweltering day, to march unflinchingly a third time into the face of death. An emotional pride arose in Langdon for these faceless soldiers, from England, Scotland, Ireland, and Wales; from Yorkshire, Cornwall, Somerset and Kent; from London, Exeter, Edinburgh and Lincoln – marching unquestioningly at the order of their commander, to defend the legislative jurisdiction of parliament and the honor of their country, all in the name of their sovereign. Tears formed involuntarily in his eyes at the grand, awful spectacle, trickling down his cheek when he tried to blink them away. "What incredible bravery," he repeated.

The flashes and smoke appeared from the rebels again, as before, when the British columns approached to within a hundred feet of the redoubt. This time the long, thick columns seemed to absorb the pummeling with little visible effect. Langdon saw some of the men in front drop, their bodies stepped over by the men in back of them as if they were so many fallen logs; but the columns moved inexorably forward across that last deadly thirty yards. The rebels' fire was noticeably lessened this time, and Langdon suspected General Burgoyne was correct in his supposition regarding lack of ammunition. The fire which the British were able to return was necessarily lessened due to their approach in columns rather than rows; but it reminded Langdon of a hefty battering ram, thin but very heavy, and unstoppable once in motion.

The British columns of the left flank reached the ditches directly in front of the redoubt. The trickle of fleeing Americans out the back of the earthworks turned into a stream as those with no powder or shot fled from the inexorable onslaught.

The final rebel volley sputtered out like an old candle mere seconds before the redcoats, with a vengeful roar, surged over the earthen walls and, with the cold steel of their bayonets, put to death or flight what remained of the defenders. The pent-up fury of their two failed attempts sought recompense in the blood of rebels. Cries for quarter were cut brutally short by the thrust of sword and bayonet, and any who stumbled or fell in his retreat found his final resting place under the glint of deadly metal. The discipline and drill of the highly trained grenadier was finally allowed to hit home with devastating effect in the fresh dirt of the rebel bunkers. For hundreds of Americans, the sixteen hours of backbreaking shoveling to create defenses turned out to be the digging of their own graves.

All along the rebel line of defense, figures were scampering, ant-like, back towards the narrow causeway which connected Charlestown Neck to the mainland. Even here they were allowed no respite as the withering fire of the *Symmetry*, *Glasgow*, and the two scows pursued them across the strip of land. Dozens more fell as the grape and round shot of the offshore vessels ripped through the retreating ranks.

Langdon found himself still watching when there was little more to see – long after General Burgoyne had departed wordlessly. What little resistance remained was quickly quelled, prisoners taken, and fortifications invested. A smaller force – Langdon thought it led by the distant form of General Clinton – pursued the fleeing rebels up and around Bunker Hill, down the other side, and onto the thinnest part of land.

Ahead lay the arduous work of transporting the wounded back to Boston, securing the prisoners, inspecting captured arms and ordnance, burying the dead, and investing the rebel works. And for the officers, there were the voluminous written and verbal reports which would be required over the next few days, detailing their and their units' performance in the action.

Langdon took leave of the battery and made his way through Boston to the wharves. A steady stream of boats was arriving with moaning injured. If their cries had not been so disturbingly heart-rending, the comparative stillness of the afternoon, with all guns around the bay silent for the first time in twelve hours, would have seemed overwhelming. Langdon felt a conflict of conscience as he saw the sheer number of wounded. As a clergyman he felt he ought to remain and assist in ministering to them; but as admiral's secretary he knew he was compelled to return to the flagship for any duty the admiral should see fit to assign him.

He found Admiral Graves on board in a frighteningly quiet and melancholic mood. Langdon made no inquiries, keeping his own counsel, and set about the small handful of tasks the admiral had for him in the writing and copying of letters, reports, and new orders now that the battle was over and different tasks faced the squadron. The work of an admiral and his aides is never over, Langdon reflected.

*

"WELL, YOU'VE WITNESSED your first battle, what?" Lieutenant John Graves said to the clergyman at dinner that evening in the wardroom, where newly minted Lieutenant Collingwood was their guest on his last evening aboard the *Preston*.

"Yes," Langdon said tiredly, "and hopefully my last."

"Come, it wasn't as gruesome as a naval action, let me assure you."

"Oh, it was not the gruesomeness of it – although seeing the flood of wounded in Boston after the battle was rather distressing – no; it was the horror of seeing British killing British, and bleeding on grass which lately had peacefully pastured English Guernsey cattle. *That* is why I hope it is the last battle I'll ever see. Of *this* war, at any rate."

"It is not the last of this war, whether you see any more of them or not, you may depend upon it," put in Lieutenant Graeme.

"What effect do you think this battle will have on the course of the war?" Langdon inquired of Old Grim.

"Very little. All it has proven is that Americans can hold their own against British regulars in a pitched field battle."

"Then General Howe was right, this morning," Langdon mused.

"Why? What did he say?"

"He said the battle was a tiresome but necessary burden, and that the only benefit to be gained from it was to keep the rebels from breathing down our necks."

"Damned fool," Graeme said. "Gage could have accomplished that objective as late as yesterday without the loss of a single man had he thought to do so, as the admiral advised after Lexington and Concord," he observed to much nodding of heads around the table.

"But do you really think the battle will have no effect on the course of the war, and the morale of the rebels?" Graves persisted. "The fact remains that they broke and ran, deserting the field to us entirely."

"Yes, after felling 400 highly trained, regular soldiers, 150 of them mortally. The entire tenor of the war changed today. All the previous skirmishes, raids and surprise attacks of the rebels have heartened them in that they could, with clever planning, outsmart a lot of stodgy, unimaginative old-world officers. But this battle has proven that they can confront the flower of Britain's army face-to-face and emerge from the field with their honor intact. It will do wonders for their recruitment efforts, I shouldn't wonder. There will be a surge of hotheaded young men pouring into the rebel General Putnam's camp over the next month," Lieutenant Graeme predicted.

"Rumor has it that a General Washington has been appointed by the Continental Congress to lead the army, and will be arriving within weeks to supercede Putnam," said Collingwood.

"Washington. That name sounds familiar," said Graeme.

"He was with Wolfe at Quebec in '59," Marine Captain Johnson said. "Fine officer, by all accounts."

"Don't you think the driving of the rebels from the entrenchments they so pointlessly built will be seen as a defeat for them?" Lieutenant Graves put in yet again.

"Pointless?" Graeme exclaimed with some irritation. "You think inflicting 400 casualties, and causing the army ignominiously to retreat twice from the field to regroup, is pointless?"

"We possess the entrenchments now, so, yes, the effort to build them was rather pointless," Graves argued.

Graeme shook his head. "You think just like one of those bloody generals – that to possess the field afterwards, no matter the cost, is all that counts. Fat lot of good it'll do us now."

"What were the respective losses, by most recent accounts, does anybody know?" Mr. Gefferina inquired.

"We've 150 dead, twice as many more, nearly, wounded--a good number of which will doubtless die before the week is out. The army counted about 75 bodies of rebels in the earthworks and along the Neck, and took another 30 prisoner," Captain Johnson replied.

"'Tis said," Lieutenant Graeme added, "that 40 or more of the dead rebels were so disfigured that they must have been killed by cannonfire – that is, by the navy's bombardment."

"Let's hear it for naval gunnery," Collingwood piped triumphantly, lifting his glass, "where a few dozen sailors inflict more damage on the enemy than 2,000 infantry do!"

*

On the following day, a Sunday, while the chaplain performed divine service for the officers and crew aboard the flagship, Vice Admiral Graves inspected Charlestown, to survey the extent of the damage.

When he returned, he dictated a report for General Gage wherein he specified the efficacy of the bombardment, adding that a coordinated landing of marines to help the fires along and to set others, would have brought to completion the impressive but spotty work wrought by the heated shot of the ships and the Copp's Hill battery. He recommended in his report that this be taken as an example of what might be done all along the New England coast to chastise those places where rebellion could not be quelled in any other way.

After Graves had finished dictating, he asked, "Do you recall Lieutenant Jorden, naval *attaché* to General Gage?"

"The one who reported to you about the council of war yesterday morning, yes," Langdon said.

"Shot through the head by a rebel in the battle. Carried dead from the field."

Langdon shook his head in shocked sorrow.

"God-damned rebels," the admiral said quietly. "I've decided, following intelligence I received this morning regarding American fishing boats, who have been informing trading vessels of the location and activity of Royal Navy cruisers, to revoke their exemption from impressment. Beginning immediately, Royal Navy ships will be able to stop fishing boats and press their crews into the service. I've had enough of their treason."

Although Langdon knew this would inflame the ire of the rebels, he did not mention it. He had no doubt, however, that the Battle of Bunker Hill had turned the corner in the admiral's mind concerning the stiffness of measures necessary to deal with the seething revolt of the colonies. Langdon regretted it highly but knew there was no other course.

*

LETTER FROM THE REV. MR. THOMAS LANGDON TO DR. DAVID BAILEY, SURGEON OF H.M.S. CANCEAUX [extract]

SUNDAY, JUNE 18, 1775. H.M.S. *PRESTON* IN BOSTON HARBOUR. (. . .) So it is to be all-out war. The army is nursing its wounds, and accusations are flying in every direction regarding the lack of imagination among the leadership in planning and executing the battle. General Henry Clinton seems to have emerged as the hero of the day, if there be any heroes from such an ignominious action. His scheme is deemed to have been the one that should have been adopted; and his gallant last-minute arrival in Charlestown to rally the leaderless left flank (General Pigot had been carried away wounded) was the stuff of portraiture. With those who died of their wounds overnight, British losses have mounted towards 200, and American losses are estimated around 80 dead and 30 taken prisoner.

Admiral Graves, rather than being in high dudgeon about the failure of the army (as I would have expected, and which is the dominant emotion among most of the naval officers around me), seems to be very excited about the damage inflicted on Charlestown. He is convinced that this should form the model of other actions along the New England coast, chastising those localities which have committed depredations and carried out treasonous designs against His Majesty's government and armed forces. While I can understand his resolve, I nevertheless feel that there is little to be won from the destruction of personal property and the chastisement of civilians, no matter how treasonous and concerted their actions. If this rebellion is to move towards war, then it must be carried out by armed forces on the field of battle, rather than by depredations committed against civilians, no matter how deserving.

During my sermon this morning it began raining, so I curtailed it. The rain is felt as a great blessing, washing the blood from the grass of Breed's Hill, and the smell of gunpowder and the ash of Charlestown from the air. (. . .)

Chapter Twenty.

"Gentlemen," Vice Admiral Graves addressed the assembled officers around the great table, which included Flag-Captain Robinson, all the lieutenants, and the sailing master. It was a week after the Battle of Bunker Hill. "I have observed that the construction of men-of-war's boats render them rather unfit for going up the narrow creeks, inlets, and waterways which abound in this and other New England bays. If they take to the ground – which is very easy owing to their great draught of water – and there is not room for them to turn about quickly, it makes retreat impracticable and makes the crew easy prey to rebel marauders. I have made some sketches of a new kind of boat – " he indicated several sheets of paper lying in front of him, which were blackened with sketches, calculations, and measurements. He had a glint in his eye which communicated clearly to those who knew him that he was enamored of his idea, and not a little proud.

"If we were to have vessels like this at our disposal," he distributed the sketches, "we'd be able to chase the rebels right back into the holes from whence they creep out to annoy us."

He remained silent for a moment, allowing them to examine the sketches. Then he resumed his description: "The boat is 36 feet long, and nearly 12 in width, which makes for a shallow draught – drawing nine or ten inches at most; but the real genius is that the keel would curve upwards to a point at either end, causing the greatest draught to be precisely amidships, and the boat would have neither bow nor stern . . . that is to say, both bow and stern would be identical, and the oar locks could be placed in such a way as to allow the boat to be rowed with either end foremost. By means of her curved keel, she would be admirably formed for mooring quickly forward or backward, without the necessity of turning round, so in all cases to approach or make off from the shore with equal ease and speed as occasion should require. I believe that a four-pounder placed in a wooden groove at either end, and a half-dozen swivels along the sides, would make the boat a menacing sight to any rebel. If she were to run aground from eagerness of pursuit, or in the night, the rowers have only to face about on their seats, pull in the contrary direction, and she'll be off in a moment. She could hold up to 75 armed men, or fewer when, say, a week's provisions were also aboard for an extended coastal or amphibious operation."

"What sort of leeway do you think she would make, given the shallow draft and wide beam?" asked the sailing master.

"Ah, that remains to be seen, obviously, and, true, it could be a possible weakness. We won't know for certain until we've made one."

"How would she be steered?" Captain Robinson inquired.

"By an oar in a grummet which could be moved to either end," he replied, pointing at a drawing in the corners of one of the sheets. "I am going to have an artificer make a neat model, which I will send to their lordships at the admiralty. I believe it would be a formidable weapon in our arsenal for the kind of warfare we are experiencing. Additionally, I think it would be an able support vessel to a squadron which was ordered, say, to set a town afire. As I learned by inspecting Charlestown following the battle last week, heated shot and carcasses do well enough by themselves, but are not exhaustive or comprehensive in either their destructive or incendiary capabilities. Thus, if it is deemed necessary that a party of marines make forays ashore to assist in the igniting of buildings, a boat like this would be ideal to set them ashore and take them out again, with the ease and quickness of lightning."

Captain Robinson was nodding thoughtfully. After a moment, he said, "Do you really think there will be much burning of towns?"

"I do. I think it an apt chastisement for treason, and a formidable weapon in our dealing with rebellion in the magnitude to which it has grown. I have proposed the idea to General Gage, and he has indicated his initial approval."

All were silent for a moment. Captain Robinson began cautiously, "I must say, sir, that I have certain grave reservations about the burning of colonial towns. I think the non-differentiation of military and civilian targets might weaken our claims of defending the right of parliamentary and royal jurisdiction over the colonies, and instead make us seem like tyrants committing depredations."

"I thought much as you do, Captain Robinson, during the first year or more of my command here. But, as the rebels have turned this disagreement of theirs not only into an armed conflict, where they presume to hold His Majesty's forces beseiged in Boston, but into all-out warfare, I feel not only justified anymore, but *compelled* to this step. For instance, have the rebels themselves differentiated between military and civilian targets? Have they shown themselves to be respecters of non-combatants – of the private property of loyalists, like our chaplain, who have been savagely driven from their homes, their livings, their belongings, with nary a scruple? I am persuaded that we must begin to return fire with fire. It is apparently the only language they choose to comprehend. We must begin to punish treason – and *that* is what it is – with measures appropriate to the gravity of the crime."

*

AS THE SUMMER DREW ON, the rebels continued to prosecute the siege of Boston with vigilance, never again attempting to take Charlestown Neck, which General Gage fortified after the battle; but threatening to entrench on Dorchester Heights to the south of Boston, and this time with much more forethought and skill than they had done on Bunker and Breed's Hills.

General Washington, who took command of the American army in early July, proved to be a skillful opponent – skillful in that he exhibited more restraint and professional soldiering than his hot-headed predecessors. This made for fewer raids and less bloodshed on both sides, but also promised that the siege would not be lifted anytime soon, and that it would now be next to impossible to dislodge the rebels, even with an army of 10,000.

This change in American leadership led to much grumbling among the British, both in army and navy, as people realized that the rebels, although not yet a disciplined army, were certainly not the impetuous, disorganized mob they had been. Rather, they were a force which could at any moment put a plan into execution that would require the British to defend themselves or be driven into the sea. The governor's prior efforts at placation and his resultant complacency in fortifying his position were now seen as having been a serious misjudgment. British entrenchments on Roxbury Neck were fortified, and the redoubt built by the rebels on Breed's Hill was strengthened and augmented by another on Bunker Hill.

Greater thought was given to defense of the city, and intelligence as to the rebels' number and disposition were now eagerly sought. It was well known that Gage had quietly expanded his use of spies and informants in his gathering of information about the rebels.

The criticism of prior complacency was also leveled at Admiral Graves. There were murmurs from every quarter that he had not prosecuted the affairs of the squadron with adequate vigilance, firmness or spirit, but had fallen back on the comforts afforded a harbor admiral and accustomed himself to lethargy. Langdon took these rumors to be extremely unfair, and knew the admiral felt them keenly, despite his silence about them.

A week after the Battle of Bunker Hill, it was heard that Governor John Wentworth of New Hampshire had been forced to flee his residence in Portsmouth and seek refuge in Castle William and Mary, where he and his family feared daily an attack by rebels. That rebels would be able to carry the castle was very likely, in that the governor had only his personal guard – about a dozen men – and another dozen armed Loyalists with which to garrison the fortifications.

Admiral Graves immediately sent the sloop *Falcon* and a transport ship to Portsmouth, to remove from the castle all munitions and anything which could conceivably be of value to the rebels. He also strongly recommended in a letter to Governor Wentworth that he retire aboard the *Scarborough*, as "it is highly dangerous for Your Excellency to trust yourself anymore among the people." To Captain Barkley of the latter vessel, he wrote,

> Upon considering the whole of your recent correspondence and that of Governor Wentworth, I can draw no other conclusion than that the New Hampshire people are as perfectly disposed toward rebellion as those of Massachusetts Bay, and that they will endeavor by force or

stratagem to drive you away or destroy you. The few good thinking people in Portsmouth no doubt naturally disavow such outrages and base behavior, and would gladly restore and support order and legal authority; but what are their feeble efforts opposed to a whole province under the worst influence?

His Majesty's servants and good subjects should be discriminated from the rebels and have what favor can be shown them; but, in my opinion, they ought no longer to risk themselves in the power of the people, without the least security from lawless and deliberate acts of cruelty and oppression.

On the first of July, word reached Boston that the schooner *Margueritta*, which had been dispatched the previous month to Machias, Maine, to protect His Majesty's timber, masts, and spars stored there, was boarded by rebels from a number of small craft in Machias harbor, her commander killed, and the crew taken prisoner. The timber and masts, needless to say, were also carried off.

Similarly, a dispatch arrived in early July from the frigate *Rose*, stationed off Providence, Rhode Island, detailing a similar action by rebels in small craft who captured the *Rose*'s tender. The tender's crew escaped ashore, from whence they made their way back to the frigate without the loss of a single man; but the tender itself fell into rebel hands.

These reports and intelligence from many other quarters indicated increased audacity on the part of the rebels in fitting out small coastal craft to harrass and threaten the more modest of the King's ships and transports in North American waters.

Several troopships with reinforcements arrived in July, bolstering the army's number by an additional third. Although this was reassuring from the military point of view, it also meant many more mouths to feed and needs to be met, thus manifoldly increasing the want of adequate supply in the besieged city.

On July 12, a landing was made by the rebels on Long Island in Boston Harbor, where they destroyed a number of storehouses and barns filled with hay and other supplies before being driven off by His Majesty's sloop *Senegal* and a number of armed boats. Two or three rebels were killed in this action.

The news which most distressed the admiral during July came in a packet of letters from the Admiralty, conveying intelligence of an illicit trade of munitions to America from such places as Hamburg, Cuxhaven, Amsterdam, Dunkirk, Brest, Lisbon, Cadiz, and St. Eustatia in the West Indies.

"This is bad news indeed," Graves shook his head as he went over the dispatches with his secretary one morning. "Not only does it mean that our opponents in the last war are militating anew against us, thus making our work all the more difficult; but it will mean a lesser chance of real reinforcements for me. It will frighten the lords of the admiralty into thinking it is more important to have adequate forces at home, to protect against a potential threat, than to send forces far away, where the threat is actual but distant."

In conjunction with this news of illicit international trade with the colonies, General Gage sent a letter to Admiral Graves as follows:

Boston, 15th July 1775

Sir,

Since the information I sent you on Sunday in regard to the endeavors of the rebels to procure powder, I have advice that within these few days they have received 37 half barrels which was brought from New Haven in Connecticut, where it was imported from St. Eustatia. They have made application to the

Continental Congress to assist them, and have likewise employed persons at Casco Bay, where they hope to import ammunition. I think it proper to give you this notice that measures may be taken to prevent their schemes.

I am, with great regard and esteem, sir,

Thos. Gage

"Do you know who these people might be, whom the rebels have employed in Casco Bay to import ammunition?" Admiral Graves asked Langdon.

The chaplain shook his head. "It could be any one of a dozen merchants in Falmouth, sir, or someone from a neighboring town, even. Although Falmouth is by far the largest port on Casco Bay, it is not the only one."

"Do you think it could be Enoch Freeman, whom Mowat often mentioned in his dispatches as the leader of the rebellious faction?"

"Unlikely, as he is not a merchant; but I cannot say for sure."

Graves nodded, and said after a moment's cogitation, "This sort of thing distresses me very much, and I shall have to take some sort of action. I'm expecting the *Canceaux* back from Halifax within the month, and, as Lieutenant Mowat is familiar with the waters around Casco . . ." he shrugged, leaving his thought unfinished, but raising great curiosity in his secretary, and engendering a flood of pleasant associations at hearing the name of that ship and her commander again.

Not long after that it was learned that Governor Wentworth had been obliged to remove himself and his family to the *Scarborough*, as Graves had recommended. The move being rather more precipitous than he had anticipated, however, owing to the exigencies of the situation, the greater part of the New Hampshire treasury was left to the rebels, which angered General Gage and Admiral Graves immensely, as Governor Wentworth had been explicitly recommended to remove it to the *Scarborough* weeks before, and as the monies would allow the rebels better to arm and provision the army around Boston.

Admiral Graves immediately issued an order to Captain Barkley to blockade Portsmouth, allowing no provisioning or trading vessel of any kind to enter or leave the port, and to send any vessels at once to Boston which he apprehended in the attempt.

Rumors abounded around July 17 that some sort of action was to be taken by the rebels against the King's troops, as it was exactly one month after the Breed's Hill battle. This apparently came to pass on July 19, when a group of men landed on Thatcher's Island in the middle of the night and destroyed the lighthouse there. Langdon was ordered by the admiral to issue a proclamation to all ships, transports, and seamen of Boston:

> This is to give notice, that the lighthouse on Thatcher's Island (commonly called Cape Ann Lights) and the lighthouse at the entrance of Boston harbor, are burnt and destroyed by the rebels.
>
> And further notice is given, that all seafaring people be careful that they are not deceived by false lights, which the rebels threaten to hang out, in order to decoy vessels into destruction.
>
> By command of the Admiral,
>
> Thos Langdon
>
> *Preston*, at Boston, 20 July, 1775

In his next letter to the admiralty, dated 24 July, 1775, Admiral Graves made a none-too-subtle plea for reinforcements:

> The rebels have collected near 300 whale boats in the different creeks around this harbor, and make expeditions to

the islands. A few days ago 105 boats, full of men, landed on Long Island and carried off all the stock. By the boats' lightness, and drawing little water, they can not only outrow ours, but by getting into shoal water, and in calms, they must constantly escape. It is not possible to guard every island in this harbor from such piratical attempts without more armed vessels and men than can be had.

Various are the conjectures about the design of the rebels in bringing so great a number of whale boats here. Robbing the islands and burning the houses and hay thereon most certainly distresses the garrison by depriving them of fresh meat, vegetables, milk, fruit and many other advantages; but it is generally believed the boats are principally intended to land a body of men in the night at the most defenceless parts of Boston, when a general attack should be made on the lines, hoping, with the assistance of disaffected people in the town, to occasion great confusion and terror, finally leading to the defeat of His Majesty's troops.

Others are of the opinion that in a calm night they mean to surprise one of the frigates of the squadron and carry her by suddenly pouring in great numbers of people. And this leads me to mention that the very low complements of His Majesty's ships at present make the duty extremely hard in this harbor. We are obliged to keep a number of men and officers in flat bottomed floating battery boats, placed in shoal water, to flank Boston and Charlestown Necks; to man an armed transport and a sloop; and occasionally to lend men to the transports ordered on service, in the place of theirs who have deserted. In the squadron, the frigates, sloops and schooners are seldom without lent men on board. These drafts are from the three large ships, which by that means are sometimes unavoidably left in a weak and almost defenceless condition. I beg leave likewise to observe that the 20-gun ships and sloops with their present low complement of men are objects of the rebels' attention, who in their large schooners and sloops fancy they shall succeed by boarding when the King's ship is at anchor.

And then again four days later, by another packet, he wrote:

In this harbor there are only the *Somerset*, *Boyne*, *Preston*, and *Lively*, the others all sent on patrol or to procure stores from other coasts. Never were ships more wanted than at present for various services, in particular to seize every thing intended for support of the rebels; also to meet and protect those that may arrive and fall into enemy hands; and finally, to remain and form a proper force in different parts of the harbor.

The *Scorpion* arrived in Boston on July 28 from a cruise to the southern colonies, and this occasioned Admiral Graves to add another letter to the admiralty with a plea for naval reinforcements, as well as a clarification or amplification of his orders:

I transmit copies of letters I received from the governors of North and South Carolina to show their Lordships how pressing it is that an additional number of ships and small vessels be stationed on this coast.

In regard to the application of His Majesty's governors along the continent for ships and vessels of war, their Lordships, I trust, are fully apprised that it is entirely out of my power to comply with any part of their requests until reinforcements arrive from England, and until I am instructed concerning the measures Great Britain intends to pursue in consequence of the revolt of her colonies on this continent.

A few days later, during the night of July 31, another landing was made by the rebels on Thatcher's Island. The entire detail repairing the lighthouse, with their guard of thirty marines, were captured and taken before General Washington.

General Washington proved himself to be a man of civility and honor when he issued an order to his army which made its way into Admiral Graves' hands:

> The General thanks Major Tupper and the officers and soldiers under his command for their gallant and soldierlike behavior in possessing themselves of the enemy's post at the lighthouse and for the number of prisoners they took there; and doubts not, but the Continental Army will be as famous for their mercy as for their valor.

Flag Captain Robinson — who by coincidence was near the island with a number of boats full of men intended for an amphibious operation in which they had been frustrated by turncoat pilots — managed to make it to the source of the noise and commotion in time to take two of the rebel whaleboats and a handful of rebels prisoner himself. It was also suspected, although the darkness of the night forbade visual verification of the fact, that a number of rebels were killed and wounded as their boats were fired upon by Robinson's men as they fled the island.

On August 2, in a conference held in the governor's residence where the governor, the vice admiral, the three major generals, the chief justice and attorney general of the colony, and the customs controllers of Boston were present, the Boston Port Act was nullified, thus allowing any and all vessels wishing to trade with Boston to be allowed access. Indeed, the move was long overdue, as the original intent of the act had been to punish those inhabitants of Boston responsible for the Boston Tea Party. Since the vast majority of inhabitants remaining in Boston were either loyalists or members of His Majesty's armed forces, it was ridiculous to continue enforcing the act. The leaders of the conference laid themselves open to charges of willfully disobeying an act of parliament, but they were so strongly persuaded that the king and his ministers, and parliament itself, would concur with their decision, that they felt confident in taking this concerted action, and therefore took care to have every single British official of any standing in the province to be present and give concurrence.

After the conference, General Gage took the admiral aside and communicated to him the fact that he had received particular advices that two people in Falmouth, Enoch Freeman and Jedediah Preble by name, had been contracted by the rebel congress to build a number of whaleboats in Casco Bay, and were also the persons mentioned in earlier intelligence as intending to import ammunition from abroad for the use of the rebel army at Boston.

A week later, the *Falcon*, which had been sent to patrol the coast between Boston and Cape Ann, entered Boston, and the following letter was sent in by her commander, Captain John Linzee, to Admiral Graves:

Nantasket Road, 10 August 1775

Sir,

I beg leave to inform you that on the 8th instant, cruising off Cape Ann in His Majesty's sloop under my command, I discovered two schooners under sail standing in for shore. I made sail after them and very soon came up with the sternmost and detained her, putting the master and thirty men aboard her as prizemasters; the other got into Cape Ann harbor, whither I followed. On my anchoring there the same day, I sent Lieutenant Thornborough with the pinnace, long boat and jolly boat manned and armed in order to bring the schooner out. The master coming in from sea at the same time in the prize schooner, I directed him to go and assist the lieutenant.

When the boats had passed the point of rocks that was between the *Falcon* and schooner, which prevented my taking the ship any closer, they received a very heavy fire from the rebels who were hidden behind rocks and houses and behind boats aground at wharfs; but notwithstanding the heavy fire, Lieutenant Thornborough boarded the schooner and was himself and three men wounded from the shore. Upon the rebels firing on the boats, I fired from the ship into the town to draw the rebels' fire from the boats. I very soon observed the rebels paid little attention to the firing from the ship, and seeing them continually firing very heavily into the schooner, I made an attempt to set fire to the town of Cape Ann, and, had I succeeded, I flatter myself would have given the lieutenant an opportunity of bringing the schooner off.

But our attempt to fire the town failed, as the powder for that purpose was set afire before it was properly placed, and was thus rendered ineffectual.

There followed a long, detailed description of how both schooners were eventually retaken by the rebels, and the thirty people placed aboard the first schooner as a prize crew, including the *Falcon*'s master and gunner, were taken prisoner. Lieutenant Thornborough and his men, however, managed to escape and get back to the ship.

The admiral, after reading this account, slammed it onto his desk in anger, and, removing his spectacles, exclaimed, "This *does* it, God damn their eyes! I can take no more. I must use those few weapons at my disposal to show these bloody Americans we will not sit idly by while they do everything in their power to insult the king and his ministers! When the *Canceaux* has returned from Halifax, which I am to expect any day according to my most recent dispatches from Governor Legge, I am equipping a small squadron to proceed to Cape Ann, and Portsmouth, and Falmouth, and Machias, and to burn them to the ground should they not surrender the principal instigators of sedition immediately! I shall demonstrate that, with rebellious actions comes swift and deserved chastisement."

Noting the look which exhibited itself on Langdon's face, the admiral continued, "I am sorry that the innocent must suffer with the guilty, Mr. Langdon; and I am mindful of the pain it must cause you, to think of all that you once held dear being sacrificed for the sins of a few; but so it must be."

Langdon said sadly, "I pray only that God will take out of harm's way those for whom such retribution is not intended, and who are undeserving of it."

"That is what we always wish in times of war, and, although it seldom comes to pass, it is one of those things which we must accept with resignation," he said, handing him Captain Linzee's letter to copy for the admiralty.

*

The Rev'd Mr. Thomas Langdon's Journal

Friday, 11 August, 1775. Boston Harbour. The admiral seems resolved to a course of action which, if undertaken six months ago, may have had a minor effect on the course of events; but, as things have now moved very much in the direction of civil war between Great Britain and her New England colonies, I think his scheme of laying waste to offending ports will be ineffective and perhaps even counterproductive.

Unlike any other war I have read about in my study of history, this one seems to have involved an inordinate amount of manipulation of public opinion. Perhaps this is the case with many wars in their beginning stages, each side attempting to wrest the public sympathy to its benefit, and thereby winning the first (and perhaps most important) battle of the war, viz., the mantle of honour through righteousness of its cause, as perceived by the masses. Then again, perhaps when a war is between two differing peoples – the Romans and barbarians, for instance, or the English and the French – public opinion is fixed, as each people assumes its own rectitude; whereas in a civil war, factions of the same nationality are attempting to prove that their cause is the righteous one, as there is no national interest to automatically determine for the people which opponent has God on its side.

So far the rebels have been winning this battle of public opinion, so maddeningly persuasive and overbearing have been their advocates, and so disjointed and uncoordinated have been their opponents, who have erroneously felt that the apparent rectitude of their arguments needed no advocating in order to be clearly understood as the right ones. And, with the momentum strongly in their favor, I wonder whether it can be turned around at this point without interposition of military force?

No, I must continue to assert that military force alone will not turn the hearts and wills of this disaffected people, which is ultimately where this conflict is to be decided; for no military effort, no matter how strong and well supported, can possibly have any hope of lasting success except through ultimate consent of a majority of those affected.

Chapter Twenty-one.

On 8 August, the Rev'd Langdon's heart leapt within his breast at the sight of the *Canceaux* coming into Boston. He snatched a telescope from a rack near the wheel and, training it on the ship, made out the familiar, stocky form of Lieutenant Mowat on the quarterdeck.

The moment the sound of the *Canceaux*'s salute had died away, the *Preston* signalled for her commander to come aboard. Langdon made sure he was one of the side party who greeted Lieutenant Mowat's arrival at the entry port fifteen minutes later.

"Mr. Langdon," Mowat said, his face lighting up with a wide smile. "What a pleasure to see you again."

"The pleasure is mine, I assure you," Langdon said, beaming from ear to ear.

"And how have you been getting on as admiral's secretary here in Boston?"

"Very well, thank you, sir," he replied. "I am eternally indebted to you for the fact that I am risen to such a position."

"Nonsense," he said. "It is your abilities which have put you where you are. You must come and sup with me aboard the *Canceaux* one evening while I am in port. It will seem like old times again, what?"

"It would be an honor, sir."

"Is there anyone else you'd particularly like at table?"

"Dr. Bailey, if possible."

"Ah, yes, you were well acquainted, I recall. Very well. How's tomorrow evening at four o'clock?"

"I shall have to beg leave of the admiral, but barring his disapproval, four o'clock – or, *eight bells in the afternoon watch* – " Langdon smiled, "will be fine."

"I see you have not been idle in your nautical education! Good. The purser should be able to scare up something in the way of fare, I hope, befitting so treasured a guest."

"Probably not from any stores he will get from Boston," Langdon shook his head. "We are quite limited at present as to the provisions available to us, because of the siege."

"Ah, yes. Well, I think we'll have plenty left over from what we shipped at Halifax, so do not be afraid of going away hungry."

"That is something of which I have never been afraid at your table, Mr. Mowat," Langdon smiled, and Mowat, touching his hat to the lieutenant of the arrival party, was led aft to the admiral's cabin.

*

GOING ABOARD THE *CANCEAUX* AGAIN, even though only three months had intervened since Langdon had tread her planking, reminded him of those times when, having been away at college in New York for term, he had returned to Falmouth for the summer months and entered his parents' house for the first time: There was a distinct and comfortable familiarity about the house, yet it was disturbing, somehow. He remembered feeling melancholy at the thought that Falmouth had somehow gotten along very well on its own, without him. So it was with the *Canceaux*.

Master Hogg and the midshipmen, Messrs. Larkin, Barker, and Samuels, greeted the parson as he came aboard, all of them beaming with pride that their former friend and colleague was now the admiral's secretary and chaplain of the flagship. A good dozen sailors also stood smiling and bobbing as Langdon recognized them and shook their hands. In fact, he became aware of the feeling of pride, almost like a palpable substance emanating from her people, even when his boat had been hailed as it approached the ship, and the reply had been "H.M.S. *Preston*; Admiral's secretary to come aboard." At that moment, feeling himself the popular man, he'd just as soon have messed with the common sailors on the orlop deck – and had a jolly good time of it, too.

He was surprised to find in himself something like nervousness as he entered the great cabin, in anticipation of seeing Dr. Bailey. He and Mowat stood sipping sherry on the far side of the room.

They looked towards Langdon as the sentry announced his arrival, and both their faces lit up with smiles.

"Mr. Langdon," began Mowat, turning towards him. As Langdon advanced enthusiastically toward them, his head suddenly banged painfully into a deckhead beam and he nearly fell over.

"Damn...!" he said, reaching up and holding the injured area of his forehead. He was instantly aware that he had blasphemed in the presence of the other two and began apologizing for his language.

They were both immediately at his side. "Nonsense," Mowat said of the parson's apology. "I'd have cursed much worse . . . and much louder! Oh dear, it's bleeding. Dr. Bailey, could you . . ."

"I've become accustomed to the flagship's somewhat more generous proportions, it appears," Langdon said, looking at his hand and seeing the blood on his fingers in verification of Mowat's observation. It began to trickle down his forehead, collecting in his eyebrow. "And I forgot myself upon seeing you both again in such pleasantly familiar surroundings."

"Captain Mowat, sir, would you mind passing the word for a bowl of water and a bandage from the orlop deck?" the doctor said.

"Of course," he stood and left the room immediately. Bailey helped the stricken chaplain to a chair.

Langdon tried to disguise his embarrassment by saying, "How

very good it is to see you again, David. I've missed you."

David smiled broadly. "Likewise, I assure you, my friend," he said, returning his attention to the cut.

At this moment Lieutenant Mowat re-entered the room with a bowl of water and explained that Mr. Larkin was fetching the bandage.

Although Langdon did not have opportunity to address Dr. Bailey in confidence again that evening, the two sentences they had managed to exchange stood out in Langdon's mind as the chief content of the evening, the rest of it being a mere footnote.

*

O<small>N</small> A<small>UGUST</small> 17, barely a week after her arrival, Admiral Graves sent the *Canceaux* to the Piscataqua, escorting a storeship with provisions for the *Scarborough*. The *Somerset*, too, was ordered away, to Halifax, partly because she was in need of heaving down and repairing, but also because there had been some disturbing reports about the vulnerability of the King's installations in that northern harbor and their inadequate defenses against rebelliously inclined raiding parties from Maine. A 64-gun guardship would put that matter to rest, Admiral Graves was confident.

The *Canceaux* returned in company with the *Sphynx* and *Scarborough* on the 25th, the latter with Governor John Wentworth of New Hampshire on board.

On the 26th, H.M. Sloop *Hunter* arrived from England after a lengthy passage of nearly two months' time. Her commander, upon coming aboard, frustrated Admiral Graves in that he carried with him no orders or dispatches from the admiralty save to place himself under the admiral's command.

"They have now surely had word of the skirmish at Lexington, and should have no question as to the warlike intentions of the populace here," Graves said to Langdon disappointedly after his meeting with the commander of the *Hunter*. "I should therefore have thought that I would have clearer directions as to what the ministry's policies towards the colonies are." He paused. After a moment he continued.

"As you know, Mr. Langdon, I have been very suspicious of Americans ever since taking command of this station," he began. "I have witnessed too many incidences of betrayal and deceit to feel confident in employing them in positions of any responsibility whatsoever. Certainly, I am more than happy employing loyal Americans as common sailors – indeed, in the last war, every British man-of-war had a few Americans aboard, and they were generally recognized as among the ablest and most industrious of our people. Since the unrest began, however, if there is any trust to be invested in a position or an order, I have advised my officers to place such trust in an Englishman first, a Scotsman second, a Welshman or Irishman third, and an American last."

Langdon wondered what he was getting at.

"What astonishes me, therefore, given this distrust," he continued, "is that I have taken an American as my secretary, to copy all my most confidential and important letters and orders, with little more than Lieutenant Mowat's word as to your loyalty. But, for some reason, I have trusted you from the very first moment I laid eyes on you."

Langdon stammered his thanks awkwardly.

Graves smiled almost furtively. "Perhaps it was your leg, dripping with water, in our first meeting!" Becoming more serious again, he continued. "It is this quality which leads me to tell you what I am about to tell you. I admit, I am curious as to your reaction to something I have decided to do, and am desirous of having your opinion of it."

"I will do my best to provide satisfaction," Langdon said.

"Here is my situation, Mr. Langdon: Until now I have waited with great impatience for a large reinforcement from England with orders as to what my future proceedings should be – or hoping that an accommodation might yet take place between Britain and her colonies. I have thus confined my operations to intercepting the supplies coming to the rebels and guarding those intended for the King's army. Yet I remain without the least instruction for my guidance respecting the rebellion; and finding the North American provinces seriously preparing for war, and considering the manifold insults which have been dealt the cruisers of my squadron and the loyal subjects of His Majesty, I am determined to wait no longer. I must use those weapons at my disposal – weak and under-manned as they may be – to exert the authority of the crown, and to annoy the enemy in the best manner possible. And, yes, you have just heard me refer to them as 'the enemy' for the first time. Heretofore I have consistently preferred to consider the rebels as a minority of treasonous countrymen, who must be dealt with under the auspices of the law; but I now consider them to have grown so warlike and threatening to the very livelihood of friends of government, that they have removed themselves from the realm of the civil judiciary and placed themselves under martial jurisdiction. I must now refer to them, therefore, as 'the enemy,' as much as that pains me when such words are directed against fellow countrymen.

"And what I purpose to do, concerning the heretofore mentioned weapons, is to equip a squadron to descend on certain New England coastal towns, and to lay waste to them when incontrovertible evidence can be produced demonstrating rebellious or piratical activity; and also when, having proven such activity, the town refuses to repent of its treason, swear allegiance to the king, and turn over munitions, boats, lumber, and any other material intended for warlike purposes, as well as the leaders of such foment in their midst.

"I intend to put Lieutenant Mowat in command of this squadron, as he is very familiar with the coast to the north and east of Boston, as well as having demonstrated the fiery zeal and spirit which such a mission shall require. I intend to fit howitzers and mortars into the *Symmetry* and *Spitfire*, and to request of General Gage a number of soldiers to accompany the squadron, thereby equipping it for both bombardment and landings of soldiers."

The easy and highly developed flow of his sentences demonstrated to Langdon the maturity of his thoughts on the subject, proving it had been ruminating in his head for many weeks, if not months.

"I take it that Falmouth is among those to be chastised," Langdon stated.

Graves nodded his head.

"And, I assume the intent is not to execute the persons who reside in such towns, but merely to destroy the property with which they carry on their rebellious preparations?"

"Precisely."

"May I speak freely, sir?" Langdon asked.

"That is precisely why I have brought you into my confidence."

"Then I must say that I am convinced the rebels will use such a show of force as another demagogic tool to accuse the British of oppression, depredation and tyranny, thus aiding their attempts at swaying the opinions of the remaining moderate, undecided colonists to their side."

"Well, that is unavoidable whatever we do," Graves observed. "I am proposing to pursue that strategy which in the long run I believe will be most beneficial to His Majesty's authority, dignity and honor in the colonies, without regard to how the demagogues will pervert the intentions which underlie my actions." The admiral paused reflectively for a moment. "Do you have any other opinions to express – as an American – about this course of action?"

Langdon felt troubled at heart. He felt that his opinions were being polled and interpreted as representing all or many Americans, and that therefore there was a great burden on him to speak representatively rather than personally. Would the admiral's decisions actually be affected by anything Langdon had to say? Or was the admiral's mind made up, and he was merely testing his decision on the only American he had to hand?

Speaking carefully, Langdon said, "I am aware that you are anxious to move from the defensive stance you have of necessity adopted over these last eight months and to take the offensive. Whereas I agree with this sentiment wholeheartedly, I'm not sure the particular tactic you have chosen will be as efficacious as hoped.

"On the other hand," Langdon continued, "whereas I would prefer to see the might of British arms demonstrated fairly in the field of battle against an army raised to oppose it, this is not the mode of warfare being offered by the rebels. They are, rather, marauding and raiding by night, secretly in small parties composed of all manner of persons, military and civilian alike. Likewise, they have not hesitated to confiscate and destroy the property of those who disagree with them – loyalists such as myself – which is simply what you are proposing to do in reverse. To return fire along such lines, although it would seem only logical, will be labeled barbarous by the Americans as preying on innocents, although we know that we are merely employing the same tactics as they have been using these last six months."

"Fighting fire with fire," the admiral stated.

"Yes," Langdon nodded. He felt profoundly sad, having just argued himself into espousing the admiral's scheme by his inability to positively refute it.

The admiral considered the parson's words for a few moments. Stirring himself after a time, he said, "I thank you for your thoughts, Mr. Langdon. Let us begin a letter to General Gage. I will dictate it, if you are ready." Langdon took up his pen.

"'Boston, 1st of September, 1775. Sir, Although the rebels' attack upon the King's troops on the 19th of April and their subsequent behavior would, I think, have fully justified my exerting the whole force of His Majesty's squadron under my command against the New England provinces several months ago; yet I have hitherto forebore, hoping this unhappy people would either have returned to their duty, or that before this time the final determination of Great Britain concerning them would have been known. But after repeated insults and losses which His Majesty's squadron has sustained,' --and you may later enumerate a few of these, Mr. Langdon, like the burning of vessels, the killing and imprisoning of troops, the interruption of commerce, the destroying of lighthouses and other installations, etc.-- 'I can no longer delay using the means in my power to prevent the progress of such rebellious and piratical transactions.'

"New paragraph: *'With your Excellency's approbation and assistance, I propose to lay waste such seaport towns in the New England governments as have recently dealt us injuries and insults, and are not likely to be useful to His Majesty's stores, and to destroy all the vessels within their harbors. To this end I must beg your Excellency to assist me with such men, artillery forces, ordnance, munitions etc., as His Majesty's squadron is not at present provided with, and are genuinely requisite for the intended service . . .'"

*

GENERAL GAGE'S REPLY three days later seemed cooperative to a point, promising that "I shall do all I am able in the present moment to forward the plan you have formed," but at the same time saying that he wished "that something of this kind had been proposed at an earlier period, when it would have been more in my power to furnish the supplies you demand." Gage directed the officer commanding the Royal Artillery to provide the admiral with an account of which ordnance and stores he would be able to furnish, and whether or when the artillery carpenters would be free to assist in the fitting out of the *Symmetry* and *Spitfire* with howitzers.

In the first days of September two more Royal Navy ships arrived from England, the armed schooner, H.M.S. *Halifax*, Lieutenant John De la Touche, and H.M. sloop *Viper*, Captain David Price, the latter bearing a letter from the admiralty informing Graves that he was, at last, to be reinforced.

"They've finally recognized the need," the admiral commented with a mixture of relief and bitterness. "Listen to this – this is the sort of condescension for which we British are famous:" He lifted the document and, like an actor declaiming his lines, read with sarcastic drama, "*'It being apprehended that the number of ships at present under your command may not be sufficient for effectually securing a due obedience to the laws passed in the last sessions of parliament . . .'* That's rich! After I have virtually prostrated myself before their feet in supplication for reinforcements, they inform me from out of their store of infinite wisdom that, after due consideration, they have determined that the number of my ships is insufficient. And, do you notice, there is still no clarification of my orders, or any word as to what the ministry's final determination concerning her rebellious colonies is? Only that the late acts of parliament be enforced."

"Do they specify what the reinforcements are? What ships and how many?" Langdon inquired.

"Three sloops – the *Hunter* and *Viper*, already arrived, to be followed by the *Raven* – and four frigates of 28 guns, the *Actaeon*, *Lizard*, *Milford* and *Solebay*."

"Seven more ships!" Langdon observed. "That's marvelous, isn't it?"

"I could use another dozen and still have need of more, with this rebellion spreading like it is," the admiral observed. He was silent for a moment. "But you are right: Seven ships will be very helpful, especially the frigates, as I have only these rather useless battleships on the one extreme, and a raft of tiny armed brigs, sloops and schooners on the other extreme. Four frigates will be very beneficial indeed."

"Does this promised reinforcement," began Langdon cautiously, "have any bearing on your intentions regarding the offending coastal towns . . . ?"

"Do you mean, does it weaken my resolve to lay waste to them? No, I am afraid not, Mr. Langdon. I'm sorry."

*

THE FITTING OUT OF THE SQUADRON to be commanded by Lieutenant Mowat dragged on for weeks, owing to a certain intransigence on the part of the military powers ashore, and their reluctance to provide the necessary stores without the most detailed description of what the admiral's intentions were; and also, because Graves suggested that Mowat carry out much of the preparation by night, in order that rebel spies would be unable to observe the goings on and report them to General Washington. Hence, the transport of the howitzers and mortars to the *Symmetry* and *Spitfire* took place under cover of darkness, as well as of other ordnance and munitions, and the more visible aspects of installation and fitting out. Those activities which appeared routine or could be easily disguised, or were within the hull of the ships themselves, could be done, of course, during the day; but oftentimes, the carpenters, sailors and artificers stood idle for the better part of the day, awaiting nightfall to commence their work.

Meanwhile, the administration of the fleet continued and grew, including the growing number of prizes and their cargoes sent in by the cruisers on various stations, owing to Graves' increasingly forceful orders to that effect to his ships. The supply needs of the army continued to be met virtually on a hand-to-mouth basis, even with the many prizes captured by the cruisers; and transports were now beginning to return from missions to the Bay of Fundy and points southward, laden with livestock, lumber, and other materials. Although the immediate needs of the garrison were thereby now being met, there was the realization that, come Winter, the situation could become potentially catastrophic, when fuel would be more in demand, and supplies more difficult to procure.

Complicating Admiral Graves' work was the report in mid-September that an armed schooner called the *Hannah*, fitted out by General Washington and the Continental Congress, was cruising in the waters off Cape Ann and had already, on September 7, taken its first prize – the storeship *Unity*, filled with dried fish for the army at Boston. Additional reports arrived later in September that four substantial privateers were being armed in Connecticut, including a 14-gun sloop, which could conceivably pose a threat to any King's ship of equal or lesser armament. This report concerned Admiral Graves considerably, and he dispatched word to Captain Wallace of the frigate *Rose*, stationed off Providence, Rhode Island, to investigate and verify the existence of the vessels, and, if possible, to destroy them. To the King's ships cruising from Cape Cod to the Piscataqua, he gave special orders to keep a sharp eye out for the *Hannah*, as its presence lent a new menace to Britain in an arena where she had hitherto been used to complete control and was therefore especially vulnerable.

Admiral Graves one day said to Langdon, "I've been thinking about having you accompany Mowat on his mission up the coast."

Langdon was surprised. "I will, of course, serve in any way you deem fit, but . . ." It took no acuteness of observation for Graves to realize that the parson was clearly shaken by the idea.

"I've decided, actually, that the presence of an American – and a fairly prominent loyalist, as you've deservingly become – might lend a sort of moral weight to the proceedings. I would instruct Mowat to employ you as an emissary to town officials in regard to negotiations. And perhaps, as an observer, you could provide me with an account of the effects of the actions, which might prove valuable to me should I be called upon to give a defense of the mission, and to provide the justification for any future such missions in the spring." He paused and watched Langdon, as if assessing his reaction.

"Naturally, I shall do as you ask," Langdon said, attempting to conceal any shakiness in his voice.

"Good. Would you be so kind as to write a letter to Lieutenant Mowat, informing him that you will be a passenger on the *Canceaux*, or whichever ship of the squadron he deems best, for the duration of the mission. I shall have to get along with Mr. Gefferina as my secretary *pro tempore* during the weeks you'll be away."

Langdon wrote the letter to Lieutenant Mowat but exploited his position as secretary to alter the admiral's wording slightly to exclude the phrase "or whichever ship of the squadron he deems best." If he was forced to go, he wished very much to be aboard the *Canceaux*.

*

IT WAS DURING A LECTURE on the Peloponnesian Wars to the four "young gentlemen" who were to be made midshipmen that the sound of distant cannon-fire reached the upper gundeck of the *Preston*. Cannon-fire was so common in Boston, for a variety of reasons, that they did not know whether it were a ship arriving in port saluting the admiral's flag, a signal or notice from one ship to another, or another instance of rebel aggression.

"Mr. Tyler, you are excused to go on deck and, giving my

compliments to the officer of the watch, find out what is afoot," Langdon bid the youth.

Two minutes later he was back. "'Tis the *Cerberus*, frigate, newly arrived from England," he reported. "Admiral's already signaled her captain to repair on board."

"Of course he has," thought Langdon. He was sure the name *Cerberus* was not among those vessels mentioned in the last dispatches as one of the reinforcements Graves was to expect. This made the appearance of the ship very intriguing.

"H.M. Frigate *Cerberus*, sixth rate, 28 guns," reported Mr. Gibbons, one of the other pupils, breathlessly, having snatched up a copy of the navy list close to hand and looking up the frigate. "Captain John Symons."

"Can we go on deck and watch her captain come aboard?" Mr. Barker inquired very enthusiastically.

Overlooking for now his erroneous use of the word 'can,' Langdon said in the voice of a pedant, "*If* one of you can tell me what the name Cerberus means." Mr. Barker excitedly waved his hand. "Yes, Mr. Barker?"

"Oh, sir, it is a multi-headed dog, sir!"

"Indeed. And its origin, Mr. Tyler?"

"Greek mythology, sir."

"And what is this creature's duty or function, Mr. Mason?"

Mr. Mason looked terrified at the question. "T-to kill its enemies, sir?"

"More specifically. Mr. Gibbons?" Langdon turned to the fourth of the quartet, despite Mr. Barker's enthusiastic waving to be recognized.

"Um, to protect, er . . ."

"Mr. Barker, you are apparently with child to give us the answer. Go on then."

"To guard the gates of the underworld, sir. To prevent the dead from leaving. He is sometimes referred to as 'the Hound of Hades.'"

"Very good, Mr. Barker. Yes, Mr. Tyler?"

"Cerberus was captured by Hercules, sir, as one of the twelve tasks he was supposed to, um . . ."

"'Labors,' Mr. Tyler, not tasks. Mr. Mason and Mr. Gibbons, you must attend to my lessons a bit more closely. You will not always have Mr. Barker and Mr. Tyler about to answer questions for you."

"Yes, sir," the two replied sheepishly, but only perfunctorily, Langdon knew; and with a pounding of shoes they disappeared from the cabin.

Langdon was waiting expectantly half an hour later when word was passed by the admiral for him. He knew from experience that the appearance of a ship from England meant the arrival of dispatches and orders to copy.

The admiral was aglow for the first time since Langdon could well remember. He seemed a totally changed man. "Langdon," he exclaimed, "the admiralty is finally taking the rebellion seriously. They're making this a station worth commanding, at last, with real reinforcements. Look at this:" he handed him a dispatch with numbers and tables. "They're recalling the three guardships – the *Boyne*, *Somerset*, and *Asia*, which is just as well, as they are of limited use to me – and they are sending in their place . . . Just look at that abstract!" he tapped a list at the bottom of the document, summarizing all the tables. He then began counting off on his fingers, "...four more 50-gun fourth rates, two 44-gun two-deckers – (odd ships, those: neither fourth nor fifth rates, really) – and 14 more frigates of 28 and 32 guns. Combined with what's already here – and not including a separate force they plan to send to guard Halifax – that's 50 ships in all. Soon I shall be able to give my orders some real teeth, which should put the fear of God into the rebels!"

"Congratulations, sir," the chaplain said enthusiastically. "I wish you joy of the news. It is much deserved."

"They've also been apprised of the supply situation and are to begin sending regular provision ships with everything we may want to effectually carry out this war and keep the men healthy," the admiral observed as an afterthought.

"That is an even greater comfort," Langdon observed genuinely.

"Although, with the *Hannah*, and God-knows what other privateers lurking about now, I shall have to post a couple of cruisers on permanent escort duty in Massachusetts Bay, running between here and Marblehead in order to protect these incoming supply ships."

*

The Rev'd Mr. Thomas Langdon's Journal

Tuesday, 26 September, 1775. Boston Harbour. (. . .) Some hours later it was learned throughout Boston that the *Cerberus* had also brought a recall for General Gage, the king personally calling him to London for consultations, "to learn the true state of affairs in America, and to coordinate an overall strategy for the prosecution of the war." Many, including myself, have ventured to wonder whether this is not actually a permanent recall of the governor, disguised in order to dishonour Gage as little as possible before replacing him. Major General Howe, a man for whom I have little love, has been made acting governor during Gage's absence. Even with all the ill-will that passed between Gage and Graves, I doubt the admiral is any happier with the prospect of having to deal daily with Howe.

Graves spoke to me at length today about the respect he has for General Howe's brother, Admiral Richard Howe. I admitted that I had not heard of him; but then, up until this last April, I had paid very little attention to the doings of the Royal Navy, and apart from Admirals Hawke, Anson, and Boscawen (who are bywords to every Englishman, having distinguished themselves so signally in the last war), I could not have been expected to have heard of anyone. Oh, and the famous Captain Cook, of course.

A chilly morning provided the first harbinger of autumn; but as the day advanced, the temperature moderated.

Chapter Twenty-Two.

During the Night of October 2, 100 marines and their officers embarked on the *Symmetry*, armed transport. Also on that day, as the schooner *Hope* had grown so leaky as to require being laid ashore for repairs, the admiral ordered her people into the *Symmetry* as well, for the manning of the new mortar and howitzer which had been placed in her. The ships of the squadron were ordered to complete their provisions to sail within the week.

The next morning the admiral received a cordial note from Governor Gage saying that, as he was aware of the great scarcity of warships, he had ordered a transport got ready for his trip back to England, and requested only a convoy out of American waters. Langdon was ordered to write a similarly cordial reply, assuring him of a convoy over St. George's Bank.

On October 4, the third of the sloops promised as reinforcements, the *Raven*, arrived. Langdon was in the midst of collecting some things in a trunk to have transported to the *Canceaux*, but the advent of this sloop, again with numerous dispatches, delayed his transfer for another day, as there was much to copy, information to be disseminated, and replies to be written.

"Here, read this, Mr. Langdon," the admiral said upon his coming into the great cabin. He took an impressive, official-looking document from his desk and handed it to the clerk. Langdon saw the king's escutcheon at the top, with lion and unicorn flanking it. "It just arrived by the *Raven*."

By the King, A Proclamation for Suppressing Rebellion and Sedition.
George *Rex*.

Whereas many of our subjects in diverse parts of our colonies and plantations in North America, misled by dangerous and ill-designing men, and forgetting the allegiance which they owe to the power that has protected and sustained them, after various disorderly acts committed in disturbance of the public peace, to the obstruction of lawful commerce, and to the oppression of our loyal subjects carrying on the same, have at length proceeded to an open and avowed rebellion, by arraying themselves in hostile manner to withstand the execution of the law, and traitorously preparing, ordering and levying war against us;

To the end therefore that none of our subjects may neglect or violate their duty through ignorance thereof, or through any doubt of the protection which the law will afford to their loyalty and zeal; We have thought fit, by and with the advice of our Privy Council, to issue this our Royal Proclamation, hereby declaring that not only all our officers civil and military are strictly charged and commanded to exert their utmost endeavors to suppress such rebellion, and to bring the traitors to justice; but that all our subjects of this realm and the dominions thereunto belonging are bound by law to be aiding and assisting in the suppression of such rebellion, and to disclose and make known all traitorous conspiracies and attempts against us, our crown and dignity; and for that purpose, that they transmit to one of our principal secretaries of state, or other proper officer, due and full information of all persons who shall be found carrying on correspondence with, or in any manner or degree aiding or abetting the persons now in open arms and rebellion against our government within any of our colonies and plantations in North America, in order to bring to condign punishment the authors, perpetrators, and abettors of such traitorous designs.

Given at our court at St. James's, the twenty-third day of August, One thousand seven hundred and seventy-five, in the fifteenth year of our reign.

God save the King.

"What do you say of that?" Graves ventured when Langdon had finished reading.

"Pretty stern stuff," he said, unsure of what the admiral was getting at. "Also the longest single sentence I have ever read."

"Wouldn't you say it is the closest thing to a declaration of war that a mother country can make against her own colonies?" he probed.

Langdon considered the question for a moment, reviewing a few of the phrases in the text. "Yes, I suppose it is," he said.

"It leaves little doubt in my mind, with words like, 'all our officers civil and military are strictly charged and commanded to exert their utmost endeavors to suppress such rebellion, and to bring the traitors to justice,'" Graves quoted without looking at it, having committed that phrase already to memory.

Graves then reached to his desk for what Langdon recognized as admiralty dispatches. "And *this* is what I've been waiting for all along – definite orders *'to carry on such operations upon the sea coasts of the four governments in New England as you should judge most effectual for suppressing the rebellion now openly avowed and supported in those colonies . . . and further, if any violences should hereafter be done to officers of the crown or peaceably disposed subjects, it would be your duty to proceed by the most vigorous methods against such persons or towns in open rebellion.'* With this squadron under Mowat, together with the recent orders I have sent to commanders from Savannah to Quebec, I have anticipated their Lordship's order, and am able to implement it immediately," Admiral Graves stated with no little satisfaction and pride.

*

Commodore Mowat's orders

Whereas the four New England governments are in open and avowed rebellion against His Majesty, and they have been daring enough to make seizures of several of His Majesty's ships and vessels, and to send the crews to prison, and have also fired upon and killed and wounded many of the King's subjects serving aboard His Majesty's ships; and whereas there is undoubted intelligence of their fortifying their seaports, and of their determination to cut off and destroy His Majesty's subjects serving in his fleet and army whenever it is in their power;

And whereas I have caused the *Symmetry* transport and *Spitfire* sloop to be armed and fitted in the best manner the situation of our affairs would admit, in order to proceed along the coast and lay waste, burn and destroy such seaport towns as are accessible to His Majesty's ships; and whereas from your having been employed many years on the survey of the coast to the eastward of this harbor, you cannot but be qualified to carry on this service from your knowledge of all the harbors, bays, creeks, shoals; and having full confidence in your integrity, loyalty and naval experience, and in particular for your late spirited and judicious conduct at Falmouth, I have thought proper that you should command this expedition.

You are therefore hereby required and directed to take the *Symmetry* and *Spitfire* under your command together with His Majesty's schooner *Halifax*, as well as the ship under your own command, and proceed with them as soon as possible to Cape Ann Harbor, that town having fired in the month of August last upon His Majesty's sloop *Falcon*, wounded her people and taken many prisoners; you are to burn and destroy and lay waste the said town together with all vessels and craft in the harbor that cannot with ease be brought away. Having performed this service you are to take advantage of wind and weather, or any other favorable circumstances, to fall upon and destroy any other towns or places within the limits aforesaid, and all vessels or craft to seize or destroy.

My design is to chastise Marblehead, Salem, Newbury Port, Portsmouth, Ipswich, Saco, Falmouth in Casco Bay, and Machias where the *Margueritta* was taken, the officer commanding her killed, and the people made prisoners, and where the *Diligent* schooner was seized and the officers and crew carried prisoners up the country, and where preparations I am informed are now making to invade the Province of Nova Scotia.

You are to go to all or to as many of the above-named places as you can, and make the most vigorous efforts to burn the towns, and destroy the shipping in the harbors. And as the number of marines you carry in the vessels are too few to land and maintain any post, you are to be careful not to risk their lives or the lives of any of your people by attempting where there is no great probability of success, but to content yourself with falling upon the rebels, doing what you can with expedition and coming away before they can assemble to cut off your retreat, and never risk your ships aground or where you cannot put to sea at all times of tide, wind permitting.

You are to bestow your whole attention to annoying the rebels and the security of your own vessels; to observe in all your operations the strictest discipline, not to suffer plundering on any account, as I will make an example of whomever shall presume to be guilty of it.

Whenever you can distinguish the persons or property of those who have taken no part in the rebellion and have given proofs of their attachment to the constitution by refusing to concur in the unwarrantable measures that have been adopted to subvert it, you are to protect and defend them in the utmost of your power.

I leave entirely to your own discretion where to go and when to return, relying on your zeal for His Majesty's service and the good of your country for the steady and effectual execution of these orders.

Given under my hand on board His Majesty's Ship *Preston* at Boston the 6th of October, 1775.

Sam[l] Graves.

By Command of the Admiral
Tho[s] Langdon

Compared to most of the orders Langdon had copied for the admiral since early June, these were some of the longest and most detailed he had yet encountered, attesting to the importance and non-routine nature of the expedition.

Once aboard the *Canceaux*, Langdon was berthed in that space so familiar to him from letter-writing of old, the chart room, and was plied with coffee and breakfast the moment he had come aboard.

The squadron set sail the following day with the wind in its favor but the sky to the west looking threatening. Indeed, having come up to Cape Ann and anchored, the squadron was suddenly beset by squally weather: intermittent downpours, generally gusty and unpredictable winds, and a constantly changing swell. The dinner that had been planned in Mowat's cabin that evening with the commanders of all the vessels was cancelled due to the perils of sending boats out in such weather, and the impossibility of setting a table. Langdon dined on cold ham and a hard-boiled egg with Dr. Bailey in his cabin.

"An inauspicious beginning to the mission," the parson said at one point before lifting a pewter tankard of small beer to his lips. An unexpected plunge of the ship to starboard caused foam and no little of the beer to slosh over his upper lip and down his chin onto his waistcoat. He cursed as he wiped it away.

"That's the second time I've ever heard you blaspheme since we've returned from Halifax," Dr. Bailey observed. "It appears the sailors have had rather more of an influence over their chaplain than the opposite!"

"I can assure you that my godly life has had a most wholesome effect on the *Preston*'s people, such that they neither curse nor blaspheme anymore."

Dr. Bailey laughed.

"And they beg the admiral to allow divine service not just on Sundays, but every day of the week!"

"And the admiral no doubt says Morning and Evening Prayers with you at the beginning and close of each day."

". . . on his knees," Langdon added. "He has had me bless his every possession, asks my godly advice on every decision he makes for the good of the fleet, and were I not so staunchly against popery, he would no doubt have given me his confession by now."

When their laughter had subsided, Dr. Bailey asked, "What's he really like, Admiral Graves?"

Langdon pondered for a moment before replying. "He is very opinionated and quick to judge, but that often makes for a resolute leader, I think, whatever other faults such a nature has. His temper is quickly ignited, which frightens me on occasion; but I have also seen him privately confused and full of doubt, and thus know there is softness under the brittle and hard exterior. He can be a whirlwind of energy when the situation calls for it, such as on the day of the Bunker Hill battle. And I have twice seen him laugh and smile like a boy when given good news or shown something which amuses him. I am told he is a personal friend of Lord Sandwich, the First Lord of the Admiralty – and that that's what he owes his command of this station to – but privately he is very frustrated with both Sandwich and the ministry. Again, this is in spite of the fact that he is politically a Tory, and therefore publically sympathetic to them."

Dr. Bailey nodded wordlessly. "Reminds me a little of Mowat," he observed after a time.

"Now that you mention it, yes, although I think Mowat is fairer minded to all people, regardless of station and rank. Admiral Graves is highly suspicious of Americans, and has that air of snobbery commonly associated by colonists with the English. Mowat judges each man on his proven merits, rather than his nationality or background."

"Still, their similarities may account for Mowat being given the command of this squadron, even though Lieutenant De la Touche of the *Halifax* – who is part of this expedition – is senior to him."

"Very likely so," Langdon nodded, "although Mowat's knowledge of the coastline between here and the Bay of Fundy was the deciding factor, I think."

*

BOTH THE *SYMMETRY* AND *SPITFIRE* were blown broadside to leeward by a mighty gale of wind from the northwest that struck the squadron at 1 a.m. Consequently, after a fruitless beating up and down in front of the entrance to the harbor the following day, Mowat signalled the squadron to bear up for Cape Cod, where he could shelter the ships for the next night, until the storm blew over.

When they came to under the cape just before dusk several hours later, a schooner was sighted under the east shore, and Mowat signalled the *Halifax* and *Spitfire* to pursue. At about 7 o'clock in the evening, the darkening sky was lit up with the flashes of gunfire, but the sound was lost in the heavy wind. The two ships returned around 10 p.m. and reported that they had run the schooner ashore.

Mowat got the convoy under way at 3 a.m. the following morning and came up to the town of Cape Ann at daybreak. Langdon happened to be on deck with a cup of coffee as Mowat conferred with Mr. Grant, the artillery officer appointed to the expedition by General Gage, who had earlier come across from the *Symmetry* by a boat.

They both looked at the harbor and the town, using telescopes and pointing here and there as their conversation continued.

"I am much afeared of the number and quality of the carcasses and charges shipped at Boston, Cap'n Mowat," Grant said, shaking his head. "If the buildings of the town were closer together – where a single carcass could ignite several – why then, I'd be more confident of success. But with so few carcasses, and what with a number of 'em probably being spoilt by the wet weather already, I think the likelihood of doing any significant damage to the town with just mortars and cannon is very slight. An' it would therefore take so much of our ammunition stores, t'would exhaust our entire supplies on the first town."

Mowat, hands clasped firmly behind his back, continued to survey the town which lay full off the larboard broadside about a mile distant. A muscle tensed along his jaw as he clenched his teeth. "Very well," he concluded. "Considering the ill consequences of a disappointment in the first attempt of this expedition, and the advantage of encouragement it would afford the rebels, we will not execute a bombardment at this time. You may return to the *Symmetry*, Mr. Grant, and tell her master that we will be taking advantage of the favorable wind this morning to go as far up the coast as possible today."

Coming to the parson's side, Mowat said more quietly as Mr. Grant clambered to his boat, "We will head for Machias next, even though it is the most distant. The wind is in our favor, so we will gather rosebuds while we may, what?"

Langdon nodded. He dared not voice his concern that Mowat was passing Cape Ann Harbor without a shot fired, as it was so specifically mentioned in his orders. Langdon recalled one of the final sentences of that document, however, which would give Mowat opportunity to defend his decision, namely, "I leave entirely to your own discretion where to go and when to return."

The squadron made it a good way up the coast, only to be met by another storm which delayed it yet another day, spent at anchor in Townsend Bay, Maine, which was very near Falmouth. During this time, as the weather had taken a great toll on the state of the ships and men, Mowat decided that they would sail directly to Falmouth, and do their first work in that port instead of Machias.

*

When the town of Falmouth first came in sight as the squadron rounded Hogs Island the following day, Langdon's heart leapt into his throat as the familiar contour of buildings and structures hove into view. The steeple of St. Paul's Church caught his eye particularly, and it took a physical effort to keep back the tears which threatened to break forth.

As the squadron approached nearer, however, Langdon was appalled at how changed the town was in its details. Where once white-washed siding had presented its cheerful face to the bay, now stained and sullied walls draped depressively in sagging fish netting looked haggardly out on the newcomer. Where once window panes had reflected the light of the sun, now gaping holes and the jagged vestiges of shattered glass told of the abandonment and looting of many buildings. Where once carefully trimmed grass and hedges had lined the commons and roadways, now mud, defaced earth, and misshapen weeds told of the comings and goings of angry multitudes, and the loss of civic pride which came from the remaining inhabitants' fear and uncertainty of the future.

Dr. Bailey stood silently next to the former vicar of St. Paul's as they approached the familiar town. Langdon searched out his house – or its roof, at any rate – behind the storehouse of Moses Pearson which his father had so hated for obstructing their view of the bay.

"I am realizing by what a tenuous thread hangs the public peace and the order of our lives," Langdon observed.

"How so?"

"Remove the overall authority in a society – even one as distant and relatively unthreatening to Massachusetts as Great Britain, with her liberal constitution and humane philosophies – and fear immediately replaces security in the minds of its people, thus leading to anarchy," he replied.

"Pray continue," Bailey remarked, not having quite picked up the line of his thinking.

"What was it previously that allowed the people of Falmouth to prosper and take pride in their society? What was it that allowed them to beautify their surroundings, better their lives, and to be kind and generous to their neighbors?"

Dr. Bailey reflected a moment. "Security. The assurance of a stable society," he replied at length.

"Precisely. The knowledge that no one could come along and take from them the fruits of their labors. The knowledge that they had certain rights guaranteed by a constitution and enforced by the courts and their ministers of justice. And what backs up the authority of these? The king and, if need be, his military officers. So, in short, I can work hard to better my life because I know that if any man threatens me in my lawful livelihood, or steals the wages of my efforts, the courts will prosecute him and restore what is rightfully mine. With this assurance, I can well afford to be kind to my neighbor, knowing that he has no unfair advantage over me; and I can beautify my property, knowing that it is safe from injury or defacement, and that the crown stands ready to protect me in the enjoyment of all these rights.

"When this assurance is removed, however, and an unruly mob threatens to violate my rights and take my property because they no longer recognize their duty to that authority which has heretofore protected everyone's rights, the entire arrangement is upended. A small minority have thus dictated anarchy for all."

"But will not courts rectify this in your hypothetical example, and bring the minority to justice, thus restoring that authority for all?"

"That's just it, though – when the minority becomes large enough to disregard authority with impunity, saying that that authority no longer *has* authority over them; and they know that the courts cannot hold them accountable any longer, the logical and inevitable end to this situation is anarchy. Deprived of the assurance that an overall authority administers impartial justice and general equality over its subjects, each individual finds that he himself is his only advocate, and he must therefore fight for his very life if he is to survive. His society has been removed from order and commerce, reduced to the primitive state of savages. For what is commerce but the civilized interaction of equal men under the assurance that the government protects each of their individual rights.

"Hence, the only difference between the happy Falmouth which I inhabited nine months ago, and the hopeless, decaying heap which now lies before us, is that a portion of its inhabitants decided not to adhere to the social bond to which their fathers and forefathers had subscribed. For some ridiculously fabricated notion of grievances, trumped up by demagogues as tyranny and oppression, they overthrew the peaceable pursuits of society in favor of anarchy and the rule of mobs."

"It is an unfortunate paradox," observed Bailey, "that the government should threaten its wayward subjects with violence — the very oppression of which the colonists earlier complained, in fact — in order to restore peace."

"This paradox plays directly into their hands by appearing to justify their complaints," Langdon agreed.

"Excuse me for playing devil's advocate for a moment, Thomas," Bailey said, "but couldn't you conceive of a situation where a people would be theoretically justified in rising up against a cruel and tyrannical government?"

"Of course," Langdon said. "There are numerous examples throughout history where a society — or a segment of it — is subjugated or abused, or even threatened with extermination by its rulers. But do you honestly think that Britain — the most liberal and free nation in Europe — has really enslaved the colonists, as some of them claim; or has oppressed them enough to warrant such widespread unrest and misery? I hardly think that a minor question of taxation, or the occasional ill-calculated act of parliament, or even the threat of creating and sending Anglican bishops, is grounds for such unrest. For when individuals rise up in opposition to their government, even if for a righteous cause, is the result proportionate to the cause? I hardly think so in this case. Did the rebels have any right to bring such general calamity down upon *all* our heads? Certainly not. In fact, it's damned bull-headed of them to presume that they can disrupt every American's – and Briton's – life, and cause such heartache and tragedy, merely due to their selfish and elusive grievances.

"I mean, look at it, David," Langdon touched Bailey's shoulder and gestured towards Falmouth, feeling the tears begin to well up in his eyes again. "Look at the misery and ugliness which are yonder. Is it right that a handful of Falmouth's inhabitants should have turned a happy, well-tended society into *that*? Is it right – no matter the reason – for one group of people to force the *whole* into civil unrest and its unhappy consequences? I find it difficult to justify, especially when I consider that it all happened simply because of a silly objection to certain taxes, or some minor philosophical differences with a heretofore benevolent and suppliant government. It is un-English, un-Christian, and a damned shame."

"The remaining people of Falmouth may not keep up the town as well as the old inhabitants once did," Dr. Bailey observed, "but what of the potential destruction to come, from the guns of this very squadron? How will that be any better than letting it fall to wrack and ruin on its own?"

"The rebels have brought the coming retribution upon themselves," Langdon said with something akin to sulkiness. He was conscious that he did not entirely believe his own statements. Just as a young man who is rejected by a potential lover claims irrationally that he hates the very one with whom he so desired intimacy, so Langdon vented his wrath on those he felt were responsible for his misery by saying they deserved to be struck a blow. "Although I grieve to see my hometown laid in ashes, the treason which this people has committed deserves such punishment, I'm sorry to say."

Bailey remained silent, allowing his friend to be sullen without judging him for it.

*

The Rev'd Mr. Thomas Langdon's Journal

Monday, 16 October, 1775. H.M.S. *Canceaux* in Casco Bay, not distant from Falmouth Harbour. The squadron sailed up the coast from Townshend Bay into Casco, and anchored in the lee of Hogs Island, within sight of Falmouth. Many people gathered intermittently on the shore to watch our slow progress up the bay to our anchorage (a strong north-westerly prevented our direct approach). They seem untroubled by our appearance. Mowat has said he intends to send a letter ashore on the morrow informing them of his intentions, and giving them two hours to remove themselves from the town before it is bombarded. I heartily wish Graves had not sent me on this mission.

Chapter Twenty-three.

The squadron ahchored before Falmouth at 4 p.m. on October 17 with the *Canceaux* in the van, furthest to the northeast, the *Halifax* behind her, and the *Symmetry* and *Spitfire* behind and closest to the main part of the town.

It was difficult to tell from the deck of the *Canceaux* what the town's reaction to the squadron's appearance was. A few souls stood on the wharves, shading their eyes from the sun – which was an unexpected but welcome change from the storms experienced during the first week of the mission – but others could be seen scurrying from building to building, pointing with alarm.

Mowat immediately dispatched his barge with Midshipman Larkin to shore, bearing a letter Langdon had assisted him in writing earlier in the day informing the people in simple terms of his orders; that, because of the treasonous offences committed by the town's foremost authorities, he had been ordered to destroy the town and its shipping. If they consented to deliver up to Mowat's custody Enoch Freeman and Jedediah Preble, as the most prominent of said authorities; surrendered all arms and ammunition; and agreed to declare their renewed allegiance to the king, he would spare them from bombardment. If not, then he would begin bombardment in the morning, and advised that inhabitants vacate the town by dawn.

When Mr. Larkin returned half an hour later, he reported scenes of confusion and panic, with people running hither and thither in great alarm. He also said that a committee of gentlemen, namely Dr. Nathaniel Coffin and Thomas Pagan, had been formed by the town to wait upon Commodore Mowat in order to learn the reason for his orders.

Langdon was filled with a mixture of emotions at hearing those familiar names spoken. He felt alternately a strong desire to see them – especially as they had been parishioners of St. Paul's – and yet a desire to distance himself from the whole situation and disappear below decks. The admiral's purpose in having him accompany the mission, however, dictated that he be present in the cabin when they appeared, which they did within the half-hour.

"Good afternoon, gentlemen," said Mowat when they stood humbly in the great cabin, hats in hands. Both seemed somewhat surprised to see their former comrade Langdon at the commodore's right hand. "Be so good as to tell me your business," Mowat continued in a business-like but not unsympathetic tone of voice.

"With all due respect, Commodore Mowat," Dr. Coffin began hesitantly, "the town has appointed us to wait upon you, desiring to know the nature of the chastisement apparently ordered upon us by Admiral Graves."

"My orders are to burn the town and destroy its shipping, in punishment for its crime of treason and rebellion against His Majesty; and for its subsequent role as a clearinghouse for smuggled ammunition to the rebels. Should you choose to deliver to my custody Enoch Freeman and Jedediah Preble as prisoners, as Admiral Graves has had intelligence that they have been the principal smugglers of said ammunition; and you declare renewed allegiance to His Majesty the King as a community, I have the discretion to spare you from this destruction," he said in clipped, emotionless tones.

"What, if I may ask, Commodore Mowat," Dr. Coffin ventured, "are the specific charges of treason against us?"

Mowat sighed. "Must I really rehearse the well-known outrages committed by certain inhabitants of this town against not only myself, a King's officer, and the people and property under my command; but also – and more grievously – against the loyal subjects of His Majesty who, until recently, continued peaceably in your midst, but have lately been compelled to flee for their very lives?"

"There are some loyal subjects, including we who stand before you," interjected Dr. Coffin, "who continue here, despite the outrages you have alluded to, Commodore Mowat. Is not the burning of the entire town a much too broad and severe punishment for the crime of a few, especially to those of us who have persevered in our loyalty?"

"Indeed, I have been authorized to distinguish those who have never taken any part in the rebellion and have given proofs of their attachment to the constitution. I shall do my utmost to spare the property of such persons, including yourselves and anyone else you may wish to bring to my attention. This may be, in the end, impracticable, but I shall do my best."

"What would become of Messrs. Freeman and Preble in your custody?" Mr. Pagan asked.

"They would be transported to Boston, and there stand trial before the governor for treason, smuggling, and possibly other charges," Mowat replied.

There was a brief silence. "The delivering up of arms might conceivably be effected, Captain Mowat," Dr. Coffin said. "But even a man loyal to the crown such as myself would not venture to ask my neighbor to submit himself to arrest and trial, in order to save my personal property from destruction. I speak only for myself, of course, but I cannot imagine that your terms would be found acceptable by even the few remaining friends of government still residing in Falmouth, not to mention those disposed to rebellion."

"What am I to say?" Mowat asked. "I had entertained hopes that Mr. Freeman might come to his senses when he assisted us in escaping from that odious Colonel Thompson. But, as you have heard, he has been identified as smuggling munitions through Falmouth. Do you have any information on this score?"

"Mr. Freeman had a hard time of it after assisting your escape," Dr. Coffin stated. "But then he renounced his actions, said he regretted them, and proclaimed publicly that if Mowat and the rest of you were in captivity again, he would kill you all himself with no pang of conscience, in order to advance the cause of liberty. He was absolved of the £158 he had promised to pay, which, I think, was partly responsible for his changed tune. Nevertheless, he has gone on to become the loudest voice of sedition in town – the loudest of many very loud voices, now."

"I am very sorry to hear it. I had come to hope more from him," Mowat said. "But to be absolved of a debt of that magnitude is a very great motivator, I have no doubt."

"We shall represent your demands to the town council, Commodore Mowat," Dr. Coffin said quietly, "although I am certain that it will not be in its power to acquiesce."

"Well, see what can be done, and I shall await your communication no later than 8 o'clock tomorrow morning, gentlemen."

There followed a long silence, broken by Dr. Coffin, who asked quietly, "Is there no way we can prevent you from carrying out your orders, Captain Mowat?"

"I *must* obey my orders," Mowat said simply. "Before morning you may acquaint me with the location of the homes and properties of loyalists, that I may attempt to spare them." He turned to Langdon, "Do we have a map of the town, Mr. Langdon?"

"I can easily draw one," he replied. Turning to Coffin and Pagan, he said, "I am much aggrieved."

At this point the conference was ended, and the gentlemen of the town left the cabin. Langdon followed them onto deck and managed to engage Mr. Pagan in a brief conversation before he descended over the side.

"How is your family, Mr. Pagan?"

"We are much in want; but we survive as long as we keep our sympathies to ourselves. It is the same with Dr. Coffin and any other loyalists still about. Dr. Coffin is shown more deference than most of us, as he is the only reputable physician remaining in town, and is therefore needed by everyone, regardless of his political sympathies."

"What of St. Paul's? Do any of the parishioners still meet for morning or evening prayers?"

He shook his head. "A number of us persisted for a few weeks following your departure; but then crowds of angry people began forming outside the church on Sunday mornings, glaring at us threateningly as we emerged from the church, thus intimidating us into disbanding the congregation. The churchwardens attempted for a number of weeks thereafter to keep the keys of the church in their hands, but were eventually compelled – on threat of violence, vandalism, and even death – to surrender them to town authorities, the church to be turned to civic use. In fact, it is where the smuggled arms and ammunition have sometimes been warehoused."

"I am devastated – and *enraged* – to hear this. The use of a sacred space for such a thing! It is a desecration!"

"Rumors around town would have it that you were appointed chaplain aboard Admiral Graves' flagship, yet here you are, still aboard the *Canceaux*."

"I am indeed chaplain aboard the flagship," Langdon replied, choosing not to say that he was also the admiral's secretary.

"But why are you here, then?"

"Admiral Graves wanted me to accompany Mowat on this mission, that I might bring back an accurate report," he said, unwilling to divulge anything more. "Tell me of Mrs. Ingersoll," Langdon said.

"She persists, like us, by remaining as quiet as a mouse. But she is much in want. St. Paul's was her life, and she has nothing to occupy herself with anymore."

"Have you heard from the Oxnards? Has Polly been delivered of her child?"

"I have not heard of them since they left town in May," Mr. Pagan said. Then, after saying he was happy to find his old vicar in good health, doffed his hat and took his leave.

At 8 o'clock that evening, Dr. Coffin returned with six stand of arms as token of his willingness to attempt to fulfill the commodore's terms, but reported sadly that Colonel Thompson's hot-headed rabble from Brunswick had arrived in Falmouth's environs over the course of the day, in response to the appearance of the squadron, and had sent representatives into town with the threat that if they complied with Mowat's demands, they themselves would burn the town down.

"So it appears," said Mowat, "that the town is to be destroyed, either way."

"God have mercy on us," said Coffin, utterly deflated, "for I do not know what we have done to deserve this."

"Such is the evil of the times," Mowat responded.

Dr. Coffin thereupon beseeched Mowat to hold off the carrying out of his orders until 9 o'clock the following morning, as it would take at least that long to clear the town of women and children. Mowat gave his word that he would do so.

*

LANGDON SPENT MUCH OF THAT SLEEPLESS NIGHT on deck, unable to sort out the multiplicity of emotions which surged back and forth within his breast. A feeling of dread anticipation of the coming day's events made the time seem to creep agonizingly by. Dr. Bailey remained with him until about an hour after midnight, and they talked of people they had known and places they had visited.

At various times during the night they heard far off drums being beaten or distant reports that sounded like gunfire (Langdon told Bailey of Lieutenant Collingwood and the sport they had made of the youth's ability to identify gunfire from a distance). It was Bailey's opinion that these were alarms being sounded, either to summon "minutemen," which had gained such notoriety at Lexington and Concord, or to warn the inhabitants in the countryside around Falmouth of the impending danger.

At the beginning of the morning watch at 4 o'clock, the people began preparing the ship for the coming day's expected bombardment. Langdon attempted to stay out of the way as much as possible, and joined Mowat in the great cabin for coffee and a light breakfast at about 6 o'clock.

"How are you feeling about all this, Mr. Langdon?" Mowat asked at one point, brushing some toasted breadcrumbs from his waistcoat. He had noticed that the parson was eating very little, poking ineffectually at his food, and looking not a little haggard from lack of sleep.

Langdon did not answer immediately, assessing the variety of impulses in his breast. He finally said, "My heart seems to skip a beat every minute or two. I have not ceased to hope that the town is compliant this morning, agreeing to your demands, and that Falmouth will thus be spared, setting an example for other New England towns as to how this conflict can be peacefully resolved."

"Do you really think there is any chance of that happening?"

"Very little," Langdon said with intense sadness.

Mowat nodded. "I'd have said none."

Punctually at 8 o'clock, Coffin and Pagan were rowed out to the flagship of the squadron and met with Commodore Mowat.

"I am afraid to report, commodore, that no significant part of the inhabitants of the town could be brought together, either last night or this morning, in order to debate your proposal, as all are in the utmost panic to remove their belongings," Dr. Coffin reported. "Mr. Preble and chairman Freeman have fled the town, having become aware of your terms." He paused, aware that they had reached the end of the line. "We therefore respectfully request that you forebear only long enough, Commodore Mowat, that we can get ashore to remove our families from their dwellings, sir."

Langdon's heart tightened, as if he had just heard the pronouncement of a death sentence.

Mowat nodded. "I am damned sorry about this, gentlemen," he said. "I had hoped that I would be able to intercede for you to Admiral Graves, as I have a genuine affection for many of you in this town. I am sorry to hear that it will not be possible. I bid you adieu, and grant you an hour to return to your families and remove them out of harm's way."

"Thank you, sir," Dr. Coffin said with visible emotion.

Mr. Pagan's eyes turned to look at Langdon pleadingly before they departed the cabin, as if he, as admiral's chaplain, might have the authority to issue a last-minute reprieve of mercy. The clergyman, filled with anguish, raised his arm and did something most uncharacteristic of him, yet which he felt somehow compelled by a higher power to do: He made the sign of the cross over them. The three gentlemen did not flinch, as one would expect Protestants to react to such a High Church, Popish gesture; but they received it almost as a measure of special favor, the horror and import of the moment seeming to warrant such a sign.

Then they were gone. Mowat looked with sympathy at the stricken priest but remained silent.

When, at length, they stirred themselves to action, Langdon left the room wordlessly, and Mowat asked Midshipman Barker to signal the commanders of the vessels in his squadron to repair on board immediately, along with Mr. Grant, the artillery officer, to confer about the day's coming action.

*

Master's Log of H. M. Armed Vessel Canceaux

Wednesday 18 Octr 1775. At single anchor with a spring on the cable, entrance of the town of Falmouth. At 9 AM light airs and fair. 35 minutes after 9 made the signal to engage. 40 minutes after 9 a smart fire begun from the *Canceaux*, *Symmetry*, *Halifax* and *Spitfire* which was keeped up by all. At 10 several houses was on fire. The fire broke out with great violens in two or three houses of the southernmost part of the town. At noon the fire begun to be general both in the town and vessels but, being calm, the fire did not sprede as wished for. At 1 PM small breezis from the south'rd. At ½ past the town house and the English Church begun to burn. A brisk fire was keeped up by all the squadron. At 2 fresh breezis and hazey weather. There being several houses toward the southernmost part of the town that could not be set on fire from the ships, at 3 the lieutenant with thirty seamen and marines went on shore to set them on fire. When on that piece of duty they ware attacked and fired upon by numbers of rebels, but the alertness of their brisk officer keeped them off, and they performed the duty they ware set upon. At 4 they came on board without the loss of a man and only one slightly wounded. At 5 ceased firing as most of the houses and all the vessels at and about the town ware destroyed to the number of 13 sail. At ½ past made the signal to get under sail, we being the last ship that got under way. We was fired upon by numbers from both sides of the water. There being little wind it was some time before we got out of reach of their musquetry, which did us no damadge. At 8 anchor'd in Hog Island road in 10 fathoms water as did all the rest of the squadron. At 10 dark cloudy weather with rain.

COMMODORE HENRY MOWAT, R. N., TO VICE ADMIRAL SAMUEL GRAVES [extract]

Canceaux in Casco Bay, 19th October 1775

Sir,

(. . .) Perceiving women and children still in the town, I made it forty minutes after nine before the signal to engage was hoisted, which was done with a gun. At the same time the cannonade began from all the vessels and continued till six. By that time the body of the town was in one flame, which would have been the case much sooner, had the wind favored in the forenoon as it did in the evening. Altho' a regular cannonade was kept up all the time, numbers of armed rebels were employed extinguishing the fire before it became general, which made it absolutely necessary for some men to be landed, in order to set fire to the vessels, wharfs, storehouses, as well as to many parts of the town that escaped from the shells and carcasses.

Notwithstanding this resistance, everyone's duty was executed with the greatest dexterity, to the no small credit of Mr. Grant the artillery officer, who employed his people not only onboard but on shore also, and whose spirited conduct in the execution of his duty does him every credit that could be expected from such a service, and indeed every man that was with him. And with equal justice I can say, that all the officers and men on this command shew'd the greatest readiness, and acted with the greatest composure and harmony in their respective duties; and with no less satisfaction I acquaint you, sir, that notwithstanding the vast numbers of armed rebels that assembled in and near the town on occasion, Falmouth, with the blockhouse and battery, the principal wharfs and storehouses, with eleven sail of vessels, several of which had cargoes, were all laid in ashes, including a fine distillery. Four vessels were also taken; and all without the loss of one person, and only two slightly wounded, Mr Larkin Midshipman of the *Canceaux* and one marine.

At the same time I am sorry to say, that had we not been situated close to the town, we should without a doubt have found great difficulty in accomplishing this piece of service, as we soon experienced the insufficiency of the artillery stores, not only in goodness, but in quantity, the particulars of which shall at a more convenient opportunity be laid before you, sir, which I am sorry to observe will not reflect great credit on the ordnance store at Boston. And with equal concern I observe, that the want of a sufficient number of troops has prevented an effectual sweep being made of all the arms, ammunition, cattle and other fresh provisions belonging not only to the town of Falmouth, but also of many islands and villages in Casco Bay, which I am very certain could have been compleatly done with five hundred men.

Our carcasses excepting a few belonging to the howitzers are all expended, and these are rendered useless by the carriages being disabled, which happened early in the bombardment. The *Spitfire* sloop is also much shattered, so that I shall be under the necessity of repairing to Nantasket to have these wants supplied before I can attempt any other place. The troops are also in great distress for want of necessarys, many of them having embarked without a second shirt, from which cause they are rendered incapable of their duty, and are falling sick very fast. My intention was to dispatch the *Halifax* immediately with this letter, but having four prize vessels to man and take care of, I consider it most prudent to keep our small force together till we are nearer. I have the honor to be with the highest respect, sir, your most obedient and humble servant,

H. Mowat

Chapter Twenty-four.

Langdon had spent little time on deck during the bombardment of Falmouth. His associations and memories of nearly every building were as old as childhood; and to see them being destroyed, with cannonballs plowing into wooden siding and flames of fire licking at gaping holes and shattered windows, was too painful for him. He emerged on deck perhaps four times to survey the extent of the damage and to stand a moment with Mowat on the quarterdeck. During one of these brief forays on deck – almost fatefully timed, as it turned out – he witnessed the destruction of the steeple of St. Paul's Church, collapsing into an inferno of flame.

After dark, and the squadron had moved across the bay to anchor near Hogs Island, a slow, light drizzle began. The fire in the town continued to rage despite it, and appeared as a distant, flickering orange glow in the blackness of the night, reflected eerily in the calm water of the bay.

"I have the feeling that I am peering across the river Styx into hell," Dr. Bailey said at one point to his melancholic companion as they leaned on the larboard rail, sheltered from the drizzle under a canvas awning that had been rigged for the officer of the watch.

Langdon was silent.

"I'm surprised the fire continues, what with this rain," Bailey observed.

Again, no sound emerged from the parson in response, so Bailey decided to give up trying to make conversation, and instead merely stood silently with his friend.

The squadron remained in the vicinity of Hogs Island for several days due to the shattered state of the *Spitfire*, Mowat allowing her the opportunity of repairing as much as was possible without the aid of a naval yard. Her old timbers had been shaken mightily by the firing of the mortar which had been fitted into her.

During this time the rain continued without respite. The fire in Falmouth continued to rage all the next and part of a third day before burning itself out.

"I am very concerned about Mr. Langdon," Bailey confessed to Mowat some days later when alone with the commodore. "He has not uttered upwards of two sentences these three days past. And even those were sparsely worded."

"Mr. Langdon has suffered quite a shock, I fear," Mowat agreed. "But he'll come round. He just needs to be left alone a while." He paused. "Is there something medical you could do for him? Prepare a physic, perhaps?"

Dr. Bailey smiled, considering the potential effect of a placebo, then shook his head.

"Well then, there is nothing but to wait. Isn't it you doctors who are always saying things like 'time is the greatest healer'?"

"Aye, it is."

"Well, there we are then."

*

THE SQUADRON WAS BESET WITH ROUGH WEATHER and heavy gales on its return trip to Boston. Two of the four prize vessels taken in Casco Bay were lost track of at night during storms. It was nearly a week – on October 26 – before the battered squadron limped into port.

Langdon returned aboard the *Preston* and was plunged immediately back into his duties as secretary. The distraction helped him forget his melancholy somewhat, but the increasingly ugly weather counteracted any improvement of spirits which he might thereby have experienced. Divine Service aboard the flagship on Sunday the 12th of November was canceled due to a storm of intermittent snow and icy cold rain, both driven by a bitterly cold wind which raged for three days. As a result, the army went into winter quarters a few weeks earlier than normal, especially as local almanacs and seasoned weather-sages were predicting a long, cold winter. Not able to spare a single ship, the *Canceaux* and *Halifax* were immediately sent back out to patrol the bay for rebel privateers, giving them barely enough time to replenish their stores.

Matters in Boston had grown much worse during the squadron's absence; the army's want of provisions promised to grow acute before the winter was too far advanced; and a veritable flotilla of rebel privateers now plied the approaches to Boston, capturing enough transports and supply craft to intensify the lack of provisions in town.

On December 3, the worst such news arrived in Boston when it was learned that the *Nancy*, a heavy transport vessel bearing ordnance, artillery, and ammunition for the army, had been taken by the rebels and escorted triumphantly into Cape Ann Harbor.

The impoverished spirits which had descended upon Langdon after the Falmouth affair now infected many in the army and navy at this news.

Admiral Graves sat glumly at his desk on the dark afternoon that news of the *Nancy* arrived, his eyes glazed over as the rain made a soft patter against the panes of the stern windows, trickling like tears down the glass.

"I have learned to dread the coming of darkness, Mr. Langdon," the admiral said softly, "as I wonder what mischief the rebels will commit *this* night. The promised reinforcements, which so reassured me in September, have not yet materialized, except for the *Phoenix*. And what cruisers I *do* have are so battered by the ravages of weather as to make me fear for their crews. Yet I cannot afford to have a single one remain in harbor when reports daily indicate that enemy privateer activity is increasing manifold. The rebels, who have every advantage over King's ships in point of sailing, and being light vessels drawing little water, can lie under the land and, upon observing a vessel or two unguarded, dart upon them suddenly and carry them off even in the sight of King's ships. It is a method of warfare damnably difficult in countering."

He remained silent for a moment, only the sound of the rain and the melancholy creaking of the old flagship's timbers to be heard. "I was raised in a navy, Mr. Langdon, which challenged the enemy to pitched battles on the open sea, confronting each other in an honorable, manly way, and emerging either victor or vanquished through might and skill of arms. This surreptitious skittering to and fro, boat actions and raids and piracy – while by no means new ideas in the mind of mankind – are carried out by these rebels on a scale of such magnitude, and with such insolence and boldness, as to render the forces at my disposal almost entirely ineffectual. The ministry, the admiralty, the parliament, all have failed entirely to anticipate the scale and nature of warfare to be waged by the colonists, and have equipped me so inadequately as to embarrass me. I am at wit's end."

Langdon was silent in response. He felt that perhaps his spirits had never been so low, listening to the admission of impotence by a man in whom he had heretofore almost desperately put all his hopes.

The greatest sadness in Langdon's life had been caused by the death of his parents eight years ago; but the pang of that personal grief now seemed distant and small in comparison to the universal tragedy and national calamity besetting his homeland and upending everything Langdon had previously held dear. His way forward had been clear at his parents' death: He would miss them sorely, but his vocation as a priest and his calling to the parish of St. Paul's provided him with the means to go forward. At this moment, on the other hand, the future ahead of him was as unfathomable as the ocean on a dark night, or as unsearchable as the frozen fog of a December morning.

"I fear for the safety of my ships at night, what with the guardships so undermanned, lending their people to the cruisers doing the heavy work out in the bay," Admiral Graves continued softly, peering out the stern windows of the great cabin at the quickly darkening sky. "The danger of a hundred whaleboats, brimming with rebels, approaching the *Preston* or *Lively* unobserved on a stormy night of low visibility, boarding and overwhelming our skeleton crews, fills me with an indescribable alarm."

"It is the most depressing time of the year," Langdon added in a subdued voice.

A few days later a rebel armed brig, the *Washington*, was taken by H.M.S. *Fowey* and brought into Boston. Admiral Graves, thinking to send her back out immediately, before word of her capture could reach the rebels, sent Lieutenant George Dawson and 70 men aboard her with orders to put to sea and take advantage of the unsuspecting rebel privateers – who would recognize her as one of their own – to go alongside and board them before they realized what was happening.

Lieutenant Dawson, however, reported that the brig was not fit for sea. Graves immediately ordered Captains Symons, Robinson and Linzee to take their ships' carpenters with them and go aboard the *Washington* to determine her state of repair. These also reported that, aside from being very leaky and rotten, and her masts sprung in several places, the brig's cannon and other arms were totally unserviceable.

Not wanting to forego this prime opportunity for a *ruse de guerre*, Graves went aboard the *Washington* himself to ascertain the truth of the reports with his own eyes. He found their reports not to be exaggerated in the least.

Governor Howe and Graves agreed to send the entire rebel crew of the *Washington* – save two persons who proved to be deserters from the *Glasgow* and *Swan* – back to England in the *Tartar*, to be tried *en masse* for treason. They hoped that this information – and perhaps the subsequent news that the entire crew had been hanged – would perhaps discourage some rebels from serving in privateers.

Graves likewise issued a proclamation, which was carried by the *Phoenix* to New York, that any town found to have participated in rebellious activity such as the raising of a militia, or the provisioning of men to the rebel army, or the construction of a fortification, would suffer the same fate as Falmouth come spring.

Meanwhile the hellish weather in New England was wreaking havoc on the cruisers in the bay and its environs. Darting from port to intercept transports, as the rebels could do, was one thing, requiring little in the way of stamina or wear-and-tear; but to cruise back and forth on the open sea, attempting to keep station in bitter cold and violent storms, was exhausting the ships and men of Graves' squadron to the point of collapse. Provisions were scarce; planking, masts, cordage, and canvas for the upkeep of the ships were dwindling quickly; and death, desertion, and illness were denuding the ships of their all-important crews.

Admiral Graves suggested to General Howe, as the only solution to keeping transports from falling into rebel hands, that the ports of Marblehead, Salem, and Cape Ann – all lying on the approach to Boston – be taken and either completely destroyed or occupied.

Howe at first ignored the admiral's repeated suggestions, then replied peremptorily that he lacked sufficient troops for any such effort, which caused a renewal of coldness to develop between the admiral and the governor.

*

THE SKY WAS OVERCAST and threatened rain, but the temperature was moderate on the last day of 1775. It being a Sunday, the Rev. Langdon celebrated Divine Service on deck – a thing he had done only twice since returning to Boston, owing to the inclement weather. He was just coming to the end of his sermon, pointing out that 1775 had brought them a bounty of woes, but that 1776 would perhaps improve their fortunes, when the masthead lookout called apologetically to deck that several ships – two of them line-of-battle ships – had just come into sight, approaching the harbor.

Anticipation that these were some of Admiral Graves' long-awaited reinforcements became almost palpable among the crew. By the time the service had been hastily concluded – the final prayers and benediction being read at almost incomprehensible speed – three of the ships had been identified: the 50-gun *Chatham*, wearing an admiral's flag; the *Renown*, her twin in armament; and the 32-gun frigate *Niger*. The rear admiral's flag flying from the foremast of the *Chatham* almost certainly indicated the arrival of Rear Admiral Molyneux Shuldham, promised to Graves as a second-in-command last August. Shuldham's name was well-known in America as he had been the commander-in-chief of the Newfoundland Station from 1772 to early 1775.

"Hopefully this is a favorable omen, what? Indicative of a change in our fortunes from one year to the next, what?" Graves said with something like hopefulness to Langdon as they waited in the great cabin for the inevitable dispatches and letters to arrive.

"I said something very similar just moments ago in my sermon," Langdon replied.

"I'm hoping the *Chatham* and *Renown* will have the increased complements promised me in earlier dispatches from the admiralty," Graves continued. "Normally ships of that size would have a complement of 300; but, owing to our woefully undermanned state, I requested and was granted an increased complement in any ships bound for North American waters. I'm hoping therefore they will each have upwards of 350 aboard, to help fill out our existing crews. They would be the first such reinforcements, if it is so."

"Yes, let us hope so," Langdon echoed.

"Now that I have clear orders giving me a free hand militarily, the rebels will begin to feel the real weight of an English fleet, by Jove!"

"I am heartily glad of it, sir."

"First I will send a good capital ship south to Virginia and the Carolina Capes to assist the handful of sloops I have already sent thither. Reports seem to indicate a potential for raising significant loyalist support in the region, which I think, strategically, will be of great benefit to us. In fact, I may send Rear Admiral Shuldham to be commander of everything south of the Chesapeake, as the region may require a person of authority nearer to hand.

"Then I will turn my attention to Cape Ann: Not only is the town a threat to the safety of all vessels entering and exiting this harbor, it is also in need of a hearty chastisement. It must be destroyed as a base of operations for privateers.

"Then, with Halifax reinforced and placed on a good defensive footing – about which I am at present very concerned – I will perhaps begin a major naval initiative off Providence or New York." He paused. "Yes, that's a good start. For the spring, anyway."

"It's good to see you feeling your old vigorous self again, if I might say so, sir," said Langdon.

"Yes, I feel the blood coursing through me with my old wonted fervor again. This winter will have aged me a decade before it's over, I fear. That's a process I can ill-afford at sixty-two. But perhaps, before this old year of 1775 is fully played out, it will have left us with the hope of a better one to come, eh?"

"I wish it as heartily as every man in the fleet, sir."

A lieutenant from the *Chatham* arrived within the half hour, and Langdon was present for the interview, as Graves expected there would be a major amount of dispatches, orders and correspondence to attend to.

Indeed, the lieutenant bore a satchel of considerable weight, which he set on the Queen Anne table in the great cabin, and, after paying his respects to the admiral, looked uncomfortably at Langdon.

Graves, sensing the unease, said, "Lieutenant Curtis, this is the Rev'd Mr. Langdon, my secretary and chaplain. He is here by my leave."

Lieutenant Curtis gave the clergyman a curt nod, then, turning to face the admiral, said, "I have been asked to point out *these* dispatches particularly," he held out an additional, smaller canvas envelope to the admiral, "as requiring your immediate attention, sir."

Graves examined the envelope, addressed as usual by the flowery hand of an admiralty clerk. "By all means, lieutenant."

Lieutenant Curtis remained stiffly silent.

"Do they require you to remain until I have examined them?" Graves asked, going behind his desk to get his letter-opener.

"No, sir."

"Very well, then, Mr. Curtis. You may return to the *Chatham*, conveying my respects to Rear Admiral Shuldham, if you would be so kind."

Lieutenant Curtis saluted and departed.

Langdon tried to mask his curiosity. Admiral Graves took out his reading spectacles and removed the tightly written sheets from the envelope he had just opened. He had read but a few sentences when his face turned as white as ash.

Without looking up, he said quietly, "Please leave me, Mr. Langdon."

"I – "

"I said to leave me," the admiral repeated, his voice betraying emotion kept barely in check.

Langdon nodded silent assent and left the cabin. Not wishing to be alone, Langdon ascended to the quarterdeck, where he found Lieutenant Graeme.

"What news, Mr. Langdon?" the latter asked affably. The appearance of reinforcements had spread a contagion of happiness around the fleet, even to Old Grim.

"I dread something awful," Langdon said quietly, sorry to dampen the spirits of the first lieutenant, but not wanting anyone else to overhear him.

"Oh my," said Graeme. "Why so?"

"Lieutenant Curtis from the *Chatham* drew the admiral's attention particularly to one set of dispatches. When Graves caught sight of the first words, he turned as white as a ghost, and asked me to leave."

"I see," Graeme said.

They brooded in silence for what seemed like hours but was actually little more than ten minutes. Eventually Midshipman Saunders emerged onto the quarterdeck and approached the chaplain.

"Admiral's compliments, Mr. Langdon, and would you report to the great cabin immediately, sir," Saunders said somewhat nervously.

Langdon glanced at Lieutenant Graeme, who raised his eyebrows in sympathy.

As he entered, he beheld a very brief glimpse of the admiral slumped in his chair, the dispatches limply grasped in his hands. But he immediately drew himself up and hid his emotions behind an icy visage. He said in his old businesslike tone, "The admiralty is recalling me. Rear Admiral Shuldham has been sent to replace rather than assist me. My performance has apparently been the cause of some discontent in Westminster, although I've previously had no indication of this, and . . ." He turned to look out the stern windows to hide once more the involuntary manifestation of emotion crossing his features.

Langdon was speechless at the announcement. "I . . . I don't know what to say, sir. This is most frightful abuse, sir."

Graves wordlessly handed him the single sheet whereon his fate was written. It read,

Admiralty Office, 21st Septem^r 1775

Sir,

His Majesty's Service requiring your return to England; I have it in command from my Lords Commissioners of the Admiralty to acquaint you therewith and to signify their direction to you to hold yourself in readiness to return to England accordingly with all the third rates under your command or such of them as may be assembled at Boston as soon after the arrival of Rear Admiral Shuldham as conveniently may be, shifting your flag from the *Preston* (which is to remain in North America) to such one of the said third rates as you shall judge proper. For all which you will receive their Lordships' order in form by the said Rear admiral. I have the honor to be &c.

Philip Stephens
Admiralty Secretary

"There's no indication here of discontent," Langdon remarked, knowing it was rather useless to point this out but feeling bound to do so. "And it's so brief, so matter of fact . . ."

"Here's a private letter from my friend Lord Sandwich, the First Lord of the Admiralty," he handed him another sheet of lighter weight personal stationary, this written in a much more crabbed, scribbled hand, somewhat more difficult to decipher.

Hinchingbrooke, 17th September 1775

Sir -- It gives me great concern to be obliged to inform you that I have received His Majesty's commands for your returning home at the close of this year. In a letter I wrote to you not long ago, I mentioned that the world in general expected something essential to be done by both the fleet and army, and General Gage's return to England has made my resistance to your being recalled utterly ineffectual: the torrent has been too strong for me to be able to withstand it.

You may however be assured that I shall in every place, both public and private, do you the justice you deserve, and declare my opinion that it has been more owing to accident than to misconduct that the operations of the fleet during this summer have not carried the importance with them that the nation expected. I am, sir, &c. Sandwich

"'Accident rather than misconduct,'" muttered Graves when Langdon had handed the letter back to him. "The king clearly blames me for the failure to do 'something essential' this summer.

And this reference to Gage – you see how he continues to attempt to destroy me? 'Something essential' was expected of both army and navy, but since Gage was called upon first to defend his actions – that is, his *inactions* – he used me as the scapegoat, apparently heaping all the blame on me! And where the real blame lies will never become public: With the admiralty lords themselves, and parliament, tying my hands by never giving me clear orders, and equipping me inadequately to do even the little I was able to do; then holding me accountable for the inaction which they virtually forced me into, until it was too late. Too late for me, anyway, and perhaps too late for all America. 'Something essential . . .' – *Damn them!*"

"You have been most frightfully used . . ." repeated Langdon, shaking his head. "Is there no way you can remonstrate? All this was decided before the Falmouth affair. Surely they will have heard of Falmouth by now, and found you not wanting in decisiveness in that instance."

Graves shook his head with resignation. "No, there's nothing I can do. There will come no reversal of this order. 'Something essential' failed to happen this summer, and they must have a scapegoat. The public clamors for one apparently, parliament requires one, and the king will have one."

Langdon did not respond for a moment. "Is Admiral Shuldham now in command?"

"No. I am senior and therefore still in command," Graves shook his head. "I shall continue for a few weeks, in order to provide a smooth transfer of authority, allowing Shuldham to familiarize himself with his environs. We will send him all of our standing orders from admiralty, make copies of the more recent orders I have sent to my ships, prepare a disposition of the ships on the station, and otherwise acquaint him with the state of affairs in North America. For example, he has no doubt heard nothing of Mowat's action at Falmouth, much less of the loss of the *Nancy* or the capture of the *Washington*. It will mean much work for you, I'm afraid, copying and assembling documents."

Langdon nodded. "And when will you be shifting your flag, as specified in the orders? When you resign the command, or before?"

Graves shook his head. "Probably not at all. The third rates specified in the orders are not available for me: The *Boyne* is already *en route* to England; the *Somerset* is in Halifax, detained by Commodore Arbuthnot for the imperative defense of that place; and the *Asia* is in New York. No, I will probably remain in the *Preston* and take her back to England with me. She is in need of a refit herself, having been on this station with me now over two years."

Langdon nodded again. "It gives me great pain, sir," he repeated, unable to think of anything more appropriate to say.

*

The Rev'd Mr. Thomas Langdon's Journal

SUNDAY, 31 DECEMBER, 1775. BOSTON HARBOUR. (. . .) I personally cannot imagine what more any man in Grave's position could have done to turn the tide of rebellion. I can find a number of faults with the governor and army to be sure – the stupidity of leaving Breed's and Bunker Hills unprotected; the senseless frontal assault and subsequent prosecution of that battle – and even more fault do I find with the government, in taking so long to make up its mind either to placate the colonists with redress of their perceived grievances, or firmness in bringing them to a right sense of their duties. But Graves and the navy, with extremely limited means, have been the most effective arm of government in prosecuting British interests in the colonies to this point. Graves has, in my opinion, been diligent in every aspect of his duties, treading the fine line between provocation and mollification, and all the while keeping his ships and men in the highest degree of readiness that is possible given the circumstances. Although he should be much commended for making the best of a bad fist of cards, he will apparently be vilified in England by those whose inaction has actually caused his downfall, but cannot afford to admit it.

As for myself, I am placed at another cross-roads. What does Graves' recall to England mean for me? I little wish to return to England with him, although a number of Loyalists (we are now so decided a body that I have seen the word capitalized of late) have already taken this course of action. Yet the new admiral doubtless has brought his own clerical staff with him, and will have no use (and less trust) of me. I do not wish to go ashore, as there is still too much upheaval here – and throughout the continent, not just New England. My emotional inclination is to ask for transfer back to the *Canceaux*, serving as clerk to Captain Mowat; but this will represent a greatly reduced salary. Still, it will provide the room and board that I need during this time, until the colonies are restored to their sanity, and peace and stability resume on her shores. Would that that time would come soon, and not tarry.

CHAPTER TWENTY-FIVE.

THE *CANCEAUX* LIMPED INTO HARBOR on January 5, her sails patched and frayed at the edges, and the paint of her hull stripped and pale, splotched with great salt stains. Her constant service since her refitting at Halifax, including the bombardment of Falmouth and two month's beating up and down the length of Massachusetts Bay, pummeled by wintry squalls and punishing storms, had left her in a visibly sorry state. Mowat sent word to the flagship that he believed the ship to be unfit to keep the sea, in response to which Admiral Graves ordered a survey.

Langdon went to dinner aboard her the next evening, pleased to be with his friends Lieutenant Mowat, Dr. Bailey and Master Hogg once again, and with the familiar and comforting form of Penfold moving quietly amongst them.

When conversation turned to Graves' recall to England, Langdon said, "I regret the admiral's removal terribly, not least for you, Captain Mowat."

"How do you mean?" Mowat asked.

"Admiral Graves has a very high opinion of you, as I have learned this past year. Were he to remain, I have little doubt of your promotion. With a new admiral however, unfamiliar with your merits . . ."

"I am heartily glad to hear of Graves' esteem," Mowat began, "but, even if Graves were not to be removed, I believe my own return to England would be shortly forthcoming. The *Canceaux* was surveyed this morning, and the surveyors agreed with me that she is unserviceable and must return for a major overhaul and refit if she is to sail and fight again. And personally, I have many accounts to settle, having been away from home for these last four years and more. I intend to travel to the Orkneys briefly to see my family."

"You and the *Canceaux* are to be returning to England, then?" Langdon asked, his weak voice and fallen countenance betraying his disappointment.

"What will Graves' recall mean for you, Thomas?" Bailey asked.

Langdon did not respond immediately, pondering his answer. "I think it would be best for me to remain in America, which would mean transferring ships and abandoning the admiral before he departs. But another part of me acknowledges that all my circle – my remaining friends –," he gestured to the men around the table, "are sailing to England."

"I wish that inviting you to transfer to the *Canceaux* would suit you, Mr. Langdon," Mowat said, "but, as you have said that you do not wish to go to England, transferring to the *Canceaux* would be the same as remaining in the *Preston*. Perhaps there is another ship in the squadron to which you could be appointed. What about the *Chatham*?"

"I have made discreet inquiries and learned that Admiral Shuldham is in need of neither chaplain nor clerk."

"Well, there must be another ship in Boston that is in need of a chaplain," Mowat said.

Langdon nodded, unable to hide his sudden sense of abandonment.

*

ON JANUARY 18 ANOTHER 50-GUN SHIP arrived in Boston, the *Centurion*. On the same day Admiral Graves received a letter from Rear Admiral Shuldham, requesting that Lieutenant Mowat be transferred to a ship remaining in North America as he was "well-acquainted with the coast." Langdon was asked to write a note with this information to Mowat. This gave Langdon a brief hope that Mowat might reconsider and be put in command of a ship remaining on the station.

Mowat's reply, however, said that he was "very desirous of returning to England, having many years' accounts to settle," and that his retention in America would be much to his personal detriment.

Shuldham thereupon wrote a letter to the admiralty, to be conveyed back to Britain by Mowat, wherein he represented

"Captain Mowat's services and usefulness on this coast, requesting that he might therefore be returned to America without loss of time in a ship fit to do justice to his experience of the station." A more certain recommendation of promotion could not be imagined, and Langdon could think of no commander more deserving of the tribute. Langdon hoped it would not be too many months before Mowat would be back in America. And this thought decided him upon a course of action.

"Admiral Graves, sir," began Langdon one morning soon thereafter, as they sat down to the day's business in the great cabin. "Far be it from me to presume to communicate my wishes to the one who has been my benefactor these last eight months – "

"But you are going to anyway," the admiral interrupted with a smile, conveying clearly to Langdon that he welcomed the intrusion.

"You may understand that I, as a colonist, feel it is my place to serve in a ship which is on this station, nearer my home. I would probably be of more use to a commander in North America, being familiar with local customs and peculiarities as I am; and in case the rebellion is put down and I could resume my life ashore as a parish priest in my native land, I would wish to be as close to home as possible. I hope that I do not sound callous in this sentiment; and I assure you that I am not insensitive to the special favor you have extended to me as your secretary, and a part of me would therefore wish to accompany you wherever you may serve; but – "

"You wish me to appoint you to a ship remaining on this station?" Graves asked.

"Yes . . . and no, sir," Langdon began. "Seeing as how Lieutenant Mowat has received such a strong recommendation from Admiral Shuldham that the admiralty should return him to this station as soon as is possible; and as I already consider him something of a patron, and a friend; I was going to request a transfer to the

Canceaux. This would guarantee my eventual return to America, yet I could remain with a commander whom I respect and admire," Langdon said, his face turning slightly red at the audacity he felt in making such a personal request to the admiral.

"Mowat will in all likelihood be made post – that is, promoted post-captain – and given a sixth-rate," Admiral Graves said with assurance. "But it is by no means certain he'll be sent back to North America. The admiralty will do with him as they please, once he has settled his affairs in England and is ready for sea again, Rear Admiral Shuldham's request notwithstanding."

Langdon remained silent at this pronouncement. The mysteries of the Admiralty were a closed book to him, obviously.

"If it is your wish, however, Mr. Langdon," Graves continued, aware that he had dealt an uncomfortable blow to the parson, "rest assured that it will be done. Mowat has more promise of continued service than I have." There was a hint of sadness in the admiral's voice. "As I shall not be needing you very much after I resign my command, I'll write out the transfer before I actually step down. I shall do it before we set sail. In fact, I will make it my last official act as commander of the North American station. You cannot say prettier than that."

"I am eternally indebted to you, sir," Langdon said.

*

VICE ADMIRAL GRAVES RESIGNED HIS COMMAND on January 27, 1776, and the order that Langdon was required to copy to Rear Admiral Shuldham – immediately after copying his own appointment as chaplain and captain's clerk to the *Canceaux* – was quite brief:

By Saml Graves Esqr
Vice Admiral of the White
Commander-in-Chief &c.

Sir--:

You are hereby required and directed to take upon you the direction of the port duty, and the command of His Majesty's ships and vessels named in the margin now in this harbour, together with those whose names are mentioned on the other side; giving such orders and directions to their several commanders as you shall judge best for His Majesty's service.

Given under my hand on board His Maj's Ship *Preston* at Boston 27th January 1776

Saml Graves

Later that same day Langdon, all his worldly possessions packed in three trunks and lowered into the sternsheets of one of the *Preston*'s boats, bid farewell to Graves in his cabin, his official appointment as chaplain and captain's clerk of the *Canceaux* tucked into his breast pocket. They wished each other luck in their respective careers, and with nothing more personal than a handshake, Langdon took his leave of the great cabin for the last time.

Langdon pondered his actions as he was being rowed to the *Canceaux*. He was stepping down from a high position, invested with much responsibility and no little trust on the part of his superiors – not to mention a combined salary as chaplain, secretary and schoolmaster of a flagship totaling over £32 *per annum* – to that of a minor captain's clerk and chaplain aboard one of the smallest ships in the squadron, a position of low regard, little responsibility, and the comparatively minimal salary of £6 *per annum*. Another man in the same situation might consider it an act of sheer madness.

But Langdon, who saw his career in the Royal Navy as a

temporary one, reasoned that it was far more important to be amongst friends than to take care for hasty advancement or influential preferment. When his basic needs for food and shelter were met by his being aboard ship, what need had he of a salary? To enjoy his surroundings, esteem his companions, and feel he was doing something of real significance were far more important to him.

The *Canceaux* – that dear little ship, the first sight of which had caused his heart to leap into his throat almost a year ago as she came smartly to anchor in Falmouth harbor – loomed above them as the boat hooked onto her main chains. The sailors of the *Preston*'s launch helped Langdon to his feet and steadied him as he stepped out of the boat.

"Farewell and Godspeed to ya', parson," said the coxswain of the flagship's boat.

"Thank you, gentlemen," he replied, not daring to turn and look at them for fear of losing his balance, and instead concentrating on the narrow steps in the *Canceaux*'s side. He realized how used he had become to the larger scale of things in the flagship.

He emerged on the familiar deck of the *Canceaux* to the sound of fife and whistle – an uncommon courtesy for a non-commissioned officer.

"Welcome aboard the *Canceaux*, Mr. Langdon," said Lieutenant Mowat, who stood with Master Hogg to his right and Dr. Bailey to his left, "although, with the state she's in, you may never reach England in her!" The midshipmen Mr. Larkin, Mr. Barker, and Mr. Samuels bobbed and smiled from behind them.

"It is a very good thing to be aboard again, Captain Mowat," Langdon said with sincerity.

* * *

About the Author

As a youth, Timothy J. Krueger fell in love with the maritime novels of C. S. Forrester and Alexander Kent. It was when he discovered the novels of Patrick O'Brian in his 20s that he realized these swashbucklers could actually rise to the level of literature, and he began trying his hand at writing his own. Meanwhile, he pursued studies in historical musicology at the Royal Holloway College of the University of London; the Universität Hamburg; the University of Colorado, Boulder; and the Wheaton College Conservatory of Music. Between the work of his actual occupation as a choir director and university music history lecturer, he continues to write novels surrounding the life of his main character, Thomas Langdon, chaplain aboard 18th century British men-of-war. He lives in Denver, Colorado, with his wife and dog. He is choirmaster at St. Andrew's Episcopal Church, Denver, and is the founder and Artistic Director of St. Martin's Chamber Choir, a professional ensemble. He teaches music history classes at Metropolitan State University of Denver.

Printed in Great Britain
by Amazon